Have You Forgotten Yet?

Have You Forgotten Yet?

A.N Arthur

Have You Forgotten Yet? published by Rangitawa Publishing, Feilding, New Zealand 2020.

ISBN 978-0-9951166-7-2

www.rangitawapublishing.com

rangitawa@xtyra.co.nz

Cover Photo: Ruth Holly Photography

Cover Design: C.A.Lines

Rangitawa
PUBLISHING

Other titles in the *Memento* series

Orphanage Boys

Between Two Worlds

Kat

Forever Memory

Acknowledgments:

Strawb and Sonny

A. Crumley and C.Lines

'Have you forgotten yet?
Look up and swear by the green of the spring that you'll never
forget.'

From 'Aftermath' by Siegfried Sassoon

Part I

1922

Wellington

February

She was nearly seven and the nearly was important to her. Tyke felt at this age she should be braver and more daring. Yet, here she stood, restlessly shifting her weight backwards and forwards on her feet in their shiny, black boots with the buttons she hated and hesitant before the closed door. Her expressive face bore vivid evidence of this dilemma; *go in or not go in?* Father's angry eyes and hasty smacks hovered in her mind while her mother's voice, calm but resolute, also echoed there.

'You are not allowed in anyone's bedroom, Tyke darling. The privacy of our boarders is paramount.'

'What about your bedroom?'

'Father's and mine as well, Tyke. We need our privacy, too.'

The little girl went into this room so rarely. If the shadows of the night grew too frightening and her imagination conjured up the ghosts and monsters Emma told her about, Tyke always headed for the sanctuary of Maudie's bed. She had done ever since she could remember. *No monster would dare enter any room where Maudie was.* Her parents' room remained tantalisingly off limits and because of that, Tyke was drawn to it, wanting to explore, to linger there.

A door further along the hallway opened and one of the newer lodgers tipped his hat as he strode past her. Tyke gave him no mind, barely noticing him at all. She bit her bottom lip uncertainly. Finally on a rush of impulse she pushed the door open, careful to peep into the empty room. Only guilt made her check if anyone was there for Mama had left earlier in the day and Father was down the pub. No one had told her where he'd be but she knew.

If Father wasn't working, and he had no work at the moment, then he was always at the pub.

The room was hushed, tranquil. Sunlight slanted through the windows, dust dancing as silver sprinkles on its beams. Tyke loved it. It was the biggest bedroom in the boarding house, the one with the largest windows. There was a carpet on the floor too, a real woven carpet, not a rag-rug like the ones Maudie made. The only other woven carpet in the whole boarding house was in the rarely used, kept-for-special-visitors parlour. Uncle Hugo had given it to Maudie not long after he arrived. With her eyes fastened on the carpet, Tyke walked over it, enjoying the difference between the hard wooden floorboards and its thick softness. Uncle Hugo told her rich people had carpets on every floor, even hanging on the walls; beautiful carpets with pictures of flowers and animals on them. Tyke couldn't imagine such incredible wealth. This carpet and the little one in the parlour were luxury enough.

A faint trace of lavender warmed the air, the scent reaching out through the drawers and wardrobe to perfume the whole room. Light glinted in the mirror on the dressing table and like a moth the girl was attracted to its brightness. Greatly daring, she sat on the wooden chair in front of the table, fingers gently exploring the glass bottles and ornaments kept there. In pride of place were the lovely hair brushes Maudie had given Alex two years ago for her thirtieth birthday. They had heavy silver backs on them with swirls of patterns and roses etched into the metal. Sometimes, for a treat, Alex brushed Tyke's hair with them and now the little girl ran a grubby hand over the curls framing her face, remembering. Lifting her eyes, she caught her reflection and grimaced at the sight. *Why did she have to have red hair?* Emma McMillain told her red hair was unlucky but didn't explain why.

'Carroty top, carroty top!'

Tyke hated her schoolmates' taunts. Alex had red hair, too but it was darker, a rich auburn, nothing carroty about it. Tyke pulled at a braid then tugged at the loose curls which always defied her plaits and ribbons. She wished she was beautiful like her mother with lovely hair and bright, silver/grey eyes. Again Tyke frowned at her reflection, those strange eyes neither one colour nor another. Hazel, Maudie told her. Tyke didn't want hazel eyes. She wanted silver ones like Alex or even dark ones like her Father's. Not these strange eyes which changed colour every time she looked at them. *Best of all would be blue eyes like Emma's. Blue eyes and blonde hair. How many pitying looks had Emma given her when they compared faces?* Tyke picked up one of the brushes and ran it thoughtfully over the hair not restrained by her braids. *She did like her curls, though.* Emma had to wear rags in her hair every night to get her hair to curl and she said they were painful to sleep in but worth it. Tyke gave her curls a smug preen, for once proud of her looks.

She pretended she was Alex getting ready for a night out. There weren't many of those but every now and again Alex allowed Tyke to help her into her evening gown. Thoughts of the beautiful frock drove everything else out of Tyke's mind. Laying the hairbrush back down, she skipped to the wardrobe. She had to stand on tip-toes to reach the handle. It was stiff and resisted her fingers until she pulled at it with all her might. The door swung open with a rough groan. Anxiously Tyke held her breath but no footsteps sounded out in the hallway so she relaxed again, screwing her nose up at the musty, familiar smell of mothballs competing with the sweet scent of dried lavender. Pushing into the rack of clothes Tyke sought the fabric she was looking for. *There it was. Mama's evening gown.* It was the palest of green with a delicately embroidered overskirt. Maudie had sewn it, every stitch, and she had given one of the lovely silver buttons to the little girl who joyfully tucked it away in the special box Moss had carved for such treasures. Tyke wiped sticky palms down her white pinafore apron before she caressed the skirt. She wished she could have a beautiful gown like this. Maudie had told her she could when she was grown up. Tyke sighed. *That was so far away.* Emma already had a corset and a grown up frock to go with it. Maudie had humphed in disbelief when Tyke whined at the unfairness of this.

Emma called Alex posh. *'Too posh for Tory Street,' the girl had sneered.*

That confused Tyke for she knew her family wasn't posh at all. Posh people didn't live in a big, scruffy house with boarders and posh people didn't wear hand-me-down clothes and sleep under sheets Maudie turned and re-sewed. The older girl had hinted about a secret to do with Samuel and Alex. Not a nice secret either, because Emma said she shouldn't really be playing with Tyke on account of it.

'I'll be your friend, just don't tell my mother,' Emma had whispered. 'You're not the sort of girl I'm allowed to play with.'

Tyke wanted to know why. She pressed harder only for Emma to completely clam up, refusing to talk to the younger girl for two whole weeks. Such achingly lonely days for Tyke who had no other friend and by the nudges and whispers from all the other girls at school, she came to realise it was all because of this secret. She was different, her family was different. To be different was to be dangerous. *And lonesome.*

One night when she couldn't sleep for worrying about it all, Tyke slipped out of bed and headed to the kitchen, determined to ask Maudie about it. Instead, Moss came in from work, whistling under his breath as he stood in the foyer. Tyke changed her mind in an instant. Leaping down the last two stairs into his arms, she giggled when he ran his bristly chin over her face.

'What are you doing out of bed, Miss?'

From laughter to solemnity in a heartbeat she blurted out, 'Moss, why are we different? No one will be my friend at school except Emma and she said it was because Alex and Father had a bad secret. What is it, Moss? Why won't other girls be my friend? Don't tell Emma's mother I'm asking, will you? She won't let Emma be my friend and Emma has to pretend not to like me.'

All this was said at top speed, almost as one sentence. Moss opened his mouth, unsure of what he could say when the little girl began to cry. He eased her more comfortably in his arms before heading to his room where he sat her on the bed. Handing Tyke a clean handkerchief, Moss took time removing his jacket in front of the washstand, scrubbing the grime of the working day off his face and hands. *How could he explain things to a six year old?* Eventually he sat beside Tyke only to have her clamber onto his lap, desperate for reassurance.

What to tell her?

Because to tell the truth, Alex's relationship with Samuel had caused a scandal. She had turned her back on well-to-do parents to live with him and they married seven months before Tyke was born. Moss cursed the likes of Emma McMillain and the mother who should have known better than to speak of such things in front of anyone, especially a child. He took the handkerchief from Tyke's clutching fingers and gently wiped her tears away. 'The secret is your mum and dad loved each other. A lot. People thought they shouldn't because Alex's parents were rich and she should have married someone with even more money but she didn't want to. She chose your dad instead.' Moss grinned at Tyke. He lowered his voice which he made plummy with mock-poshness. 'Such a thing just isn't done when one's parents have plenty of money.'

'Oh.'

Moss could see the little girl mulling this over.

'Well, I don't think it's bad to love someone who's not rich.' Tyke wiped her wet eyes.

'Me neither.'

Silence.

'Moss?'

'Mmm?'

'Do you have lots of money?'

'I get by.' Moss had the oddest feeling it wasn't the question Tyke really wanted to ask. With habitual patience, he cuddled her until she spoke again.

'Moss?'

'Yeah?'

'Are you still living the war like Father?'

He laughed. 'No, Tyke. I was too young to go to war. I'm only twenty, you know!'

'Twenty? You're really old, Moss!'

He tickled her, happy to see the shadows leave her face as she laughed. 'No I'm bloody not. I'm just a lad.'

'Well, I'm nearly seven.'

'I know, Grandma. Look whose calling *me* old. It'll be double figures for you, soon. Then you'll catch up to me.'

'You're silly, Moss.'

'I don't care.' He studied her face as he stifled a yawn, the long day's work catching up with him. 'Feeling better now?'

When Tyke nodded, he threw her over his shoulder and carried her back to her own bed.

Thinking of that conversation now, something else echoed in Tyke's memory.

'I know, Grandma.'

Why didn't she have any grandparents? Emma had two sets and one set of great-grandparents.

Maybe if your parents live a bad secret you can't have grandparents.

With a final, lingering glance at the lovely frock, Tyke made to close the wardrobe door when something else caught her eye. Tucked against the far end of the wardrobe, right behind everything else, hung Father's uniform, cleaned and brushed. He'd been wearing it when he came home from the war. Tyke touched the scratchy, woollen fabric, tugging gently at the shiny brass buttons. *Why does Father keep it so clean and tidy when he doesn't have to wear it anymore?* Once, not long ago, she asked him why and he brushed off her question so angrily Tyke hadn't dared ask again. Mama wouldn't answer the question either. In fact, she seemed uncomfortable as if Tyke had asked something shameful. Any questions about Uncle Jimmy were the same. No one said why he looked like he did. All Tyke knew was it had happened in the war. No one spoke of it. No one. *The war was like the wind; you couldn't see it now but you could see the effect of it.* Of course, the metaphor wasn't hers. It was something Uncle Hugo said and the image stayed with the little girl and here, hidden away, was another reminder of it. Tyke ran her hands down one sleeve. *Father kept his uniform spotlessly clean and Uncle Jimmy's frightening face was normal.* So many things they didn't talk about, like the way Father and Mama argued at night when they thought no one could hear them.

'Maudie, why do Alex and Father argue all the time?'

Maudie's frown wasn't not an angry one. 'Little pitchers have big ears, my girl.'

Tyke had no idea what Maudie meant or what it had to do with her question. When pushed and impatient, Maudie would mutter something about men still living the war but Tyke didn't understand that either. *The war had been over for years. How could people still be living it?* Turning all these things over in her mind now she was glad Moss had been too young to go overseas to war. *I don't want him still living it like Father does.*

With a sigh, she shut the wardrobe door and moved to the window sill where the tin soldier sat. This toy hadn't been in the house before Father came home and she wasn't allowed to play with him but he looked interesting and Tyke was bored and lonely. She picked the soldier up, giving his dirty metal face a clean on her increasingly grubby pinafore apron.

'I wonder what your name is?' she whispered to the battered face as the bedroom door swung open.

Samuel came to an abrupt halt in the doorway, surprised to see his daughter in the room. The first thing he noticed was her guilty face. Swaying a little from too much beer, Samuel kept a steadying grip on the door knob as his eyes scanned the room looking for proof of mischief.

'What are you doing in here, Tyke?'

As he frowned, Tyke gripped the tin soldier in a fist behind her back, her tummy squirming sickly. She wished she hadn't been so curious now.

'Did you hear me? I asked what you're doing. You know you're not allowed in here.' Samuel's small stock of patience began to thin. 'Tyke, answer me!'

The little girl swallowed hard. 'Nothing.'

Samuel's frown deepened at the obvious lie. His daughter's tense face irritated him and he held out a hand, clicking his fingers. 'Show me what you're hiding,' he demanded.

Pause.

'I won't ask again.'

Biting her bottom lip, Tyke held out the tin soldier. For a few seconds she thought Father wasn't going to be angry but then his eyes narrowed. Tyke instinctively took a few steps backwards as he strode towards her.

Samuel snatched the soldier out of her hand. 'I've told you not to touch this! Why did you?'

'I don't know.' Tyke's eyes filled with frightened tears. She struggled not to let them fall. Crying made him angrier.

There was no softening in Samuel's face as he glared down at his daughter. 'Then maybe you need a lesson to help you remember.' Before Tyke could react, Samuel pulled her onto his lap and spanked her. His hand was calloused and each slap against the back of her legs and buttocks stung hard enough to leave an imprint.

Once on her feet Tyke couldn't hold back the tears and fright anymore. With a sob, she ran out of the room, bumping into her mother on the way downstairs.

'Tyke?' The only reply to her question was a slammed door.

Alex paused on the landing before walking into the bedroom. Samuel stood by the window, turning the tin soldier over and over in his hand. 'What did you do to Tyke?'

'What I had to. You and Maudie are too soft on her.'

'That doesn't answer my question, Sam.'

His hand slammed down on the window sill. 'She was touching things which don't belong to her and it wasn't the first time!'

'She's just a little girl.'

'She's old enough to know better.'

'That's your yardstick for measuring good behaviour, is it? Age?' Her mouth twisted as she caught the odour of stale beer and a sharper scrutiny of his features revealed the telltale slackness of his mouth. Once again he had been drinking heavily. Alex folded her arms. 'How old are you again?'

Samuel turned to confront his wife. 'Don't start, Alex.'

'Don't start what?'

Her eyes burned into his and Samuel swung away, wanting distance from her all too piercing glare. 'I've had enough of your smart questions. Every time I come home you're at me about some bloody thing or other.' Samuel noticed the wardrobe door was ajar and he slammed it shut, shaking the whole room with the bang. 'Is it too much to ask for some peace when I get home?'

Alex made a dismissive sound. 'The only one shouting and crashing about is you.'

Samuel moved closer, a dangerous light in his eyes. 'I'm warning you, Alex.'

She stood her ground, not without a twist of dread. 'Warn away.' Alex watched Samuel's fists clench and unclench. She lifted her chin, expecting him to lash out again. Maybe he noticed her glance because with an angry hiss, he spun round instead, reached for the door. 'Where are you going?'

'What the hell does it matter to you?'

'I'm your wife!' A cry from the heart.

Silence.

Samuel moved so close his beery breath warmed her face. His fingers grazed her cheek and in a sudden movement he pressed his mouth against hers. Alex jerked away, her fear and distaste too obvious to hide.

Samuel's mouth twisted in a bitter sneer. 'My wife? What the fuck does that mean anymore?' Without another word he left her alone in their bedroom, the venom of their last exchange lingering nastily.

Alex found she was trembling. She reached for the bed-knob and gripping it tightly, breathed with deliberate calmness to collect herself. *He hadn't hit her. She was thankful for that at least.* With a strangled sound Alex realised what she was doing. *So now she was to be grateful for not being hit?* She slumped down onto the bed, stifling the harsh, humourless laugh. She knew where Samuel was going. Sometimes she could smell the woman's perfume on his clothes. A heavy, cloying, overly sweet scent which put her in mind of locked doors, closed curtains and candles lit for effect, not light.

The day had drawn in, the room no longer filled with sunlight. The abrupt dimness seemed darker than the afternoon hour implied, the shadows in the corners of the room more threatening. Alex moved to the bedroom door. No sound other than her daughter's heart-broken sobbing. For several seconds she listened, all her energy dripping away until she closed the door on Tyke's unhappiness. She leaned her back against the solid wood and stared at nothing.

Tyke had recently become afraid of monsters, sobbing out her fear, how they hid under beds or in wardrobes and waited for darkness. Of course her mother had soothed her as best she could, fervently denying the existence of such creatures. *But*, Alex thought numbly, *she could have told her daughter, yes, monsters do exist and sometimes they didn't hide in dark places.*

Sometimes the worst monsters hid only behind a smile and looked frighteningly like the people you loved.

***

Hugo whistled as he and Moss unloaded the cartload of crates into the cellar of the boarding house. This dark, brick-lined space was perfect for their business. It wasn't huge, in fact it mirrored the floor space of the kitchen and scullery which sat directly above it. What it lacked in size it made up for by the protection of hefty wooden doors with strong padlocks. There was just the one key. No one could get in here without either Hugo or Moss knowing about it.

Four years ago Hugo had returned to New Zealand and the younger sister he hadn't seen for twenty years. To his surprised delight Maudie hadn't changed. They picked up exactly where they had left off all those years ago. Though he hadn't expected it, Hugo discovered his greatest pleasure was to be part of a family. A ship-hand for most of his life, he had been the proverbial rolling stone, happily exchanging a settled domestic routine for the rough, hard life of a sailor. Only when he lost his Ameliese to typhoid did Hugo discover just how empty life could be if no one in the world was waiting for you to come home. It took a few more years even then until he eventually turned his back on a life at sea. He arrived on Maudie's front doorstep, lugging two big sea chests full of black market goods, for Hugo hadn't returned home without a plan to earn a tidy sum of money. With his nephew Moss a willing, quick-witted collaborator and his own contacts in the major ports of the world, Hugo had established a thriving business supplying hard-to-get goods and top of the range alcohol for eager New Zealanders with cash to spare.

With a grunt Hugo set down the two crates he was carrying and wiped a hand over his wet forehead. Moss was hard on his heels. The younger man placed his three crates on top of his uncle's two. No competition in this, of course.

'Get a move on, Grandad. There's plenty to lug in.'

Hugo gave a good-natured grin. 'No need for me to bust an artery with you to do the lion's share.'

'Donkey's share, more like.' Moss replied over his shoulder as he went back out to the cart.

Left alone, Hugo ran an appreciative eye over the carefully stacked wares. *Good haul, this one. We'll have no trouble shifting the lot.* Even allowing for the cut he gave his mates at the port and on shipboard, there was a tidy profit to be made.

A clatter of boots on the brick floor and Moss reappeared. He carried four crates this time and the look he gave Hugo as he set them down was teasingly eloquent. 'Ma's asking if we want a cuppa. Take a break?'

'Why not? No need to make a penance of it and I'm as dry as a lime-burner's boot.' They walked out into the sunshine, Hugo wincing as he massaged a sore shoulder. 'We'll shove the cart off the street, though. Don't trust the light-fingered bastards around here.'

Together they heaved their precious cargo up behind the building and away from prying eyes.

Moss laughed. 'Yeah. It'd be a bugger if we get ripped off before we can rip off anyone else.'

His uncle shook his head in mock sorrow. 'I dunno where you get your appalling cynicism from lad.' He'd no sooner finished speaking than Maudie bellowed to them from the scullery door.

'You two tycoons comin' in or not?'

Sharing a grin, they wandered inside, stamping the street off their boots at the doorway. Hugo ran the water in the scullery sink as Moss leaned against it.

'Did Taylor Green pay you the money for the last bottles we sold him?'

Moss shook his head. 'Not yet.'

Hugo frowned. 'He's two deliveries behind now.'

'Well, he's not the only one.' Moss scrubbed at his filthy hands. 'I get more 'put it on the tab' than money these days.'

'Remember what I told you, lad. It's better for all concerned if we don't let anyone run up a tab. We're not a charity and it only encourages blokes to think they've more money than they do.'

As he passed over the cloth, Moss reached for a hand towel. 'Don't worry, Uncle. I know the score. I never hand over the goods without the cash, not unless I know the bloke well.'

'Good.' Hugo gave his nephew a meditative stare. 'And it wouldn't hurt to keep a weather eye out. If men can't afford their grog, there's tough times ahead.'

'I'll get the buggers to settle up before the end of the month.'

'Moss! Maudie's made pikelets!' Tyke's excited voice reached them just as they finished washing.

At the kitchen table, Moss saw a plate of warm pikelets wrapped in a clean tea towel plus a newly opened jar of jam and a fresh pat of butter. In their hardworking household it was always jam or butter never both. He sat down beside Tyke. 'Pikelets, butter *and* jam? What's the occasion?'

'If yer complainin' yer can go without,' Maudie grumbled as she set the heavy teapot in front of Alex.

'No fear.' Moss grabbed two pikelets, spreading them with butter and sandwiching them together with jam.

Tyke was horrified at his gluttony and bad manners. 'Moss, don't take two!' In reply to this Moss stuffed both of them into his mouth. 'Maudie! Moss is being a pig.'

Maudie cuffed Moss's head as she passed him to sit down. 'Remember yer manners, boy!'

Moss winked at Tyke before whining, 'Uncle Hugo, Ma's being mean to me.' As Tyke turned to see Hugo's reaction, Moss whipped the pikelet off her plate. Her squeal of rage when she discovered its loss was music to Moss's ears.

Alex hadn't caught any of the by-play. At Tyke's shriek, she jumped and scolded, 'Tyke! Quiet at the table, please.'

Moss hastily replaced the stolen pikelet. 'It was my fault, Alex, not Tyke's. Sorry.' The apology was meant for Alex but it was to Tyke he shot a contrite look. The little girl was oblivious to Moss's remorse though. She was happily munching on the reclaimed pikelet.

With peace around the table again, Maudie resumed a conversation she and Alex had broken off to serve afternoon tea. 'Are yer set on yer plans, girl?'

'Yes, Ma. I am.' Alex gave Maudie a cool stare, her lips set in a determined line.

'It won't end well.' Maudie's warning was shrugged off.

'I have to try.'

'More fool you, putting yerself through it.'

Alex's knife clanged onto her plate. 'Doom-saying doesn't help, Ma. I've explained my reasons.'

An uncomfortable silence fell, the men exchanging quizzical looks.

'What's all this?' Hugo reached for the teapot.

'Nothing.' Alex replied, fooling no one for the smallest moment.

Never one to let an uncomfortable silence fall if he could help it, Hugo related a story about he and Maudie and a plate of burnt pikelets from their childhood. By the time he'd finished, the strained atmosphere had gone. Unlike her brother, though, Maudie thrived on a bit of awkwardness, or at least they all assumed she did because of her well-known talent for creating it.

Making eye contact with her son, she asked, 'Thought Samuel was meant t'be helping yer today?'

Moss spread another pikelet for Tyke before replying, 'He was,' hoping his Ma would let it drop. He should have known better.

'Dunno the last time that man done anything for anyone but himself. What's the bugger turned into?'

There was the sudden, loud scrape of chair legs across the wooden floor. Alex left the table, plate, tea cup and saucer in her hands, all of which she dumped unceremoniously onto the sink bench before leaving the room.   Moss shot Maudie an imploring look which she mercifully heeded for once, muttering whatever else she wanted to say under her breath instead. Quick-on-the-uptake Hugo distracted Tyke so Moss could leave the table, too.

Damn it Ma. Why can't you let things drop sometimes?

He found Alex in the parlour where she had thrown herself onto the sofa, staring at the floor. She radiated unhappiness. Moss sat beside her. He didn't speak. If Alex wanted to be alone he would go without argument yet he didn't want to deny her companionship while she was so obviously unhappy.

Long moments passed before Alex lifted her eyes and eased back on the sofa. With a sigh she laid her head against Moss's comforting shoulder as he slid a brotherly arm around her. 'He's getting worse and I don't know what to do.'

Nothing hurt Moss more than the way Samuel had changed since the war. At first they all thought he was fine. Yes he'd been wounded but he had survived and there were no other scars they could see. His first few explosions of temper they put down to him needing to settle down again. *He'll have seen things*, Hugo had told them. *Probl'y done things, too*, Maudie added. These comments made sense so they all gave Samuel the space he seemed to need. Then there was the first morning Alex came downstairs with a bruised face. She knew she couldn't write it off as tripping into a door for their harsh row must have been heard by everyone.

'It's nothing,' she told them all hastily. 'It was my fault really. He didn't want to talk and I forced him to.

Maudie kept her thoughts resolutely to herself as she found a compress for the bruising and avoided everyone's eyes.

The second time it happened, Moss met Alex on the landing as she returned from the bathroom. Her lip was still bleeding. He could hardly bear the way Alex kept her head up even as she swallowed down her tears.

'Let me talk to him,' Moss demanded.

'No, please. I shouldn't have provoked him.' A watery smile. 'I can't hold my tongue when he turns up drunk.' *Sam's demands for intimacy, only achieving arousal by his anger and her fear. His strength. Her defeat.*

'Alex.....'

She laid a hand on Moss's arm, pleading. 'It's all right, Moss, I promise. It won't happen again. He's sorry he did it.'

So Moss stood to one side and he, too began to avoid his family's empathetic eyes.

They had to accept it. The Samuel they all knew and loved had gone, replaced by an angry, aggressive drunk who got into fights and, all too often, used his fists on his wife. The household rallied around Alex as best they could, trying to keep things normal for Tyke's sake.

Further down the track here was Moss offering more consolation as he held Alex. He could feel the effort she put in to keep from crying.

'What should I do?' she whispered brokenly.

'Leave him.' Moss hated himself for saying it. Like Alex he loved the tormented Samuel but how long should Alex have to live imprisoned in a painful marriage? *Love shouldn't wear bruises and it shouldn't give them.*

'I can't. He needs me.'

'He's got a funny bloody way of showing it!'

'I've done nothing but try to understand him, Moss, racking my brains for the reason why my husband is so different from the one I married and you know what? I think every outburst of violence from Sam is a really silent scream. The war did this to him. He barely sleeps. The times he does, he wakes up gasping and shaking at things only he knows. I can't desert him. Any more than Cally could desert Jimmy. Just because

26

Sam doesn't wear his wounds the way Jimmy does, doesn't mean he hasn't been grievously injured.' Now the tears came and Alex wiped her eyes. 'Poor Cally.'

Mystified by the object of her sympathy Moss frowned. 'Cally?'

'The day I took Jimmy home. The look on her face when she saw him for the first time. She hated him, Moss. Hated the way he looked, the way he'd changed from the attractive man she'd married and I felt such contempt for her! All my compassion was for the broken, ruined man. Cally wished Jimmy had died and, God! How I resented her for it.' Alex drew away from Moss, taking in his serious face as she forced herself to continue. 'But now,' her handkerchief crumpled in a tight fist. 'Now I understand what Cally meant because I hate my husband as well. And I love him. And it's my love which ties me to him and I hate him for that, too.'

What could he say? There was nothing Moss could say to make this better. He drew Alex to him in an embrace containing as much concern as it did pity.

They were silent for a long time.

'Alex, what were you and Ma arguing about earlier?'

'I'm taking Tyke to meet my parents.' She sat up once more, patting her hair tidy before offering Moss a wry smile. 'And, well, you heard what Ma thinks of the idea.'

'Have they been in touch?'

'No. It's just Tyke asked me why she doesn't have any grandparents like her friend does. Her question set me thinking. I know we parted on bad terms but how could any grandparent turn their back on their only grandchild? How long could they hold onto their anger against me once they meet Tyke?'

If they'd wanted contact, Alex, how difficult would it have been for them to find you?

There was such longing on Alex's face Moss didn't have the heart to express his doubts.

Tyke was excited. Mama dressed her in her Sunday best even though it wasn't Sunday and said they were going visiting.

'So I want you to be on your very best behaviour, Tyke.'

'Yes, Mama.'

'No talking if adults are talking. You speak only when you're spoken to.'

'I know.'

'Best manners, too. I assume you remember what manners are?' If Alex's words were sarcastic her tone wasn't. When her daughter grinned she hugged her. 'Good girl.'

Hand-in-hand they walked downstairs, pausing at the kitchen door.

Maudie gave a disapproving sniff. 'Goin' through with it, then?'

'As you see.'

'I'd wish yer luck but there ain't enough luck in the world for what your doin''

Alex chose not to take offence. Instead she moved into the room. 'Not even a hug for the condemned woman?'

It was then Maudie understood just how conflicted Alex was. She felt her trembling when they embraced and all her dire warnings melted away. She whispered for Alex's ears only, 'If they don't take yer back into their lives they don't deserve yer, girl. Think on that now.'

A final loving squeeze and Alex left Maudie's arms for the unknown.

To Tyke's delight they took a tram. She loved these rattly carriages, sitting on the wooden bench with her back straight and her hands on her lap just like her mother. Although maybe not exactly like; Alex was unusually restless, hands playing with her handbag handle or flattening imaginary creases out of her skirt. Though she had put a brave face to confront Maudie's scepticism, Alex felt ridiculously nervous. It had been seven years since she had last seen her parents and all she could remember was her father's face twisted in disbelief and anger on the afternoon Samuel asked for his daughter's hand in marriage. *Poor Samuel barely had time to ask the question when Father dismissed him.* Alex refused to leave Samuel so Edward abruptly turned her out of the family home, his daughter left with nothing but the clothes she was wearing. Maudie had taken in the distraught young woman, made sure she had clothes on her back and somewhere to call home. Alex had been pregnant then too, unwilling to tell Samuel and cast more troubles onto his head.

Again, Maudie had stood beside her, never judging, always offering support and comfort. *As every parent should.*

Alex shifted restlessly on the hard wooden seat as the tram stopped, people swarming in and out. Maudie's love had replaced both her parents' grudging affection. *So why this overriding need to try to reconnect with those who disowned her? It was the war,* she decided. *It had changed everything.*

It changed everyone and left so many people with a sense of fragility of their place in the world. The impossible had happened, the worst events of generations and there were no certainties anymore, no sense the sun would rise on a world as uncomplicated as it had been before 1914.

Staring out the window as the tram made its way down Courtney Place, Alex caught sight of a poster advertising the Socialist Hall and with a start she knew she was deceiving herself. Pre-war life had been vicious.

The Great Strike showed wealthy New Zealanders to be brutal and capable of terrible cruelty against those going without even the barest necessities. Life had been just as uncertain, then, more so. Men strove to find work, employers tried to crush rebellious strikers. Frederick Evans's murder in Waihi had brought it all to a head and the Great Strike made a battlefield out of New Zealand's cities.

You're looking in the wrong place for an answer, Alex. Her feeling had nothing to do with politics or countries. It was right here with her now. *Tyke.* She cast a downwards glance at her own daughter, sitting so proudly and felt such a surge of love she wanted to burst into tears It wasn't the fragility of the world which concerned Alex. It was the fragility of families. She and Samuel had lost their sense of family, of facing the world together against all odds and it left her exposed. She didn't diminish everything Maudie had been and had become *but blood was blood, wasn't it?* She wanted to be accepted back into her parents' lives again. Alex reached out and took Tyke's hand in hers, the little girl giving her a happy, confiding smile.

Who could prove obdurate against such a smile?

For the first time since she had made her decision, Alex felt a glow of optimism and hope.

The two-storied house on Tinakori Road looked the same. Even the roses marching up the front garden path were unchanged, the brilliant, rich flowers and buds nestled among deep green leaves. Alex closed her eyes briefly and breathed in, convincing herself she could smell their apple-scented sweetness from where they stood out on the road.

'Why are we standing here?' Tyke asked, bored with standing still for all of two minutes.

'I'm just making sure we have the right address.'

'Don't you know? Who are we visiting?'

'Tyke you're asking too many questions.'

'Only two!'

'That's two too many, darling.' Alex was debating fiercely in her mind; *should she tell Tyke who they were visiting or not?* The girl's pleasure at the possibility of grandparents couldn't be denied. *But if they didn't want to know her?* What a terrible blow for a young one to recover from. In the end, Alex decided not to say. *Better to think you have no grandparents than long for them and be rejected by them.* Taking Tyke by the hand once more, Alex nerved herself to walk up to the front door and pull on the bell. It tingled inside the house. Heart thumping, the door opened and they were greeted by a sour-faced maid.

'Yes?'

'Is Mrs Edwina Redburn at home?'

'Yes.'

Pause.

'Then may I speak with her?'

Grudgingly, the maid gestured for them to enter. Alex stood in the hallway trying to ignore the ghosts and the echoes from the past who lingered in doorways and corners. *Bobby, the world at his feet. Bobby the adored son who could do no wrong. Bobby, dead from opium and in the end loved only by the sister who had never measured up.*

The maid interrupted Alex's reverie. 'If you wouldn't mind waiting in the parlour, I shall tell Madam you're here. Who shall I say is calling?'

'Mrs Alexandra Brodie.'

The wait seemed interminable. *Was Father was in the house and if so, would Mama fetch him*?

Seeing Tyke reaching towards a china vase on a low occasional table, Alex prevented any mishap by steering her to the sofa where they both sat out of harm's way.

Tyke was mesmerised by the room. The beautiful, rich curtains and all the pretty things on the tables and in the cabinets against the walls. She wriggled her feet on the carpet. *It was just like Uncle Hugo had told her! A huge carpet taking up the whole floor so you could only see the edge of the wooden floorboards around the outside of it.* Tyke longed to lie on it and see what the all the pictures were so she could tell Uncle Hugo and Moss all about them. She had just opened her mouth to ask permission when the door to the parlour opened and an old woman came in.

Alex's first thought at the sight of her mother was, *she's aged terribly.* Her instinctive emotion was pity. Edwina's hands were trembling so much it couldn't be dismissed as mere nerves. *Mama isn't well.* Then, on the upswell of tender emotion Alex met her mother's eyes and froze.

'What are you doing here, Alexandra?' There was no forgiveness in Edwina's heavily lined face. 'We made our feelings abundantly clear seven years ago.'

Alex found her voice as she came to her feet, Tyke's hand clutched in hers. 'This is my daughter, Jeannie Margaret.'

Tyke heard something in her mother's voice she had never heard before. She noticed her tension, the way Mama held her hand so hard it hurt. *Jeannie was her real name but Mama never called her Jeannie. No one did. Mama was afraid.* Tyke swallowed painfully. *Why was she afraid?*

At Alex's reassuring nod Tyke gave her best curtsey and smiled up at the old woman staring at her. Her smile faltered when it wasn't returned.

'I fail to see why you think this would be of any interest to us.'

'Mama, please.'

The breath left Tyke's body. She forgot all her manners and tugged at Alex's hand.

'Is this your mother, Mama? My grandmother? Do I have a grandmother?'

Alex knelt down and held Tyke's warm hands in her cold ones. 'Darling, we can talk about this later. Please.' And in the final single word Tyke heard all the unspoken sub-text. *Please don't ask questions now. Please just be good. Please trust me.* To Alex's intense relief, Tyke gave way and sat back down on the sofa, hands pressed between her knees, her back ramrod stiff. Coming back to her feet Alex moved towards Edwina who lifted a hand as if to ward the younger woman off.

'Mama, I wanted you to meet your granddaughter.'

A hunger burned in Edwina's eyes and was gone so quickly maybe Alex imagined it. Instead, Edwina took refuge behind a haughty demeanour. 'You made your decision when you chose an unsuitable man over your family, Alexandra. There really is nothing more to say.'

Greatly daring, Alex reached for her mother's hand. She held it tightly, forcing eye contact. 'Are you sure, Mama? Truly sure? Look at her. Please just take one look at her.'

It was against Edwina's own will, that much was obvious, as her head turned to the child sitting upright and tremulous on the sofa.

Alex lowered her voice. 'Jeannie's your only grandchild. Father may be unbending but are you so sure you can turn us away, Mama? Because if you do, we shan't return. I will not subject my daughter to such a rejection from her family ever again.'

Edwina's unblinking scrutiny of Tyke made the little girl uneasy. She stood, flustered and unsure, only to realise she shouldn't have moved. Tyke hastily sat back down again, her eyes wretchedly seeking her mother's for reassurance but all Alex's attention was focussed on her mother as she continued softly, imploringly. 'Mama? We can meet in secret if you wish. Father need never know.'

Edwina's eyes met Alex's. This time the yearning burned there for the world to see. Alex's relief showed in her smile as Edwina broke contact and took a step backwards. The tremble of her hands and arms increased to shaking now though she held herself upright and proud.

'You made your decision, Alexandra. You having a child with that man does not make her a grandchild of ours.'

Alex heard a stifled cry from Tyke.

Silence.

After long moments, Alex found her voice. 'Is it your final word on the matter?'

'It is.'

'Very well, Mama.' Alex broke eye contact. 'Jeannie, darling?' Alex held out a hand and Tyke rushed to cling to it, tears shining in her hazel eyes as she stared up at the grandmother who was rejecting her.   Despite the tremor in her voice Alex met her mother's cold face with an aloofness of her own.   'We shall not bother you again.'   Without another word they left, Tyke falling over her feet to keep up with the swift steps her mother took to escape.

Edwina stood alone in the empty parlour.   She had done exactly what Edward had commanded.   Her hands shook so much it took real effort to lock the parlour door.   Only then was it safe to release her tears.

Late that night when Alex made her way to bed, she paused as she always did outside Tyke's bedroom before going quietly in to check she was asleep.   Moving softly, Alex approached the bed and automatically pulled the blankets more snugly around the sleeper. A furry head appeared from under the top blanket. Fluff the cat taking his comfort where he could find it. He pressed his face against Alex's fingers, his purr a deep rumble.

Alex rubbed his ears and whispered, 'You soppy old thing.' As Fluff curled into a tight ball of fur, Alex kissed Tyke's curly head and turned to leave.

A little hand grabbed at her skirt.

'Why doesn't Grandmother want me?'   Tears edged Tyke's voice and when Alex stroked her face, her fingers came away wet with tears shed quietly in the dark.

'I thought you were asleep.'   Alex sat down on the bed and Tyke snuggled into her.

'I tried.'

'You need your sleep. When you sleep you grow.'

'Grandmother hates me, doesn't she?'

'Oh, darling, no. She doesn't.   But it's complicated, and unfortunately, you have ended up in the middle of all those complications.'   Alex sighed and stretched out on the bed to hug Tyke all the more closely.

Tyke sniffed and wiped her nose on the sleeve of her nightgown. 'Is it to do with you not marrying a rich man?'

'Who told you such a thing?'

Moss could get into trouble for telling the secret! Tyke hastily scrambled for a believable reply. 'I heard people talking. They said Father was too poor and you shouldn't have married him.'

Alex listened to her daughter's voice in amazement. *Firstly, how could anyone speak of such things in Tyke's hearing, and secondly, how simple it sounded spoken in the words of a six year old.* 'Well, yes. It is true.'

'And my grandparents were angry?'

'Yes. They were. Very angry.'

Silence.

Tyke settled more comfortably, feeling her mother's arms tighten around her. She was drowsy now, the excitement and emotion of the day falling away. 'Would you be angry if I married a poor man?'

'No. Not if he loved you and you loved him.'

'What if I married a rich man?'

Alex laughed teasingly. 'Of course, that would be best of all!'

'Would it?' Tyke missed the irony.

She seemed so genuinely interested in the possibility Alex hastened to amend her mockery. 'No, darling. I was only teasing. Money makes life easier though not necessarily happier. I think happy is always better than easy because if you're happy, the difficult things don't seem so difficult and if you're miserable and unhappy, even paying the bills won't make you any more content.'

Pause.

Alex could feel Tyke's body growing heavier in her arms as she relaxed. 'Do you understand?'

'I think so.' Tyke's voice was sleepy now. 'Mama, I'm glad Grandmother doesn't want us. She was very angry and we have enough angry with Father.'

There was absolutely no denying it, Alex thought, again admiring the way her daughter went straight to the heart of difficult things and accepted them in her guileless way. She sat up on an elbow to stroke the soft face. 'Do you think you can sleep now?'

'Yes.' Tyke reached for her doll, the one Moss had bought for her third birthday. Louise was a bit tatty now. Her dress had been patched by Tyke in her first sewing lesson with Alex but however worn she was she never left Tyke's pillow, always there to welcome the little girl after her busy days.

Alex slid off the bed and drew the blankets up to Tyke and Louise's chins, kissing both faces, running her fingers along Fluff's silky coat. 'Goodnight, darling. Sleep well.'

'G'night.'

Tyke was asleep before Alex closed her bedroom door.

***

Murchison
July

Once inside the barn Matthew shook the raindrops from his hair and shoulders, shivering a little as he shrugged more snugly into his outdoor coat. It was a typical Murchison winter day. In fact, it was one in a fortnight of neverending typical Murchison winter days and Matthew had had enough of them. *Day after day stuck in the house with Father made each and every hour wretched.* He and his twin sister Fee couldn't make a noise. They could barely speak above a whisper, tiptoeing from room to room because no one ever knew what would set Jimmy off. Fee took her brother to task over his lack of sympathy for their father only to have Matthew rebuff her anger with his own bitterness. *It wasn't his fault the old man was a wreck, was it?* Last night, as Fee helped their mother clear up after dinner, a saucepan had slipped out of her hands into the sink, breaking a plate in the process. Jimmy had shoved away from the table, hands pressed to his ears, screaming. Matthew watched the distraught, writhing man in disgust, leaving his sister to calm him. Then in the early hours of this morning, the whole house had been disturbed by one of Jimmy's bad dreams. Home felt more like a tomb than ever. The oppressive atmosphere weighed Matthew down until he couldn't stand it a moment longer. Grabbing his coat and ignoring his mother's questions, he left. From the window above the sink, Cally watched her son's escape. Through the rain he raced across the sodden paddocks in a futile effort to outrun his frustration, finally coming to a panting halt against a closed gate. Leaning on the wet, wooden spars Matthew stared down into the gully where the river ran deeply, sniffing back the hard lump in his throat. *No tears. Tears were for cissies! What would Drover or Colin say if they knew he cried?*

The chilly rain pelted down harder and Matthew hunched further into his coat, wishing he'd thought to grab his cap as well. He didn't want to stay out here freezing. He needed shelter. *But where could he go? No way he was going home nor did he want to see his grandparents because Grandma had too sharp an eye.* She would ask Mathew why he was upset no matter how hard he pretended he wasn't and Matthew knew he would find himself telling the truth because he just couldn't lie to Emily and his honesty would only upset her. After some thought he decided to head for the barn.

So here he was, angry, resentful and restless. Matthew paced, kicking sacks of feed and bales of hay aggressively. The hard mass in his throat choked him as a queasiness surged through his stomach. He fought valiantly against the tears even as his lips trembled and his eyes welled.

Maybe he could run away? But where could he run to? And what would he do for money?

'I hate father,' he told the empty barn, unable to keep his voice from shaking. 'Hate him! Why doesn't he just bloody die or something?'

But the barn wasn't quite empty. To the boy's horror, his grandfather came limping out from the little tack room in the back corner. Matthew was in awe of his grandfather. Emily he loved unconditionally and always felt comfortable in her company while John was a quiet man who never spoke much to anyone and rarely to his grandchildren. They could never tell what he was thinking. There was also the boy's instinctive understanding that Emily would forgive them any misdemeanour whereas John would not. The thought made Matthew stutter in panic as the old man drew nearer. 'Grandfather, I'm sorry! So sorry! I didn't mean it! I....'

'It's all right, lad.'

To Matthew's amazement John's hand lay briefly on his wet head in a rare caress. To his shame, the hot tears he had been struggling against ran down his cheeks and he hastily brushed them away as he looked into his grandfather's lined, gentle face. 'I'm so sorry. I shouldn't have.....'

'Hush, lad.   No one heard but me, the rats and mice and maybe the spiders, if they have any interest in our doings.' John had bridles and girths in one hand and he waved them towards his pale-faced grandson. 'Come and help me clean this lot. I could do with an extra pair of hands this morning.' Without waiting to see if he was followed, John limped back to the tack room. Inside, he gathered the oil and soft cloths, drawing his comfortable wooden chair near to an upturned box onto which he placed everything. He looked towards the doorway where Matthew hovered, still nervous and uncertain, his face smeared with dirt and tears. John pulled another crate close, upended it and patted the seat it made. 'Sit you down, lad. I won't bite.'

Hesitantly Matthew joined him. He took the bottle of oil and the rag John passed him, tipping the oil onto the cloth to rub it into the leather the way he'd been taught. There was no sound except the swish of cloth on leather, the muted jangle of the metal harnessing and bits as they worked. Matthew began to relax in the familiar routine of his labour.

John kept one eye on the grandson who looked so much like Jimmy. Without effort, the old man conjured up the Jimmy he first knew at the orphanage in Stoke all those years ago. *He was right there in the bones of Matthew's face, the set of his head, even in the shape and colour of the lad's eyes.* Not much similarity in their characters though and John had spent long hours wondering if it was a good thing or not. 'How old are you now, lad?'

'Don't you remember, Grandfather? I'm seven in six days.'

'So you are. I seem to recall your Grandma mentioning a party.'

Matthew's face lit up, all tension flown at the magical word. He'd badgered his mother for weeks, alternately pleading and sulking until she'd finally given way, her misgivings obvious to anyone other than a single-minded six year old who could see no further than his first, proper birthday party.

'Grandma's baking me a cake and everything.' Matthew rested his chin on his elbow, the tack cleaning briefly forgotten. 'And do you know, Grandfather, I'm the only person in school to have a party this year.'

'It's Fee's party as well, isn't it?'

Matthew made a dismissive noise as he picked up the cloth again. 'Well, I suppose it is. But it was me who got Mother to agree to one because Fee said she didn't care if we had a party or not, so really, it's more my party than hers.'

John hid a smile. Here was the difference between his son and grandson. Matthew's cockiness, his assuredness, all his bolshie attitude was poles apart from Jimmy as a boy and as a man. No wonder they clashed. John knew he should reprimand the lad for his attitude but every time he resolved to have a word with him, Matthew would grin and John lost the heart for growling. *He was young yet,* he reasoned. *Plenty of time for tellings off.*

'How's school going?'

Matthew scowled. 'It's all right, I suppose. I only like arithmetic. Fee doesn't. She likes writing compositions. That's just like a girl, isn't it Grandfather?'

'I don't rightly know, lad. I was never a hand for writing or numbers. Mind, I left school at twelve when my father needed help on the farm.'

'Twelve?' Naked envy coloured the boy's voice. 'I hope I can leave school at twelve. Then I could do real work.'

'What would you work at? Farming or something else?' John was sincerely interested in Matthew's reply. A farmer worked for the future and always hoped his own blood would take over the land he had slaved to clear and make productive. *Of course, his expectation had always been for Jimmy to take over the farm.* Here John stopped his train of thought. *No point travelling the well-trod road.*

Matthew gave the question deep contemplation. He'd always expected to end up running home farm like his

Grandfather.   To be questioned about any possible alternatives made him stop and think. *It wasn't only farming he enjoyed.   He loved motor cars too, and the machines his uncles worked on in their workshop in town.*   When he didn't have chores, Matthew spent many happy hours getting covered in oil and filth as he helped Wally and Ben tinkering, repairing or even building machinery.

'I think I want to be a farmer like you, Grandfather but using tractors and machinery like Uncle Ben and Uncle Wally work on. They say machines make farming so much easier. They say there's more money in machines than horses.' Matthew reached for the oil again.   'Can't we get a tractor, Grandfather?' The boy's eyes shone excitedly at the possibility.

'Your father couldn't cope with the noise, lad.'

All happy expectation drained out of Matthew's face. He concentrated on the bridle in his hand. 'Yes. Of course. I forgot.'   Matthew rubbed oil into the leather as if his life depended on it.

John watched him silently for a few moments before reaching over and laying his work-roughened hand with its swollen knuckles over his grandson's smooth, dirty one. 'We don't know what the future holds for us, lad. Maybe we can get a tractor one day. Maybe you could think on it anyways. Just in case. If we do get one, you'll know all about them, won't you?'

Matthew's smile lit the miserable day as his enthusiasm took flight. 'I'll learn everything I can from Uncle Ben and Uncle Wally. There's nothing they don't know about engines.'

'You do that. Now, tell me all about this party, then.'

The boy dropped the rag and bridle and drew in one big breath.

***

It was everything Matthew hoped. He had invited his three best mates, Hamish, Colin and Drover, the boys keeping their distance from Fee and her friends when they wanted to play party games.

'Boys and girls don't mix.' Matthew told his twin disdainfully.

Because it was a special occasion, John had given permission to play in the barn, so the boys gleefully refought the Great War to their satisfaction, killing the Hun while winning medals and glory. They had no doubt war was glory and fighting always done for honour and the King's Empire. Colin's father had won the Military Medal for bravery and Drover's had died at Ypres. Hamish's dad made it home with the Star, the War Medal and the Victory Medal and unscathed. No one ever mentioned Matthew's father. This party was one of the rare occasions the boys had seen Jimmy. At the sight of him Colin and Drover exchanged aghast looks and these exchanges made Matthew burn with humiliation. Hamish offered only pity which was so much worse though Matthew couldn't explain why.

It's all Mother's fault! He had asked to have the party at Grandfather's or his uncles' workshop in town but she'd refused, knowing only too well her son's reasoning.

'If you want the party, Matthew then of course your father will be there.'

'But my friends will see him!'

Cally's lips tightened. 'You have to live with him, Matthew as do we all.'

Thankfully, Father kept to himself for the most part and Matthew made sure his friends spent ages in the barn. After taking a particularly tricky gun emplacement, the four boys threw themselves on top of a pile of sacks, panting hard.

'Wish we could go to war,' Colin said, aiming his finger-gun at a sparrow high in the rafters. 'I could win a medal like dad.'

Drover picked up a clod of dirt and hiffed it at the bird, which flew away in fright. 'Yeah, and I bet I'd survive. Not like my old man.'

'Well, at least he died a hero, eh? Mum says all the men who died in the war were heroes.' Hamish dug into his pockets and pulled out a ragged bag of humbugs which he generously handed round.

Matthew said nothing. He sucked on the sweet and ignored the way they studiously avoided his eyes. After the last of the humbugs had been eaten, Hamish made to screw up the paper bag when Drover caught his eye and shook his head, finger to his lips. Careful to make sure Matthew's attention was elsewhere, he took the bag from the curious Hamish, carefully folded it up and tucked it into his jacket.

Hamish mouthed, *what you gonna do with it?*

Drover just grinned wickedly.

Janet moved through the sitting room, anxiously seeking her brother-in-law among the people gathered there. Jimmy didn't like crowds and Janet was unhappy her sister had arranged this birthday party for the twins. *She could have held it at Emily and John's, even in Wally and Ben's workshop.* Instead Jimmy's sanctuary had been invaded and for no good cause in Janet's opinion. *Children did not need birthday parties.* She scanned the room impatiently. *Where was he?*

Movement out the window caught her eye as Jimmy's familiar shape limped passed. Offering bland smiles to anyone in her path, Janet wandered outside, looking around the well-tended garden until she caught Jimmy's back heading towards the river. Taking a moment to put on her coat, Janet jogged nearer, careful not to startle him.

'Lost your party appetite?'

A wan smile. 'Not my cup of tea, really.'

They were comfortable enough in each other's company to walk in relaxed silence. Jimmy held his good arm out for her, offering the ghost of the cheeky grin Janet remembered from before the war. With an ironic bow she took it regally, changing her usual lope for an elegant strut until he laughed. In a few minutes they reached the willow tree near the river bank. The crumbling edge was much closer to its trunk after regular winter storms, so close in fact, when they sat and rested their backs against the bark, their heels hung out over the brink.

Jimmy drew in a deep, contented breath. 'This has always been my favourite place in the world. I spent hours up in those branches as a lad.' He leaned his head back, squinting through the skeleton of intertwined tree limbs. 'Hiding away from the world.' His voice drifted off.

Seeing his distraction, Janet drew him back with a nudge. When he turned to her she wished it was always so easy.

'What?'

'You were gone for a moment there.'

His eyes darkened. 'Plenty to go from.' Jimmy ran a hand over his bad leg before impatiently and awkwardly tugging his twisted jacket sleeve down his stiff arm. When his fingers fumbled with the fabric, he swore, swotting Janet's hand away as she tried to help. 'I'm not a bloody child, Janet!'

'I know.'

'Do you?' There was heat in his burned, ruined face, scepticism in his roughened tone.

'Yes, Jimmy. I do.' Janet held his glower placidly until he looked away with an unwilling nod. *It never got any better*, she decided long ago, praying for the day she could see Jimmy and forget the good looks and wicked sense of humour he used to have. Every memory of him was spoilt because his exuberant past had proved so fleeting, so heart-breakingly fragile. Eight years ago he had sailed off to war. It seemed like no time and a lifetime all at once. She knew Cally continued seeing Jimmy's old friend Jeff. Sometimes Janet would catch a look on Jimmy's face at the sight of his wife and the poignancy of his expression was enough to make her wonder whether he knew, too. *Coward as she was she would never ask him. She hated what her sister was doing but by God, she understood why she did it!* Years ago with Jimmy at war, Cally had confessed how much she hated him, telling her sister one anguished night not long after he came home that he was drowning her and she couldn't cut him free. Society's expectations, duty, marriage vows, all these things tied her to Jimmy and for Cally there was no escape except for those stolen hours with Jeff.

And me? Janet peeped sideways at her brother-in-law. She still loved him and irony didn't come any stronger or more bitter. The same tethers binding Cally to Jimmy were the same ones which kept Janet from him. *No point dwelling on these things!* She clicked her fingers at the recumbent Jimmy. 'Come on, lazy lump. The twins can't cut the cake without their father there to see.'

Jimmy wriggled upright, Janet fighting the impulse to offer him her hand. 'Damn lot of nonsense for young ones,' he grumbled.

'Oh, don't be a killjoy,' Janet replied, inwardly smiling at her own hypocrisy for Jimmy's comment had been her own thought not half an hour since.

'Well,' he muttered, refraining from further complaints.

When they walked back into the living room, Cally was talking animatedly to Jeff.

Jimmy dragged his gaze from them. 'I wasn't even missed.'

Janet pointed at Fee, joyfully heading straight for them. 'I wouldn't bet on it.'

'Da, where'd you go? I looked for you.' Fee took his hand, automatically grabbing his good one to lead Jimmy towards the kitchen table where the birthday cake sat in delicious isolation at the head of the table.

'I needed a few moments of quiet, love.' He noticed Cally's start when she realised her husband was close to her once more; the way she abruptly drew away from Jeff as if caught out. *She'd have been better to stay where she was,* Jimmy thought, returning Jeff's smile with a meaningless one of his own.

As the family gathered around the table, Matthew and Fee's friends formed a huddle near the middle. Drover's hand slipped into his pocket, fingers curling around the paper bag. He made sure he had Colin's attention then with slow, backward steps, retreated unobserved behind all the adults. Hamish was standing at Matthew's shoulder, the latter proud to be the centre of attention as he and a shy-looking Fee were placed behind the cake as its candles were lit. Cally led them all in singing happy birthday and Matthew felt a surge of pure happiness. When the twins blew the candles out, he wished it could always be like this. Then Drover brought his hands sharply around the tightly blown up paper bag. The explosion caused panic. People spun around to find the cause. Fee's friends screamed and Matthew's greatest nightmare came horribly to life.

Before Janet or Fee could prevent it, Jimmy hit the floor, shrieking. 'Get down! Get down! Jesus Christ, save yourselves!'

In front of horrified eyes, he cringed under the table, sobbing and incoherent, as a dark stain appeared through his trousers and pooled around him. There were long moments of awful silence until Drover burst out laughing, the sound smashing into the hush. The looks he received only made him laugh harder. With a strangled gasp Hamish threw a punch which collided with Drover's nose. Eyes watering, Drover swung a fist in clumsy retaliation just as Jeff grabbed his arm, wrenching it painfully behind the boy's back. Jeff ignored Drover's protests, hauling him out the house, telling Cally, 'I'll deal with the little bastard.'

She didn't hear him. Cally had frozen, staring at her husband. Her friends left in mortification as Fee, Janet, Emily and John clustered together to hide the traumatised Jimmy from view. Colin disappeared out of the house before anyone realised he'd gone and Hamish could think of nothing to say. He touched Matthew's shoulder and opened his mouth only to be shoved aside as his friend fled the scene, white faced and shaking. Even though he felt like an intruder, Hamish didn't want to just slink away. He approached Cally warily. 'Mrs Benn, can I do anything to help?'

Matthew's mother didn't move, so Hamish repeated his question and this time she turned to him. 'No, Hamish. I think you had better go.' Cally's voice dropped to a whisper and the boy could barely make out what she said but he thought it was, 'There's nothing anyone can do.'

***

The rain didn't let up. Monday meant school and Matthew dragged his feet. He was reluctant to get out of bed, slow to dress, driving Cally to distraction with his moaning.

Mathew clutched dramatically at his stomach. 'I feel sick,'

'So do I,' was his mother's exasperated reply, 'although I will improve wonderfully when you two are at school.'

Matthew pointed out of the kitchen window and scowled at the teeming skies. 'It's raining.'

'And Aunt Janet said she'll take you in the covered cart. She has to pick some things up from town and will drop you off on the way. Oh, good girl.' This last to Fee who had deftly plaited her hair and now had her coat on ready to go.

Matthew scowled at his sister. 'Trust you to be a Miss Goody Two Shoes,' he hissed under his breath.

Fee ignored him as she so often did, remembering to pick up the brown paper bags containing their sandwiches for lunch. She understood why her brother was being such a pain and she wanted to let him know she understood. However Fee also knew he would angrily rebuff any overtures of sympathy so she determined to bite her tongue and keep a watchful eye on him. *They were exactly the same age so how come she felt so much older?*

She thrust his lunch bag at him as their mother went to dress Jimmy. 'Look, come on.' Fee dragged him out the door to wait on the veranda. 'If you're like this with Aunt Janet she'll make you walk.'

It was no idle threat for the no-nonsense Janet had done it before, sick to the back teeth of Matthew's whinging.

'Aunt Janet's a cow.'

'No, she's not. You're just in one of your moods.' Quiet and painfully shy among people she didn't know, Fee was unsparing of her opinions around those she felt safe with. When it came to her twin she was even capable of merciless, brutal honesty.

Reluctant to admit she was right, Matthew lapsed into the sulky silence which proved Fee's diagnosis spot on. He kicked his heels away from his twin, letting the rain splash onto his hot face until the doors to the barn were flung open and Aunt Janet led the horses out, the cart hitched behind them.

'Morning you two. Jump on quick. I'm a bit late so we'll have to get a wriggle on.'

Matthew instantly brightened up. Late meant a quick trip and he loved speed. The faster the better. By the time they reached the single-story weatherboard schoolhouse sitting in a paddock, he was over his sulk. Leaping down from the cart with a crow of goodbye, he raced the raindrops to the little foyer behind the front door. Fee was hard on his footsteps, giggling as she shook herself free of her coat and hat. Quickly placing outdoor things and bags on their hooks, the twins walked through to the school room where the desks sat in lines down its length and the cast-iron stove exuded much needed warmth on this chilly day.

It was the boys' job to see there was enough wood chopped and stacked in the woodshed to keep the fire burning over the cold months, the girls' to clean the stove and sweep up the ashes.

By the time the twins reached their desks, Matthew became aware of sniggering. He met the devilish glint in Drover's eyes and felt a chill of apprehension as he hastily dropped his gaze. All around the twins, children whispered behind their hands.

'Settle down, settle down.'

At their headmaster's words, attention left the Benns to focus instead on the blackboard. But, not quite all the attention. Colin and Hamish sat either side of Matthew, Drover in the desk immediately behind. As soon as he was safe from detection, Drover grabbed his ruler and poked Matthew's back. 'Great party, Benn,' he whispered. 'The floor show was hilarious.'

'Shut up,' Matthew hissed over his shoulder.

Drover leaned closer, his eyes cautiously on their headmaster busily drawing a map on the blackboard. 'If you'd said, we coulda brought our mum's buckets and mops. You know, to help clean up all that conchie piss. Your old man pissed himself even at the thought of war, eh? Like the bloody coward he is.'

With a roar of rage, Matthew spun round and launched himself across the bigger boy's desk, pounding him as hard as he could with both fists. All around them boys shouted encouragement while Fee leapt to her feet and pushed through the press of bodies, frantic to reach her brother. She made it just as Drover recovered enough to retaliate. He heaved against the enraged Matthew with all his might, his elbow swinging back and colliding with Fee. The girl stumbled backwards into a desk, completely off balance. She lost her footing, hitting her head on the hard corner. Fee collapsed to the floor unconscious. Nobody noticed at first. Bodies were jostled to and fro, some in eagerness to be close to the action, some in fright to get away from it. The headmaster tried to restore order through the pandemonium of his usually orderly classroom. He grabbed his cane and dragged Matthew off Drover, the boy spitting and writhing in his frenzy.

'Enough!' His bellow brought the uproar to a sudden halt.

Matthew grappled to reach Drover until the painful grip on his shoulders tightened and he stopped, red-faced and panting.

Glaring around, the headmaster demanded, 'Someone tell me what on earth happened here.'

Before he could get a reply, Fee's friend Mary gave a scream. 'Sir! It's Fee. She's dead, sir!' Mary pointed to the unconscious Fee.

Chaos ensued.

With one hand gripping Matthew's shoulder, the headmaster pushed through the fascinated audience to where Fee lay, blood oozing from her head wound. Even as he knelt down, the little girl groaned and began to sit up. Holding Matthew onto the nearest chair with a warning which kept the boy unmoving and rigid, the headmaster then scooped Fee up in his arms and lay her down on a bench under one of the high windows. Swiftly he grabbed the first aid kit and skilfully administered to her wounds.

'She will be all right,' he told the assembled press of children, all watching with bated breath. 'Who rode to school today?' Two pairs of hands shot into the air. The headmaster sized them up, choosing the most reliable and the least excitable. 'David, ride to the Benn's and let Fee's mother or aunt know what's happened. Tell them I think it would be better if they picked her up and kept her at home for a couple of days.'

Not even pausing to acknowledge his orders, David strode out, a hero to the more susceptible youngsters, a source of envy for the older ones. Any immediate danger over, the headmaster turned to confront the cause of the uproar only to find Matthew had gone.

Where was Matthew?

Hamish wasn't the only one concerned as the day stretched into evening and he hadn't managed to track down his friend. Instead of staying at home after school, Hamish went to the Benn's. He wanted to put Matthew's side of things to his family for the headmaster didn't know Drover and Colin had wound Matthew up and the head's version would have reached the Benns along with the injured Fee.

Hamish didn't even have to knock. Cally had caught the sound of boots on the veranda and instantly expected her son to walk in. Instead she swung the backdoor open on an apprehensive Hamish.

'Oh, Hamish. Is Matthew with you?' Cally impatiently scanned the background.

'No, Mrs Benn. Sorry. I just came to see if he was all right after what Drover and Colin did.'

Cally stood to one side to let the boy enter.

'How's Fee?' Hamish asked.

'Tucked up in bed and anxious about her brother but she will be right as rain. Now, what were you saying about Drover and Colin? Your headmaster told me Matthew caused the fight.'

Hamish shook his head vigorously. 'No, Mrs Benn. It was Drover and Colin. They were whispering to Matthew behind the head's back. It set him off like anything.'

'What did they whisper that was so bad?'

Hamish shuffled awkwardly, reluctant to meet her eyes. 'Well, it was stuff about the party. You know,' he finished lamely.

Cally did know only too well. *The damned party!* She patted Hamish on the shoulder. 'Thank you for telling me. I'll make sure to put things straight at school.' With a sigh Cally sat at the table. 'So you haven't seen Matthew at all?'

'No, Mrs Benn. I came here to see if he was home.'

'Matthew's run away like this before though he has always turned up before it got dark.' She saw the worry in Hamish's eyes and hastened to reassure him. 'I'm sure he'll turn up like the bad penny he can be.' Her eyes drifted back to the window and the increasingly dim light of late afternoon as she stifled the swoop of panic. 'I just hope he'll be home before dark.' Cally forced herself to smile and it must have seemed genuine enough because Hamish visibly relaxed.

'I'll go have a look around our hiding places, shall I?'

'Would your mother not want you home?'

'I'll let her know what I'm up to. She won't mind.'

So Hamish began looking for his friend. Knowing he would only have a winter moon to see by, he had taken his dad's torch not bothering to ask permission. Their gang had several places to play or hide away in and there were only two Hamish hadn't explored. By the time it was full dark, he stood on a gravel road debating which one to try first; the disused pump-house or the quarry up behind Drover's family farm. Hamish reasoned anything to do with Drover would be out, so saving his torch batteries for when he really needed them, he relied on the moon to light his way. Off the gravel road to the creek where the old pump-house sat hidden beneath a tangle of overgrown broom, gorse and a venerable macrocarpa tree. There used to be a farmhouse somewhere on this site, Hamish's dad said, a substantial one, too. The gang had spent hours trying to find its old midden. All old places had the hole where they threw away their rubbish. On his uncle's property Hamish had found lovely old blue bottles made of heavy glass, some complete with the glass stoppers. However, apart from a couple of broken plates the gang had found nothing of interest on this site and the pump-house rarely served as a hut now they knew they weren't going to discover any lost treasure.

It was eerie at night. Hamish flicked on his torch as he edged down the steep bank to the creek. He heard the sound of stones being thrown into water and called out, signalling his arrival. 'Matthew? That you?'

There was a flurry of movement and the creaking of a wooden door being hastily shut.

Silence.

Hamish slid the last couple of feet, scratching his bare legs on the unforgiving gorse and swearing loudly. 'I know you're here.' He swung the torch beam towards the old shed. Nothing moved. 'It's just me, you idiot. I'm alone.'

Finally there was a scrabble and the pump-house door opened enough for Matthew to stick his head around. 'No lies?'

'Nup.'

'Did Mother send you to look for me?'

'Sort of. I was going to anyway but she knows I'm doing it.'

Matthew pushed against the unyielding door to give Hamish room to squeeze past him. The rusty hinges groaned in protest. Both boys jumped at the unexpected sound. Exchanging sheepish looks they huddled down at the back of the shed, sitting shoulder to shoulder for warmth. Matthew lit the stub of candle in an old tin they had tucked away when they had spent all their spare time here. Even the little bit of light and warmth soothed his jangled nerves. Hamish being here helped, too not that Matthew would tell him so. *You expected friends to know such things.*

'Is Fee all right?'

'Yeah.'

Matthew let out a big sigh of relief but there was irritation in his voice as he spoke. 'Why'd she get involved anyway? Stupid!'

Hamish shrugged.

'Dunno. Maybe she was worried about you.'

'Stupid.'

'You or her?'

'Fee, of course.'

'No of course about it, mate. You attacking Drover was stupid. Bloody stupid.'

Matthew bridled. 'He deserved it!'

'I know. But now it's you in trouble.'

All anger fled from Matthew's face as worry returned. 'Real trouble?' He had reason to fear their headmaster's cane.

'Well, not as bad as it might be 'cause I told your mum about Drover and Colin. She'll tell the head, too so he'll know you had reasons for what you did.'

'Thanks.'

'Doesn't mean the old bugger won't give you a whack, though. You know, for disturbing the class.'

Disturbing the class was a great sin in their headmaster's eyes. They shared wry looks, acknowledging the truth of it. As Matthew poked at the guttering candle wick, Hamish reached deep into his coat pocket and pulled out a packet of sandwiches. 'And here. Your mum wouldn't let me go without bringing you something to eat. She knew you'd be starving.' His friend wolfed into the bread and cheese and seeing how hungry Matthew was, Hamish refused the offer to share. He stared into the flickering candle-light until a satisfied Matthew screwed up the paper from his sandwiches and chucked it into a corner.

Pause.

'You know what? I'm jealous of Drover.'

This surprising statement startled Hamish. 'What? Why?'

'His father died.'

Hamish shifted uneasily, wanting to offer comfort, completely unable to think of anything useful to say.

Maybe Matthew picked up on his friend's discomfort because he abruptly changed the subject.

'Did Mother look really angry?'

'Nah, I told you. More worried than anything else.'

Matthew shivered and did up the top button of his coat. 'Maybe we should head back, then.'

'Yeah.'

They carefully doused the candle before beginning the long walk back to Matthew's. Needing to think about something else, Matthew remembered his weekend plans. Chances are he would be grounded but thanks to Hamish, maybe not. *Worth planning towards something in any case. Took your mind off things.*

'Hey, do you wanna come to my uncles' workshop in the weekend? They're getting a new truck and promised to take me for a drive.'

'Would they mind me tagging along?'

'Course not! They're great. It'll be a laugh.'

Hamish needed no further urging.

***

Berlin

The music was deafening, the huge dance hall opulent beyond belief. Eighteen year old Wilhelm had never seen affluence like it. Enormous chandeliers splintered light into gilded mirrors creating spangled radiance and spotlights shone on the scantily clad bodies of dancers decorating a vast stage. Waiters glided through the throng, skilfully balancing silver trays laden with glasses as they side-stepped improvised dance from couples seized by the jazz rhythms pulsing through the room. Wilhelm was jolted into one amorous couple who were kissing deeply and passionately, his apology dying on his tongue when he realised it was two men. He hastily averted his gaze only to witness a woman caressing her female companion in an erotic performance which left nothing to the imagination. Completely disconcerted Wilhelm concentrated on following his cousin through the crowded room, striving to hide his awkwardness and discomfort.

Joachim wasn't fooled, though. There was no concealing the nervousness of Wilhelm's body language. 'It's all right, you know,' he shouted.

'Should we even be here?' Wilhelm asked. Joachim didn't hear him through the screech of trumpets and shrieks of voices so he grabbed his cousin's arm and shouted the question directly into his ear.

Joachim didn't reply straight away. After sizing Wilhelm up, he dragged him to an alcove which gave an illusion of privacy in this packed, heaving dance hall. 'This isn't my scene really but you did say you wanted to see everything Berlin had to offer. Top to bottom you said.'

'I know, it's just....' Wilhelm's voice tailed away. Uninhibited behaviour raged full flight wherever his glance fell.

'It's not New Zealand?' Joachim guessed with a grin.

'No. Not at all.'

'Which is a good thing, isn't it? You said how backward the place was and you were living in the capital city apparently.' Joachim slapped Wilhelm on the shoulder. 'Look, we're only meeting Kristel then we'll go somewhere a bit less shocking.'

Wilhelm bristled, interpreting Joachim's care as condescension. 'I'm not shocked.'

'No?'

'No. It's just....' Again words failed him.

'Not New Zealand?' At his deliberate repetition Joachim grinned wickedly and it proved contagious.

Wilhelm gave way before it. 'No. It certainly is not.' Unwilling to seem even more provincial, he kept his mouth shut and his face neutral as they ordered drinks at the bar. 'Do my aunt and uncle know you and Kristel come to places like this?'

Joachim almost spilt his drink. 'No. No they don't and for Christ's sake don't tell them.' He wiped his chin and added, 'Best not to mention it to Inge either. She can be awfully pi.'

'Pie?'

'Pi as in pious. Self-righteous. Inge would not approve for the smallest moment.'

Wilhelm was roughly jostled to one side.

'Schumann. Where've you been hiding?'

'Heinrich.'

A tall, roughly dressed man with an oddly elegant beard shook Joachim's hand. After being briefly introduced to the newcomer and dismissed by him, Wilhelm let his attention wander.

What a city Berlin was. He'd been offered a wrap of cocaine for five marks and a prostitute for three all within minutes of setting out tonight. Wilhelm tried to convince himself it wasn't the louche atmosphere which disturbed him so much as the gaping difference between this world and this one he'd been introduced to three weeks ago. He had arrived at his Uncle Sigmund's apartment in a chauffeur driven car, rendered speechless by the expensiveness of the area and the grandeur of the apartment. His father's brother lived a respectable if wealthy life far beyond Wilhelm's imagination. He couldn't help but think back to his parents' struggle in New Zealand during the war years, the grinding poverty and despair. *Why did this rich uncle never offer to help?* It never occurred to Wilhelm that maybe his father's pride kept their troubles secret. If Sigmund and Freya noted the shabbiness of their nephew's clothes and his few possessions they were far too well-mannered to mention it. Instead they gladly threw their home and lives open to him, teasing that the two year old German boy who had emigrated across the sea all those years ago would need to be reminded again of what it meant to be German.

What it meant to be German.

As he gazed around him, jostled by the ebb and flow of the exuberant crowd Wilhelm wondered if this was what it meant to be German. *Maybe it was the pimps, prostitutes and drug-dealers? Or perhaps the concerts his aunt and uncle took him to? The art galleries? The restaurants?* It was all so removed from the simple, parochial life he had lived. The out-of-placeness he felt on his first day seemed even more entrenched, forcing an unhappy thought to the front of his mind. *If he didn't fit in New Zealand and he didn't fit here where did it leave him?*

Of his cousins Wilhelm liked Joachim best though his handsome, cosmopolitan maturity was daunting. Thankfully his youngest cousin, Kristel was Wilhelm's age and acted it. She was pretty and kind but closed off in a way the out-going Joachim could never be. She also reminded him strongly of his sister Lottie, with her blue eyes and widow's peak, her smile even. Wilhelm missed nothing of New Zealand except his mother and sister. *Maybe Kristel would help him overcome his homesickness for Lottie.*

True kinship would never develop with Inge though. That had been obvious from day one. Inge was the middle of the three and from the first had looked down on this new arrival from one of Britain's colonies. She was patronising and scornful in turn, particularly of his clumsy accent.

Joachim hastened to reassure Wilhelm. 'Patronising scorn is a well-known Inge trait. She looks down on Hindenburg himself,' he laughed.

It didn't stop Wilhelm's sense of shame and hurt.

The Weimar Republic was simply dazzling. Its architecture soared while its sophisticated culture pushed the boundaries of acceptability and daring to a scandalous degree. Wilhelm could barely understand what he saw and heard let alone approve of much of it. Inge delighted in Wilhelm's ignorance, lecturing him on the glories of German Expressionism, the way it influenced Europe and led the world. She spoke to him at length of Bauhaus and his architectural designs, the literature of Döblin and Berlin Alexanderplatz. When Joachim first witnessed his cousin's open-mouthed wonder at Inge's sweep of knowledge he let it go. It wasn't until he realised Wilhelm actually took Inge's opinions for gospel that he let the teasing commence.

'Inge has never finished reading even one book, you know,' Joachim remarked to Wilhelm in front of his infuriated sister. 'She reads reviews and talks to her better-read friends to get the headlines of an education as it were. Inge likes to appear educated, don't you darling? Without all the bother of tedious learning.'

With a toss of her head, Inge would rage only to fall into Joachim's trap again and again in her desperation to be respected as thoroughly contemporary. Whatever Joachim said, however, Wilhelm found Inge painfully crushing and he avoided her company unless politeness or family occasions demanded otherwise. Tonight, they were thankfully without her company. *It did make him smile, though; picturing Inge here among this wildness.* Through the press of bodies and the din Wilhelm heard his name shouted. Kristel was shoving towards him, a hand raised in recognition.

'You really are seeing all the hot-spots,' she grinned. 'You won't tell Mama or Papa Joachim brought you here, will you?'

'I've already promised.' Wilhelm raised his glass as he added, 'or Inge.'

Kristel's expression was pure comedy horror. 'God, no! Never Inge.' She introduced the tall good-looking man who had arrived with her. 'Cousin Wilhelm meet Jost Vogt. He is unbearable but I'm afraid you, like the rest of us, will have to bear him nonetheless.'

Jost listened to this with an engaging smile. He reached out a hand. 'Welcome to Berlin, Wilhelm.'

As Wilhelm returned the firm handshake, Kristel reached across to grab her brother's shoulder. Joachim pointed to his glass, then her and Jost. Kristel nodded vigorously. Handed his glass, Jost downed his drink in one gulp, smacking his lips in appreciation as he banged his empty glass on the bar top.

Heinrich turned at the noise. At the sight of Jost his face twisted into a sneer. 'Fucking hell. I thought there was some unspoken gentleman's agreement not to let communist shit drink in here.'

Jost sighed. 'The Socialist Democratic Party isn't the Kommunistische Partei Deutschlands Heinrich. Not sure how often you need to be told.'

'Fuck all difference from where I'm standing. Russian lackeys the lot of you.'

'We're really not,' Jost began.

Joachim shook his head warningly. For once Jost heeded his friend and ignored Heinrich. Instead he whistled to try for the attention of an overworked barmaid. As he raised an arm, his glass was knocked out of his hand and smashed on the floor. Jost wrenched out of Heinrich's grip, launching a couple of punches, the speed of his attack forcing Heinrich onto the back foot. With a roar Heinrich grabbed a bottle from the bar. As he swung it over his head Jost stepped in close and threw an uppercut, lifting the man off his feet. Like a felled tree,

Heinrich hit the floor, the bottle slipping uselessly from his hand to come to a rolling stop at Joachim's feet. Wilhelm became aware of the unnatural hush from those nearest the bar. The silence radiated out until the music and every tongue was still. Two men appeared from a door behind the bar. They caught Jost's eye as with a dangerous, metallic click, switchblades appeared in their hands.

'Jost you bloody fool.' Joachim hissed.

'Off, I think.' Jost murmured. He led them quickly through the silent crowds, elbowing gawping idiots to one side as the four of them made their way down the stairs onto the street. The two armed men followed with deliberate intent. They went no further than the shadowy doorway however, one of them tossing his deadly blade from hand to hand.

Jost gave them a wave. 'Do you think we will be welcomed back?'

Kristel faced him angrily. 'Don't you dare find this amusing! Why does our every night out have to end with you in a fight?'

'To be fair, Kris, it wasn't Jost's fault. This time. Heinrich started it.' Joachim tried to catch his sister's eye but Kristel stalked away in front of the three men, muttering under her breath.

'What about acknowledging the fact I laid out big bastard Heinrich with one punch?' Jost complained.

Joachim lit a cigarette. 'It was three punches actually and you have been told to keep out of trouble.'

'It's not as if I don't try.'

'It's not as if you try hard enough.'

Jost gave an irritated hiss. 'You're beginning to sound like Inge.'

Before Joachim could hotly deny this, Wilhelm spoke up. 'What's Heinrich's problem anyway?'

Jost cadged a cigarette from his friend. 'It's easily explained. In a Germany of increasing nationalism I'm one of the enemy.'

Wilhelm frowned, confused at Joachim's mocking laughter. 'What d'you mean?'

'Jost's a damn socialist, Wilhelm and he absolutely refuses to see sense.' Frustrated anger tightened Joachim's voice.

Jost, in deliberate contrast, kept his tone light. 'The Socialist Democratic Party is the only answer to the rise of Adolf Hitler and his N.S.D.A.P and if sensible men like you continue to refuse to see it Joachim, then this country is headed for calamity.'

Joachim stopped in the street, forcing other pedestrians to skirt around him. 'Keep your lectures to yourself. If you're going to talk politics I'm off home.'

'You were happily talking politics to Heinrich,' Jost countered swiftly. 'Is it only the politics of the Nazis you're interested in?'

An exasperated sigh. 'What's wrong with listening to someone's point of view? Just because it isn't your opinion, doesn't make it invalid.' Joachim made to move away as Jost grabbed his friend's arm.

'It's wrong because what they're saying is dangerous.'

'Jost, let it rest, will you?'

'Are you coming on to the meeting?'

Joachim shook his head. 'No. I've had enough of your friends and their opinions.' He began to walk away.

'What about Kristel?' Wilhelm called after him. To his shame he really wanted to ask *what about me?*

'She knows her way around,' Joachim replied. 'Are you coming with me or carrying on with this fool?' He pointed at the unconcerned Jost. Wilhelm hesitated too long. Joachim turned on his heel. 'Suit yourself,' he said shortly and left them.

Wilhelm's turmoil showed in his face so Jost slapped him heartily on the back to reassure him. 'Never mind your cousin. This isn't the first time he's left us to our devices to head home in a self-righteous sulk.' His mouth contorted. 'He continually lets Heinrich fill his head with bullshit. Come on, we'll be late.'

'Late to what?'

Jost flicked his cigarette butt at Wilhelm's feet. 'You'll see.'

It turned out to be a smoky basement room in the working class district of Wedding. No jazz music here, no well-stocked bar. The atmosphere was sombre yet heightened, too. The room buzzed with expectancy and the conversations were all muted excitement.

Jost hovered in the entrance, eyes scanning the crowd until he spotted what he was looking for. 'This way.'

Wilhelm was aware of garnering sharp, examining looks as they made their way to the table where Kristel sat, her body language stiff and unyielding.

Jost pulled out a chair next to her and threw himself onto it. Unaware of anything else he stared into her troubled blue eyes. 'Forgive me?'

'No.' She slapped him across the face. It wasn't hard but it stung. 'You know they're already looking for excuses.' Kristel's voice revealed the strain.

Jost rubbed his hand over his cheek. 'We have to defend ourselves.'

'What you did to Heinrich tonight went beyond defence, Jost! He will report it and things will only become more dangerous.'

'You think they won't anyway? The Nazi Party is dangerous.'

'Damn it, Jost! You....'

To Wilhelm's shock Jost pulled Kristel to him and kissed her. A woman at a table to their right nudged Wilhelm and grinned. 'Fight and kiss. Fight and kiss. It's their way.'

Before Wilhelm could make any reply, those seated nearest a small stage in the furthest corner of the basement began to clap and cheer. Kristel settled into Jost's arms as their attention was taken by a middle aged woman standing on the stage. Plump and plainly dressed she faced them all with noticeable authority. The applause died away and like the leader of an orchestra she let the silence stretch out as the expectation built.

'Three years ago.' Voice softly pitched she met pairs of eyes throughout the room. 'Three years ago Rosa Luxemburg and Karl Liebknet were murdered for their beliefs in a Free Socialist Republic. *'Freedom only for the supporters of the government, only for the members of one party – however numerous they may be – is no freedom at all.'* These were Rosa's words and they resonate more strongly today as support for the N.S.D.A.P increases. They would have one party. One set of beliefs – their beliefs. They fear the left because they know we have the strength and force of will to fight against them. The Kommunistische Partei Deutschlands and the Socialist Democratic Party. We can resist the rise of Adolf Hitler and his Nazi Party.'

As groups around tables began to whoop and cheer the woman raised a hand to quiet them.

'But, there are widening gaps between us on the left, comrades. Socialist and Communist must work together or we will fail.' From behind Wilhelm boos and hisses erupted. The woman remained undaunted, nodding, accepting the challenge. 'We continue to let each other down, I know this! And we cannot afford to do so. Hitler calls Berlin the reddest city in Europe after Moscow and we are proud to be so! We are proud the Nazis fear who we are and what we stand for. Do not be daunted by their rhetoric of hate. Only fear makes them hate us so. But we must stand together. We must learn to fight together.'

A female voice from deep in the audience, brave in her anonymity shouted, 'How?'

The question was picked up and repeated until the woman raised a hand. 'How?' She made a tight fist. 'We learn how to fight by fighting. Rosa told us, *'The modern proletariat class does not carry out its struggle according to a plan set out in some book or theory; the modern workers' struggle is a part of history; a part of social progress and in the middle of history, in the middle of progress, in the middle of the fight we learn how we must fight. The great masses of the working people must first forge from their own consciousness, from their own belief, and even from their own understanding, the weapons of their own liberation.'* Cheers rang out. 'Comrades whether you are Communist or Socialist we have to fight the same fight against a common enemy. Whether we stand or fall, whether we succeed or fail depends on our ability to understand and appreciate what brings us together not what divides us.'

Jost stood, his fingers in his mouth, whistling. Kristel joined him, cheering. Some tables shouted disapproval, others support. Questions were shouted towards the stage, voices heckled only to be silenced. Everyone had an opinion and wanted to voice it. Wilhelm eased back in the chair, eyes wide.

Or perhaps this is what it means to be German?

Kristel and Wilhelm walked slowly back home, each lost in their private thoughts. They had been quiet for long minutes until Kristel lightly touched Wilhelm's arm.

'So what did you think of your night?'

'Honestly? I don't know.'

'You won't say anything, will you? To Mama or Papa? Not about the drinking or the politics?'

'I promise. Would they be so angry?'

'Papa's all for Chancellor Hindenburg and the Republic. He doesn't approve of socialists or communists, In fact he seems unwilling to tell us apart.'

'What are the differences?'

Kristel took time to marshal her thoughts. 'Well, the K.D.P are violently opposed to the Republic and any form of government control. They want to tear down democracy and replace it with a Russian-style communist dictatorship.

Whereas the S.D.P are strong supporters of both democracy and the Republic.'

'The woman tonight was calling for unity between the two? Forgive me, cousin if I say it sounds impossible.'

Kristel's expression was wry. 'You're not alone in your thinking but we do have common ground. It's where our strength lies, if only the extremists on both sides could see it. We both want social welfare programmes, labour unions, progressive taxation and equal opportunities for women.'

'And this Adolf Hitler and his Nazis?'

'Like the K.D.P they are violently opposed to the Republic though where the K.D.P want all wealth to be distributed equally among everyone and not in the hands of government or the rich, the Nazis want an economy run by and for industrialists and wealthy land owners.'

Wilhelm blew through his lips, shaking his head. 'So which party dominates?'

'Since 1919 the S.D.P have received the most votes in the national elections and have the largest legislative delegation but the pressure from the K.D.P grows stronger within our ranks. I worry if the left can't hold firm common ground, the right will find a way through.' They walked in silence for a while. 'What's the government like in New Zealand? Who holds the power?'

Wilhelm made a dismissive sound. 'The wealthy landowners. There's a strong union movement which gains a bit then is pushed back but the rich control parliament and the working class suffers. I can't see it changing.'

Kristel regarded Wilhelm thoughtfully. 'Your country's on the other side of the world and facing the same problems.'

'The working class in New Zealand doesn't have true representation in parliament, though. At least the S.D.P and the K.D.P understand the struggles facing the poor.'

'I've seen how factory workers live, the terrible struggle of their lives whilst their bosses grow fat. And once you've seen it, you can't forget it. Jost made me understand. If you see injustice then you have to do something about it or you're as bad as the unjust.'

They were silent once more, Wilhelm uneasy in the face of such intensity.

'How long have you known Jost?'

'He's been friends with Joachim for years. He lives in Wedding – to the disgust of his father. Jost has a job in one of Papa's factories. He spends his days working and every other hour pushing the union and S.D.P agenda wherever he can.'

'And Joachim?'

'Father tries to make him interested in his business but he's not had much success so far. I don't think even Joachim knows what Joachim wants to do. I wish he was more like Jost.'

'It's easy for Jost, though isn't it? '

'What do you mean?'

'Well, apart from a handful, everyone in the hall tonight were working class, completely dependent on the goodwill of a boss who will strip them of their job if they agitate. They risk everything to fight so the fight means everything. What risk to Jost? To you? If the fight is lost you go back to your easy lives and you find another cause.' Wilhelm was already regretting being so open. He didn't need the shuttered look on Kristel's face to let him know he'd overstepped the mark. *Too late for him to temporise now, though. And she did ask.* 'It's easy to fight,' Wilhelm repeated, 'if you can escape the consequences of that fight.'

Kristel wanted to hotly deny this but she shut her mouth around an instinctive denial to consider more deeply what he meant. 'So you're saying we just see the problems, live our comfortable lives and ignore them?'

'No. It's commendable you care.' An exasperated Kristel slapped a hand on his sleeve and brought them to a stop. 'Then what do you think we should do?'

Wilhelm gave her a half-smile. 'I don't know. I'm just saying it's different for you.' She was still bemused, and Wilhelm couldn't blame her for he felt confusion, too. 'Look, cousin, I've barely set foot back in a country I've mostly forgotten. Maybe I'm misreading things and being too harsh.' He eyed her warily. 'Friends?'

Kristel punched his shoulder. 'Just,' and smiled to belie the smack and the words as she slid an arm through his. 'Wilhelm, can I ask you a personal question?'

'Of course.'

'Why did you leave New Zealand?'

He didn't answer at once, conjuring up the intensity of his hatred for a country he wanted to forget. Almost of their own volition, the words formed. 'During the Great War we were Germans living in a land at war with Germany. Our ties to the Fatherland condemned us without hesitation, without justice. The New Zealand government interned us and enslaved us. They treated us like the enemy. People we believed to be friends, turned on us. With violence they ran us out of town, beggared us, refused to trade with us.' *It all came back. The helpless anger. The churning shame as his father gave way again and again.* 'Father and I were taken away and put into nothing more than a chain-gang where they worked us laying railway lines.' Wilhelm bit down on his bottom lip, unable to hide the emotion. 'Father sickened. He was denied any treatment, even basic humanity until the bastards guarding us had no choice. They sent him home where he died from their treatment or rather lack of it. Mother couldn't even let me know. I didn't find out till after I was released well after the end of the war. A friend of ours committed suicide. Jesus.....' He withdrew his arm from Kristen's and wiped apologetically at his eyes. 'I swore I would leave, that I would come home.' Now he met her concern, an unconvincing smile barely covering his grief. 'So here I am.'

'And are you?'

'Am I what?'

'Home?'

Wilhelm sighed, all the confusion of the night inherent in the sound and uncertainty made him answer wearily. 'I'm not even sure I know what home means anymore.'

***

For days after his heart-to-heart with Kristel, Wilhelm felt awkward for having revealed so much. His biggest concern was she would share it with Joachim or, God forbid, Inge. *How would he feel if Inge showed him patronising sympathy? Or worse, tried to befriend him out of pity?* After a few weeks with no change in anyone's behaviour, Wilhelm began to relax and accept his trust in Kristel hadn't been misplaced.

One evening after dinner he was summoned to his uncle's study. He went there apprehensively. *Had his jaunts out with Jost and Kristel been discovered*?

Instead, Sigmund smiled benignly from behind his beautifully polished mahogany desk. 'I managed to secure your new passport, Wilhelm. It took a bit of string pulling to get it so quickly but what's the use of contacts in the government if a man can't help his family?'

Wilhelm swallowed the hot rush of guilt. He hadn't lost his passport. He'd deliberately destroyed it. In the years after the war, his mother changed their family name to Shearman, ashamed of their German heritage and beaten down by the effects of the Great War. All Wilhelm had felt was bitterness. *How dared anyone condemn him for his name?* They had done their best to break him during the war years and it was his one source of pride he'd refused to be broken yet he couldn't deny his mother and sister's aching need for acceptance again. So Shearman they became.

Not anymore.

With effusive thanks to his uncle Wilhelm held his new

identification. William Shearman, New Zealander was gone forever. Herr Wilhelm Schumann, German was reborn.

Sigmund bent his head over his desk again as Wilhelm cleared his throat. 'Uncle, I wondered if you would keep an ear out for any work for me? You've done so much already, I hate to ask but I need something. I can't live off your generosity forever.'

Laying down his pen, Sigmund nodded his approval. 'I can enquire. What sort of work were you looking for?'

'Anything. I will turn my hand to any manual work and be grateful for the opportunity.' Wilhelm shifted under his uncle's scrutiny. He must have passed some kind of test for Sigmund nodded again, more emphatically this time.

'I'm sure we can find something for you, Wilhelm. Now, if you'll excuse me?' He gestured to the mound of paperwork in front of him.

Wilhelm backed out. 'Of course, Uncle. Thank you.'

Back out in the foyer he grinned. *It would be good to be making his way in the world again.*

A new start.

Sigmund proved to be a man of action.

Not long after their conversation, alone in the apartment and unaccountably restless, Wilhelm made his way to Sigmund's small but impressive library. With characteristic generosity, Sigmund had given permission for his nephew to make use of the room whenever he wanted.

Wilhelm liked to throw himself down onto the leather sofa and burrow deep into any book which took his fancy; German history, political tracts, Jung, Goethe, he read voraciously, trying to understand the country of his birth. Even on nights with only a slight chill, Aunt Freya would ensure a fire burned in the hearth and so it proved tonight. Wilhelm relaxed in the peace and quiet, revelling in the comfort and warmth. He hadn't been reading for long when the library door creaked open and his uncle's head appeared. 'Thought I'd find you here. I may have found you work.'

Reading forgotten, Wilhelm stood. 'Uncle, thank you!'

Sigmund raised a cautionary hand. 'You need to be interviewed. There's no guarantee. Calev Altmeyer is the manager at my electronics factory and I've told him if you don't suit, he is under no obligation to take you on. If he does hire you, he will expect hard work. As will I.'

'I won't let you down, sir.'

His uncle seemed gratified by Wilhelm's enthusiasm and with a smile which conveyed approval he left his nephew with the satisfaction of a duty willingly done.

Too excited to read anymore, Wilhelm prowled the room before settling against the ornate marble mantle-piece surrounding the fire. He added another log into the hot ashes, nudging it carefully deep among the smoldering red. Kneeling, he blew gently, encouraging the embers to glow and catch into flame and when they did he sat back to survey the result.

His life was like those embers, banked down all these years, waiting for something or someone to breathe into them the spark of blazing animation.

If Germany didn't feel like home up until now, maybe it soon would.

***

1927

Wellington

A clear blue sky day. Tyke pushed the hat back off her face to enjoy the cloudless expanse of forget-me-not blue above the city streets. Summer or not, Maudie made no concessions to the heat, leaving Tyke to scratch at wool-clad legs, itchy with sweat behind the knees. She begged to be allowed to wear long, white socks but Maudie wouldn't hear of it, horrified at the thought of bare legs.

'They won't be bare, Maudie. I'll be wearing long socks.'

'Above your knee long?'

Tyke hesitated, feeling her argument slipping away. 'No.' She rallied valiantly. 'Nearly, though.'

Maudie folded her arms. 'Nearly ain't good enough, girl.' And she pointed back to the hated woollen stockings lying neatly washed and darned on Tyke's bed.

There was no doubt about it. She would need to enlist her mother's support - if she could hold her in one place for more than five minutes for Alex was rarely at home. She rushed from this struggling family to that one, taking soup and bread or medicines, finding jobs for those without them, trying to help the growing number of distressed people who lived within her and Maudie's awareness.

Never mind the poor children. Alex needed to worry about her own daughter a bit more, Tyke grumbled, but never, ever out loud.

Resigned to being hot and scratchy, she tugged her hat back into place and continued on, kicking stones in and out of the gutters and jumping to avoid the trams. She was late to school as per usual, taking her desk after making up a plausible lie for her teacher Miss Taggett.

'One of our boarders took sick and there was only me to run for the help.' Tyke's steady gaze reflected the concern on her face.

Accepting the innocence of face and voice, naïve Miss Taggett swallowed another one of the girl's fibs as she motioned for her to sit.

Emma leaned across their shared desk. 'Was it true?'

Tyke kept her face straight. 'What do you think?'

'I think she'll catch you out one day.'

'Nah, she won't.'

'She will if someone tells her.' The slightly unpleasant glint in Emma's eye was missed by Tyke who was trying to hide the sight of Maudie's neat darn on the knee of her right stocking. Emma had a sharp eye for such details and had shamed Tyke because of them. Emma never wore darned clothes or hand-me-downs. *Lucky Emma whose father was a lawyer and her mother didn't spend too much of the housekeeping on strangers.* Tyke tugged at her frock hem only to meet Emma's expression of obvious pity. She burned with the disgrace. It was unusual but she sided with her father who regularly took Alex to task over giving their money away to *'bludgers and wastrels.'*

Making sure Miss Taggett was busy at the backboard, Emma gave Tyke's hand a condescending pat. 'Never mind. It's not your fault you're poor and anyway you're not as badly off as Phyllis.' Emma's mouth twisted into a sneer. 'Look at her. She's not wearing stockings or socks today.'

Tyke leaned across her desk to see and sure enough Phyllis's thin, somewhat grubby bare legs ended in nothing but an old pair of shoes. Now Tyke came to think about it, Phyllis hadn't brought lunch to school for the past week, either. Her sympathy stirred at the sight of the other girl's lanky, unwashed hair and pinched face.

Emma's spiteful voice whispered on. 'I'm going to let Mother know how standards are dropping at this school. She wants me to be taught privately, you know. I'm sure when Father hears about the scarecrows I have to see every day he will finally do the right thing.'

Senses alerted Phyllis to the fact she was the object of attention. Emma pointedly stared at Phyllis's feet and with a flush of humiliation the mortified girl hastily lowered her eyes over the desk. Emma dismissed her with a tut while Tyke felt a rush of sympathy for Phyllis's bare legs and sockless feet. A painful nudge from Emma's elbow snapped her attention back to the blackboard, Phyllis's hungry face lingering in her mind.

The morning dragged on, more boring than usual. *Who cares about arithmetic?* Out of the window, the faultless blue tugged Tyke's ragged attention, teasing her with summer scents and green parks. The hands on the clock over Miss Taggett's desk seemed glued to its face until at long last someone from the headmaster's room rang the lunchtime bell. With a whoop, everyone pushed away from their desks. Tyke grabbed her paper bag to follow Emma. Skipping side-by-side the girls made their way to their coveted place outside under the oak tree where they sat in their select group every break. The older girls chose to sit with their backs to the tree and their eyes on the boys. For once, Tyke wasn't contributing to the giggles. Phyllis sat listlessly away from everyone else and she wasn't eating. Tyke felt the weight of the sandwich in her hand. In her lunch bag there was also a piece of cake. For long moments the girl weighed up whether to do the right thing or not. That she found this surprisingly difficult dismayed her. *Maudie or Alex wouldn't hesitate.* Ignoring Emma's bemused query, Tyke stood up, gripping her sandwich and lunch bag.

'Where are you going?' Emma's haughty, demanding query disregarded.

With stares on her back Tyke made her way over to the other side of the playground. Giving the suspicious Phyllis a grin, she plumped herself down. 'No lunch today?'

Phyllis shrugged as if it was of no importance. 'I forgot it.' She tried to keep her eyes from the thick slices of bread and cheese.

Tyke went along with the girl's fib. 'That was silly of you. Would you like to share my sandwich? I don't want it.' Young as she was, Tyke was old enough at eleven to read the internal tussle playing out on the pale face beside her as pride fought with hunger.

Phyllis dragged her gaze from the sandwich, fingers restless in her lap as she shook her head. 'No thanks.'

'Please?' Tyke held it out. 'You know what Miss Taggett is like if we don't eat all our lunch. I don't want to do a hundred lines because I'm wasting good food.' Phyllis held out, lips clamped tightly. Tyke tried once more. 'You'd be doing me a favour.'

Phyllis swallowed. 'Why?'

'I hate writing out lines and I've still to do the ones I got for not cleaning the dusters yesterday.' Tyke proffered the food once more.

This time Phyllis surrendered. She ate each mouthful in its turn though she wanted to wolf it down.

Tyke opened her paper bag and gave an exasperated sound of pretended disgust. 'Maudie's given me a piece of seed cake, too.' She screwed her face up. 'I hate seed cake.'

With her defenses down and mouth half-full Phyllis replied, 'I don't mind it.'

Tyke put it on the girl's lap. 'Then you can have it.' She mimed vomiting to seal the deal.

Phyllis gave her a shy smile. 'Thanks.'

'Don't mention it. And I mean that. Never mention it. If Maudie finds out I've given away her cake she'll wallop me.'

'I won't say a word. I promise.'

Phyllis held out her pinky finger. Tyke solemnly wrapped her own one around it, shaking to seal the promise. Absorbed in each other, neither girl noticed they had company until a shadow fell across them.

'Tyke, why are you sitting here?' Emma glared down, arms folded across her chest, a disdainful twist to her lips.

'Just talking.'

Emma sneered at the hapless Phyllis now frozen into immobility. The seedcake crumbled in her fingers as she withered beneath Emma's scorn.

'Letting her scrounge food off you, you mean.'

Colour flooded Tyke's face as she scrambled to her feet. 'No. She didn't scrounge anything. I gave it to her. She didn't even want it.'

Emma's disbelieving laugh drilled into Phyllis who slumped further down, trying to hide the tears which came upon her so easily these days.

'We're not supposed to share food,' Emma continued remorselessly.

Tyke grabbed Emma's arm to pull her away. 'Leave her alone.'

Shocked at this treatment, Emma jerked herself free. 'Why are you defending her? She's nothing but a beggar. A dirty scrounging beggar.'

'Don't say that.' Tyke's hands were fists now.

'Why not? It's the truth.'

They had a wider audience now. Those with an ear for trouble had drifted eagerly forwards. Phyllis dropped the seedcake on the ground. Drawing her knees up she wrapped her arms around them and buried her face in her sleeves.

Emma played for the watchers. 'I don't know how you can bear to be seen with her. She's dressed like a scarecrow.' There were titters from some of the other girls. 'And she smells.'

One of the boys trod on the piece of cake as he bent over the slumped Phyllis. He sniffed loudly, holding his nose and dry retching to laughter. Tyke was angrier than she had ever been in her life. Once more she tried to drag Emma away from Phyllis only to be shoved away

'You're looking shabby yourself, Tyke. I suppose living in that hovel of a boarding house is finally showing. If it is a boarding house.' Emma's voice trailed off suggestively.

Tyke frowned, catching behind-hand smiles and sniggers. 'What do you mean?'

'I've heard it's more bordello than boarding house.'

Tyke had never heard the world bordello before but its meaning took shape in the shocked looks from the girls and the obscene gestures of the older boys. She confronted Emma in a rage. 'You take that back!'

Emma smirked. 'Make me.'

With a yell Tyke pushed her to the ground and fell on her, slapping every bit of bare skin she could reach. As Emma howled, their audience cheered. Rough hands dragged Tyke onto her feet as she thrashed to and fro. A head-ringing slap across her face stopped her with a gasp.

'The little wild-cat, Jeannie Brodie.' Mister Harvey's lip curled distastefully. 'But of course.'

Miss Taggett, all rushed and flustered panic, helped Emma to her feet. The girl's face bore bright red patches where Tyke slapped her.

'She attacked me, Mister Harvey! I didn't do anything.'

Tyke gasped. 'That's a lie! She…' Whatever else Tyke wanted to say was bitten off as she was shaken into silence.

'Enough! Come with me.'

Dragging a protesting Tyke behind him, Mister Harvey marched towards his own classroom. Emma sobbed out her side of the story, garnering all the sympathy. Phyllis cried, isolated and forgotten. Tyke was at the steps into the building when she remembered the thick leather strap Mister Harvey used all too regularly. Fearful of pain and punishment, her face stinging from the slap, she kicked out with all her might. He yelped and released his hold. As Mister Harvey roared her name, Tyke fled. Shoving the schoolyard gate open she disappeared down the street.

Hugo was in the storeroom trying to find a crate of whisky when he heard the thump of running feet and panting breath as someone dashed passed the cellar. He reached the entrance in time to see the door into the woodshed dragged shut. After a pause came muffled, despairing sobs.

Tyke?

Hugo's instinct was to go to the girl immediately but he floundered, wondering what to do for the best. He had little experience with children and young girls were particularly mystifying at times. Still, he couldn't leave Tyke crying alone in the woodshed. Maudie and Alex were out and Moss had headed down to the wharf an hour ago. *It was down to him.* Rocking back and forth on his feet Hugo bit at a ragged nail as he pondered.

Damn it! He had to do something.

Whistling under his breath as he did whenever he felt awkward or out of place, Hugo made his way to the woodshed and stopped, uncertain. Feeling a little foolish he knocked gently.

'Tyke, lass?'

The sobbing hiccupped into a ragged silence before a voice, thick with emotion replied angrily, 'Go away.' The crying began anew.

Hugo leaned against the door, not willing to intrude, unable to leave. 'Well I can't, can I? I can't just ignore the fact a girl I like very much is obviously unhappy.' Again Tyke's crying quieted into gasps. 'Would you like to talk?'

Pause.

Hugo persevered. 'I won't make judgments or anything, you know, if you've done something terrible, or think you have.'

Silence.

'Tyke?' He began to think he would be better leaving her.

'All right.' The reply was muffled as if her head was buried in something soft.

Hugo carefully shoved into the woodshed, taking his time to close the door. There was Tyke sitting huddled on the chopping block, hat askew down her back, hair coming out of tidy plaits, her face buried in her arms. She cried less noisily yet to Hugo she sounded more hopeless, too. His heart went out to her. Again, taking his time he cleared away the splinters and sawdust beside the chopping block and settled there.

'So, you're not having a great day.' It wasn't a question though Tyke answered anyway, shaking her head to and fro, her whole body swaying with the movement. 'Oh. Still don't want to talk about it?' More vehement shakes. 'Righteo.' Hugo fiddled with the chain of his fob watch. 'Well, whatever scrape you got into I bet it wasn't as bad as my day.'

Tyke lifted a tear-stained face, wiping wet cheeks with her sleeve as she sniffed. 'Why? What happened to you?'

'I've lost a crate of whisky, Tyke. Top quality Scottish single malt. Terrible times indeed.' The tease was risky but Hugo didn't have any other weapons in his arsenal. He held his breath until the girl gave him a fleeting if sad smile. *You're a fighter, lass, whether you realise it or not.* 'So, you know, compared to my suffering how bad can your day have really been?'

This time Tyke's watery smile came with ironic amusement. She rolled her eyes at Hugo, succumbing to his wiles. 'I got into a fight with another girl.'

Hugo sat up straighter as he handed Tyke a handkerchief to blow her nose. 'Who got the worst of it? You or her?'

'Emma did.'

'Did this Emma deserve a smack?'

'I think she did. She was mean to Phyllis who was only hungry. And poor. Poorer than us.' Tyke's face darkened with anger this time, not upset. 'Emma had everyone ganging up on Phyllis. It was awful.' When hot tears threatened, Tyke wiped at them impatiently with the soggy handkerchief. 'Mister Harvey gave me such a smack, Uncle Hugo. He was going to give me the strap so I kicked him and ran home.'

'Who's this Harvey bloke?'

'Our headmaster.'

Tyke couldn't read Hugo's expression as he gaped at her, mouth open.

'You kicked your headmaster?'

'Yes.' Tyke bowed her head.

Hugo gave a great shout of laughter. 'Good on you, girl! Any bloke giving a wee lass a smack deserves his comeuppance. Good on you!'

As relieved as she was at the support, Tyke knew not everyone was going to be as supportive of her behaviour as Uncle Hugo. *Father for example....* Tyke's momentary flame of bravery snuffed out. 'I'm going to be in big trouble,' she whispered. There was such sympathy in Hugo's face she clambered off the chopping block to sit beside him.

He put his arm around her. 'Well, thinking hard about it all, would you do the same thing again?'

Tyke took her time to consider. 'Yeah.'

'Sure now?'

'Yes.'

'So really what you did was a matter of principle?' At her questioning look Hugo simplified his question. 'I mean, it was something you felt strongly shouldn't have happened?'

'Yes. What Emma did was mean.'

'Then you have to know something, lass. Sometimes you have to rock the boat, even if you fall into the water. There will always be people who disagree with you, always. So you have to decide what's worth getting into a fight for. And, if you believe something's important enough to fight for, then you have to understand there will be people who believe you're the enemy.' Tyke's bright hazel eyes remained glued to Hugo's face. At the intensity of her concentration he smiled, running a rough hand over her untidy hair. 'For what it's worth I think it's always right to stand up and fight for the underdog.'

Silence.

Tyke snuggled into Hugo's comforting arms, mulling everything over. She was feeling better about her part in the day although there was no denying, 'I'm going to be in such trouble.'

'Yes, you are. But, think hard, Tyke. Do you still think it's worth it?'

'Yes,' she said decisively. 'Yes, I do.'

Hugo hugged her. 'Then you won't face the trouble alone, lass. I'll stand up beside you.'

For the rest of the afternoon and to help keep her mind off her predicament, Hugo gave Tyke chores in the storeroom. After shifting innumerable boxes and re-counting dozens of crates they found the missing whisky.

Lifting the precious cargo up, Hugo gave it a smacking kiss. 'Come to daddy,' he told it, making Tyke laugh. Wiping his sweaty face he turned to his helper. 'Have you been to the movies lately?'

'Not for ages and ages. Not since Moss took me to see Gold Rush.' Tyke sighed. 'I love Charlie Chaplin.'

'So you haven't seen The Jazz Singer, then?'

Tyke gasped. 'The talkie? Oh, I would love to see it!' She tugged on Hugo's sleeve. 'Can you take me? Really?'

'Well, I was thinking about it as a thank you for all your hard work but you don't seem very keen.'

Ignoring the joke Tyke threw her arms around him then danced her way out of the dim cellar into the sunlight. 'Can you afford it, Uncle Hugo?'

'I've a little put by for emergencies like this.'

'When can we go? Tomorrow? Next week?'

Hugo locked the doors behind them. 'Maybe tomorrow.' Once back out in the sunshine, he noticed how grubby Tyke was. 'You better have a wash and brush up, lass. Before Maud and Alex see you.'

At the mention of family, Tyke's dancing faltered. 'I won't be able to see the talkie, Uncle Hugo. I won't. Not after Alex and Father find out about what I did.' To have such a treat promised and taken away was unbearable.

Hugo tapped the side of his nose conspiratorially. 'There's ways and means, lass. There's always ways and means. Just keep the treat between you and me, promise? Now, seriously you look like a sweep, so go and have a clean up before I get the blame.'

Worry lingered in Tyke's relieved smile as she obediently ran inside to tidy herself up. Hugo watched her go, frowning in concern.

Things weren't going to be easy for you this evening. Couldn't blame you for having a good heart, though.

Alone for once in the kitchen Hugo put the kettle on before sitting at the kitchen table to ponder Tyke's problems.

The front door opened and closed and moments later Moss wandered in. 'Kettle on?'

Hugo pointed his thumb at the stove. As his nephew joined him at the table he asked, 'Get the list to Jonty?'

'Yep. Find the whisky?'

'Yes but we're not letting it go without cash up front. We've lost too much to defaulters lately so no more grub-staking any bugger. I don't care who he thinks he is, if he doesn't pay up front he doesn't get the goods.'

'Fair enough.' The kettle began to scream so Moss lifted up from the table to make the tea. 'There are more businesses going to the wall every day. D'you think it'll get worse? It can't go on this way, surely?'

'I dunno but it's a fair sign of trouble no two ways about it.' Hugo nodded his thanks when Moss placed the cup of tea in front of him. 'By the way, speaking of trouble, our Tyke's got herself into a bit of strife.'

Moss's teacup clattered into its saucer. 'She has? How?'

Careful not to overstate the case, Hugo brought Moss up to date and raised an eyebrow at the stream of expletives his nephew released.

'That bloody little snob, Emma! She's always been able to make Tyke cry. Her mother's no better, either.' Taking a calming gulp of tea Moss added, 'You'll know her father – the lawyer from up near Parliament House. Callan McMillain.'

Hugo whistled. 'Arrogant bugger. Single malt whisky without an e. Laphroaig by choice. Likes the good stuff. It's his crate Tyke and I found today.'

'Wish you hadn't now,' Moss grumbled into his tea. 'Hey, Slugger.' This to a tidy, angelic-looking Tyke who had appeared in the doorway. 'Glad you gave that little snob a bit of what's due to her.'

Tyke glared at Hugo. 'You told him?'

'Couldn't keep such a juicy piece of gossip to myself, lass. I reckon we could earn money betting on you in a ring.'

Moss got to his feet, ducking and weaving about Tyke, his fists up, shadow punching her until with a pout she elbowed him back onto his chair to sit on his lap. Tyke poured more hot tea into his cup which she drank in one go, smacking her lips appreciatively.

'Help yourself why don't you?' Moss was mollified only when she topped his cup up once more.

With a sigh Tyke left Moss's lap to sit in a chair between the two men, her elbows on the table, chin in cupped hands. 'I know you and Uncle Hugo think I did good Moss, but Alex and Father won't.'

Tyke was right to be wary. Hours later, with the supper dishes still on the table, Tyke's untouched, Alex and Samuel were in rare accord. The moment both her parents started shouting, Tyke reached for Hugo's hand and gripped it hard under the table.

'What on earth were you thinking of, Tyke?' Alex demanded, hands on hips.

Samuel leaned over the kitchen table, glaring down at Tyke's bent head. 'She wasn't thinking at all. That's the problem.' True to his word, Hugo remained with her, ignoring Maudie's blatant gestures and signals to leave the table when she did. Moss hovered until Tyke shook her head and only then did he reluctantly follow Maudie out of the room.

'Mister Harvey is threatening not to let you back. Honestly, Tyke!'

Tyke lifted her head, eyes flashing. 'School's horrible and so's everyone there. I don't want to go back.'

Samuel's slammed both hands down on the table top making her jump violently. 'Not an option, young lady!'

'If Mister Harvey won't let me…..' Tyke didn't both to finish the sentence, her eyes meeting Samuel's defiantly.

'Then perhaps boarding school would be better.' The words were out before Samuel had thought them through. In seconds he was pounced on.

'We can't afford it, Samuel. Be reasonable.' Alex, reverting to what Samuel deemed her usual stance of opposing everything he said.

'I'm *never* going to boarding school! If you make me I'll run away!'

Samuel loomed over the back of his daughter's chair. 'You are in no position to bargain, Tyke. You will do what we say and finish your schooling.'

'Did you?'

The question stopped Samuel mid-argument. 'This isn't about me.'

'And Moss hardly ever went.'

'That's not…..'

'And Maudie left when she was twelve. Maudie said school was no use at all for teaching people about the world.' Tyke stated this as the bottom line. She sat back in her chair, took her hand from Hugo's and folded her arms to glare mutinously at the cluttered table. 'I'm never going back. Never.'

Samuel's face took on a dangerous, angry red. In a rage he yanked his daughter out of her chair, fist raised.

Hugo stood, calmly setting Tyke behind him as he faced the furious man. 'Nothing will be resolved tonight, Samuel. Tyke's too upset. Why not sleep on it, eh?'

For a heart-stopping moment Alex expected Samuel to lash out at Hugo. From experience she knew it was touch and go. Samuel held Hugo's steady gaze, the older man balancing his stance ready for a fight. *Wouldn't be the first of his life.*

Samuel managed to unwind drop by drop until he broke eye contact with Hugo to point at the terrified Tyke. 'I will not be disobeyed. You may have the rest of the family sticking up for you but I am your father. You think on that! This isn't over. Not by a long shot.' Without conceding anything to Hugo or Alex, Samuel left the room.

The front door slammed on his exit.

Behind him an unsettled silence throbbed in the kitchen. With imploring eyes, Tyke reached out a hand in entreaty to Alex.

Her mother's face remained implacable. 'I'm not going to pretend to be on your side in this, Tyke. You have to be punished for what happened whether that happens here at home or at school.' Alex moved past Hugo only to stop beside him. 'You were brave to confront him,' she said softly. 'But it doesn't alter the fact Samuel and I are Tyke's parents and it will be we who make the final decision on this incident. Violence can never be condoned.' And if there was a bleak glance between mother and daughter, Alex didn't acknowledge it. 'I will discuss this with Maudie, Tyke although you can understand this much as of here and now– you are grounded for the foreseeable future. And that will be the least of your punishment.' Alex walked out of the room, both Tyke and Hugo holding their breath until they heard her feet on the stairwell.

Tyke sat back down at the table, feeling shaky and sick. She'd been hit by Samuel repeatedly over the years but those times paled into nothingness compared to the dark threat he just directed at her. There was nothing of love in the final look he gave her, not a glimmer of any emotion beyond vengeance. Hugo took Tyke's hand and she scrapped her chair as close to his as she could manage, hiding her face in his chest, feeling cold even though he hugged her tightly.

'I'm not sure it was worth it after all,' she whispered.

Hugo bent his head to hers. 'It might not feel like it, lass, but it was.'

It had gone midnight. Tyke lay on her bed, staring up into the darkness doubting her uncle's certainty. She pictured the look on Samuel's face and bit her lip. As much as she wanted to say it had been worth it, she couldn't. *She wasn't so brave. Not now.*

It was hot, too hot to sleep even if she could quiet her mind long enough to let sleep come. True to her word, Alex had spoken with Maudie. She relayed the result in the cool, detached voice Tyke hated. 'We decided nothing would come of forcing you back to school so you are to stay at home. I will give you lessons and every other hour you will spend working, either in the house with Maudie or assisting me in my work with families in need. This will be no holiday, Tyke.'

Tyke didn't need the warning. It was there in her mother's stance, the way she held herself in as if clenching unwanted emotions to her chest. Then Alex sent her to bed. Keeping her head high, Tyke went, Uncle Hugo's wink reminding her of his promise – somehow they would see the new talkie. Again however much she wanted to believe him, Tyke couldn't see how they would manage it. She wasn't going to be left alone for any length of time. Maudie might give way to her in some things but she never gave way in anything Alex wanted.

Tyke fidgeted restlessly, pushing the long sleeves of her nightdress up her arms as high as she could. Maudie didn't believe in bare skin even in bed. Finally, Tyke threw back the covers, hot feet welcoming the cool floorboards as she made her way to the small window overlooking the back of the boarding house. The window resisted her effort to lift it until it gave way with a groan. Tyke pushed it as high as it would go. She leaned over the sill, breathing in the warm night, longing for a cool breeze instead of this unusual stifling Wellington air. She wished she could have talked the day over with Moss but he had disappeared on some errand and hadn't returned.

Out in the dark, someone stumbled into the tin fence at the end of the yard. Straining her eyes Tyke made out the black shape forcing through the gate behind the woodshed. The shape swore, pushing the gate backwards so hard, there was a crunch of breaking timber. More swearing. Moonlight fell on Samuel's face. He tripped heavily and in righting himself, his head fell back. *He'd seen her!* Heart racing, Tyke rushed back into bed. She dragged the heavy eiderdown up to her chin and lay there, hardly daring to breathe.

All too soon Samuel's boots sounded on the stairs. Squeezing her eyes tightly shut, Tyke prayed he would just go to his own room and forget he had unfinished business with her. The footsteps came to a stop outside in the hallway and her stomach lurched unpleasantly. Tyke's door swung open and when she screwed up enough courage to peek, a heavy darkness loomed in the doorway. Her father took a step into the room and closed the door behind him. A sharp click of the latch.

'Get out of bed.'

Tyke gripped the eiderdown with white knuckles. 'Father, please. I know what I did was wrong. I'm sorry. So sorry. I.....'

'Get. Out.'

There came the unmistakable sound of his leather belt being removed. Trembling, Tyke's feet found the floor. She pulled her nightdress sleeves down, as if the thin fabric would protect her from what was coming.

'You constantly disobey me, Tyke.' Samuel's words were

slurred as he fumbled to gather the belt into one hand. 'Alex, Moss and Maudie, they gang up on me. They think I don't know it but I do.'

Tyke had pressed herself against the bed, one hand reaching out. 'Father….'

'Be silent!' It wasn't Tyke Samuel saw. In the half-light it was Alex, dressed for bed, taunting him with a lust he could no longer satisfy. Something snapped. Samuel yanked Tyke towards him, swinging the belt over his head. As his rage took over he heard nothing. Not the slap of thick leather on tender skin, not the pleas of his daughter, only a ringing in his head as frustration consumed him.

Candlelight danced flickering shadows over Tyke's tear-stained features. The mirror was clean though its edges had corroded over time. It left strange sullied shapes on the edges of her reflection. Placing the candle holder onto the sink bench, Tyke turned on a tap. She bent stiffly over the sink, lifting handfuls of cold water to douse her face. She didn't stop until she was gasping. Lifting her dripping face she confronted her image.

See? The tear-stains were gone. Washed away as if they never were.

There wasn't a bruise on her face, just one red mark where the belt-buckle had gone astray. It would have faded by morning. Gingerly, Tyke unbuttoned her nightdress, easing it down over one shoulder then the other as she turned slightly. Big welts, one or two with broken skin scored her back. Tyke ran her fingers over a particularly deep cut on her left shoulder. *This one would leave a scar.*

With great deliberation Tyke pulled her nightdress back up and buttoned it before lifting the hem up her thighs where bruising already shadowed her skin. One by one she ticked off the wounds, tallying up the damage done tonight. Finally, she straightened upright and grimaced at her echo in the tarnished mirror. *She wouldn't tell anyone about this.* She felt shame as much as anger. *This was their secret.* She would remind him of it every time he looked at her. *But,* Tyke lifted her chin, *never again would he make her cry.*

***

Maudie was turning bed sheets middles to ends when Alex and Tyke appeared in the kitchen.

'I thought you were going to buy new to replace these old sheets?' Alex lifted the kettle from the woodstove. She waggled it at Tyke who shook her head.

'I was gonna, girl until them two buggers in the attic rooms cleared off with two month's rent owing.' Maudie unwound some more thread, biting it off between her teeth.

Alex filled the waiting tea pot, leaning against the mantle as it stewed. 'They seemed such nice men.'

Even as she spoke the second word, Maudie had expletives voiced. 'Seemed. Seemed,' she muttered bitterly. 'Everyone's a nice seeming bugger when they want summat.'

'Can I stay and help you, Maudie?' This from a hopeful Tyke who didn't relish the thought of more time spent with her still angry mother.

'Nah. Yer got stuff to do. The way things are headed yer'll be helping me do more of this soon enough. Tea ready yet, girl?'

As her mother drank, Tyke watched Maudie's needle flash in and out as she sewed. A thought suddenly occurred to the girl. 'Why aren't you using the sewing machine?'

A not-quite-look passed between the two women.

'S'being repaired.' Maudie said and bent her head over her work.

'Oh.' Alex drank the last dregs of her tea, avoiding Maudie's eye as Tyke continued heedlessly. 'You sent Moss with it to Mister Benge's to be repaired ages ago. Shall I chase it up?'

Alex held out Tyke's hat and gloves. 'Come on,' she said sharply. 'We've a full day ahead of us.'

Tyke sighed. 'We always do.'

The summer day promised to be a scorcher as Tyke trailed her mother onto Tory Street. Turning right they headed up the hill. The smell from the wharf was only too evident today, a wind from the north blowing its stink over Wellington streets. Screwing up her nose, Tyke hastened after Alex, the string bags she carried bumping against her leg. 'Where are we going this morning?'

'Aro Valley. We have several visits there today.'

'I hope there'll be no one I know.'

'It doesn't matter in the least if there is. You'll just have to keep quiet and help where you can so we can leave all the quicker.'

'I know. You tell me every day.'

'Because every day you complain about the same things.' Alex stopped on the roadside for a moment, shifting the packages more comfortably in her arms. 'Look, Tyke. You brought this all on yourself.....'

'I know!' Tugging at the handles on the strong bags, Tyke stalked off.

An exasperated Alex let her go. There was no doubt about it, her daughter had changed. She smiled less, seemed quicker to take offence or be angry. Maudie put it down to growing pains which Alex accepted as a possibility although it didn't really explain the girl's attitude to her father; the way she never spoke to him and he never appeared to notice her. Alex glanced up to sight the blue straw hat with the yellow ribbons bobbing along in front of her. *Perhaps they had both given up pretending.* Alex deliberated her smiles after a bad night with Samuel, the way they all pretended not to know what they all knew too well; the strain which pretence had in the household.

Tyke's way was the more open way to live. An honest display of her emotions didn't make the girl easier to live with though, did it?

The run-down cottage was tucked up a path little more than a track cut into the bush. Panting under the weight of their combined loads, they toiled to the edge of the clearing where the little home sat. It was cool here even in the heat of summer for the trees had been left untrimmed and they blotted out the sky. Tyke smelt dampness mingled with the reek from an outhouse she couldn't see. Giving her daughter a reassuring glance, Alex walked up to the peeling front door. There was no veranda or porch, not even a piece of roofing iron to protect the door from the elements. Two thin cats came enquiringly out from under the house, purring appealingly. Tyke automatically bent to pat them only to recoil at the fleas crawling around their ears. Shuddering, she tried not to flinch as they both smooched around her legs, meowing and obviously hungry. Eventually the front door was opened by a girl of Tyke's age. She held a youngster bawling on one hip and held another by the hand. *Phyllis.* Aghast Tyke tugged at her hat brim, hoping to hide her face as she slipped casually behind her mother.

'Is Mrs Henderson at home?'

'Yes.'

'She's expecting me. I'm Mrs Brodie.' Alex smiled gently.

Phyllis eyed her suspiciously before holding the door back. 'You better come through, then.' She seemed oblivious of Tyke until they were side-by-side in the hallway and the name Alex had given clicked. *Brodie.* 'Tyke?'

Alex vanished down the short hallway of the three roomed cottage, disappearing into the kitchen at the far end. Tyke gestured after her mother, her face red with embarrassment.

'I better....' Her voice trailed off as Phyllis laid her free hand on Tyke's arm.

'Give me a sec.' Phyllis soothed the sobbing baby.

The toddler gawked at Tyke until he found her boring. An old shoe abandoned on the floor grabbed his interest. Picking it up and chewing on it, he wandered off, leaving the two girls and the crying baby.

'She's teething, poor thing.' Phyllis put her finger gently into the baby's mouth, running it over the hard gums. 'One's coming through. See?'

Tyke peered into the wailing mouth to see the tiny piece of white tooth beginning to break through swollen red gums. As she screwed her face in sympathy the baby smiled and gurgled at her.

Phyllis looked at Tyke in surprise. 'She doesn't smile at anyone! Wonder what's so special about you?' They exchanged grins.

'How old is she?'

'Nine months. Do you want to hold her?'

Lowering the string bags gently onto the hall floor, Tyke gave the little one a pensive look. 'I've never held a baby.'

'Lucky you. Look, I'll pass her to you…. Perfect. Just keep her head against your arm like that.' The baby continued to smile up at Tyke, gurgling through the fingers crammed in her mouth. 'Well, I'll be! We have to show mother. Come on.'

Down the hallway they went, Tyke glancing into the two bare rooms either side. Nothing in them she could see but a big bed in each piled with grey pillows and old blankets. The small kitchen was just as bare. A sink against one wall, the wood stove unlit and at the table sat Phyllis's mother, her big belly proof of another baby on its way. Two boys of about eight and nine were crouched outside on the grass sorting through some sacks of rubbish.

'Look, Mum! Little Margery has taken to Tyke.'

Mrs Henderson's weary face lit up with a lovely smile. 'You've got the touch, my dear.' She turned to Alex. 'Is this your daughter? I thought so. She looks a lot like you.'

Tyke tried not to stare at the signs of real poverty. For the first time she had an inkling of what Alex threw her strength and time at. *Bare rooms with empty shelves. The smell of unwashed bodies and clothes. The hunger in gaunt faces.*

Seeing Tyke's distraction, Phyllis gestured to the back door and the two girls found somewhere outside to sit, the now sleepy baby happy in Tyke's arms. Her eyes lingered on the busy boys. 'What are your brothers doing?'

Phyllis fidgeted uncomfortably. 'Oh well, you know. They go through people's rubbish and stuff. In case something's good and we can use it or pawn it.'

'Oh.'

Tyke knew people were hungry but she'd never seen a completely empty kitchen before or children sorting through other people's rubbish in the hope of finding something to live off. She knew times were tough; bread-with-jam-or-butter-never-both times but she had never appreciated people went without jam and butter because they didn't even have bread. She strove to find something to say when Phyllis spoke in a rush.

'Tyke, I'm sorry. So sorry. I didn't mean for you to get into such trouble. All you did was be nice to me and you were expelled! I'll never forgive myself! I'll never....'

A shocked Tyke finally found her tongue. 'I wasn't expelled!'

Phyllis stared at her, round eyed. 'You weren't?'

'No. I left and told everyone I wasn't going back.'

'Is that really true?'

'Yes!'

Phyllis eyed Tyke doubtfully. 'You told lies to Miss Taggett all the time.'

'Well I'm not telling one now. It is true. Alex is teaching me at home and I have to help her....' Here Tyke faltered, not comfortable with telling Phyllis she was helping her mother with some of the poorest families in Wellington. Of course they both knew why she was here but even so. It felt wrong to put it into words. 'I have to help her,' she finished lamely.

'Who's Alex?'

'My mother.'

'You call her by her given name?' Phyllis was shocked.

'Sometimes.' Tyke cut the girl off as she opened her mouth to question her further. 'Look, I wasn't expelled. Cross my heart.'

Pause.

Phyllis's wary eyes searched Tyke's intently. 'Emma told us all you'd been expelled.'

Tyke gave a snort, startling the baby who grizzled briefly. 'She's a liar. I'll never forgive her for what she did to you.'

It had been a revelation to Phyllis; *someone risking so much just for her!* In all her twelve years no one had stuck up for her the way Tyke had. Shyly they looked at each other.

'I can't do anything to thank you.'

Tyke reached out and held Phyllis's hand. 'You don't have to. It's what friends do for each other.'

'Friends?' Phyllis looked so dumbfounded Tyke thought she'd made a mistake and took her hand away only to have Phyllis clutch it closely one again. 'I've never had a friend before.'

Through Tyke's mind Emma appeared over the years. With the recent confrontation in her mind, the scenes shifted somehow and all the older girl's patronising sneers became crystal clear. With sudden clarity she was able to return Phyllis's grip and say, 'Me neither until now.'

As they grinned one of the boys gave a whoop of success and lifted an unopened tin above his head.

'Hey, Phyl! We've got some meat!'

Tyke joined in the happiness as they went to inspect the find.

***

A few days later, Tyke was in town with Maudie. She

waited what felt like an interminable time for Maudie to stop gossiping on the street with an old friend. Growing bored she wandered further along, aimlessly window shopping, coming to a halt outside a pawn shop display. Phyllis's brothers popped into her mind and she wondered if anything there had come from them. Tyke's eyes fell on a sewing machine. Not just any sewing machine. It had once belonged to Maudie.

The days of no bread, no butter or jam were heading their way, too.

***

Murchison

Fee was bored. Matthew had promised to play cards but here it was, well after seven in the evening and there was still no sign of him. He always lost track of time when he worked in their uncles' workshop.

No excuse to leave me bored and lonely, though! And he did promise.

Fee was coming to understand how Matthew's promises were like God – you could have faith but the truth was no matter how hard you wanted to believe, you invariably ended up alone and wishing they were real. She had asked him once if she could join him at the workshop only to be rebuffed with, *'Girls don't work with motors and don't like getting dirty.'* A patent lie which Aunt Janet gave proof to every day. Aunt Janet said girls could work anywhere they damn well wanted. Shockingly, as well as swearing, she even wore trousers, something Fee's mother hated as unwomanly. Fee had a sneaking suspicion that was one of the reasons Aunt Janet wore them. Unbeknown to Cally, Janet had given Fee her own pair of trousers. They were hidden under everything at the back of Fee's wardrobe. She wouldn't dare wear them in front of her mother though she had tried them on, amazed at their comfort and sense of freedom. *A bit like being with Aunt Janet.* In fact, if it wasn't for Da, Fee would happily live with her aunt. *I couldn't leave Da alone with Mother and Matthew though. He has to have someone in the house who loves him.*

Fee's restless pacing came to a stop. She'd never put those unexplored feeling into words before but there was no denying their truth now she had. *Poor Da. It wasn't his fault he was the way he was.* Aunt Janet related stories about Jimmy before the war, about his teasing, his jokes and what a wonderful dancer he had been. She told Fee how he had fought on the side of the farmers during the Great Strike only to discover his long-lost brother, her Uncle Samuel fighting on the opposite side. How he regretted that fight. How he joked about it and the brother he loved. Aunt Janet would pick up the photo of Jimmy and Cally on their wedding day and smile at his good-looking face.

'He was one out of the box, your Da.'

Fee wished so much she'd known Da then! Wished he was like that now.   Every once in a while there would be a glimmer of his old sense of humour. He would tease her or Aunt Janet and Fee would ache all the more. *So that was who Da used to be.*

Her grandparents' house became too confining. Fee checked she wasn't being watched before slipping outside.

Where are you, Matt?

Cicadas chirruped noisily from the trees around the old farm house, their family home further down the road, not too far away but out of sight from where Fee paced. They were staying with their grandparents for the weekend.

'*To give your mother a rest,*' Emily had said.

Fee was hard put not to bitterly laugh out loud. For though Fee loved the way Emily cared for them all, Grandma did not know Cally didn't need a rest. *Aunt Janet did most of the caring for Da, actually.*   Emily didn't see it for the care was as unobtrusive as it was unfailing. Fee also acknowledged her own efforts. *Da quieted around her.* She could always bring him back when he was lost in his head – *well,* she amended honestly, *mostly she could.*   There were those terrible times when he was away for days, staring blankly at a wall or lying rigid in his bed and she would sit or lie beside him, stroking his hand and whispering, '*Come back, Da. I miss you.*'

Cally refused to see Jimmy during those times. She left the house and Fee never liked to ask where she went. She assumed her mother went to Mrs Stewart's place though when she mentioned it to Janet, her aunt's face had become a mask.

'Yes probably,' she replied leaving Fee as doubtful as when she broached the subject.

So, lovely as it was to be away from home, even if it was just down the road, Fee felt Emily had been taken advantage of, offering help for all the wrong reasons.

It was all so complicated.

Fee walked further down the farm road to where she could sight the road into town.

Still no sign of Matt.

Sighing heavily she walked back towards home farm and just in time for she heard Emily calling.

Fee began to run. 'I'm here, Grandma!' Panting, she arrived at the back door.

Emily waited for her. 'I wondered where you'd got to, love, that's all.'

'Just waiting for Matt. He promised he'd be home in time for us to play cards before bed.'

Emily moved to the stove to heat some milk for cocoa. 'You know what the boy's like. He'll have had his head under the bonnet of one of your uncles' vehicles and completely lost track of time.' Fee nodded her agreement. She sat at the well-scrubbed kitchen table as Emily asked, 'Would you like some cocoa? Grandfather and I are having some.'

'No thank you.' Fee couldn't sit still. She cocked an ear to the hallway. 'Is Da all right?'

'He's sound asleep. Stop worrying, love. I brought you three here so you could relax and let me take over for a change.'

'Hardly a change, Grandma. You care all the time.'

'Well, what else is my time for?' Emily's eyes fell on her granddaughter's sturdy figure, slouched against the door onto the hallway. Her feet tapped restively as she bit on her nails and gazed anxiously down the hallway. 'Fee, why don't you go for a walk and burn off some energy? When Matthew turns up I promise I will scold him for you and feed him so when you return you can start playing cards straight away.' Fee turned a smiling face towards her.

'You wouldn't mind?'

Emily chivvied her out of the kitchen. 'Come back when you're ready and not before.'

Pausing only to kiss Emily's cheek, Fee dashed off. Thinking of her twin it occurred to her she had stupidly left Matthew to remember his pyjamas and change of clothes for Grandma's. *He never remembered to pack them, no use thinking he would have today.* Wishing she had just packed them when she did her own, Fee jogged towards home, whistling under her breath. She reached the top of the rise in the road where their cottage came into view, tucked against a stand of native trees. Fee frowned. There was a light on inside and there shouldn't have been. It didn't occur to her to run back to get her grandfather. John hadn't been well and he tired easily these days. With only a fleeting want for Matthew's company, Fee ran to the cottage, keeping to the grassy verge of the road so no one would hear her feet on the gravel. Once on the veranda outside the back door, she pressed her ear against the wood. Nothing stirred. *Probably just a light left on by mistake.* Nonetheless, something made her cautious. As quietly as she could, Fee eased the door open and stepped into the kitchen. A deep sigh sounded from somewhere down the hall. Fee reached for the rolling pin, feeling immediately better for clasping something heavy as she investigated further. More soft sounds. She couldn't make out any words. Now Fee was standing in the hallway, straining to hear. There was movement in her parents' bedroom and she stepped soundlessly towards it, rolling pin raised in her hand, heart hammering in her chest. Taking a moment with her back against the hallway right beside the bedroom door, Fee nerved herself. Someone groaned.

Mother?

She no longer hesitated. Fee sprang into the room and froze, her brain struggling to understand what she was seeing. Cally was naked sitting astride a man. They both leapt in shock and

Fee saw the man's face. *Uncle Jeff.* Innocent as she was, Fee wasn't a fool. As she met her mother's horrified eyes, Fee turned and walked out, dropping the rolling pin to the floor.

Don't follow me. Don't follow me.

Fee reached the back door and threw it open just as her mother's voice called her name. The girl didn't look back. She took to her heels and ran, pounding down the road, arms pumping like pistons her brain screaming to forget what it had witnessed. Too shocked for tears Fee ran until her breath came in gulping, heaving gasps and she had to stop, muscles burning, head spinning. Stumbling on shaky legs she found a corner fence post to lean over. As her stomach reacted to the flood of violent emotions, Fee retched helplessly.

It was there Matthew found her. She didn't hear him call out, didn't know he was anywhere near. He was several yards away before realising something was very wrong with his twin. 'Fee?'

Nothing.

Reaching her, Matthew laid his hand on her shoulder, recoiling as she spun round, her face twisted as she struck out blindly.

'Don't touch me!'

Matthew held his hands high above his head. 'It's me, Fee. It's me.'

Fee's vision cleared and her brother swam into view. Unable to stop, she threw herself into his arms, trembling.

'What the hell's wrong?'

She couldn't find the words to tell him, tightening her grip around his neck.

Frightened now, Matthew wrestled free, holding Fee's hands. 'For God's sake, Fee. Tell me! Is it Grandfather?'

Fee noticed how he instantly claimed John for his concern, not Jimmy. It's Mother.' Fee wiped at her burning eyes. And stopped. *How could she tell him?*

'What about her? Fee! What about her? Tell me!'

'She was in bed with Jeff.' *He'd been Uncle Jeff for as long as she could remember but never again.* 'They were in Da's bed together!' A strange immobility came over her brother. *Had he heard her? Did he understand?* 'She was naked, Matt. With him.' Fee's voice faltered. 'In Da's bed.' *Among all the awfulness of her discovery why did that stand out?* Matthew hadn't moved. He didn't show any emotion at all. 'Do you understand, Matt?'

Now he was angry. 'Of course I bloody understand.'

When he met Fee's eyes there was a strange expression in them. *Was it pity?*

Silence.

Fee felt a sick throb of comprehension. 'You knew.' She grabbed his arm. 'You knew and didn't tell me?'

'What the hell could I have said?' Matthew twisted out of her grasp. 'You wouldn't have believed me anyway.'

'You could still have given me a warning!'

'Bloody how? Tell me how, Fee? I wanted to say something as soon as I suspected but explain to me how the bloody hell I could have told you!' His voice dropped. 'I felt so guilty, Fee.'

That threw her. Dazed and confused she shook her head to clear it. 'Why?'

Matthew tried to speak. He cleared his throat, tried again and this time his words were ragged and thick. 'Because I love Mother and you don't. And you love Da. And I don't.'

They were twins. Sometimes they hated each other more than any person in the world. Sometimes they didn't need to speak to understand what the other was thinking. And then there were times like this when they knew each other's truth and appreciated no one else would forgive them for it.

Tentatively Fee stepped closer. Matthew hugged her. Together they rocked silently to and fro as the night darkened around them.

Fee found excuse after excuse not to leave their grandparent's home. She didn't want to go back to the house now forever tainted by the image seared into her brain. Eventually, as Matthew pointed out, they either had to tell Grandma the truth and explain why they wanted to stay or go and leave her untouched by the revelation. They left.

Home again in their own cottage, Cally tried to act as if nothing was wrong, even as the atmosphere threatened to choke them all. Her daughter wouldn't look at her, would barely acknowledge her beyond the barest of words. Matthew too seemed distant. He wouldn't speak about Fee even when Cally asked him direct questions. He began avoiding his mother, spending longer and longer hours down in town with Wally and Ben in their workshop. His absence left Fee and Cally alone in the cottage with Jimmy as the walls closed in.

Fee couldn't sleep. She tossed and turned in her bed, trying to empty her mind of the images of Cally and Jeff. *All those nights when Mother had left her and Janet to cope with Da she had been with Jeff.* The sense of betrayal swept her so completely it brought Fee upright, gasping a little for breath as she placed both hands over her chest to will the feeling away. Slowly it receded, leaving a lump in her stomach, a knot too tight to unravel. After minutes of useless fretting, Fee got out of bed. Taking her dressing gown off the hook on the back of the bedroom door, she slipped it on to make her way to the kitchen. Jimmy groaned in his sleep. Fee paused in the hallway to make sure he settled only to remember how she had stood in this exact spot seconds before discovering her mother's adultery. *Why did she keep torturing herself like this?* Exasperated, Fee walked straight through the kitchen to the sink under the window. Moonlight played with the shadows in the room and outside it was as bright as day, just a day without colour. Sighing, Fee turned to lean her back against the sink.

Cally was sitting at the kitchen table.

Fee found her voice. 'How long have you been in the dark?'

'Since 1915.' Cally remembered another occasion. *Discovered sitting in the dark after running from the monster Jimmy had become.*

Pause.

'I don't want to listen to your excuses, Mother.'

'Why not? You excuse your father every single day.'

'That's different!' Not wanting to wake the sleepers, Fee pitched her voice low though it ached with intensity. 'Da did not choose what happened to him.'

'Neither did I.'

'Why do you always have to make it about you?' Fee began to tremble and gripped the sink bench briefly, gathering her strength to leave the room. 'It's not. About. You.' She nearly made it through the door when her mother stepped in front of her.

'We have to talk.'

'No. No, we don't. You just want to justify what I saw.'

'Please, Fee.' There was something in her mother's voice Fee hadn't heard before. She hardened her heart against its appeal. 'I have to explain.' Cally held Fee's shoulders only to be shaken off.

'Explain it to Matthew, then. He might listen and forgive you.'

Cally's tone flattened. 'But not you?' She had her answer in the embittered pause but Fee gave it words anyway.

'Never me.'

Fee pushed past Cally and left her alone in the kitchen. Left her in the dark.

***

Jimmy wanted to leave the house. This was such a rare occurrence his daughter gaped.

'Just somewhere near the river. For a picnic,' he told Fee yearningly.

When Janet arrived with Jimmy's latest prescription from the doctor, Fee bailed her up and told her of Jimmy's wish. She hadn't bothered mentioning it to Cally.

'Shouldn't be a problem.' Fee smiled. That was Janet's response whatever anyone asked of her. 'When were you thinking, Fee?'

'Tomorrow? If we leave it Da will either change his mind or the weather will pack it up.'

Deal done.

The next day seemed as if it would hold to its early morning promise so Fee packed up a simple lunch along with a flask of cold tea. Cally watched silently, offering no help, asking no questions. It was as if the two women were in different rooms. Different houses. Different worlds. At the sound of pony trap wheels and a set of hooves, Fee picked up the basket, a thick blanket and her father's coat, despite Jimmy's grumbles about not needing it.

'You never know,' was his daughter's irrefutable reply.

The sun beat down on them as they made their way further up the Matakitaki Valley. Janet whistled, Jimmy smiled, and Fee gradually relaxed, enjoying the regular rhythm of the horse's hooves clopping on the road in the warmth of the day. She leaned into Jimmy's shoulder – his good side. He picked her hand up and kissed it briefly before tucking it under his arm.

'Janet, remember this?' Jimmy cleared his throat and sang, with a voice rough with disuse.

'I'm a Yankee Doodle Dandy. A Yankee Doodle do or die.

A real life nephew of my Uncle Sam. Born on the fourth of July.'

Janet whooped and joined in.

'I've got a Yankee Doodle sweetheart. She's my Yankee Doodle joy.

Yankee Doodle came to London. Just to ride the ponies.

I am the Yankee Doodle Boy.'

Laughing together, Fee watching them in bemusement.

'A great song from before the war,' Jimmy told her.

'And your father butchered singing it back then!'

'All right,' Jimmy countered, 'how about this one? *We're strolling along on Moonlight Bay.'*

'I know this.' Fee enthused and joined in.

'We could hear the voices ringing, they seemed to say,

'You have stolen her heart.'

'Not don't go 'way.'

As we sang love's old sweet song on Moonlight Bay.'

It was so lovely they all sang it again and again. Fee added a harmony, Janet a second. Three parts in complete unity drifted over the head of the horse, on over the green fields. On, on and out of sight. In no time at all they found the old dirt road which cut off through paddocks down to the river. The road was so dry dust furled up behind as the horse pulled the cart along, bouncing through potholes. Jimmy laughed as Fee was almost jolted off the seat, laughing harder when she scolded him for being an unnatural father to find humour in her predicament.

Jimmy pointed to their right. 'Over there. Under those willows. Perfect spot for a picnic I reckon.'

'You're not usually right about anything,' Janet teased, 'but let's see, shall we?'

He was right and made much of the fact. Janet unhitched the horse and set her free to graze the paddock behind them leaving Fee to lay the blanket over a springy patch of ground on the shadowed edge of overhanging trees. Jimmy took hold of the basket, swotting Fee's hand away when she would have taken it from him. A sharp look to make sure she hadn't offended him. *No, he was smiling.* Fee began gathering the particular round, flattish stones required for skipping across the water.

'Remember teaching me, Da?'

Jimmy came to a rest beside her. 'Of course I do. Bet I can still beat you.'

'Bet you can't.'

Fee offered some of her own stones only for Jimmy to mock her choices. He scoured the river bed for the perfect ones, Fee's taunting making him growl in mock anger.

'Samuel always beat me at this.' Jimmy turned a stone over in his fingers before letting it fly across the water. It sank after two skips.

'And here you are, about to be beaten by your daughter.' Fee squinted as she bent slightly and took aim. The stone flew from her fingers with the perfect flick and she crowed as it skipped nine times.

'A lucky shot.' Jimmy scoffed, rubbing his next stone between his fingers.

Janet sat on the blanket, happy to watch them. *When was the last time she had seen Jimmy so happy?* It worried her she couldn't remember. Jimmy's shout made her start but he was cheering.

Janet cupped her hands together. 'Get him, Fee! You can't let him win!'

Her niece's reply went unheard, only her delight echoed back.

It didn't take long for Jimmy to tire. All his damaged and twisted right side ached, he could barely drag his leg along as he headed for the blanket. Unable to lower himself, two pairs of willing hands gently took his weight and guided him down to the welcoming softness of the picnic spot.

'Shall we eat?' Janet asked. 'I have to say, I'm starving.'

'It amazes me you're not the size of a house the way you stuff yourself.' Jimmy retorted, his words slurred with effort.

'I don't stuff myself!'

Exactly the response Jimmy was aiming for. Happy to let Janet spout on, he accepted the piece of pie Fee passed him. They munched in silence, Jimmy slumping further onto his left side until he was prone on the blanket. His movements gradually slowed until the next time Fee glanced at him, he was asleep, the last of the pie crumbling in his hand. She pulled the edge of the blanket over his lower body and removed the crust from his open hand.

'Shall we wake him?'

'Let him sleep. He's had a strenuous morning. Any pie left?'

Fee handed Janet the last piece and reached for a biscuit. She had no idea how preoccupied she looked until Janet nudged her.

'Penny for them?'

'They're not worth a penny.'

'A ha-penny, then?'

A shake of the head.

'Must be worth something. You don't look happy.' Janet finished the last mouthful, dusting her fingers off on her trousers. 'You're hiding it well in front of your Da but I know you, remember?' Shrewd eyes studied her. 'Actually Fee, you've not seemed well for a while now. What's wrong?'

Fee agonised over the need to spill everything out versus her loyalty to her mother. In the end her confusion and unhappiness weighed the balance.

Janet saw her uncertainty. 'You don't have to tell me if you don't want to,' she said softly.

'I do. I do want to. I need to.' And with a final despairing look at her sleeping father, Fee let it all out.

What she saw.

Finding her mother sitting in the dark kitchen.

Her own stubborn refusal to forgive.

'I don't want to hate Mother, but I do. I hate what she's done. I hate her betrayal of Da.' Fee covered her face. 'I hate her.'

'Oh, Fee....' Janet wasn't one for hugs but confronted with such anguish she shifted to put an arm around Fee's shoulders. A long silence as Janet deliberated. 'I want to tell you something. It may help, it may not, I don't know but from what you've just told me, you have a right to hear it anyway.' She stopped.

All Fee could see was her aunt's profile, unnaturally subdued. 'Tell me, please.'

Pause.

'I knew about them, Cally and Jeff. I worked it out years ago.'

Fee gasped. 'How many years ago?'

Janet hesitated. 'During the war.'

'What did you do?'

'What could I do? I told Cally I knew and, well, protected her, I guess.'

Fee pushed free of Janet's encircling arm. 'Why? Why would you? It was wrong!'

'She was still my sister, Fee. I had to.'

It was unfair, Fee knew yet she felt betrayed by her aunt. *Another betrayal on top of her mother's.*

Janet accurately read her niece's mind. 'Wouldn't you protect Matthew? Don't you every day? When you know he's done something wrong?'

Fee was too honest to lie, too dispirited. 'Yes.'

'Then you must understand why I couldn't say anything.'

Silence.

'Fee?'

'It's so hard.' A cry from a broken heart.

'I know but there's only one person we have to worry about.'

Together they looked down at the sleeping Jimmy.

Silence.

'How do I live with her?' Fee asked, not taking her eyes off her father.

'Day by day. And Fee?' Janet waited till her niece looked up. 'This will be hard to understand, probably the hardest thing of all, but remember Cally knows you know. Being discovered by you will be one of the worst moments in her life. Maybe the worst. Every time she sees you, even hears your name mentioned, your mother will remember the look on your face at what she was doing. It's a life sentence for her, too.'

Fee's face hardened. 'I don't care. She deserves it.'

Janet didn't push it. This was something Cally and Fee would have to work out. Or not. Nothing anyone else could do.

***

Berlin
February

The day had stretched on and on. Wilhelm should have finished work hours ago, yet he was behind his desk frowning over the mass of invoices, receipts, orders and miscellany which always ended up on his desk. *The more successful the business, the greater the swathe of paperwork.*

His uncle had been one of the first manufacturers in Berlin to support innovative work with electricity. This factory, his flagship, had been directly involved in producing the science required to provide Berlin with its startling electric street lighting, the wonder of visitors from all over the world. Sigmund actively encouraged new developments in electrical manufacturing, his support found behind some of the newest products and ideas. None of this had been known to Wilhelm five years ago when he came to work for his uncle.

After less than six months as a glorified cleaner and messenger, Wilhelm had been given the opportunity to work on the production line. As his interest grew, he asked to be shifted through the various departments, quickly learning how the factory operated and to his own surprise he developed a skill for management. Sigmund's business manager, Calev Altmeyer, a cynical observer of this nepotism eventually came to appreciate the younger man's ability and drive. He gave Wilhelm ample opportunity to develop his talents, making him a foreman who proved to have a deft, empathetic way with the employees under his watch and a keen eye for ways to increase productivity.

Wilhelm's eyes lost focus briefly. *Five years. He'd hardly noticed it pass.*

And now with an office and desk to call his own Wilhelm tried to make sense of the mass of correspondence and wondered at the loss of all the hours in all his days. A headache made its presence felt. Massaging his temples

Wilhelm reminisced with some longing on those times when his work finished once he'd removed his overalls.

Shouts and pounding feet in the street startled him out of his lethargy. He peered through one of the larger windows onto the alleyway where their dispatch trucks were parked. Someone stood there, looking up, tossing a dark lump from hand to hand. Another shout. Three men raced down, arms gesticulating wildly at the figure standing there before disappearing. The man's arm thrust back, the rock in his hand sent crashing through the window. Wilhelm leapt back, showered in broken glass. He expected more missiles but instead another group of men ran down the alley. The window-breaker bolted, shouting at his pursuers. As they raced under a street lamp the light brought the chasers' uniforms into sharp relief. Brown-shirts. Their numbers had grown over the past few years. There were gangs of them roaming through Berlin's streets, disrupting political meetings, looking for violence and if they couldn't find any, they caused it. Wilhelm watched the pursuit before studying the shards of glass clinging to the edge of the window frame. If it wasn't a fascist who broke it then it must have been K.D.P. A new member, perhaps who didn't know the factory he had targeted for his rage held men sympathetic to the left. He had simply seen the size of the factory and attacked a probable capitalist.

'Little bastard.' Wilhelm grumbled as he moved to his desk.

The factory was quiet. *God only knew what time it was. No use trying to recover his concentration for the work sitting on his desk.* Wilhelm was debating whether to nail some boards over the broken window when another noise came, this time from the cellars. He snatched a hammer off a workbench as he made his way down the stairs. *Bloody Brown- shirts or K.D.P. Whoever was down there would learn a short, sharp lesson.* Near the bottom he stopped. Someone was breaking in through one of the smaller wooden doors. There were hurried, anxious whispers, a groan of pain and after a pause, the door was forced open. A shadow stumbled in, righting itself to rub a shoulder.

Taking a firmer grip on the hammer, Wilhelm moved swiftly. He grabbed the shadow, one arm around its neck, the hammer raised. 'Don't move or I will knock your brains clean over the floor!' To his amazement the shadow began to laugh. Wilhelm tightened his grip.

A strangled voice gasped, 'It's me, you fool. Let me go.' It took a moment for Wilhelm's hold to relax. Jost fought to get free, grumbling as he rubbed his neck. 'I thought you didn't like fighting?'

'What the hell are you doing breaking into the factory in the middle of the night?'

'Escaping. Didn't you hear the bloody Nazis?' A moan from outside the door brought Jost to his senses. 'Marc!'

As Wilhelm watched, one ear listening for more trouble outside, Jost half-dragged, half-carried an older man into the cellar and laid him carefully on the floor.

'What happened to him?'

'One of Goebbels Brown-shirts. We had an S.D.P rally tonight. They came smashing in, police at their sides, blowing whistles, screaming blue murder that we were breaking the peace. Marc here got flattened by some bastard flailing a baton. They were going to drag him away to God knows where but me and a couple of K.D.P lads managed to get him out.'

Wilhelm knelt beside the injured man. As he tried to see just how bad his wounds were, Marc heaved himself onto an elbow, pushing Wilhelm away.

'I'm well.'

'Are you sure?' Jost helped the older man to his feet, keeping a grip on one shoulder as Marc swayed.

'Don't fuss, Jost.'

'You should see what I'm looking at,' Jost replied for blood stained Marc's shirt and jacket, one side of his face already purpling and swelling into an impressive bruise.

'I'll be alright once I'm home.'

'Can I help you?'

'No,' Marc grumbled. 'Just piss off.' He stopped at the door with a half-glance back over one shoulder. 'Thanks for getting me outta there.' Then he left them.

'Stubborn old bugger,' Jost muttered half under his breath. 'He'll be back out tomorrow night.'

The two of them fixed the broken lock on the cellar door, tidying up the mess before Wilhelm found a good-sized board and some nails to go with his hammer.

'Some little bugger smashed window upstairs, too. Lucky it wasn't more, I suppose.'

'Who smashed it?'

'K.D.P, I think. He and a group were running from the Brown-shirts.'

They wandered back upstairs, Jost lending a hand to cover the lost pane.

'Could be. There are rumours it's industrialists who are funding Hitler. Maybe someone's whispering about your uncle.'

Wilhelm paused in the act of hammering a nail. 'Uncle Sigmund supports the Republic.'

'I know but that's hardly in his favour, is it? Not to the K.D.P. You know, we seem to spend as much of our time fighting the damn communists as we do the Nazis.' Jost ran a hand over his face as if trying to wipe his weariness away. 'Have you seen this?' He handed over a much-creased newspaper.

Wilhelm studied it. 'Der Angriff?' He frowned. 'The Attack. Who wrote this?'

Not bothering to reply, Jost stabbed a finger at the leading article.

'We Demand. Joseph Goebbels. 'We demand the right of work and a decent living for every working German. We demand homes for German soldiers and workers. If there is not enough money to build them, drive the foreigners out so Germans can live on German soil.'

Wilhelm sat on the wide windowsill as he read on in growing astonishment.

'These days anyone has a right to speak in Germany – the Jew, the Frenchman, the Englishman, the League of Nations, the conscience of the world, and the Devil knows who else! Everyone but the German worker.

Germany for the Germans!'

Unable to tear his eyes away, Wilhelm began to read aloud, ' *'Why are we Socialists? We call ourselves a workers' party because we want to free labour from the chains of Capitalism and Marxism. 'We are the army of the swastika. Raise high the red flags! We want to clear the way to freedom for German labour!''*

It took Wilhelm long moments to gather his thoughts and as he did, Jost snatched the paper from his hands.

'The Nazis are dangerous because they're smarter than us on the left. They are using our own symbols against us – the red in their swastikas, calling themselves Socialists, using every weapon to get the worker on their side; our voters.' With a curse Jost shook the pages. 'It's like the establishment of Christianity, Wilhelm. You take the symbols of paganism, some of its important images and beliefs and you wrap them up in something similar but so different that before anyone knows what happened, you've created something stronger and more powerful. You have a weapon strong enough to control the world.'

Wilhelm failed to mask his scepticism. 'I think you're being melodramatic.'

'Do you?' Jost showed no expression at all. 'I hope I am but do you want to know the very worst? Do you know who gave this to me in the spirit of brotherhood? Joachim. He told me the Republic is failing, communism is failing, socialism is failing but there is a fourth way. And he handed me this. This piece of shit.' For a second nothing showed in Jost's face until with a roar he ripped Goebbels' attack into shreds, showering them both in tumbling black and white.

***

Kristel circled the room, drink in one hand, feeling nothing but nervous about tonight's gathering. She paused in front of an ornate gilt-edged mirror to run a hand over her hair, carefully pinned tightly back off her face. *When was the last time the whole family were under one roof? That fact alone should make it a night of celebration. Instead….* A frown passed over her features as a cough sounded from the doorway. Kristel focussed on the reflected surface to see her cousin waiting tentatively in the hallway.

'Look at you, hovering like a servant. You don't have to announce yourself, you know. Not after all these years.' Yet Wilhelm's modesty was one of the things Kristel liked. She moved swiftly to kiss him lightly before slipping her arm through his and escorting him into the large room, all prepared for a cocktail party.

Wilhelm tugged at his waistcoat, grimacing slightly at its tightness. 'Never cared much for fancy dress,' he grumbled.

'Don't know why. You look very glamorous. Drink?'

'Please.'

'I know I need something before the crowd arrives.'

For the first time Wilhelm noticed the shadows under Kristel's eyes, shadows her makeup couldn't quite hide. 'You're nervous? Why? Uncle Sigmund has been planning your birthday for weeks.'

With a swift movement, Kristel emptied her glass, refilling it immediately. Expecting judgment she wagged a finger at her cousin. 'Don't say anything. I need this.' There was more than a hint of desperation in her actions, enough to worry Wilhelm who stopped her pouring a third gin.

'Tell me what's wrong.'

'I can't.'

'Yes, you can.' Wilhelm guided her to a sofa near the back of the room. 'Sit,' he commanded.

For a moment it looked as if she was going to ignore him until she slumped down and buried her head in her hands. 'I wish Papa hadn't organised this party tonight.'

Wilhelm pulled a chair in front of the sofa. From there he studied his cousin with troubled eyes. 'He's thought of nothing else.'

'I know and it just makes it worse.' Kristel rubbed her hands over her face. 'It wouldn't be so bad if it were only family here tonight but it's not, is it? Weber and Koing will be here, among others. And you know Jost. He is increasingly unwilling to compromise. Imagine him in front of Papa's guests! Imagine, Wilhelm! Imagine Jost in this room with fascists and tell me I have nothing to fear from tonight.' Her eyes pleaded with him.

How Wilhelm wished he could allay those fears. Jost had a point – *Christ! Some of the things happening around them.* But Wilhelm owed Sigmund a nephew's loyalty and the thought of Jost confronting businessmen under his uncle's roof, well, it concerned him, too. He opened his mouth to say something soothing but he'd let the pause drag on too long. As he reached out a placatory hand, Kristel began to pace.

'So you are worried. And something's wrong between him and Joachim. Something's changed.'

'You mean apart from their politics.'

'Don't be glib! They've been friends for as long as I can remember. Surely there has to be more to it than damn politics?'

What could he say? If Kristel refused to see the obvious, there was little Wilhelm could do to change her mind.

'We'll keep an eye on him.' Wilhelm felt no resentment when Kristel gave a spurt of mockery. 'We can only try, cousin.'

'And that has worked so well in the past.'

Their eyes met and on cue they both began to laugh, a ragged, uneven sound. Whatever else they might have shared was lost as a voice broke in on their privacy.

'You've started the party already? Where's my gin?' Inge was dressed to the nines, the lights catching the diamonds at her throat. Wilhelm hastily came to his feet. Whereas Kristel had greeted him warmly with a kiss Inge merely bent her head in his direction, instantly dismissing him as she faced her sister. 'I hope you've told your communist to keep away.'

'I assume you mean Jost. And no. Firstly, he is not a communist and secondly, he is my friend and has been invited along with everyone else on the guest list.' All Kristel's former anxieties were swept away in the sudden rush of dislike for her sister. Inge's haughty face didn't just register disapproval, there was hatred there, too and though Kristel knew it wasn't directed at her, it still stung.

'Friend,' Inge mocked. 'Just a friend? I can't approve of him,' Inge began.

Kristel cut her off with an impatient gesture. 'Lucky for me then I don't have to seek your approval before inviting those I like to my own birthday party.'

'Does Papa know?'

'Of course.'

'Then he's as much a fool as you.'

'A fine thought for a daughter to have.'

Inge spun round as Sigmund entered the room. 'Papa, I....'

'Think your father is a fool. I know. I heard you the first time.' Although Sigmund had never demanded unquestioning obedience from any of his children, Inge's casual words angered him even as he acknowledged she was right. *He was a fool. It was a dangerous thing to let Kristel invite Jost, yet how could he deny her when he had invited Calev?* They were friends and Sigmund's instinctive loyalty led his heart. Although none of his close friends were Nazi Party members, acquaintances like Doron Weber and Alfons Koing had joined because Adolf Hitler appealed to a certain type of businessmen; businessmen who happily put profit over morality, who wanted no union interference from their employees. They wanted to make greater profits with no pressure to reward those who helped make them. And both those men would be here tonight.

A conflicted Sigmund glanced at his daughters. Yet, Kristel was right, too; friends deserved loyalty, especially in troubled times, whereas Inge understood the need for reality in the face of growing threat. Wilhelm stepped into his uncle's line of vision, a glass of cognac held out with a smile and some of Sigmund's tension ebbed. Here was someone who saw both sides of any argument and this one particularly, for Wilhelm's quiet understanding was reflected in troubled eyes. *Thank heavens for this steady young man.* Sigmund took the glass, smiling at the empty ones in his daughters' hands. With an effort he shrugged off his worries. 'Happy birthday, my darling Kristel.'

As she was drawn into his embrace, Kristel caught Inge's expression. Deep resentment was written there.

The evening began and as inconspicuously as he could, Wilhelm kept an eye on Kristel, noting with admiration how she hid her worries behind a convincing social veneer. He took it upon himself to watch out for Jost and finally spotted him being welcomed through the front door. A quick look towards his cousin to make sure she was preoccupied and Wilhelm acted. Jost had just been relieved of his overcoat when Wilhelm appeared in the foyer. With no greeting he brusquely dragged Jost into a box-room barely big enough for the two men to comfortably stand in.

'What the hell are you doing?' Jost grabbed for the door knob only to be swung back round to face the other man. The threat on Wilhelm's normally dispassionate face brought Jost up short. 'What?'

'You have to show some self-control tonight. For Kristel.'
Before Jost could protest, Wilhelm shut him down. 'You
know who's here tonight. In fact, I'm warning you now;
Koing is parading his brand new S.A uniform out there like
the thug he is but you cannot challenge him. Not here. Not
under this roof.'

'Why the hell not?'

'Don't be obtuse Jost and don't take me for a fool. You
damn well know why not. Kristel is compromised by her
attachment to you and by association, so are we all. Uncle
Sigmund is under increasing pressure to – and these are not
my words – re-establish German purity among his staff and
associates. You know what that means and you can be bloody
sure Sigmund does, too and he's resisting even as men like
Koing just wait for the axe to fall. You must not make things
worse tonight.' Wilhelm took in a breath and actually begged.
'Please, Jost. If not for Uncle Sigmund then for Kristel.'

Silence.

Having braced himself for rage, Wilhelm was surprised
when a rueful smile tugged the corner of Jost's mouth.

'Look at you, all het up. You have been worrying, haven't
you?'

'Yes.'

'I suppose Inge has predicted a dire fall-out because of my
presence?'

'The whole works. I'm surprised she hasn't mentioned fire
and plague.'

'If that bastard Koing says anything....'

'Count to ten and walk away from him. He's looking for
any opportunity to bring Sigmund down. Don't give it to
him.'

Jost leaned a shoulder against the wall. 'I suppose there is
something to be said for smiling pleasantly at those who hate
you.'

'Surely you will have had plenty of practice?' Wilhelm

risked a grin, pleased at the grudging smile in return as Jost held out a hand to seal his promise.

As soon as she saw Jost, Kristel rushed over to him, scolding even as she hugged him. 'Where have you been? I was beginning to think you wouldn't show.'

'I had to pick up some S.D.P flyers on the way here. You know, to hand out to everyone.'

The utter shock on her face gave Jost a guilty pang. Instead of a facile remark he grabbed her hands. 'I'm joking, love. Of course I'm joking! You must think the worst of me if you thought I actually would. Tonight of all nights.'

'To be honest, Jost, I wouldn't have put it past you.'

'I know but don't worry. Your cousin has already lectured me about being on my best behaviour tonight and I promised.'

Kristel lightly kissed his lips in her relief. 'I am surprised.'

His arms tightened around her. 'That I promised?'

'That you even know what best behaviour means.'

Against all expectations Kristel began to enjoy her party. She avoided Herr Koing and Herr Weber, finding pleasure in dancing and ignoring Inge's disapproving frown as Jost expertly swung her round. As the music died away to applause, Kristel searched faces. 'I wonder where Joachim is?'

'He'll be here. You know how he loves to make an entrance.'

'Have you seen much of him lately?'

Jost shook his head. 'We argue more and more. I think he's been deliberately ignoring me.'

'Well, he'd better make it. He promised me a surprise.' Her voice died away as Wilhelm made his way towards them, his face tense.

He grabbed her hand and Jost's arm, his voice rough with urgency. 'Joachim's here.'

Kristel's face lit up. 'Where?'

'Cousin, it's not good.'

From happiness to fear in a heartbeat it was Kristel's turn to clutch Wilhelm's hand. 'What's happened to him?'

Wilhelm cursed, shaking his head, trying to keep his voice low. 'It's not what's happened, Kristel. It's what he's done.'

Jost spun around to follow Wilhelm's unhappy gaze so he saw before Kristel. 'Fuck him,' he breathed out in shock.

In dread Kristel turned. There stood her brother next to another man. They were both dressed in immaculate S.A uniforms, their matching black ties and black caps revealing something else, something darker. They had joined the S.S, an elite unit within the S.A. - the Schutzstaffel - Hitler's protection squadron. Around them people began to applaud. Wilhelm glanced around in despair. He caught sight of Calev Altmeyer disappearing out through the cheering room.

How she managed to smile through the rest of her party, Kristel couldn't say. For through the dancing and drinking, the laughter and eating she was aware of Jost's desperate strain and Joachim's proud bearing in his new uniform. Keeping a brave face she manoeuvred through the press of people, accepting birthday wishes as her stomach churned. Since her brother's arrival the atmosphere of the party had changed. Now people slanted glances at her and Jost. Kristel was suddenly aware of whispered conversations breaking off at their approach. Needing privacy, they sat in a quiet corner, neither of them speaking and there Wilhelm found them.

'Calev left.'

'When? I didn't get a chance to thank him for my present.'

'Just after Joachim and his companion arrived.' Wilhelm joined them briefly on the sofa until restlessness drove him back onto his feet once more.

Jost's right leg was pumping like a piston. He glanced at Wilhelm. 'Do you know who the other man is? The one who arrived with Joachim?'

'No.'

'He's Emil Seidel. Destined for big things I hear.'

Kristel lowered her voice to match Jost's.

'How did you hear?'

'Through the usual channels. We have to know who the enemy is. And Emil Seidel...' Jost hesitated. 'He's old friends with Joseph Goebbels.'

Wilhelm frowned. 'Goebbels?'

'Someone else we watch closely.'

The three of them sat in silence as the room emptied around them. They had begun to talk quietly again, when raised voices reached them. Kristel recognised unusual anger in her father's tone so she hastily sought him out, Jost and Wilhelm close behind. Sigmund was hemmed in by Inge, Joachim and Emil Seidel, the scene, looking for all the world like dogs at a bear-baiting.

'It is increasingly dangerous to do business with men like him, Papa. I understand you have known him for years but they are dangerous people.'

With a glance at Emil, Sigmund lifted a hand in a warning gesture to his son. 'We are not going to discuss it now.'

Inge spoke up. 'He's already shunned. How can we be seen to be friendly with him?'

'Calev is a good businessman and a better friend. Idle chatter does not concern me.'

'It is not idle chatter, Papa. Already people speak against you and your willingness to negotiate with the unions. They say you are their puppet. Men like you who support the Weimar Republic are failing Germany by letting unions dictate too much. Look at the unemployment benefit. Why should those unwilling to work be handed free money at the demands of the unions?' Joachim gestured to his new friend. 'Tell him, Emil.'

Sigmund swallowed his growing anger. 'Keep your voices down and your opinions to yourself. I am answerable to no one. And how dare you question Calev. He saved my life in a Belgian trench and means more to me than most. I will not abandon him.'

'Then you risk your business,' Joachim replied flatly.

With chill enunciation his father replied, 'It is mine to risk.' And with the barest acknowledgement of Emil, Sigmund left them.

As Inge grumbled about her father's lack of respect to a guest, Joachim noticed Kristel for the first time.

'Kris! Happy birthday.' He hugged her, seemed not to notice her lack of response. Reaching into a pocket he pulled out a prettily wrapped present. 'Open it.' The pause stretched out. Kristel remained unmoving. Joachim finally comprehended something was wrong. 'What is it?'

Emil cast a condescending glance at Kristel. 'I think your sister would like some time with her family.' He clicked his heels, bowing to Kristel before taking Inge's hand to his lips. 'Perhaps Fraulein Inge would do the honour of showing me out?'

Inge slanted stealthy triumph Kristel's way. Sliding her arm through Emil's she gestured to the hallway.

'Not before time,' Jost muttered just loudly enough.

For the first time Emil reacted to Jost and Wilhelm's presence. He looked then over with mocking eyes and an equally mocking bow. A haughty glare from Inge and they left the room.

Unaware of all this by-play, Joachim placed the gift into Kristel's hands. 'Happy birthday anyway.'

Finally Kristel found her voice. 'How can you choose the Nazis after all we've seen and heard together?'

'So that's what all this attitude is about?'

'Just answer her.' Jost's rough demand.

Silence.

Brother and sister watched each other, the twisting, intertwined pathways of shared childhood diverging at this moment.

'It was easy,' Joachim said flatly. 'It was because of all we've seen and heard.'

'Though I appreciated the thought, and continue to do so, you should not have invited me, Sigmund.'

'Why ever not?'

Calev remembered a woman at Kristel's party who gave him nothing but contempt. Meeting his eyes she had shifted her gaze but only after her lips twisted in a derisive smirk. 'Your associates were not happy to have a Jew in their midst.'

Sigmund snorted. 'I will not be dictated to by bigots. You are beyond being merely my right-hand man, Calev. We have been friends for more years than either of us would care to count.'

'And yet, you should not have invited me.' He forestalled Sigmund's heated denial. 'I'm not speaking as your friend but as someone intimately connected to your business interests. You only damage your reputation by openly employing me.'

'Damn them,' Sigmund hissed. 'I'm breaking no law by doing so.'

'Yet,' Calev offered softly.

Sigmund was only barely hanging onto his temper. He strode around from behind his desk to drag a chair closer to where Calev and Wilhelm sat. Outside his office the factory continued its work, the three men confident in that if little else.

'I have communists damning me for being a capitalist and dealing with the Republic. Now I have fascists damning me for dealing with Jews and unions! If all those bastards have their way we'll have no business at all.' He shook his head as if trying to shake the madness away. 'What the hell can anyone do but the best they can?' Seeing the concern on their faces Sigmund drew in a steadying breath.

Calev leaned forward in his urgency. 'I just want you, no, I need you to be aware of what's being spoken of around Berlin and Germany. Hermann Tietz's takeover of Adolf Jandorf's interests has only added fuel to the fire of speculation and accusation that Jews are running Germany for their own profits at the expense of German businesses.' Calev lowered his voice. 'They are making us into the enemy, Sigmund. There are reasons they are doing so.'

Wilhelm spoke for the first time. 'It is also unfair, Uncle, to expect Calev to mix with those who refuse to hide their dislike.'

Calev raised his palms up. 'Such a consideration was not my concern,' he protested gently.

Sigmund frowned. 'But my nephew has a point, old friend. One I should have given thought to. I put you in an untenable position and though I despise having to give way to pressure, I shall for your sake only.'

They held each other's eyes for a moment silently acknowledging the changing world they feared.

***

The room was dim. Even on a sunlit day, the light hardly reached into the small, grimy windows of Jost's attic room. There were a dozen other small rooms in an area which had once been an open space until an enterprising landlord appreciated the opportunity it afforded. Thin walls failed to contain the noisy domestic lives lived here. Babies cried, there were shouting matches, slamming doors, crashes and bangs, all of it the background to Jost's life. Most of it he scarcely noticed, having grown attuned to the sounds like someone living near a railroad track who never hears the trains. Two things he loved about his attic room; few visitors wanted to climb the stairs or face the poor streets of Wedding to get here. One of his last visitors had been his father. Paul had stayed long enough to disown the son who refused to alter his politics.

'I'm losing clients because of it, Jost. For God's sake see sense!'

'No.'

Sometimes when he couldn't sleep the look on his father's face haunted Jost. It spoke of love denied, love forgotten, love withheld and he would wonder if he should have compromised. Thankfully the night would pass and so would his doubts.

It was already growing darker outside, adding to the gloom. Three meagre hours of sunlight in a Berlin winter did little to warm body and spirit. With his breath showing on the air, Jost reached for his overcoat, glad of its thick warmth as he shrugged it on. He was reaching for his hat when the knock sounded on his door.

Who the hell...?

As he swung the door inward, he couldn't keep the surprise from his face. 'Joachim.'

'May I come in?'

Pause.

Jost stepped back as Joachim walked passed him to stand in the middle of the room and mutter, 'It's colder in here than outside.'

'Then by all means stay outside.' Joachim studied Jost's face for a hint of humour and found nothing but enquiry. 'Not wearing your fancy uniform tonight?'

'I don't wear it every damn hour.' Joachim winced at his defensive tone.

'Unlike your pal Emil. I have a bet on with Kristel that he sleeps in it. Does he?' Jost adopted a relaxed pose leaning against the nearest wall, enjoying Joachim's obvious discomfort.

'I didn't come here to put up with your bullshit.'

This time Jost didn't even reply. He just opened the door and bowed.

Silence.

When Joachim didn't move Jost shut the door and enunciated with chill precision. 'What do you want?'

'Are you intending to be at the Pharus Hall tonight?'

A shrug.

'What about Kristel?'

'Have you asked her?'

Joachim made an angry gesture, turned away from Jost's searching gaze. 'Kristel hasn't spoken to me since her birthday. She walks out of any room I'm in. Thanks to you my sister has cut me out of her life.'

'Kristel's intelligent and perfectly capable of rational thought. She makes up her own mind without any influence from me.' Try as he might, as betrayed as he felt, Jost couldn't distance himself from Joachim's pain and confusion. He knew how conflicted Kristel was, too. He spent hours listening as she tried to reason why the brother she loved could be following an ideology so alien and frightening. Jost could offer no insight, for he had also loved Joachim, assuming their friendship would last despite their growing differences. It hadn't survived being clothed in an S.S uniform.

'Just tell me what you want.' Jost moved from the door to sit on his bed, pointing at the only other chair in the room.

Joachim stayed on his feet, needing to be on the move. 'Don't go to Pharus Hall tonight.'

'Why not?'

'There's increasing trouble between communists and you socialists.'

'Jesus, Joachim. Tell me something I don't know. The further the K.D.P move to an extreme left, the further it moves from our moderate stance in the S.D.P. I blame Ernest Thalmann. He claims policies have to become increasingly aggressive to answer the Nazi threat. I understand why he's demanding the change but he's alienating good, loyal socialists.'

Joachim gave a bitter laugh.

'Good, loyal socialists? Now there's a phrase that doesn't bear analysis.'

Jost's boots hit the floor with a resounding thud as he propelled himself off the bed to confront Joachim eye-to-eye. 'Get the fuck out.'

Silence.

Joachim was a heartbeat from storming away. 'Don't go tonight. Don't.'

Silence.

'The Nazis are coming to us for the first time. Of course I'll be there.' The look of frustrated anger on Joachim's face brought Jost's defiance to a halt. He took a breath. 'Do you know something we don't, Joachim?'

'Goebbels is trying to force confrontation. He wants to break the largest population of communists in Berlin. Tonight is a step towards it.'

Jost studied Joachim's face. 'He's forcing us to retaliate?'

Pause as Joachim's inner conflict raged. 'Wedding's a powder keg, waiting for a spark. Goebbels will push till you light it.'

Silence.

'I can't stay away. If there's trouble, we'll face it together.' Jost lifted his chin.

A light snuffed out in Joachim's eyes. He opened his mouth in anger only to swallow it back and bury his pride. 'Then at least promise me you'll keep Kristel out of it.'

'Kristel will do what she feels is right.'

'I want my sister to be safe.'

Pause.

'Then you should stand beside her and not beside those bringing it all down.'

Their last spark of friendship died.

From his eyrie Jost watched Joachim burst out from the building and march out of the alley.

He didn't look back.

***

Wilhelm was already regretting his impulse to accompany Kristel to tonight's meeting. The closer they came to Pharus Hall the denser the crowds, the greater the buzz of excitement and fear. Everywhere he looked Wilhelm saw groups of men talking furtively. Once or twice he saw knives disappearing up sleeves, cudgels tucked into deep pockets. It was a relief to see Jost waiting for them on the corner as arranged. *Should he warn Jost? No. He would know about the danger and not care.*

Jost hailed Kristel's blithe figure, a red beret on her head and lifted a hand to point at it. 'Aren't you asking for trouble?'

'What? No one can wear red and not be a communist?'

'Kristel...'

'What?'

For a moment indecision played over Jost's features. Then, he took Kristel by the arm, beckoned Wilhelm and found a doorway where they could talk without being overheard.

'Joachim visited me earlier.' Two incredulous faces gaped. 'To give warning.'

'What warning?' Wilhelm glanced over his shoulder, suddenly aware of the milling crowds a few steps away.

'Goebbels is using tonight to provoke an attack.'

Kristel gave a skeptical snort. 'What makes tonight different from any other when his Brown-shirts start brawls at our rallies and meetings?'

'Because tonight, he wants us to throw the first punch, then he has every reason to smash back and hit hard. By tomorrow morning the headlines will scream of unprecedented violence shown by the left and we will be damned as troublemakers while Goebbels piously claims the Nazis were merely spreading the gospel in Wedding.'

Kristel frowned. 'Why did Joachim tell you this?'

Pause. Jost met her eyes.

'Because he's scared you will get hurt,' he said softly, not breaking eye contact.

'Bit late for that. The hurt started the moment he put on a

bloody S.S uniform.' But both men caught the betraying huskiness in her voice.

Wilhelm shifted uneasily. 'Maybe we should listen to him.'

'No.' Kristel shot the word out. 'If my brother was truly concerned about people getting hurt, then he shouldn't have joined the Nazis. What he told Jost tonight was about appeasing his conscience towards someone he knows, nothing more.' She stood her ground. 'I'm going in. Whether you two join me or not.'

Jost grabbed her hand, kissed her fingers. 'You're not going in there alone, right Wilhelm?'

In spite of the tension, the look of trepidation on his face made them both smile.

There were plenty of K.D.P gathered around the hall itself, milling on the road, merging with the shadows and lost in the heavy grey mist.

Inside was bulging at the seams.

'Gotta be nearly a thousand people here,' Jost shouted above the noise.

Brown-shirts were everywhere with a small number of S.S beside them. Kristel peered through the press of people, half-expecting, half-fearing to see Joachim but there wasn't a sign of him. Emil Seidel was there, though. She watched as he strode importantly in the direction of the stage before being lost in the crowd. There were Communist Party members scattered throughout, people standing on stools and chairs against the walls for a better view. They couldn't even see the platform at the end of the hall through the press of bodies. A sharp whistle to their right and a gesturing arm beckoned them further on. A couple of Jost's friends had claimed two tables, shoving them together to stand on. Grinning, they held out hands, hoisted the three up with them, part of Wilhelm wishing he'd stayed on the floor, undetected, unseen.

Kristel pointed to the platform as someone walked onto it. 'There he is. Goebbels.'

His arrogant bearing was unmistakable even from their position, an arrogance made all the more menacing framed as it was by more than twenty S.A and S.S troops standing along the front of the platform.

The noise in the hall increased as Wilhelm leaned towards Kristel to shout in her ear. 'I see our new friend Emil is here.'

'I know. Thank God Joachim isn't.'

'You do know Emil's seeing Inge?'

'Yes.' Kristel's face tightened.

Noting her discontent Wilhelm changed the subject. 'So what's Goebbels speaking about?'

'The collapse of the bourgeois class state ostensibly.' Kristel's mouth twisted expressively. 'But that's not what he's really here to say.'

Wilhelm was lost. 'What do you mean?'

'Look at him, Wilhelm! Surrounded by the Nazi Party's private army. He's telling us all he's coming for us.'

'The Communists?'

Kristel nodded, her eyes glued to the front of the hall. 'Communists, socialists, trade unionists, anyone left of the Nazis.'

Wilhelm strained to hear her. Goebbels was shouting his message at a crowd of disbelievers. He knew he was and didn't care. With every sentence the noise increased, the soldiers in front of Goebbels waiting for their moment. Goebbels raised his voice and a man stood on a chair on the opposite side of the hall and shouted, 'Point of order!'

He was ignored.

Jost hissed. 'We were given the right to question!' He cupped his hand to his mouth. 'Point of order!'

Every time Goebbels paused for breath the man on the chair yelled. 'Point of order!'

The meeting quickly degenerated into chaos. Wilhelm saw two Brown-shirts, one of them Emil break away from the stage front. He kept his eyes on them as they shoved down the side of the hall until they reached the man on the chair. In seconds they dragged him down, hauling him back to the stage. No one seemed to have noticed until Jost happened to glance around and saw Wilhelm staring open-mouthed. At the sight of the communist being taken, Jost leapt off the table, roaring at those around him and suddenly everyone knew. From somewhere in the crowd a beer mug sailed towards Goebbels and smashed at his feet. It was the spark the explosion needed.

Jost grabbed Wilhelm's arm. 'Get Kris out! Now!' He turned away, squaring up to an officer in S.A uniform.

 Desperately Wilhelm tugged at Kristel's arm. 'We've got to get out!'

She pushed him away, almost unbalancing them both from the table top. Just when they righted themselves, two men crashed into the table, sending them all smashing to the ground. The fighters didn't pause. Table legs were torn off and used in combat, blood spraying over those huddled against the wall amidst the shattered table. Kristel favoured her right shoulder as she tended to Wilhelm who had blood streaming from a cut above his left eye. Head ringing, he pointed to the nearest door. Kristel cast a final frantic look at the heaving chaos trying to spot Jost but it was hopeless. Following Wilhelm's lead they left the hall.

It wasn't much better out here. Communists surged forward, eager to join the fray, equal numbers tried to get away from it. Into it all marched the police and they came in swinging. Wilhelm kept one arm up over his head and one around Kristel's shoulders in a hopeless effort to protect them from batons, pistol handles and fists as he fought through the melee. Finally they found a deserted alleyway. Here they came to a stop, gasping for breath, shocked and too stupefied to speak. Chaos raged around them; chaos signalling a shift in the Nazi's policy of dealing with the political parties opposing them.

1929/1930

Wellington

Very nice. Moss's first thought as he surveyed Callan McMillain's office. Thick brocade curtains draped the bay window, elaborate plaster cornicing edged the beaten copper panels on the ceiling. *And chandeliers like that don't come cheap either.* Moss moved his muddy boots across the carpet. Silk in the mix he'd bet his life and ratcheted up the cost of it even as he left traces of dirt on the gorgeous weave. Anyone else who spent so much on a Persian rug would hang it on a prominent wall. It explained a lot about Callan McMillain that he chose to put it on the floor in front of the leather chesterfield sofa and the inlaid walnut occasional tables. Moss raised his eyes to the attractive woman behind the desk with the fashionably crimped hair, typing with efficient concentration. He had already been up to the desk twice and she wasn't so good looking he would bother to approach her again. Moss's patience with McMillain's stalling tactics ran out. He deliberately ground the heels of his dirty boots deeper into the carpet then stood. The receptionist shot an anxious look his way only to snub him once more.

Right. That's bloody it!

Moss marched passed the desk. He ignored the squawk as he pushed open the door into McMillain's office, the receptionist protesting at his heels. They found the lawyer studiously bent over his desk, the picture of concentrated industry.

'Oh, Mr McMillain! I'm so sorry. This man wouldn't wait. He...'

A large white hand cut off her spluttering protest. 'Thank you Miss White. You may leave us.'

Giving Moss a final glare, the receptionist closed the door with pointed obedience.

McMillain barely raised his eyes from his paperwork. 'You have upset Miss White.'

'Damn Miss White.' This forced the intended response.

McMillain eyed him disapprovingly. 'You and your partner were given explicit instructions to never visit me at either my office or home.'

Moss grabbed one of the two chairs in front of the desk and sat down, deliberately exaggerating the boorishness of his pose. 'And you were given a deadline for payment. I wouldn't be here if you weren't in debt.' Pause. 'Considerable debt.'

For the first time emotion crossed the bland face. McMillain tried to hide it but worry flashed before his professional impassiveness reasserted itself. 'You will get your money.'

Moss's smile was anything but reassuring. 'Oh, we know.' Settling back as if he owned the place he studied the fixtures of the elegant room. 'You're hiding it well, McMillain but we're not the fools you take us for.'

The lawyer shifted irritably.

'I have no idea what you are referring to.'

'Really? Because the way I hear it, the bailiffs are days away from knocking on your door.' Moss had the satisfaction of seeing the anguish written clear in the lawyer's eyes. 'We gave you six months, McMillain. Six months good faith and it's finished, right here, right now. Either you settle your debt or I walk out the door to chat with your wife.' He leaned forward solicitously. 'You have told your wife about your debts? Or how about your clients? You will have notified them of your difficulties, of course. All their money given to you in trust. Gone.' Moss snapped his fingers.

Silence.

McMillain's eyes slid away from Moss, fear, anger, guilt all fighting for dominance. He gave up any pretence of work, throwing his pen onto the desktop, ink splattering the pristine wood.

When he finally spoke his voice shook.

'If you take what's left you'll ruin me.'

Moss's glare was unrelenting. 'You've ruined yourself, mate. We're just the lucky ones who'll get what you owe them.'

Silence.

Moss walked out of the office, ignoring the receptionist's haughty sneer. He removed the roll of notes from his pocket, letting her see the thickness of it. Licking his thumb he unpeeled a ten pound note and laid it on the paperwork in front of her. 'I'm guessing he hasn't paid your wages for a while now. It probably won't cover what's owing but at least you'll get something out of the old bastard.'

She couldn't take her eyes from the money. 'What do you mean?'

Moss tipped his hat. 'You'll find out soon enough.' He felt her eyes on his back as he walked out.

He didn't feel good about what he'd just done. It hadn't been the first time he'd had to lean on people either. Although he had little sympathy for the lawyer, identifying him early on for a shifty bastard, there were men who had just been unlucky, not greedy. Men who had borrowed to tide them over for better days only for those better days never to dawn. *Many of those poor bastards had fought through the Great War.* They'd been looking forward to peace and for a couple of short years most of them found it. Then things began to falter. They had battled through the mud and blood of the war and now struggled in peacetime to feed their families. First they sold those wedding presents they had never used, the silver fish knives and forks, the ugly vases from well-meaning aunts. Then the carpets on the floor – *we don't need carpets.* The extra pots and pans. *We can make do with one large, one small.* Then it was the curtains, the clothes worn only on good occasions until children went barefoot wearing sacks for raincoats and the family ate potatoes or bread and dripping for every meal.

Moodily Moss pulled his hat low, not wanting to make eye contact with beggars while he had a pocketful of money. He passed a man with a half-full flour sack dragging over one shoulder. Swaggers. There were more and more of these men in worn down boots heading out of the city in search of work.

Might be me soon.

Back at the boarding house, Moss threw the money onto the kitchen table in front of Hugo.

'The old bugger paid up.'

'Easily?'

Moss scoffed. 'What do you think? By the way, it's a tenner short. I gave it to his receptionist.'

Maudie cuffed his head. 'Trust you t'be sympathetic t'the lassies.'

'It's not like I fancied her, Ma. She's a right snooty cow. It just seemed the right thing to do.'

Hugo counted the money into three equal amounts. One he slid across the table to Moss, the other he handed to Maudie. 'This is the last of it,' he told them sombrely. 'We've got a bit of stock left but who's going to buy it? No one's buying whisky or cognac these days.'

Scooping the money up and shoving it into her apron pocket, Maudie got on with fixing dinner, making a mental note to get more oatmeal because adding oatmeal to any meal stretched it further.

Moss tapped a shilling on the table. 'I might know a place we could shift the rest.'

'Where?'

His nephew shot a look at his mother's back as she worked over the stove only to be given proof she had eyes in the back of her head.

'Might as well spit it out, boy. I'll find out one way or t'other.'

No denying that. Moss cautiously named the den he had in mind.

Even Hugo's eyebrows shot up in surprise. 'You do know who runs that.'

'I know he's rolling in dough.'

'If we get into his bad books....' Hugo didn't bother finishing the threat. He didn't need to.

Moss spun the shilling on its side, concentrating on its twirling path across the table-top.

'We wouldn't. We'd be supplying him not owing him.'

Maudie tasted the contents of her stock pot then laid down the wooden spoon. 'Them buggers are worse than the Chinese.'

In exasperation Moss slammed his hand on top of the spinning coin. 'Well, do either of you have any other ideas? We either shift the stock we've got left, the stock we paid out good money for and recover our costs at least, or we sit on it and go broke.' The widening silence answered his question. 'Right. Well, then. I'll pop along and see him tonight.'

Maudie hefted her wooden spoon again. 'You make it sound like you're calling in for afternoon tea,' she grumbled.

'If you're going, make sure you keep yourself safe,' Hugo said seriously.

Moss patted his jacket. The dagger Alex and Samuel had got him from Cairo never left his pocket. He drew it out as Exhibit A when Tyke wandered in. All conversation ceased and Moss surreptitiously tucked the dagger back in its sheath.

Not surreptitiously enough. Tyke had seen it and the accompanying silence made her instantly suspicious. 'What's going on?'

'Nothing.'

'Were you talking about me or something?'

'How was work?'

She answered Moss's question with a glower. 'Don't change the subject. What were you lot saying that needed your dagger on view? Talk about guilty faces!'

'Don't talk tosh, girl.' This from Maudie. 'Get an apron on and help me out.'

Tyke did as she was told, her eyes never leaving Moss's face.

Haining Street hadn't changed. Areas like this never did. Dreary slum homes, the rare businesses, potholed roads leading down dank alleyways. He didn't come here often but whenever he did, Moss remembered the night Samuel dragged his friend Cass from the opium den. Samuel had paid ten year old Moss to track Cass, more than upset when Moss revealed where he was to be found. Tonight, slipping further into the jumble of rough buildings, Moss passed the same opium den. *Wonder why the coppers never touched it?* They were forever congratulating themselves on the lack of organised crime in Wellington even as the black market flourished. *Gotta be coppers too who liked to chase the dragon.*

Moss knew a shadow moved stealthily behind him. *Clever, my friend but not quite clever enough.* Throwing a stone against an opposite wall as a distraction he ducked into a lean-to and waited. The shadow made its cautious way passed. Moss grabbed it and heaved it against the nearest fence, his dagger already in his hand. 'Why the fuck are you following me?'

The figure squirmed under his restraining hand. 'I wanted to know what you were up to.'

Moss let go in astonishment. 'Tyke?'

She straightened her coat. 'You're so bloody jumpy, Moss.'

'Don't swear!'

'You sound like Alex.'

'No I don't. You wouldn't dare swear around your mother.'

An amused chuckle exhaled softly. 'Maudie, then. You sound just like Maudie.'

Moss gathered his wits. 'Stop trying to change the subject,' he admonished, angry because she already had. 'You're not supposed to be out at night.' He grabbed her arm. 'Come on. Home.'

She yanked free. 'Whatever you're here for is obviously important.'

Moss tried to get hold of her again, only to be smartly evaded as Tyke dodged round him.

'So?'

'So, I'm not stopping you doing it.'

Exasperated he hauled her into a small spill of light thrown onto the dirty alley through an uncurtained window. 'There is no way I'm taking you where I have to go. No way.'

'Why not?'

'For God's sake, Tyke! You shouldn't bloody be here.' He lowered his voice, concern tightening his tone. 'These aren't nice people I have to see.'

For the first time Tyke hesitated. 'Is it dangerous?'

Movement further down the alleyway. They held their breath, waiting until they were quite alone again.

'Yes, in a way. And you shouldn't be here,' he repeated.

Pause.

'If I promise to go home will you tell me tomorrow what you were doing?'

Moss prevaricated. 'As much as I can.'

To his intense relief Tyke seemed to accept that. She gave him the once-over. 'Promise?'

'I've said haven't I?' Moss checked his pocket-watch by the yellow light. 'Look, bugger off will you or I'll be late.'

Tyke saluted him jauntily. 'Buggering off, sir.'

To make certain of her intention, Moss kept Tyke company till they were back out on Tory Street. 'Straight inside the house. No unseemly loitering.'

This time the gesture Tyke gave him wasn't so polite. Moss reached out to clip her ear but she ducked under his arm and jogged off. Wondering at her audacity Moss checked his watch anxiously. He noted the time and swore under his breath as he retraced his steps into the back-alley haunts of Haining Street. *Snowy wasn't someone you kept waiting.*

It wasn't just a brothel, though Snowy made good money from his girls and boys. It wasn't just a drinking den either, even if alcohol flowed through in happy resistance to the temperance movement in Wellington and throughout the country. Anything you wanted could be found here. Want to know the bent coppers? Want to arrange a bit of pressure on some debt defaulter? Snowy would know it, learn it or arrange it for you. It cost, though. Cost a lot. Most people thought the money well spent and those who didn't, well, they never complained. If they did, they didn't complain for long.

All this went through Moss's mind as he waited to be shown into Snowy's office. Once in the inner sanctum he was offered a chair. There was no desk in the room. Snowy's business didn't require a lot of paperwork. The chairs were shabby leather and they were placed in front of a fireplace. The two men took each other's measure. Moss couldn't tell from Snowy's face how old he was. His skin had a leathery look and his hair was white but according to Maudie, Australians often had tough, weathered skin and bleached blonde hair. *The sun in Australia did that to yer, lad.* However old Snowy was he was venerable in experience. Even the Chinks kept out of his way, Moss had heard.

'So yer've got how many crates of grog?'

Picturing Hugo's face if he heard his precious single malt whisky and top of the range cognac called grog! 'Couple of dozen. Might be more.'

Snowy rubbed his chin. 'Anything else?'

'Yeah. Got some stuff.'

'Wanna share what it is or do yer reckon I'll cough up some dough on spec?' Sinister figures sniggered from where they leaned against walls. It did them no favours. 'If yer wanna have a laugh yer'd better fuck off. We're not here to amuse you bastards.'

Silence, Moss careful not to smile. Exit sinister figures.

Snowy sniffed hugely then spat thickly onto the floor. 'Did yer think to bring a sample of this grog with you?' As Snowy reached into for two glasses, Moss removed a sizeable hip flask from his jacket. He poured two generous measures, confident in their product. The Australian took a swig, eyes widening in pleasure. 'Hey, this is bloody good.'

'Only the best single malt, Snowy.'

Narrowing of pale blue eyes. 'It's Mr Peakes to you, sonny.' Snowy waited to see if offense had been taken.

'Fair enough, Mr Peakes. And it's Moss, not sonny.'

Pause.

Snowy lifted the glass to the light, studying the toffee coloured liquid. 'Two dozen crates like this you say?'

'Yep. P'raps more, depending. Maybe a dozen of the cognac.'

'Do I get a taste of it as well?'

Moss did the honours, Snowy smacking his lips in appreciation. 'I'm not a cognac man partic'ly but can't deny you've got good stuff here.'

'Only the best.'

A slight change in the atmosphere. A certain hardening. 'What about the other stuff?'

'If it's all right with you, Mr Peakes, let's do this deal and see how we work together.'

'What if I say it isn't all right?'

Moss toughened his voice to match. 'Then it will only prove what we've heard about Snowy Peakes.'

'And what's that?'

'He's a hard bastard, just not a clever one.'

Utter silence.

Moss let the hush settle. *Don't blink, don't fidget. Don't so much as breathe.*

'You've got some fucking cheek.'

'Yeah, so I've heard.'

Not so much as a ghost of a smile on the Australian's face. 'How much yer want?' Moss grabbed a handy scrap of paper and pencil. He scribbled a number then passed it across. 'Steep.'

'But not exorbitant.'

Moss made a show of pouring a final measure.

'How 'bout I add fifty pounds and you blokes get me some other stuff I'm having trouble sourcing?'

'I'd need to talk to my partner, Mr Peakes.'

Snowy knocked back the single malt. 'You do that, sonny.'

With heavy emphasis on the last word and a gesture towards the door, Snowy brought the meeting to an end.

Back out in the alley, Moss checked his pockets. *Dagger. Check. Wallet. Check. Testicles? Check.* He hadn't been sure he would get to the end of the night with any of them safe and sound. Reliving the meeting Moss decided it went as well as could be expected. *Did they want to have more to do with the Australian, though? Whatever the money?* It would take some pondering.

A woman screamed. There came the crack of a hand on skin and another scream, this time with curses. Moss picked up his pace as he tried to get his bearings. The scream came from behind the nearest huddle of buildings but there appeared to be no breaks or gaps between them. *Where to get through?* Finally Moss spotted a gate closing off a tight path. It was barely shoulder width as he jogged down it, the fight growing louder. As he burst out into a small courtyard a flying brick missed his head by inches, bringing him to a sharp stop. Two men had two females pushed against the back wall of a building. One of the women was struggling in fury. It took a few seconds of horror for Moss to recognise Tyke's voice.

'Get your bloody hands off me! And leave Phyllis alone, you big bastard!'

Tyke's knee swung up with all her weight behind it and it connected spot on. With an agonising soft crunch the man collapsed on the ground, groaning and retching. Moss was torn between alarm and pride. *Glad I taught her that.* The fallen man's companion gave a roar of rage. One hand holding Phyllis firmly in place, he managed to twist his hand in Tyke's hair and yank her close but by then Moss reached them. He held his dagger in view, moving it deftly from hand to hand until the man's eyes focussed on the glint of its polished blade.

'This here is none of your business, mate,' he growled.

'This one makes it my business.' Moss pointed at Tyke, writhing under the man's grip on her hair.

'She's a little hell-cat. Dunno where she sprung from 'cause she don't belong here.' The man sounded more offended than anything else.

'You've got Phyllis!' Tyke yelled.

The man looked confused. 'Who's bloody Phyllis?'

Tyke pointed at her friend, like a statue against the wall.

'You mean Florrie.'

'No. She's Phyllis!'

The man's patience gave way in a roar of rage. 'Fucking enough already!'

He bounced Tyke off the back wall. Moss acted quickly. Careful to graze not slice, he ran the sharpened blade along the man's forearm. He swore and loosened his hold on Tyke. Moss forced her to one side, balancing the knife as he feinted towards the hand holding Phyllis.

The man stepped back, one hand over the cut on his forearm, both raised in submission. 'Jesus, all right!'

Tyke pulled Phyllis away from the wall but to her surprise, her friend twisted out of her grip. 'What are you doing, Phyl? Come on.'

'Tyke, you don't understand.'

'This bastard had you against the wall!'

'I know.' Phyllis was horribly embarrassed.

A light flicked on in Moss's understanding. He lowered his knife as Tyke persisted.

'I heard you cry out!'

'Yes, but Tyke, it wasn't for help.'

Tyke stared from her friend to the big man nursing his wounded arm. 'What do you mean?'

Phyllis couldn't find the words.

It took the big man to explain. 'What your friend means is, she was earning her keep.'

'But...but....' Tyke's hands lifted and dropped helplessly. 'You cried out,' she repeated to Phyllis who couldn't meet her eyes.

Muttering a hasty apology to the man he cut, Moss stood at Tyke's side. 'Come on, Tyke. Phyllis is fine.'

Tyke placed her hands on her friend's shoulders and waited until she looked up. 'Are you?'

Phyllis nodded and Tyke's hands fell away. Unable to bear anymore, Tyke bolted for the hidden path. Moss paused long enough to reassure himself Phyllis was all right. The man seemed to bear her no ill will, and was leading her to one of the doors off the courtyard. Phyllis didn't even look back. Nothing more to be done, Moss chased after Tyke. He found her at the end of the pathway, leaning on the gate. At the sound of his footsteps she straightened up, tensing in response to Moss's worried anger.

'What the hell were you doing, Tyke? You promised you'd go home.'

'I meant to.' His face was sceptical. 'I did! But I saw, well, I didn't know it was Phyllis for sure but I thought it might be and she was heading this way. I followed, wondering why she was here so late and thinking....' Tyke's voice dropped. 'I didn't know what I was thinking really. It just seemed so strange.'

Moss waited as patiently as his simmering anger would allow.

'She met a man down the alley near where you went. I watched them head down this path. And then. And then,' again Tyke faltered. 'I heard her cry out. I thought he was hurting her.' She covered her face with her hands. 'I feel like such a fool, Moss.'

His anger faded. 'There's no need to. You thought your friend needed help and tried to give it.'

'Phyllis's a prostitute.' If there was disgust in Tyke's voice there was pain, too. 'She's not much older than me.' The years melted away from her as she turned to Moss. 'Why is she doing it, Moss?'

Pause.

Moss didn't feel like smiling anymore. He sighed. 'She's poor. You've told me just how poor. Sometimes all someone has left to sell is themselves.'

'It's so wrong!'

'What else can she do?'

'Not Phyllis! The reasons why. It's not fair.' Even as she uttered those last three words Tyke was aware of the utter futility of even thinking them. Maudie's voice echoed in her head.

'The world's not meant to be fair, Tyke.'

Moss began to walk down the alleyway. He beckoned Tyke to follow him. After a moment or two she did, tucking her hand under his arm before leaning her weight against his comforting bulk. They walked in silence.

'I think you should go see her,' Moss said.

'Why?'

'Because she's your friend, Tyke and she's obviously not happy.'

'What on earth would I say to her?'

Moss thought for a few moments. 'Maybe, 'We're still friends.'?'

Tyke mulled over the wealth of the unsaid in Moss's simple words. After considerable thought and long after she was back in her warm bed again she decided she agreed with him.

The bare rooms in Phyllis's house.

The empty shelves in the kitchen.

Two boys scrabbling through bags of rubbish for something to eat.

Tyke's family didn't have much but in a blinding flash of understanding she realised a profound truth - they were richer than she had ever believed.

The next day Tyke asked if she could take the Driver's provisions to them by herself. Busy as usual and pleased to share the load, Alex consented. Together they packed the box carefully, Maudie adding a bottle of milk from their own store cupboard. Hefting it under one arm, Tyke set off. She felt a little sick as she tried to plan what she wanted to say. Two years ago Tyke and Alex had visited the family with a care parcel. The help continued as had the girls' friendship. Only now was Tyke able to really see the changes two years increasing hardships had made to this one family. Phyllis's despairing action opened Tyke's eyes with a crash and all the little signs of her family's decline were revealed in a sudden spotlight. The older boys' increasing aggressiveness towards Tyke, their sneers at the generosity they hated having to receive. Phyllis's father, Saul, home more and more often every time Tyke visited. He couldn't find work. The little the family owned had been whittled away even to the pillows on the two beds they all shared.

Why hadn't she noticed? Really noticed.

Because the family's seeping decline was their normal state. Confronted with Phyllis's despairing action Tyke understood how their decline had become a full collapse into total want and desolation.

She had long since used the back door when she came, claiming the right as an old friend. Now though Tyke faced the rotting front door, her mouth dry as she didn't want to assume a friendship Phyllis might no longer want. Lifting her hand, Tyke knocked loudly and waited. A tumble of bodies and noise thumped down the hallway as someone flung the front door open.

'Oh. It's you,' Bert said dismissively, shoving his three younger brothers aside as they snuffled like puppies at the newcomer. 'Phyl! It's Tyke.'

Bert and twelve year old Graham glared at her, elbowing past to get outside. It was left to six year old Arlo to grab the box from under Tyke's arm. Crowing, he held it like a grail as he made his cautious way down the hall to the kitchen. As the noise faded away Tyke stood in the hallway waiting for Phyllis. When she didn't come, Tyke poked her nose into the room the girl shared with her siblings. The double bed held the three eldest while a little box bed lined with old clothes against the far wall showed where Arlo slept. There, curled up on the big bed lay Phyllis, her back to the room.

Tyke hovered in the doorway. 'D'you want me to go?'

Phyllis kept her face to the wall. 'Up to you.'

'Righteo, then.'

Silence.

Unable to resist a peek, Phyllis rolled over expecting to see Tyke gone. Instead she was leaning in the door frame. 'I knew you'd have to check.' If Tyke expected her friend to melt into friendly welcome she was sorely mistaken.

Phyllis's face darkened. 'Why are you here? To laugh at me? Preach at me?'

Tyke inched into the room. 'Well, I did want to see you and say something,' she began.

Phyllis sat up on the bed, her face screwed up in shame and anger. 'Of course you did! You wanted to tell me how ashamed you are. How you hate me now. How you never want to be seen with... with a whore.' On the final word the distraught girl burst into a storm of tears. Whirling away from Tyke's pity, Phyllis threw herself face down onto the bed and sobbed.

It seemed best to let her cry. Eventually the worst of the outburst passed and Phyllis became aware she still wasn't alone. 'Why don't you piss off?'

Pause.

'Don't you want to hear what I came to say?'

'Oh, go on then. Get it over with.' And Phyllis waited, her heart sick with unhappy expectation.

'We're friends.'

Phyllis slowly sat up, her eyes sore with crying fastened on Tyke's face. 'What?'

Tyke reached out and hugged the girl's hand to her chest. 'We're still friends. If you want to be.'

Silence.

'Why?' A world of confusion in a single syllable.

'Because you're the sister I never had. Because I love you, Phyl.' The wonder on Phyllis's face melted Tyke's heart. 'Friends?'

Warm tears spilled down the unhappy girl's face as she nodded. 'Yes please,' she said.

They hugged, warm and close neither saying anything for what was left to say?

Hours later, Tyke relayed everything about Phyllis to the ever dependable Maudie only editing how she discovered her friend's work.

'Phyllis had no choice. Mr Driver got too sick to work and you know how hard it is for even a healthy man like Father to keep a job. He was arrested for stealing food.' Tyke twisted the table cloth unheedingly in her fingers. 'I didn't know! Phyllis never said anything because they were so ashamed. The magistrate gave him three months in jail, Maudie!' All the unfairness of it stung Tyke's voice. 'He had only taken enough for the family to have one good meal. With Mr Driver locked up they ended up so far behind in the rent the landlord threatened to evict them.' Her troubled eyes met Maudie's. 'So Phyllis did what she had to. She expected me to never see her again but she's my friend, Maudie. I can't turn my back on her now, can I?'

'Would yer do it if I told yer to?'

'No.'

'Then there's no help for it, is there?'

With a thankful sigh, Tyke sat back in the chair, the weight of all her worries falling away a little now she had poured them out. 'You won't tell Alex about Phyllis, will you, Maudie?'

'D'yer need to ask me?' Slightly bloodshot but very direct blue eyes met concerned hazel ones as Tyke shook her head. 'Well, then. Yer've got yer answer haven't yer?' Maudie heaved her bulk out of the chair as the soup began to boil over on the stove.

The Driver's lives took a more tragic turn. Saul Driver was released after three months. Sick and dragging his conviction behind him he couldn't find work. One early dawn, unable to cope anymore he hanged himself from a beam in the kitchen. Where Phyllis discovered him.

***

Smoko break or lunch in the workshop meant a snatched five minutes if the foreman wasn't looking so a bloke could have a ciggie and a breather. Ian was a union man who kept trying to force them to fight. Even now he ranted at them.

'Every working man's entitled to a regular lunch break. It's what the Blackball miners fought for back in oh-eight, for God's sake!'

One or two listened, maybe even agreed but Samuel could have told Ian to save his breath; there were fewer and fewer jobs which meant if you wanted to work you did what the boss wanted, you worked like a slave and shut the fuck up. Listening now as Ian raved, Samuel smoked his cigarette and watched him skeptically with narrowed eyes. *What would Cass have made of the man?*

The answer as clear as if his old friend was here beside him. *He would have agreed with everything the bastard said and joined him in fighting for their rights.*

'You always were the better man, brother.' Samuel whispered.

Ian gave up on his listless audience, turning his back on them all with a gesture of bitter hopelessness just as the outer door crashed open. Every man hurriedly picked up his tools again as their foreman marched in, his normally placid face tense.

'Mister Grieve wants a word before you lot knock off so send one of the apprentices to spread the word to those out on jobs to get themselves back to the workshop at seven thirty.'

'What's it about?' Ian demanded only to get a glare in return for his bolshie attitude.

'You'll find out seven thirty, won't you? Back to it.'

He left them muttering but resigned as Ian joined Samuel at the workbench. 'So who's for the chop tonight, then?' Ian meant it as a dark joke, his grin fading at the look on Samuel's face.

Eight pm saw them all dismayed, staring in disbelief at Amon Grieve's retreating back. He'd sacked them all. Each and every one. Those who'd been with his company for over twenty years down to the new apprentices.

'I will re-hire anyone willing to bargain new wages.'

Bargain. He'd made it clear what the bargain entailed. Re-employed at two thirds their original wages, no overtime. Or they could walk.

'Walk? Bloody where to?' An anonymous voice called from the back of the workshop. 'Who's hiring?'

'Guess it's up to you to find out.' Grieve replied. 'Whoever shows up tomorrow has a job under the new terms.' He turned to his foreman of ten years standing. 'This applies to you, too Nathaniel so if you're here in the morning, hire to fill any gaps.' Without another word Grieve left them muttering blue murder, for the first time giving some credence to Ian and threatening strikes.

To what bloody end? Samuel thought. *Plenty of blokes out there only too willing to take their places.*

'It's just like the Great Strike.' Ian sought out each pair of eyes, commanding their attention now. 'The bosses are in control of a subjugated workforce. Nothing has changed! Nothing. We have to fight!'

'If nothing changed with the Great Strike then nothing'll change now. Let it rest, Ian for fuck's sake.'

There'd be no strikes. No one would leave for where could they go? End of story.

Samuel joined a group who went to a den hidden in the maze of streets around Tinakori Road. Each and every one of them had to face their family and tell them there would be less money coming in each week. *Jesus, things were already tough!*

The defeated Ian got the next round in and they sat staring into their drinks.

***

Murchison
June

Everyone was talking about those strange booming sounds echoing round the hills of Murchison. No one knew what they were, though one or two ventured there was blasting going on, maybe for roads or quarries. After the first couple of days they stopped talking about them. *Someone's working somewhere. None of our business.*

Matthew was off to his uncles' workshop in town. He hadn't told them at home, of course. With Fee walking beside him they had left for school, forced to walk this morning as Janet was helping Emily smoke and brine a pig John and Matthew had killed the evening before.

'Did you finish your homework?' Fee asked, confident she knew the answer.

'Nah. Well, I did the arithmetic and geography stuff. Couldn't be bothered with the essay.'

'You'll get detention again.' Matthew gave Fee his I-don't-bloody-care look. 'Why do you always get yourself into trouble? You could just do the work. It's not like you're stupid.' Fee flicked him a sidelong grin. 'Not all the time anyway.'

Her brother snorted. 'Essays aren't going to help me get a job, are they? Arithmetic is different. I can see a point to that. What about you, though? Don't you want to leave school?'

'I don't know.'

'Well, what do you want to do?'

Fee rubbed her nose as she lifted her shoulders. 'Someone has to look after Da. Especially as Grandma's not getting any younger.'

Matthew shot her an incredulous look. 'That's it? That's all you want?'

'What else is there, Matt? I suppose I'll get married at some point but someone has to take care of things at home.'

'Why you?'

He'd made her angry now. 'Who else is there? Are you volunteering? Mother, perhaps?'

'There's always Aunt Janet.'

'He's my Da! Yours, too if you'd ever remember.' Fee picked up her pace as she stalked off, compelling her twin to jog to catch her up. To Fee's surprise Matthew was conciliatory.

'Look, I'm sorry. I didn't mean to upset you.'

This was so unlike her brother Fee studied him curiously for a few seconds. 'It's all right, I suppose. You just don't think sometimes.'

The schoolhouse came into sight.

'And here we part,' Matthew said.

'Oh, Matt! Not again. I'm running out of believable excuses.'

He tugged on one of her long braids. 'You're the one who's good at composition. You'll think of something.'

Fee watched him dart through the nearest paddock, the one which took him past the schoolhouse unseen. With a sigh she slowed her steps to give herself time to come up with yet another credible lie on her twin's behalf.

Matthew shot a look back over his shoulder, happy to see the roof of the schoolhouse disappear behind the hill. At fourteen he'd had more than enough of lessons. He ached to be earning a wage, heading towards the longed for goal of independence. Wally had offered him a room at the workshop. *'You can pay a bit of rent and we'll take you on full time.'*

How Matthew wanted to accept. More than once he had been on the verge of doing so only to remember how much John relied on him. Matthew loved farming. He did. He wavered equally between mechanical work and home farm, just not farming the way they were forced to because of Jimmy.

Grandfather and he shouldn't have to slave themselves to a standstill when a tractor and a truck would easily halve their slog.

New methods of farming were passing them by. *And it wasn't even as if Da was aware of what went on a lot of the time.* John remained adamant. There would be no noisy engines to trigger Jimmy's attacks. *'If we have to work a bit harder and stick to the older ways, well, so be it,'* he said and they continued to work with horses.

Easy for Grandfather to say!

Matthew's sense of fairness nudged his conscience. *Of course it wasn't easy for Grandfather.* He had farmed for his son who was too sick to take over as planned. Matthew knew he was the fount of all John's hopes for the future of home farm. *But how to tell him he didn't want to carry on the way they were?* Home farm lost a little more money every year, unable to compete with increasingly larger holdings able to burn and clear more acres of land using machinery. *It could be them.* Frustration ate at Matthew who could only continue to burn manageable sections of bush and use horses to pull the stumps out of the ground. Sometimes Wally and Ben helped if it was a really big job. Matthew could see how much his grandfather itched to be hauling on ropes or swinging off an axe. He would hover nearby giving instructions, maybe able to drive the horses but he tired so quickly. It upset him so much to have to watch there were times John wouldn't even leave the house. Emily wanted him to retire completely but he adamantly refused.

'I'm doing it for the lad,' he would say.

When he heard this, guilt seared Matthew's heart. So, he swallowed his frustration and unhappiness to rise before dawn and put in a few hours on the farm before heading to school only to head back out onto the paddocks as soon as he was home. Even the time he stole to work with his uncles added to his guilt for as much as he loved it, he knew there were things on the farm which needed attending to. *On top of it all off he had caught Grandfather leaning on a gate the other day, a hand clasped to his chest, his lips turning blue.* Matthew and Fee overheard Emily telling Cally about the heart palpitations, the shortness of breath, all indicators of the ill health John denied. The twins had exchanged fearful looks.

Damn it all to hell!

Matthew reached the road into town, kicking random stones angrily. A surge of unhappiness jolted his body into sudden movement. Picking up his feet, his arms pumping hard Matthew ran and ran until sweat poured down his face and his breath came in loud gasps. He almost ran right into town. Pausing on the roadside, a hand pressed against the stitch in his side, he thought he heard John calling his name.

'Grandfather?' In surprise Matthew spun round. *No one.*

The air boomed and the ground heaved knocking him clean off his feet as the earthquake struck.

Fee and her classmates groaned. Their headmaster had just called an oral arithmetic test.

'Clear your desks and think hard because I will be taking score.'

More mutinous muttering from behind raised desk lids as everyone packed their books and pencils away. Fee's heart sank. She was bad at arithmetic and couldn't understand how her twin found it so easy. It was no consolation for her at this moment how she found English and composition a breeze whereas Matthew struggled with both. She damned him under her breath for he had saved her during other oral arithmetic tests by the simple expedient of signing the answers in a code they had devised. In exchange she would do his English homework.

No bloody help today, are you Matt?

Standing in front of the class, the head rapped his cane on the nearest desktop. A distant rumble caught everyone's attention.

'Thunder.' Fee's friend Mary said.

Every pair of eyes swivelled expectantly to the windows, surprised at the clear skies.

The thundering increased as their desks began shaking. Now panic set in. Before anyone had the chance to cry out, the floor heaved as the roaring of the earthquake hit.

'Everybody outside!'

Screaming and frightened the school obeyed, the head carrying the two youngest pupils who couldn't keep to their feet. Tripping and stumbling, eventually crawling they made it outside where the ground heaved like waves on the ocean. Above them the huge macrocarpa trees swayed and creaked, the schoolhouse rocked off its piles. The sound of splintering wood and groaning trees added to the terror. It was Hamish who noticed the huge slip. His eyes widened in terror at the river of hillside rushing towards them.

'Look out!' he screamed, pointing.

In desperation they fought the motion of the earth to struggle to safety. Wherever they lay they all grabbed on to what they could through the heaving, rolling movement. The slip crashed through the little building leaving only its roof showing as the earthquake subsided to a shuddering halt. The ground still trembling, the head began calling his students together, naming them one by one by memory as per his roll until they were gathered around him, dirty, crying and shocked.

'Who's injured?'

'Me, sir.' Hamish nursed a broken arm, his face white under the dirt.

Others stepped forward, cuts, grazes a few sprained ankles but no one had been killed and the headmaster gave thanks. Fee, Mary and Drover were among the older ones assisting him. Using shirts and petticoats to tear into bandages they did the best they could, soothing the sobbing young ones, cuddling the terrified all the while hiding mounting fear about their families.

Matthew lay curled up in a ball, unable to do anything else

as the earthquake tore through Murchison. All around him echoed the sounds of destruction. Trees fell ahead of him, one crashed behind him as the houses nearest to him swayed. When the world stopped spinning, he gingerly uncurled. Spitting dirt from his mouth, shaking it from his hair and clothes, he cautiously rose to his feet. The edge of the road had crumbled and his gaze wandered further along seeing the huge cracks and collapses on the once even surface. *What to do?* Dread hit him. *Fee at school, his grandparents and mother at home, his uncles at their workshop. Where should he go first?*

Panic subsided as his brain kicked in. *He was closest to his uncles.* Matthew ran the last distance into town. Turning onto the main street. The broken buildings. The verandas leaning drunkenly to one side. It was incredible to find anything left standing. Matthew raced off the street, down the road to his uncles' workshop and came to a skidding halt at the pile of rubble where the building once stood.

Oh no!

Beside it stood Wally, his face expressionless. He didn't know Matthew had arrived until his nephew tugged at his arm. 'Thank God you're safe!' Wally didn't move. 'Where's Uncle Ben? Uncle? Where's Ben?'

With a roar, Wally threw himself at the rubble, heaving away roofing iron, yanking at spars of wood. Matthew joined him and they worked frantically.

After twenty minutes or so Matthew froze. 'What was that?' Wally didn't hear him, sweat pouring down his face as he fought a way into the wreckage. Matthew grabbed him as the sound came again. 'Uncle! Listen.'

Nothing.

With an impatient growl, Wally pushed his nephew to one side. He reached for the remains of the front door and suddenly heard it. Metal banging on metal.

'He's alive.' Wally whispered the words. Without another word they toiled with purpose.

People appeared from their houses or shops, surveying the damage. When they knew there was a manhunt on at the workshop, they joined in, someone calling out a warning to the rescuers about the instability of the ruins.

With the clanging to guide them they finally found Ben, huddled beneath the solid frame of the tractor they were working on. Glad hands reached under and pulled him free.

'Bout time you buggers showed up,' he coughed, choking on the dust from the workshop floor but his laconic tone couldn't hide the tremble of his hands.

Wally took a flask from his jacket pocket, passed it to Ben, who just lifted his shaking arms. For once in his life Wally refrained from teasing. He held the flask to his brother's lips and helped him drink.

Matthew's worries flew to the rest of the family. 'I've gotta get back up the valley,' he told his uncles. 'Fee went to school and,' he swallowed hard, 'the family's at home.'

'You'll not go alone.' This from a determined Wally, one eye on his brother who was thanking the neighbours for all their help. 'What's the road like?'

'I only know the bit I ran after the earthquake but it's a mess.'

'Can we get a car along?'

Matthew was doubtful. 'Maybe,' he temporised, 'maybe some of the way at least.'

'We'll check next door – at least the bloody house is still standing! We'll grab some rope and whatever tools we can find.'

'What if...' The words stuck in Matthew's mouth.

Wally patted his shoulder. 'Let's get on our way, eh? We will deal with whatever we find.'

The three of them ended up walking most of the way, leaving the car in a paddock. They met no one on the road, awestruck by the amount of damage all around them. By the look of the Matakitaki River, she must have been dammed somewhere deeper up the valley and just the thought of a slip so big reduced the men to silence. Matthew pushed the pace, desperate to get to his twin. They came near what was left of the schoolhouse, the mass of debris.

Matthew gasped. He stumbled into Ben, eyes staring in horror. 'Fee.' The single syllable weighted in despair fell from his lips.

A flurry of movement caught their eyes.

'Under the macrocarpas, Matthew. Look.'

Matthew followed Wally's pointing finger to where the school pupils huddled. He didn't hesitate, running over the uneven ground towards them, calling for his sister. Hearing Matthew's voice, Fee leapt to her feet and ran to meet him. They hugged, unwilling to end the embrace.

The headmaster joined Wally and Ben.

'Everyone all right?' Ben asked.

'As much as we can be.'

'What'll you do here?' Wally asked, his eyes on the children under the trees.

'Wait. I thought it would be the best thing at the moment. One or two of the older children have left. They wouldn't stay. I sent Drover into town to notify whoever he can find that we are all well. Hamish broke an arm.' He cast a quick glance back towards the children. 'I set it as best I could. Drover will try to find a dray or vehicle of some kind.' He gave the men a questioning look.

'Won't get a cart or vehicle up here.'

The head grimaced, resigned. 'Then we'll wait. There may be aftershocks and I don't think the littlest ones would cope.' He met Ben's eyes. 'Is it bad?'

'Yep. Not heard of any deaths so far.' Ben's tone made it clear he expected some.

'Right. Well. I'll get the children sorted so we can at least be warm tonight.'

Ben exchanged a quick glance with Wally who read his twin accurately.

'Might as well.' Wally replied answering the unspoken question. 'Me and Matt'll take Fee and do what we can till you return.'

Ben nodded. 'I'll help here and see you at home farm sometime, then.'

Leaving Ben, they continued the difficult journey towards home, dreading what they would find.

It could not have been worse. They could see from the road the size of the slip behind the old farmhouse. They ran, clambering over muddy rocks, a fallen tree and reached the brow of the rise. The slip had shunted the farm house a good fifteen metres off its piles. Earth flooded around it on three sides, stacked up to the windows on the bottom storey. They were frozen, gaping at the awful destruction until coming to their senses.

'Grandma?' Fee headed towards the barn, shouting as loudly as she could. 'Grandfather?'

She came to a shocked halt as Matthew staggered into her. All that remained of the barn was a pile of shattered timber.

'Oh, God...' The words slid out of Matthew's mouth on a shaky breath.

Wally steadied him. 'The cottage,' he said.

There was no road to it now, just huge fractures and holes where it used to be. Fee leaped one crack and landed awkwardly, twisting her ankle. She cried out at the sudden pain, brother and uncle immediately at her side. Fee gently pushed them away as she sat on a rock, massaging her foot. 'I'm fine, truly. Go.'

Matthew cast one glance back to her as they shot off.

The cottage appeared to be undamaged. Two trees behind it had fallen and lay sprawled across the garden, the end of which had given way where the ground had collapsed under it. The white picket fence stuck out here and there among the broken branches and piles of earth. Matthew reached the back door first, falling through it as he shouted. Cally appeared from the hallway with a cry. In three strides Matthew held her, his mother trembling violently.

'Darling, you're safe! Have you heard if Fee.....?' Cally couldn't finish the sentence.

'Fee's fine, Mother. She's here. She's coming.' Matthew searched her face. 'Grandma and Grandfather?'

Cally raised a hand to his face. 'Grandma is injured but she will survive.'

'And Grandfather?'

Pause.

'I'm so sorry, Matthew. It was too much of a shock.'

The tone of her words alerted him. 'He's dead?'

Cally nodded. 'Heart attack.'

Matthew bit back the rush of pain. 'Is he... is he at the farmhouse?'

'No. He's here.'

Wally spoke for the first time. 'I'll go to Fee. Let her know.'

Cally led Matthew through to the sunroom where John lay on the daybed, his face battered, a leg lying crookedly. Matthew reached out a tentative hand to lay gentle fingers on the cool skin. With a gasp he sank onto his knees beside the bed, gripping John's wrist, his head pressed into the soft mattress.

Cally left him as soon as she heard footsteps in the kitchen. Her daughter asked the question Matthew hadn't. 'Where's Da?'

Cally cleared her throat. 'In our bedroom.'

Leaving Wally to comfort his sister, Fee went straight to her parents' room. She hesitated in the doorway at the sight of Janet, sitting on the end of the bed staring at the wardrobe.

'Mother said Da was in here.'

Janet nodded her head towards the wardrobe. Confused, Fee shifted to see. Jimmy was huddled into the gap between the wardrobe and the wall. He had his back to the room as he crouched and muttered incoherently.

'I can't get him out.' Janet said brokenly. 'I've tried but he refuses. He doesn't know it's me. He's somewhere, Fee, somewhere not here.'

The girl knelt down and laid a hand on her father's shoulder. 'Da?' she said softly. 'Da, it's Fee.' Nothing. 'Da, please?' Nothing. This time when Fee increased the pressure on her hold, Jimmy's muttering became agitated and he tried to cram his body further into the recess.

'Best leave him, I think,' Janet whispered. 'He'll come round when he's ready.'

Fee's legs felt wooden when she tried to stand. She faltered and Janet helped placed a firm hand under Fee's shoulder, assisting her upright. 'Uncle Wally said Grandma's been injured but she'll be all right.'

'Yes. We put her in your bed.'

Fee nodded. 'Can I see her?'

'Hopefully she'll be asleep but of course you can.'

Someone had drawn the curtains in her room, though the brightening day outside pushed fingers of light through the gaps. Fee sat carefully on the bed. Emily lay on her side facing her, white hair in disarray, smudges of mud on cheeks and hands.

You look so old, Grandma. So fragile.

Emily's right arm had been bandaged, her hand, too. As Fee gently pushed the fall of hair from Emily's face, her eyes fluttered open. At the sight of her granddaughter, Emily smiled, so much hurt in the smile. 'Darling,' she whispered, her voice little more than a rasp. 'We were so worried. Matthew, Wally and Ben... we were so worried.'

Fee stroked Emily's hand, careful not to touch the bandage. 'We're all safe, Grandma. Uncle Ben's helping the headmaster at school but Uncle Wally and Matthew are here.'

Tears slid down Emily's cheeks. 'Your grandfather, Fee. He didn't survive.'

'I know, Grandma. I'm so sorry.'

The sight of Emily's tears triggered Fee's. Emily drew her granddaughter down onto the bed beside her. Holding each other closely, they let the tears fall.

Twilight had come and gone. The moon rose high. Janet, Cally and the twins sat around the kitchen table, exhausted and picking at bread, cheese and cold meat. Ben had arrived a few hours earlier. Once he had shared in the sadness of John's death and reassured himself they were as well as they could be, he and Wally packed some provisions from the pantry and returned to help out in town. There were homeless people to shelter, tents to erect and shocked, injured people to feed and care for. Fee wondered idly where her uncles found the energy. She could do nothing but sit lethargically at the table.

Jimmy remained cowered in the bedroom.

'I think it's for the best.' Janet said. 'As long as he's lost in his own world, he's spared the pain waiting for him in this one.' She privately dreaded him knowing about John. *Would it tip him into his darkness forever?* She kept these fears to herself though, unsure if Fee was already thinking them and not wishing to put them in her head if not. *Time, as always, would tell.*

Matthew had a slice of bread on his plate, reducing it to crumbs with restless fingers. 'Grandma will be all right, won't she?'

'She's had a terrible shock but we think so.' Irritated by his messy plate, Janet pulled it away from him. 'Either eat or not. Don't bloody play with it.'

'Sorry.'

Cally leapt to her son's defence, shooting Janet a glare. 'You have nothing to be sorry for, darling. Aunt Janet's just on edge.'

Janet threw her napkin down. 'Oh, for God's sake, Cally....'

Fee raised her voice. 'Can we please not do this?'

At her pleading expression Janet and Cally relaxed back in their chairs, suitably chastened.

Silence.

'I can't believe anyone managed to survive the slip.' Fee couldn't suppress a shudder. 'When we first saw the farm house....'

'It was John who saved us.' Janet said. 'Emily and I were in the smokehouse cutting up the pig when we heard a rumble. We thought it was thunder until John ran in. He shoved us out and told us to head to the cottage. We dropped everything and obeyed.'

Matthew frowned. 'And Grandfather?'

Janet made a strangled sound. 'His bloody dogs! I thought he was right behind us but when I looked back he was disappearing round to the kennels. I sent Emily on, dashed back and dragged John with me. Then the landslide crashed down the hill. We were running ahead of the bloody thing until it ploughed through the barn and the farmhouse. John couldn't help looking. He called out for his dogs and collapsed, the road giving way under him.' Janet used the napkin to wipe her eyes. 'Emily had been knocked off her feet. She cracked her head on something as she fell. I thought....I thought we'd lost both of them.' Janet met her sister's eyes and gave a watery smile. 'I raced here, found Cally and we went back for them. Cally realised Emily had just been knocked unconscious. So, we brought them here, saw to Emily, tidied John.' She squeezed Fee's fingers. 'Nothing left to do but sit and fret about the rest of you.'

Silence.

'Uncle Wally and Ben's workshop's gone.' Matthew said huskily.

'Our house?' Janet leaned forward anxiously.

'Survived from what I could see. On its piles at any rate.'

The four of them stared at nothing.

They tried to think of nothing and failed.

***

Aftershocks continued throughout the coming days. Those without homes camped in the open or in tents, sometimes sharing sheds or lean-tos. Working together, the community ran communal kitchens, everyone contributing whatever they could. Even so, supplies began to run low. The slips dammed many rivers, the Matakitaki and Buller, the Matiri and Maruia, as well as others and this added to the locals' fears. West Coasters understood just how dangerous floods could be. So, packing whatever they could carry, many Murchison residents loaded vehicles and left. Only able to make it so far along the damaged roads, they had to abandon their cars and carts, turn horses loose in nearby paddocks and walk the remainder of the twenty five miles to Glenhope Station. There, they were able to catch trains to Nelson, grateful for undamaged tracks.

Smaller communities throughout the West Coast were unreachable for months until pick, shovel, dynamite and back-breaking slog re-opened roads. Coasters, resourceful by nature, found their ingenuity tested to the utmost.

Seventeen people died in the earthquake of 1929. Fourteen of them by landslides.

***

The day of John's funeral was bleak. Heavy, unmelted frosts had built up in shadowy places and the southerly picked up their chill, adding an extra icy flurry to the wind. Jimmy stood beside Emily, the cane he now used permanently taking most of his weight. All the family were dressed in black. Cally wore a veil Janet regarded an affectation while Matthew and Fee stood solemn and hand-clasped on the other side of their grandmother. There weren't many people outside the family group. John had been a private man, shunning company in preference for his dogs and paddocks. Several had shown up though, wanting to pay their respects to a gentle, hardworking man.

Janet tried to keep a discreet eye on Jimmy. She found it hard not to smother him in attention. He had returned to them from his darkness, thinner, paler and less able. When Emily broke the news of John's death he hadn't cried. His expression never changed.

How much do you understand? Janet peeped at him from under her hated hat as the minister intoned over the grave.

Finally they were throwing handfuls of dirt down onto the coffin. Matthew placed a collar from one of John's favourite working dogs – Wolf, long dead though John had kept his collar on a nail in the tack room. Once the collar hit the little piles of dirt on the coffin lid, Matthew couldn't take his eyes off it, couldn't move away.

Once he did, the grave would be filled in and Grandfather would truly be gone forever.

Emily gave the signal everyone was waiting respectfully for. Time to head back to the cottage for the small wake she had planned, more for the grandchildren than anyone. Seeing Matthew gazing down at the coffin, Emily withdrew her arm from Jimmy's. She passed the responsibility of him to the ever-obliging Janet to stand beside her grandson. They were silent for long moments, oblivious of the icy wind.

'I never believed in God before,' Matthew's voice was scratchy. 'Or heaven.' He wiped his wet eyes. 'I want to now though. Is that wrong?'

'No, darling. Whenever you need them they're both there.'

Silence.

'Grandma, I'm going to leave school. I want to take over home farm.'

'I'm not sure we can keep it going. The slips, the fences and animals lost. We've no barn even.'

He squeezed her hand gently, taking his eyes from the grave at long last. 'I know. But I want to try.'

Emily didn't want to crush Matthew's dream but the young were so quick to tie themselves to a dream. *Too quick. Dreams had a habit of becoming nightmares if you weren't careful.* 'You're fifteen.'

Again he had a ready answer. *How long had he thought about this without knowing it?*

'Uncle Wally said he'd help. He said Ben will, too. They don't know if they want to rebuild the workshop or not. Until they decide they're both willing to do what they can for the farm.' His eyes were ardent now. 'I'm sick of school, Grandma. It can't teach me what I need. It didn't teach me one half of all Grandfather did.'

Slowly they began to walk to the cart for the trip back home.

'Have you spoken of this with your mother?'

Matthew shook his head. 'It's nothing to do with her.'

'Well….' Emily noted a maturity about Matthew. Since the earthquake the sulky boy had been replaced by something new. She hoped it was better and would last.

'I won't let you down, Grandma.'

'Oh, darling. I never thought you would.' Emily paused to take a final glance back to where John lay. Finally she met Matthew's enquiring gaze and nodded slowly. 'You can try, Matthew. It's all anyone can do. It's all Grandfather would have done or asked.'

For a day all about endings it proved to be one of beginnings, too. Back at the cottage the woodstove warmed the kitchen and the fire in the sitting room gave heat to the rest of the house. Jimmy had been tucked up in bed. Cally was trying to urge Emily to do the same to no avail. Wally and Ben placed themselves either side of the sitting room fire, keeping it stoked and burning brightly. Fee bustled to and fro in the kitchen, laying out the food she and Janet had prepared the day before. Emily stirred a stockpot of soup on the woodstove, the smell pervading every room.

Only Matthew was idle. He sat on the window seat, fiddling with the curtains and looking outside to where they had begun the process of clearing the fence at the bottom of the garden. The garden itself could wait. It was the fence they needed to repair so they could replace stock into that paddock.

Seizing his moment Wally sidled up to him. 'Did you tell Emily?'

'Yes.'

'What'd she say?'

'She's letting us try.'

Wally punched his nephew's shoulder exuberantly. 'We'll make a go of it.'

'You'll miss the workshop both of you.'

'Yeah, probably. But nothing to stop us putting up a shed away from Jimmy's hearing, eh? We can keep our hand in, do some tinkering.'

Matthew's face lit up. 'You know, I never thought of that.'

'Which is why you need your Uncle Wally at your side. He's the ideas man.' Wally could always make Matthew laugh and he did so now, hastily smothering the sound as disrespectful. 'Life goes on, Matt.' Wally said softly. 'Gotta laugh when you can, eh?' He waited for Matthew's nod. 'And what did Emily reckon about you leaving school?'

'She never said anything about it.'

They both jumped when Cally's voice cut through their conversation like a knife. 'Whose leaving school?'

Matthew shot Wally an *O-oh* look, half-amused, half-annoyed when his uncle hastily backed away.

Better tell her now, then. 'I am, Mother.'

'You are not.'

'I'm going to run the farm.'

Cally gave a sharp, scornful laugh. 'Farm? What farm? There's nothing left worth a damn now.' Before her son could marshal his thoughts she changed tack. 'And you're far too young. Just fifteen. You couldn't do it.'

Matthew's mouth drooped mutinously. 'Grandma doesn't doubt me.'

Cally was incredulous. 'You don't mean to tell me you've talked about it with Emily? Without mentioning it to me first?'

Matthew began to pace in the confined space between the window seat and his mother. 'Because I knew what your reaction would be!'

'You will stay at school, do your exams and get a proper job.'

'What's a proper job? What's better than farming?'

'Anything! Anything's better than slaving your guts out for no return.'

'Grandfather built this farm from nothing. It's kept us all. And with Da the way he is….' Here Matthew paused. 'Well, it doesn't matter.' His chin shot up. 'I've made up my mind.'

'You can't do it alone, Matthew. Listen to me, please.' Cally pleaded.

'I won't be alone.'

Near the fire Wally and Ben exchanged panicked looks. Cally in a temper was as fearsome now as it had been when they were growing up.

Matthew continued remorselessly. 'Uncle Wally and Ben are going to help.'

'Oh, are they?' Cally confronted her brothers. 'Why encourage this foolishness?'

'We don't think it is foolish,' Ben mumbled.

'No. It isn't.'

So engrossed were they in their drama, no one noticed Jimmy appear in the doorway. Janet took an automatic step towards him, coming to a stop at the look on his face.

'Jimmy. You should be in bed.' Cally's swallowed emotion could be read in her clenched fists, the tension of her jaw.

'I heard raised voices.' His words were slow, without emphasis. 'If Ma says Matthew can run the farm, then he must.' Jimmy met his son's incredulous face. 'One of us should and it will never be me.' Leaning heavily on his cane he limped further into the room and placed a shaky hand on Matthew's shoulder. 'Grandfather would be proud of you.'

Nothing could be heard in the room except the shifting of a log in the fire, the spatter of sparks shooting up the chimney.

'If Matthew's leaving school then so am I.' Fee wiped her hands on her apron as she joined them. 'No, Mother,' she said anticipating Cally's objections even as her mouth opened. 'If the farm's going to work again we all need to do our bit. I've been doing my own thinking and I won't be talked out of it.'

Matthew felt so adult. His twin, his uncles, to Grandma, tears shining in her eyes as she listened, and Father, never had he felt such unconditional approval. Then he met Cally's eyes and looked away from what he read there.

No one expected to have any appetite yet here they were, sitting around the kitchen table doing justice to the soup and bread. Only Cally picked at her food. She could hardly bear to look at any of them as they shared stories of John. Jimmy's were the most poignant.

'Pa accepted me from the first. Never once did Pa treat me as anything other than a loved son. Ma, too.' Jimmy's voice broke. 'I've been lucky, you know. In spite of everything. So lucky.'

Those were the words they all remembered whenever they looked back on the night.

***

Berlin

'The best propaganda is that which, as it were, works invisibly, penetrates the whole of life without the public having any knowledge of the propagandic initiative.'
Joseph Goebbels.

***

Hindenburg's Great Coalition government was in trouble. It finally collapsed as the Left and the Conservatives argued over the increased costs of the unemployment benefit. In a desperate response, Hindenburg invoked the constitution's emergency presidential powers to restore law and order in a crisis. This new government consisted of a Chancellor and his cabinet who ruled by emergency decrees instead of laws passed in the Reichstag.

So ended the Weimar Republic.

The new Chancellor, Heinrich Bruning remained unable to bring unity. He laboured to keep the appearance of an effectively functioning government as parliamentary chaos reigned.

Germany lurched inevitably towards elections.

***

Kristel's nerves rubbed raw. This lunchtime, pre-wedding introduction to Emil's Austrian parents was gruelling. It wasn't the conversation, though the deliberate banality of it revealed much in itself. It came from the welter of the unsaid. And early on in the meal Kristel knew she wasn't alone in feeling the tension. Sigmund was far removed from his urbane, genial self while her mother's over-bright smile communicated an anxious unease if only to those who knew Freya well. There had been no mention of politics and this was due to Sigmund and Wilhelm veering the conversation into safe harbours if any hints appeared. When this happened, a smirk lifted the corners of Emil's mouth. *I know what you're about.* His eyes, empty, dark tunnels studied each of the Schumann family in turn. Just once Joachim returned Emil's knowing smile with an eloquent one of his own and catching it, Kristel lost her appetite for the company and the food both. She wished herself a hundred miles away. *How close was she to shoving away from the table and escaping!* The only thing preventing her was Wilhelm's solid presence at her side. At the sickening episode between her brother and brother-in-law-to-be, he had gripped her hand under the table and the warm pressure spoke volumes: *I see it, too. He wants to bait us. He's looking for any excuse to damn us. Don't give him the satisfaction.* With massive effort Kristel found a small, oasis of composure. *Tomorrow Emil and Inge and would leave this house and Joachim would return to his apartment near the Reichstag. Hold on to that.*

She was pushing untasted dessert around its bowl when Herr Seidel stood.

He delicately tapped his glass. 'This is an exciting time and not only for our families. A new Germany approaches where men such as my son Emil and Joachim will prosper.' Herr Seidel beamed proudly. 'That is something to look forward to.' He radiated approval on Inge. 'And with such a wife at his side, how can my son fail?' Pause for effect. 'My wife and I would like to bestow upon our children,' he included Sigmund and Freya with a gracious nod, 'a house of their own but during their search for something suitable, I beg our new family to offer them a home here. After all, Emil will be your son from tomorrow. From tomorrow we are one.'

Every nerve in Kristel wanted to scream no! *To have that Nazi living under their roof? Surely Papa would speak out?* She studied every face and realised, hopelessly, *what could Papa say or do?*

Sigmund was caught by every family and social convention. With no real choice he did what was expected. He raised a glass and toasted Herr Seidel. It saved him having to speak.

When the interminable meal came to an end Kristel made her excuses. 'I've a couple of errands to run before tomorrow.'

Wilhelm stood. 'Shall I accompany you, cousin?'

She recognised his question for the support it was but turned him down, her eyes sending him the message, *I just need some time alone.* Grateful for her cousin's understanding, Kristel gathered her hat and coat. She was striding off down the pavement with no real destination in mind when someone called her name.

Inge joined her, shaking out a list. 'I'll come, too. Just a few things to check on.'

Kristel could find no reasonable excuse to deny her sister so without a word she walked on.

The Depression had hit Germany hard. Hungry people were everywhere and their numbers grew daily. Bellies emptied, anger flourished, resentment and bitterness on gaunt faces. *How could Inge not see it?* But her sister chatted on about the success of the luncheon and her excitement for the wedding, oblivious to everything but self-interest.

Not only had the desolate poor increased but Brown-shirts, too. Swaggering, startling Kristel with their youthfulness, school-aged boys wore the brown uniform with an arrogance which gave little reassurance. *Hitler Youth; already brain-washed into believing fascist propaganda.*

A small girl, not much older than eight or nine huddled in a doorway. Beside her sat a wicker basket where a crying baby lay cocooned in a blue shawl. Kristel stopped.

Inge tutted. 'Come away,' and grabbed her sister's hand.

Pulling out of the grip, Kristel knelt and smiled at the girl as she handed over a coin. 'Is this your brother?'

Nod.

'Where's your mama?'

'Gone to find work.'

'Where?'

The girl lifted her shoulders. 'Anywhere.'

'Your papa?' To Kristel's dismay the little girl's eyes filled with tears. They spilled down her thin face and she began to stutter, shooting frightened looks at the haughty Inge. Kristel shifted so only she filled the girl's vision, wiping her wet face with a handkerchief as she asked softly, 'Is he dead?'

'No.' A whisper of sound.

'Is he looking for work, too?'

A shake of the head. 'The Nazis took him away.'

'Do you know why?'

'He was at a meeting. Mama said he did nothing but ask questions.'

Inge's sharp voice broke their spell. 'Communist is he? Are your family communists?'

The girl's face fell into fear at the harsh, accusing tone, the bitter judgement in the words. Kristel glared at Inge before facing the girl again. 'You don't have to answer. It doesn't matter if he is or not. Here.' Kristel reached into her handbag. She passed over some more coins and a leaflet, enclosing both small hands between her warm ones. 'This is the address of a soup kitchen. Bring your brother every day and we will feed you both until your mama comes home.'

Too scared to speak again, the girl just nodded, reaching for the screaming baby as Kristel turned away.

Inge didn't even try to hide her anger. 'If you want to give money away, why not find good, German families?'

'What?'

'Rather than support the children of agitators. Emil says….'

Kristel held up a hand. 'I don't want to hear.'

Disregarding the request Inge continued. 'He says communists are working against Germany by disrupting industry and creating the conditions necessary for their own persecution.' The words came out by rote.

Kristel laughed out loud, her rage giving it a raw edge. 'Do you even listen to yourself, Inge? Do you?' She didn't know what made her more despairing, Inge's total acceptance of the Nazi creed as spoken by Emil or her complete lack of empathy and understanding. *But then, they were the same thing.* A lump formed in Kristel's throat, a mixture of anger and despair.

'You won't be able to speak so freely after tomorrow.' Inge was checking the list in her hand so she failed to catch Kristel's expression.

'Why ever not?'

'Once Emil moves in. He won't allow your sympathising.' Inge realised her sister had come to a standstill. Pause. 'What?'

'I thought you both wanted your independence?'

'We do. But there are other matters at play.'

'What matters? Herr Seidel said it was just about you both looking for somewhere more suitable.'

Complacency exuded from Inge. 'He had to say something. Come on. We just have to check on the flowers and then we're done.'

'Tell me what matters you mean.'

'Well, Emil has grave concerns over the way Papa is running his factories. He wants Joachim to take on a more active role. Emil says it would be better if he was on hand, maybe even take full control.'

Kristel was horrified. 'That can't happen. Not to Papa.'

'It's time you grew up, sister. Papa is not the Almighty being you suppose him to be. He's employing the wrong people in his factories and his willingness to negotiate with union organisers, well. Such ideas have brought about the end of his precious Republic.' Inge gave Kristel a hard look. 'Papa's continuing friendship with Calev Altmeyer does him no good either and Emil says you need to distance yourself from Jost Vogt. The times are fast approaching when we all have to be on the right side.'

Sick apprehension swept through Kristel. *The right side. Joachim, Inge. How had she moved so far apart from her siblings? She couldn't recognise who they were anymore. She couldn't separate them from their politics and every year those politics became more hate-filled, more divisive. They were family. You were expected to feel love; you loved your family, right? Through thick and thin. In spite of the world. And yet.....*

And yet. Kristel studied Inge's bright face. She felt closer to her cousin than she did her brother and sister and if she was honest, she felt no lack. What she had been pining for was their life before politics changed them all. Today proved something Kristel had been denying - those changes were overwhelming and complete. The life they had lived and the people they had been were gone forever.

'No more.' The two words fell softly, decisively from Kristel's lips.

Inge gave her a questioning look but Kristel just shook her head and walked on, her mind in a whirl.

'Kristel?'

Ignoring her sister, she picked up her pace. *Emil in her home, of not being able to escape him.*

'Kristel!'

Papa, the life being squeezed out of him. His fear.

Kristel ran. Without conscious thought her decision had been made.

Life had changed them all. It was time she acted on those changes.

***

Jost and Wilhelm dived through the dank alleyways, their boots skidding on the filth underfoot but they didn't dare risk a glance over their shoulders for their pursuers were hard behind and gaining.

'This way!' Jost ducked into an old warehouse, slamming the metal door shut as soon as Wilhelm made it through. 'Help me,' he gasped.

They thrust their weight against the door just as it was driven inwards.

'Come out you fucking red bastards!' Outside, something smashed against the metal. The door shuddered but held.

Above Wilhelm's head was the bolt, rusted with disuse. He struggled desperately to loosen it, all the while adding his weight to Jost's. Boots thudded down the alley.

'More of them,' Jost hissed. 'Hurry up with the fucking bolt!'

With massive effort, Wilhelm loosened it. With a groan it shot home. The S.S on the other side threw themselves uselessly at the locked door, hurling insults and bricks as Jost and Wilhelm raced through the empty warehouse, clambering out a broken window to safety.

'That was too close,' Wilhelm gasped. 'Did they get a look at us?'

'Not good enough.' Jost coughed and spat onto the ground. 'Don't worry. They have no idea one of Herr Schumann's managers is an agitator.' He grinned but Wilhelm saw no reason for amusement.

'We're taking too many risks.'

'Someone has to.'

Wilhelm swung round, his face thunderous. 'A glib and ridiculous answer Jost! What use can we be to any cause or anyone, locked away by Goebbels' S.S?'

Jost opened his mouth to argue only to clamp his lips shut and give a curt nod.

They had been part of a crowd which deliberately disrupted a Nazi political rally, bang in the centre of Wedding's working class district for Goebbel's propaganda war focussed on the dispossessed, the unemployed, the lost, the angry and the resentful.

Goebbels had faced the throng, his Brown-shirts around him as he ranted. 'Who is to blame for your present unhappiness? Who? The bosses who have collaborated with the unions and the failing Republic! You have no jobs. You have no homes while foreigners live in German houses and Jewish landlords rake in the profits. Money is stolen from you, the worker, the poor, to the pockets of the entrenched wealthy, dissipated rich. And no one is listening to you. No one but the N.S.D.A.P. We are listening!'

He was cheered and howled at in equal measures. Happy with the outcome, Goebbels allowed his Brown-shirts to hustle him away. The scene became ugly as the crowd turned on itself. Jost and Wilhelm had torn down swastika flags as they ran, seen and chased by screaming S.S. They managed to dump the flags into a sewer and evade their pursuers – just.

Now they headed back towards Jost's flat. Wilhelm knew he had reached an impasse tonight, *how to break it to Jost?* He was willing to do what he could to help those who needed a job and a safe place to work but he would no longer attack so visibly. *Let Jost give and take the beatings. He was over it.*

The streets and alleys were quiet. Automatically checking the shadows for movement, they began to climb the concrete steps. In the hallway they saw light moving under the ill-fitting door into Jost's flat.

'Someone's in my room,' Jost hissed. Shoving Wilhelm to one side he reached up into a space in the rafters, pulling down a hefty cudgel. Without a word, he took a few more paces and repeated the action, passing the second club to Wilhelm who realised that for all Jost's dismissive words on the subject, he did expect reprisals.

After a pause Wilhelm followed Jost walking softly towards the door, weighing the cudgel in his hand, readying his grip. On a nodded count of three they rammed their shoulders against the door. It crashed off its hinges as they jumped into the room.

A startled Kristel faced them, a suitcase at her feet, another on the roughly made bed.

Silence.

'Who or what were you expecting?' As upset as she was, Kristel barely stifled the involuntary laugh at the sight of their faces.

'Not you anyway,' Jost said, relief in every tone as he lowered the club and embraced her.

Wilhelm shifted self-consciously, pitching the cudgel from hand to hand. 'Shall I....?' he gestured to the door. He was far from reassured at the serious look his cousin subjected him to.

'Better if you did. And, when the family ask, and they will, better if you deny seeing me here.' Kristel felt their concern like a physical touch. 'I've left home and have no intention of returning.'

'The wedding tomorrow?'

'Will go on without me.'

'What?' Wilhelm gasped. 'Why?'

'Emil and Inge are intending to live with us. They and Joachim are planning to oust Papa from his business. From something Inge almost said, Emil's father seems to at least be aware of their plot.' She moved out from Jost's arms to pace the small room. 'Inge warned me – once Emil's living under the same roof, I will be denied the right to defend or support any person or cause which isn't satisfactory to them. They want me away from you,' Kristel briefly laid her hand on Jost's arm. 'And the K.D.P and S.D.P supporters you are both hiding in the factories aren't as well hidden as you think. Emil knows. He and Joachim want them gone.'

'They can't overrule your father.' Jost's mind was racing.

'Not while he's in charge but how long will that last?' Wilhelm, straight to the heart of things in his dispassionate voice.

Silence.

Each of them remained lost in their own thoughts until Kristel slumped down on the bed. 'What can we do?'

'Whatever the hell we can,' was Jost's grim reply. 'We'll get out those we must, protect those we can. Sigmund is still the owner. He's still in charge.'

'But,' Wilhelm began, only to be cut off by Jost's dramatic gesture, his hand slicing through the air.

'But nothing. We work with what we've got in the time we have. Kristel, they'll know you're here. They will want you home.'

Shoulders back, chin thrust out. 'It's not my home anymore.'

Jost kissed her and whispered, 'And I think I know how we can make the most of it.'

'How?'

Taking in Wilhelm with a glance, Jost knelt at Kristel's feet, deliberately exaggerating the effect in an attempt to lighten the atmosphere, urgency and sincerity plain in his voice. 'Marry me.' Just when he thought she wasn't going to answer, Kristel nodded and Jost leapt to his feet, grabbing Wilhelm's hand. 'You need to return, keep up the pretence you're neutral. We need to know as much as we can to stay ahead of their plans.'

'They know I'm Uncle's right-hand man.'

'And they will need you on side because of your ability and knowledge of the business. I won't go unless they push me out so until then, be cautious. Keep away from here. Don't acknowledge me. Don't mention me and keep away from politics.'

Wilhelm had lost colour from his face as he listened. He ran his tongue over dry lips, biting distractedly on a ragged thumbnail. 'I'll do my best.'

'You'd better.'

Kristel approached them, eyes not leaving their faces as they talked. Now, she hugged Wilhelm, whispering in his ear.

'You're the only family left to me. Don't forget that.'

'I can act as go-between for Aunt and Uncle and you.' Wilhelm gripped Kristel's arms answering urgency with urgency. 'You remember that.'

He left then, stepping over the broken door as Jost called out, 'Oh, and Wilhelm?' When he turned, Jost clicked his heels, throwing out his right arm. 'Heil Hitler.'

Wilhelm exited on the blackest of laughter.

***

'There are known agitators working in your factories, Papa.'

'Not known to me.'

Joachim didn't even try to hide his impatience. 'Jost Vogt for one,' he said, enunciating each syllable.

'A friend of yours.'

'Not these past years.'

'His political stance has never interfered with his ability to work well.'

Father and son faced each other over the desk, Wilhelm a discreet presence in the background.

'There are industrialists without your wealth and influence, Papa who are supporting the Nazi Party and not just with donations but by being faithful to the ideals of our Fuhrer.'

'Adolf Hitler is not my Fuhrer.'

'The Republic is dead!'

'The ideals it always stood for are not.'

'Germany is being torn apart. The growing threat of the K.D.P, the interference by the League of Nations, by foreigners who would decide the future of the Fatherland without reference to its glorious past and potential – these threats are real, Papa. Businessmen are beginning to understand. With less interference and control over their businesses, fewer taxes from government and by destroying the grip of the unions, they are capable of leading a wave of expansionism this country has never seen. The N.S.D.A.P understands that. We want industrialists and leading businessmen to be the controllers of the economy – and it's possible. With support from men like you, we can be a force to be reckoned with outside our own borders.' Joachim was alight with a fire Sigmund had never seen in his son.

The problem with fires is when uncontrolled, they destroy everything in their path.

'Emil made me understand, Papa. How can the Fatherland be great again if Germans do nothing about those who would have it chained by Marxism and a failing economy?'

Sigmund gave an exasperated hiss. 'I do not need a party political broadcast, Joachim. It is admirable you wish to take an interest in our family business but I will make no changes to the way things are run merely on the whim of men like Emil Seidel.'

'Emil has the ear of men gathered around the Fuhrer and the Nazi Party is not a whim. There are elections due this month and we will prove we are not to be underestimated. Those industrialists who stand beside us will have opportunities they have only dreamed of.' Joachim leaned over Sigmund's desk. 'Those who do not prove worthy will find themselves friendless. No one will do business with a man not seen to be aligned to German interests.'

Silence.

From his corner, Wilhelm saw the sudden slump of his uncle's shoulders.

'What would you have me do?'

'Dismiss Jost Vogt.'

Silence.

'And if I refuse?'

Silence.

There wasn't the least hint in Joachim's face that he was talking to his father. The man who raised him. Loved him. Gave him every advantage. With cold eyes and an unforgiving twist to his mouth he replied, 'It would be better if you did not.'

***

1933

Berlin
January

A winter night in Berlin. Black, black sky, the city strangely bright under a full moon. Under flaring torches and huge spotlights, thousands of S.S and S.A troops marched through the Brandenburg Gate to celebrate the success of their Fuhrer. But, however Hitler's propaganda chose to spin it, in the November elections two months ago the K.D.P took 16.9% of the vote, gaining one hundred seats on the Reichstag, their largest representation since 1928. Berlin remained the strongest Communist city in a country with the biggest Communist affiliation outside Russia. Tonight, in defiance of those facts, Hitler intended this procession to be a telling show of strength and challenge. The K.D.P had to be beaten for with the S.D.P alongside them, the Nazis would never get their desired majority.

In immaculate uniforms, marching with slick precision, legion upon legion passed under the imposing eighteenth century edifice on their way to the Presidential Palace where Hitler with his high-ranking Nazi party members waited.

Jost and Kristel watched from the back of the crowds who lined the way, arms thrown out in salute as the thrumming of military drums stirred them to cheers. It was a sombre vision. Kristel slipped her arm through Jost's, drawing her husband closer. In concern, he bent his mouth to her ear. 'What's the matter?'

'How can they be beaten? Look at their power and how people respond to it.' Kristel pitched her voice for his hearing. 'We can't beat them.'

Jost slid his arm round her waist, laying a hand on her face he kissed her. 'We will try,' he told her softly. 'It's all we can do.'

Jost was right. Clashes between fascists and the left increased, as did the levels of violence. It suited Goebbels to give his S.S a free rein in their attacks. A frightened populace is one more easily manipulated by a show of force.

***

After a fortnight of non-stop aggression in the streets, Jost held a meeting in his room. Alwin was young, barely sixteen. While his friends and brothers joined Hitler Youth, he had joined the S.D.P, seeing it as the only sane option. His angry family ostracised him, banishing him from their lives as completely as if he'd never been born into it. Only one aunt had taken pity on him, offering him bed and board right up till her brother, Alwin's father demanded otherwise. Alwin had found more than like minds in the S.D.P, he had found friends, eternally grateful when Kristel and Jost claimed him as family.

The youngster had taken one of the few chairs. He leaned forward on the seat, both legs jiggling. 'We can stop them. Hitler may have the largest single party in the Reichstag but it hasn't given him a majority. Don't forget, the two largest parties after the Nazis are us and the K.D.P. He'll have to work with us.'

'He won't. He's already made it clear he will not work with the Reichstag as elected in November last year.'

'So what are you saying, Jost? Democratically the Nazis have no choice, surely?'

Jost's burst of laughter was cold and humourless. 'The Nazis don't want or need democracy. Why do you think Hitler and Goebbels have given such power and prominence to the S.S and S.A? They deliberately militarised an arm of their political movement to instil fear in his political opponents and spit on any democratic process.'

The atmosphere darkened as those gathered there considered his words.

Alwin blustered.

'I say we keep faith in the Reichstag and Thalmann.'

'Faith won't last long if it's up against the S.S!'

'Then tell us what you would have us do, Jost.' Kristel spoke for them all. 'It's been a month since the procession and how many of our comrades have been wounded or killed? Countless. How many fascists have the police arrested for starting riots? None. How many communists or social democrats have disappeared? Too many. The Brown-shirts swagger around the city and all we do is retaliate. The control is theirs.'

Silence.

Jost lifted a weary hand. 'Maybe Alwin is right. The elections in March. Gaining more seats will be our best hope for keeping the Nazis out of power. Maybe this increasing show of militarism will turn voters away.'

Now Jost had come round to his way of thinking, Alwin perversely changed his perspective, affecting a bitter irony. 'So, comrade. We only need to win more hearts and minds?'

'No,' Jost met each pair of eyes. 'What we need is a miracle.'

***

27th February

Kristel surveyed the cellar room, wiping her hands on the cloth she had used to clean off the trestle tables. Every night this soup kitchen fed more people. It was her dread they would have to start turning people away as had happened elsewhere in the city. *But not yet, thank God.*

A loud bang signalled another dropped pot in the small kitchen. 'Sorry!' A voice called through.

Kristel poked her head round the door as Alwin replaced the pot onto the cold stove top. 'No apologies needed from my best washer-upper. And it's late. You should be heading home or your aunt will give me what for when she sees me next.'

'She doesn't care.'

'What do you mean?'

'She had to throw me out.'

'Why?'

'Father demanded it.'

Kristel gaped. She genuinely liked Hilde. 'But she took you in! We thought she understood.'

Alwin chewed on a ragged nail already bitten to bleeding, his upset all too raw. 'Me, too.' A shrug, aiming for nonchalance and missing bravely. 'Apparently she doesn't.'

'When was this?'

'A while ago.'

Silence.

'And you said nothing.'

'Everyone has enough to deal with without me moaning.'

Poor Alwin. So young. So lost. 'Where have you been staying?'

Alwin couldn't meet her worried eyes. 'Where ever I can. I kip down at Soss's when he's not working.'

Kristel took the towel out of his hands. 'Jost and I can make room for you in the attic. Don't you ever feel there is nowhere for you to go and no one to help. All right?' She waited until he gave a nod.

'Same time tomorrow?'

'And every day you have the energy.'

A tip of his hat brim and Alwin left. Now though, Kristel found herself alone. She had been actively seeking company all day, losing herself in hard work to forget today was February 27th – her father's birthday. This would be the second one in a row she had missed.

The last time she had seen Sigmund he faced her across his office desk for Kristel had flatly refused to set foot in her old home. Unbidden came his last words to her when he had asked her to give up Jost: *There is more at stake than your heart.* He wanted her to return home. To attend Inge and Emil's wedding. To live with them all. To pretend everything was well. To do everything she could not do. And she hadn't seen any of her family since. Once she sent a letter to her parents, telling them of her marriage to Jost. Their complete silence had swamped her. Wilhelm kept in touch whenever he could, and that was rarely. He had kept to the pact they made. Jost had been fired within days of her running away so there was only Wilhelm left to protect those workers under threat by Joachim. How he managed to do so spoke volumes for his diplomacy and intelligence.

Someone thundered down the stairs, calling her name.

Recognising the voice, a delighted Kristel met him in the doorway. 'Wilhelm. I was just thinking about the last time we saw you! I…'

Dishevelled and distracted he ignored her welcoming smile. 'Where's Jost?'

'Out.'

'Out? Out where?'

'I don't know exactly. You know what he's like. What's wrong? Why are you here?'

With a curse, Wilhelm stared wildly round the empty room

before meeting his cousin's worried expression. 'The Reichstag's burning.'

'What?'

'It's bloody burning! There's already talk.' Wilhelm released Kristel's hand. 'We need to find Jost. He has to get off the streets. S.D.P, K.D.P….. the blame's headed their way.'

Kristel was astute enough to not need a fuller explanation. She thought furiously. 'The Nazi's have brought their army to Berlin with one purpose – to frighten the public and terrorize their political opponents. And now this?'

'What are you thinking?'

Kristel met Wilhelm's frown. 'You know what I'm thinking.'

Before he could reply they heard more feet thumping on the stairs and as one they turned. Jost and Alwin threw themselves into the room.

Kristel thrust an accusing finger at Alwin. 'Thought you were headed home?'

'I was but…'

Jost cut him off. 'Wilhelm. You're here?' But he had more important concerns. 'The Reichstag's on fire!'

'We know.'

Jost could barely contain his excitement. 'I was there when Hitler and Goebbels arrived in one of their big black cars.'

'Never mind the damn cars!' Wilhelm was pacing now.

'Sorry. Sorry. Hitler was screaming it was the Left. Goebbels agreeing.' Jost too was on the move. He avoided Kristel's eyes, picturing the reddened, smoke-filled sky. Though he hid it, he felt a savage twist of exultation.

'Who started it?' Wilhelm demanded.

'I don't know.' Jost saw the looks he was getting and said more forcefully, 'I don't! And there's more. Diels arrived. Hard on Hitler's coat tails. Well, as head of the Prussian Political Police I guess he would. Goebbels told him then and there it was a call to arms for a communist revolt.'

'Without a shred of evidence.' Wilhelm ran his hand over his face.

'You mean apart from the burning Reichstag?' Alwin added, shrinking back as Jost rounded on him,

'That's assumption, not fucking evidence!'

Kristel spoke for the first time. 'We have to do something.'

Not one of the three men said a word.

'He's not finished.' Even by the dim light Alwin had lost colour. Shadows threw his cheek bones into sharp relief, his pupils huge. 'Tell them, Jost.'

Jost cleared his throat. 'Hitler lost it. Jesus, I was standing behind a group gathered around their cars and he was literally spitting in rage. He screamed at Diels, told him there must be no mercy shown to those responsible. Not communist or social democrat. He wants every communist official shot where he is found and all deputies hanged.'

Alwin's legs gave way under him. He stumbled blindly onto a trestle, Kristel beside him in concern as he muttered, 'We're dead men walking.'

A prolonged silence pulsed around them.

'They lit it themselves.' Three pairs of eyes swung to Kristel.

An astounded Wilhelm gaped at her. 'What?'

'Think about it,' she urged. 'Someone needs to take the blame. Someone needs to be locked up. Blame a whole movement and you can condemn everyone in it.'

Alwin found his voice, gave a strangled laugh. 'Jesus, Kristel! That's a fucking stretch!'

But she wasn't looking at Alwin. She was staring at Jost knowing without words he agreed.

Silence.

Jost disappeared up the stairs. They heard him slamming the bolts home in the locks. Back down with them he shut the door into the cellar, leaning back on it as he studied their watchful faces. 'Wilhelm, you need to be gone. You know who they will be rounding up from the factories. Get word to them – if they haven't already heard. Tell them to get out of the city.'

Wilhelm nodded. 'And you?'

'I'm not going anywhere.' The words were barely out of his mouth before Kristel and Wilhelm shot him down. He let them rave before holding up a hand. 'We need to save who we can and those we can't? We need to protect any family left behind.'

'Why you?' Kristel's voice shook with anger. 'You're known to them, Jost. A prominent S.D.P supporter. You have to go.'

'I will. As soon as I can.'

'It might not be soon enough.' Alwin's voice was husky with emotion.

Jost grasped the younger man's shoulder and gave him a smile. 'Let's get moving.' Kristel hugged Alwin, leading him out of the cellar.

Seizing the opportunity, Jost spoke quickly to Wilhelm. 'If they do get me, look after her. Promise.' All the fear he hid from the world glittered in Jost's eyes.

'Of course.'

A quick hand-shake and Jost left, Wilhelm staring after him.

The morning papers made the position abundantly clear. Headlines screamed. Communists had burned the seat of government in Germany and the civic-minded S.S were actively seeking the culprits to save the nation from catastrophe. Hitler's dictatorship began with the political enactment the following day, his *'Protection of the People and the State'*. It took away all political, personal and property rights.

Panic ran through Berlin as men went into hiding, some escaping the city altogether.

Four thousand arrests were made with no evidence and no pretence of it.

Goebbels gloated, *'Now the Red pest is being thoroughly rooted out.'*

Only one party benefited from the Reichstag fire. The Nazi Party. Using it as an excuse to arrest the leaders and supporters of the Communist and Social Democrats, Hitler cleared the decks for the March 5th election. Even after the fire, the Nazis only polled two hundred and eighty eight seats. Hitler couldn't guarantee on the other parties not voting en bloc against him. The S.A and S.S increased their presence, the threat they invoked allowed the passing of the Enabling Act on March 23 1933. This finally gave Hitler what he and the Nazis had striven for; the ability to wield supreme power.

March 22 1933 saw the opening of the brand new Dachau prison camp. The first prisoners through the gates were the communists and socialists illegally rounded up after the Reichstag fire.

***

It was late. From the attic window Kristel stared down into the alley as she waited with growing impatience for Jost. She had barely seen him since the fire. While he assisted their friends into hiding, she kept the soup kitchen running, working longer and longer hours until she ached with weariness, unable to find the comfort and healing of sleep for sleep wouldn't come. Leaning her hot head against the cold glass Kristel shivered, too tired to even grab her shawl off the bed. Her fingers slipped into a pocket and held the necklace there. *The one piece of jewellery she'd been wearing when she left home all those years ago.* Kristel pulled it out, caressing the stones in their simple, elegant setting. It would fetch enough to see her husband free of Berlin, even Germany. As she slid the necklace back into her pocket, she noted a familiar figure turn in the alleyway. *Jost.*

By the time he reached their room she had a simple supper of bread and meat ready for him and he sank gratefully onto the stool at the table. Kristel was content to sit opposite and watch him eat hungrily. When his plate was empty, she reached for his hand and kissed his fingers.

'We need to talk.'

His smile tore at her heart. 'No we don't. You're going to beg me to leave.'

Kristel drew her hands from his. She pulled out the necklace and laid it on the table between them. 'Those are diamonds and they will see you free.'

His hands covered hers again, his fingers gently caressing her palm. 'No, my love. I won't run.'

'They've taken thousands of K.D.P and S.D.P, Jost, with no trials.' Kristel's voice broke. 'It's a miracle they haven't arrested you. You must leave.'

He didn't reply. After a time Kristel sat on his lap and there they stayed, holding each other.

Later when Kristel finally slept, Jost got out of bed to sit at the table again. He lit a candle and undid a roughly folded pamphlet a fellow S.D.P had jammed in his hand earlier in the night. It wasn't even typed. A call to arms to resist the Nazis, the writing uneven but firm and strong. *We can keep fighting. We must keep fighting. You are not alone even now.*

A sound in the alley caught his attention. Careful to remain hidden Jost saw dark shapes moving towards the laundry. *So this was it.*

His eyes fell on Kristel, sleeping peacefully. *I will miss you, my love.* Kneeling beside her he kissed her awake. Sleepy arms wrapped around his neck, warm lips seeking his.

'They're here, love,' he whispered.

'No.' But Kristel's denial was an instinctive reaction only. She was out of bed to dress with fumbling fingers as movement sounded in the hallway.

By now Jost had his jacket on, feet stuffed into his boots.

'Don't show them fear.' He reached for her. They were hugging as the door was broken down.

Shouts filled the room. Jost was dragged out of Kristel's arms, showing nothing but scorn as his hands were cuffed behind his back. The officer in charge stood before him and Jost spat in his face. His captors punched the wind out of him. As he slumped forward they dragged him away. The officer met Kristal's horrified stare.

Emil.

'I should take you with him.'

Kristel lifted her chin. 'Then do.'

Emil moved so close she flinched. He ran the back of his hand gently down her face as he whispered, 'But then I wouldn't see you ever again.'

She shoved him away his eyes never leaving her face. An unnerving smile settled on his lips as Emil turned and left.

***

Dachau concentration camp was just outside Munich. Artists, homosexuals, the mentally and physically disabled, political activists, all were taken there in railway carriages shunted straight through the forbidding Jourhaus entrance.

Using Emil's name even as she choked down her hatred of him, Kristel tried to gain entry to the camp. It was refused. She flirted, teased and begged information out of anyone who would talk to her. The S.S proved implacable. Only one man spoke to Kristel, a man already having doubts. He told her the story of Sebastian Nefzger, a Munich schoolteacher beaten to death in the camp for insubordination.

'Or so they said. Munich's public prosecutor put Dachau's commandant on a murder charge. Hitler immediately over-turned it and promptly raised an edict stating, *'Dachau and all other concentration camps were not to be subjected to German laws as it applied to German citizens.'* He gave Kristel a bleak look.

'The S.S administration will run the camps as they see fit. I hope your young man knows how to keep his head down.'

'If he did, he wouldn't be in that place.'

June 1933 Theodore Eicke replaced Hilmer Wackerle as commandant. New regulations were immediately enforced. Prisoners deemed guilty of rule-breaking were to be beaten. Those plotting to escape or advocating political views were to be executed on the spot.

Kristel never saw Jost again.

***

Wellington

They were hungry, starving even and they were marching. Wellington's unemployed were taking their message to the Forbes and Coates government in the grounds at Parliament. Homemade banners flew over their heads, those unbowed heads, as they sang their way down Lambton Quay.

In 1931 the Government initiated its Relief Scheme for the rapidly growing percentage of unemployed. By October 1933 nearly eighty thousand men were unemployed but this figure didn't include men under twenty or women. Throughout New Zealand, men worked with picks and shovels on relief work which was really government sanctioned slavery while their wives and children starved at home wearing insufficient clothes and suffering malnutrition. Businesses quickly took advantage of a hungry workforce. Staff were sacked and re-hired at relief wages. Farmers and large companies who were well able to afford a decent living wage were told by the Unemployment Department to pay only relief rates or chose to do so because they could. People worked for no wages at all, settling in desperation for bed and board. Girls were brow-beaten into accepting jobs where the men of the household could abuse them with impunity, knowing the despairing girl had no choice but to put up with it.

Empty houses filled the streets as people couldn't afford rent and became wandering homeless. Where extended families were forced to share one small home, overcrowding was rife and sickness spread through over-full households.

These were some of the abuses Wellington's unemployed were marching against. And they did get a response from the government. A well fed Gordon Coates said, 'Let them eat grass.'

***

It wasn't only the urban workforce who went hungry and wretched. Farmers with smallholdings suffered, too. In fact, Joe Savage in Parliament said,

'It is as if the farmers were struggling in water and in danger of drowning. Instead of the government throwing him a lifebelt or sending out a boat to rescue him, it had decided to throw in the worker to drown along with him.'

The big farms though, the richest landowners, they were making hay while the sun shone. They expanded their holdings, drained swamps, had hundreds of miles of fencing done, cleared land, built sheds all on relief wages. Some farmers paid no wages at all, providing bed and board as if they were doing their workers a huge favour. Many of the workers remembered the way the farmers had turned on them during the Great Strike, sons and fathers becoming a military arm of Massey's government. On horseback they had ridden down a hungry workforce, attacking with long batons and guns.

Of all they work they hated, working for these sons-of-bitches was among the worst.

***

Moss took a breather, wiping the wet off his face with a filthy hand. His cap was soaked like the rest of him but he was reluctant to shed it though for the slight warmth it offered. *Rain. More bloody rain.* It had been raining for a fortnight, grey, miserable weather and they joked darkly how they had forgotten what sunlight was. Around him the rest of his exhausted team mates shared the misery. They were never dry, even their tents were sodden and for the past four days they had been working knee-deep in water as they dug a drainage system. Sometimes they worked up to their waists for hours at a time. It was vicious, hard slog and it took a grim toll on their health.

The deep channels they dug reminded the older men of the trenches in France.

Occasionally one of them would yell, 'Watch out for the bloody Germans!' and give them a reason to smile briefly.

Thomas likened the bastard farmer they were working for to General Haig. ''Cause when did that fucker ever visit the trenches and see how we were living? Bastard never left headquarters.'

Irish disagreed. 'Haig sacrificed us for the good of the Empire, at least. This bastard sacrifices us only for his bloody pockets.'

Dark, rebellious mutterings which meant nothing except as a way to burn off steam. Nowhere to go. Nowhere else to earn even the pittance they were living off now and if they refused to work in the rural areas, the government paid nothing. No relief. Nothing.

As usual, they worked till it was too dark to see, dragging their weary, aching bodies back to camp, such as it was. The mess-tent was lit and there was soup bubbling away, the scent enticing to empty bellies. Too tired to wash, they slumped together around the trestle tables, hard bread and stew disappearing like manna from heaven.

Thomas dipped his spoon into his bowl and lifted it, letting the contents drop back with thick, unappetising plops. He called back over his shoulder to the cook, slicing another loaf. 'This is cow shit! Put anymore bloody oatmeal in our stew, Heavy, and we'll call it porridge. Thought we were gonna be given some fucking meat?'

Heavy grunted. 'Tell it to the farmer who was supposed to drop a sheep off for me to slaughter. Guess he don't wanna waste his precious mutton on you lot.' Heavy gave a lopsided smirk. 'Can't say I blame the fucker myself.' Jeers greeted this comment.

Irish hiffed a chunk of bread at Heavy who caught it smartly and popped it into the soup, stirring it in well. 'Waste not, want not as my old mum used to say.' Nothing disturbed Heavy's ponderous calm.

Outside the rain fell harder, the canvas above their heads bowing as it pooled with water. Thomas grabbed the purpose-built stick with a T-section nailed to the end of it. He lifted the canvas underneath the worst of the sag and pushed the water out of it, releasing the drenched canvas back to its proper shape.

'Hey, Irish. Thought you said the weather was gunna clear.'

Irish lifted his shoulders, his thin face completely indifferent. 'Had to say something, comrade. I thought you were going to cry.'

Thomas grabbed his coat from his shoulders and biffed Irish about the head with it until Moss yanked it free from his hands. 'Christ's sake. You two are like kids the way you go on.' He threw the coat back at Thomas, pointed a warning finger at him. 'Give it a rest, will you?'

The tent fell silent as they ate. Moss began to wish he'd let Thomas and Irish bitch – *at least their bickering blocked out the sound of the drumming rain.* They lingered over their simple meal, there was nothing else for them to do except play with dice or cards and even those games palled. *Where was the thrill if you had no money to gamble with?* Still, they smoked and chatted, reluctant to leave the relative warmth of the mess for their cold tents out there in the mud and rain.

Irish bitched about how the last camp he was at housed them in bigger tents with simple stoves for warmth. When asked why he left such luxury for this shithole, Irish grinned, relating a story of an overseer with a hatred for anyone from Ireland and his personal short fuse for bastards.

'Stood up to me, the bastard. Tell you, the fucker couldn't talk through his mouthful of broken teeth.'

They were a mixed bunch. The oldest was Tyree in his seventies, down to a handful of teenagers, all cocky, strutting for the first couple of weeks. The agony of blistered hands, the misery of continual rain and flooded tents soon calmed them down. One of the lads, Coll, went out of his head just last week, screaming he'd had enough, throwing his stew across the mess-tent and disappearing into the night. They never saw him again. The older, married men envied the bastard. There wasn't a moment they didn't wish they could run too but they had families needing the forty odd shillings they made a week. *Couldn't run when you had family depending on you.*

Even though Moss wasn't married he still supported his family. Every penny he made was sent home to Maudie. He never smoked, they never saw the inside of a pub so there was nothing for him to spend money on. Moss made twenty-one shillings a week, over half of what the family were living on.

Coll, the poor bugger. They'd watched the lad growing increasingly highly-strung, unable to do anything to help him. Eventually Moss had a quiet word in their overseer's ear. Den wasn't a bad man, just an officious one, who took refuge behind the rule-book and regulations governing their lives. If he wanted to help Coll, Moss had seen no proof of it though in the end the bugger was right – *'If a bloke's gonna do a runner who can stop him?'*

With the wayward Coll a lingering ghost at the trestle table, Moss shifted his gaze to the right, near the back of the tent. There, alone as he always chose to be, sat Gordie, a quiet, hard-working man in his fifties who offered little in the way of conversation. He'd been here from day one yet after all this time, he was the one Moss knew least about. Tall and thin with a perfect monk's tonsure of brown hair, Gordie's office-worker's hands were not toughened to pick and shovel. More than any of them he suffered. After the first day, he could barely stand, hobbling back into camp bent over like an old, old man. Sharing a tent, Moss heard Gordie crying softly through the night. Things didn't improve over the coming weeks. Before the skin on Gordie's palms thickened with blisters, they'd bled, the blood soaking into his sleeves as he pressed on. Eventually the skin hardened but he suffered torments until then. His body ached, the muscles in his arms, shoulders, back and legs all unused to the physical hardship but not once did he voice any complaint. In spite of all Moss's best efforts, Gordie didn't respond to overtures of friendship, keeping himself to himself, unable to find any respite in the black humour of the other men. He was a church-going religious man for whom the rough, irreverent companionship was failing to comfort.

Tonight Gordie hunched over a letter he was struggling to read in the lamplight of the tent. The paper scrunched in his hands and an unnatural inertia overcame him. Concerned, Moss shifted beside him, careful not to raise any curiosity from the others who were gossiping amongst themselves like housewives.

'Everything all right there, Gordie?' No movement beyond a tightening grip of the letter. 'Gordie?' A tear splashed onto hands which began to shake. Worried, Moss laid his hand on the man's thin shoulder. 'Gordie, what's happened?'

'My son has died.' Moss could barely make out the words, lost in thickly slurred emotion. 'He was sick when I left home.' Gordie raised a wretched face. 'My wife last wrote to tell me to come home and see him but I couldn't…. couldn't afford to leave here. And now he's gone and I will never see him again.' It was too much. Gordie thrust the letter into his pocket. Grabbing his hat he left the mess-tent, ignored by everyone except Moss who watched him go with troubled eyes.

Irish piped up. 'What's up with our resident monk?'

'Mind your own business, Irish.'

'Take your confession did he, Moss?' Irish hooted in amusement. 'No wonder he looked green about the gills! You terrified the poor bastard.'

Moss let them mock and laugh. *Anything to take the spotlight off the poor sod.*

Gordie was in bed when Moss turned in. There were six of them in this tent, not much room between them. Privacy was a luxury they forfeited with their poverty. Moss ached for the older man, knowing he was suffering and unwilling to become the subject of all eyes. Moss determined to speak to him in the morning, maybe talk to Den, get something done for Gordie. Turning these things over and over, Moss lay awake until dawn and knew Gordie had, too.

Must be nice to be rich enough to grieve and mourn with your family.

***

Tyke wandered into the kitchen just as one of their boarders was leaving. She gave him a cheery good morning which he completely ignored.

'What's got up Parker's whopping great nose?' she asked Maudie who was up to her arms in flour kneading dough.

'Paid his last week.'

'You kicking him out?'

'No. He's been sacked. Off to stay at the Starlight Hotel, like as not.' Maudie waved a floury hand at a small pile of odds and ends near the kitchen sink. 'Sort through that lot, will yer? He left it as payment. Fat lot of good it'll do us but at least he tried which is more'n some of the other buggers did.'

Tyke lifted a small china vase and a silver photo frame. 'This vase'll fetch a penny or two. The photo frame a couple of shillings maybe.' She ran a judgemental eye over what was left. 'The rest isn't worth anything. Well, not to us. Shall I take it to the Relief Committee? Or the Unemployed Women's Association? They'll know where the greatest need is.'

Maudie divided the dough into four, began shaping it for the tins. 'Either will do. You found work yet?'

Tyke shook her head. 'Someone told me of a kitchen-maid's job in Kelburn. I'll go see about it.' She didn't sound hopeful.

At the last whisper of work she had stood in line with over a hundred others. 'Alex at the soup kitchen?'

'Yep. Thought yer were givin' a hand?'

'Just on my way.'

Tyke hovered until Maudie finally looked up from her work. 'What yer hanging about for then?'

'How many boarders we got left?'

Maudie placed the shaped dough into the tins. 'Four.'

'It's not enough, is it? To make money from them, I mean.'

'Not really but we'll manage.'

'I overheard Father telling you to put their rent up.'

'No use chargin' the poor sods more when they can't afford what they're paying now. Yer father wasn't thinking straight.' Maudie pushed past her to get to the stove where she placed the loaf tins on the drying rack above the hotplate to rise. When she turned back, Tyke was restlessly swirling a finger through the mess of flour on the table. 'Yer still here?'

'Uncle Hugo's hawking vegetables out round Hataitai and out to Lyall Bay, Moss is at the relief camp and I can't find any work. How will we manage, Maudie?' She began to wipe down the table top, beating Maudie to it and receiving an approving pat on the shoulder.

'We're luckier than most, girl. We gotta roof over our heads and food in our bellies. It's not as much as before, but we're not starvin' and plenty are. Two meals a day 'stead of three is luxury and don't forget it.'

'Of course I won't!' Tyke's vigorous scrubbing paused briefly. 'We took food to some old men Alex heard were living in the hills around Tinakori and Mount Vic. They'd laid newspaper and pine needles in hollowed out tree trunks and that's where they were living. No blankets, Maudie. Just a couple of second-hand overcoats for warmth. Alex makes sure they come to the soup kitchen and if they don't, she's chasing up after them.'

'She's a good woman, yer Ma.'

'I know. Wish I was more like her.'

Something echoed in Tyke's wistfulness. Maudie subjected her to a searching look. Tyke was eighteen now with her mother's pale skin and dark lashes. She had freckles she hated, having scrubbed them uselessly with lemon juice until conceding defeat only in the past year. With large hazel eyes and a forthright manner Tyke was very attractive in a distinctive, uncommon way but Maudie understood she wasn't meaning her looks. 'Yer do everything yer can and more, girl. If yer not helping Alex, yer here slavin' for me. The garden yer've kept up for the past few years has been a godsend and no doubt.' Maudie patted her hand. 'Yer'll find yer place in the world, Tyke. If there's not one to be found that fits, make one that does.'

'I'm so sick of everything! I want to have an adventure like Alex did when she went to find Uncle Jimmy during the war.' Tyke sighed. 'I'd love an adventure. I'd love to see London.' She rest on her hands, a wistful face turned to Maudie's. 'Have you ever been to London?'

'Once.'

Tyke perked up. 'Really? When?'

'Years n'years ago.'

'Was it as romantic as Alex says?'

Maudie gave a huff, her disdain of romantic illusions only too obvious. 'It was dirty and foggy, girl.'

Tyke refused to be disenchanted. Her eyes wore a dreamy expression. 'I would love it.'

'How'd yer know? Yer ain't ever left Wellington.'

'That's why I would love it. Anywhere, anywhere is better than this old place! I'm sick to death of having nothing.' Tyke finished cleaning the table and leaned back to critique her work.

'Well, yer old enough t'do what yer want. Why not go overseas?'

In a perverse way, now someone was backing up her

dreams, Tyke drew back from them. Giving a laugh she threw the dishcloth at the sink where it almost made it. 'You're so keen to make a rebel out of me, Maudie. Better not let Father hear you.'

'I speak as I find. Now go or yer Ma'll think yer not gonna make it.'

'I'm going. I'm going.' Tyke reached the door when Maudie stopped her dead in her tracks.

'And by-the-by. Say hullo to that boy of yours.'

With appalling nonchalance, Tyke turned back. 'What boy?'

Maudie read nothing but innocence in the young woman's face. 'Say hullo, anyway.'

No fooling Maudie, Tyke grinned as she left the house.

She'd met Jack a few weeks ago after returning from another useless job interview where two hundred women of all ages had queued up for one vacancy in a clothing factory. Making her disconsolate way back towards Tory Street, Tyke had heard shouts, thumps and smashing glass. Frozen to the spot, trying to work out where the trouble was, two dozen young men raced around a corner and swirled around her. Police whistles shrieked, drawing alarm from the runners who apparently hadn't expected such a quick response.

One of them had grabbed Tyke urgently. 'Hug me,' he demanded. 'Quickly before the coppers come!'

Tyke had only been aware of bright blue eyes and a laughing mouth before she obeyed. He'd hastily drawn her into the nearest shop doorway, hugging his lean body to hers as the policemen dashed passed. All but one ignored what appeared to be a courting couple. An older, heavily built man came to an abrupt stop on the pavement. His uniform buttons strained across his chest trying to contain the flesh within. Breathing heavily he rapped on the doorpost. 'Oi. You two. Keep it seemly.'

Tyke drew away, her embarrassed face the best cover the young man could have had.

'Sorry, officer. Of course we will,' was his contrite reply.

'Mind you do,' the policeman's parting shot as he followed his colleagues, the thump, thump, thump of his heavy boots gradually receding.

Tyke wrenched the stranger's hands off her waist. 'You've got some nerve,' she scolded.

'It's my middle name. Would you rather I'd been arrested?' The solemnity of his expression belied by dancing blue eyes.

'Maybe I would. Better than me being mauled about by some rough boy.' Tyke made a show of tidying her already neat clothes.

'I am sorry. Although,' he adjusted his stance to meet her eyes, 'maybe not too sorry.' Tyke tried not to laugh but he was not to be denied. 'I'm Jack. Jack Tyler.'

'I'm Jeannie Brodie but everyone calls me Tyke.'

Jack bowed over her hand with amusing formality. 'Lovely to meet you, Tyke. Thank you for saving me. I owe you.'

'What did you and your friends do, anyway?'

Jack's smiling face dimmed. 'We were making a point.'

'What point?'

'I'll tell you if you let me buy us both a cup of tea from the pie cart. If you want to hear the story, we may as well be comfortable.'

Fifteen minutes later they were sitting on the top step of an empty shop tucked down off Courtney Place having promised the owner of the pie cart faithfully they would return the mugs.

With both hands wrapped round the mug, Jack blew into the steaming, black liquid. 'Unlike all my mates I've actually got a job. Holding onto it by the skin of my teeth. I'm an apprentice butcher. The only reason my boss keeps me on is I'm cheaper than a fully qualified one. In the meantime I'm good enough at what I do so he doesn't miss out. The old bugger's extended my apprenticeship once already.'

'Why?'

'Because once I've completed it, he'll have to pay me full whack.'

'That's unfair!'

Jack smiled. 'I appreciate the sentiment but I'm letting it ride. At least I've got work.'

Tyke sipped her tea. 'You still haven't explained why you were out breaking the law today.'

'Ah. Our show of solidarity. A friend of mine, Henry, and half a dozen of his workmates were sacked yesterday. The boss decided he could take on some family members from up north and pay them instead – relief wages, mind, the old bastard! Turfed Henry and the others out without a qualm and refused point blank to pay out the money owed to them. Henry's supporting his sick mother and three younger sisters and the old bugger knew it.' Jack frowned. 'We thought we'd show him a lesson by breaking every bloody window we could reach.'

Pause.

Jack sneaked a look at his companion, wondering what she had made of it all. She didn't look happy. *Bugger it.*

'Wish I'd known what you intended.' Tyke said angrily.

'Why? Turn us in, would you?'

'No! I'd've chucked a few stones myself!'

Jack had burst out laughing as they toasted each other.

They had managed to see each other four or five times since, enjoying a similar sense of humour. With no money for anything else, they happily strolled up to the Botanical Gardens or if the weather proved uncooperative, they would share a pot of tea in a café as far from Tory Street as Tyke could arrange. She had grown to like Jack quite a lot, confident Maudie would like him, too. *Alex and Father though? Not too sure about them.*

Thanks to Maudie's insightful tease it was Jack Tyke was thinking of as she sped to the soup kitchen. Moments like this, heading to London didn't seem quite so enticing. *Not compared with dancing blue eyes and a cheeky grin.* Thankfully she was in good time to help set everything out before the queues began to form, which they always did, disappearing around the corner most days. Once or twice they had run out of soup and bread. The look of resigned despair from all those who missed out haunted Tyke. By the look of things, it wouldn't happen today.

Her mother stood beaming behind a trestle table full of produce. 'Hugo dropped off some vegetables he couldn't sell and that lovely Italian family donated seven dozen meat pies!' Alex's unguarded smile was bright. 'Seven dozen! Soup and pie. We can give them a good meal today.'

The meat pies were a wondrous surprise to the hungry. Animation lit expressions of all except the most defeated. Tyke enjoyed each smile, grin and happy exclamation as she dished up. She was about ladle soup into the next bowl held out to her when she recognised the young woman holding it. *Emma McMillain.* The soup fell out of the ladle back into the big pot. *The school yard. Emma taunting Phyllis. Emma with her enviable blonde hair and blue eyes, her lovely clothes and arrogant disdain.* The intervening years since school had not been kind to Emma. All the haughty self-assuredness had gone with her father's wealth. In a well-worn frock covered by a dirty coat this Emma deserved sympathy if not pity yet all Tyke could think about was how she made poor Phyllis's poverty even more miserable. *All those memories.* Any sympathy Tyke may have had died away. She waited, the ladle dripping until Emma looked up and recognised her, too. As horror and shame flooded Emma's face, Tyke dropped some soup into her bowl and passed her some pie. 'I hope you bloody choke on it,' she hissed.

Emma scuttled to the furthest trestle in the room. As busy as she was Tyke never saw her leave. She just hoped she wouldn't return.

Eventually, Alex and Tyke were clearing away and laying

preparations for the next day.

'Shall we walk home together?' Alex asked, wiping the last plate and folding the damp tea-towel. Tyke fumbled the handful of forks she was putting away, spilling them noisily over the trestle. She was so taken aback, Alex hesitated. 'You don't have to,' she said quickly. 'I just thought as we don't see each other very often it would be nice to catch up.'

'No, I'd love to,' Tyke reassured her. *Jack was to meet her down the road from here. Alex mustn't see him!*

Arm-in-arm mother and daughter began the walk to Tory Street. Alex was more careworn these days. It gave Tyke a shock to realise how much her mother had aged. All of a sudden meeting Jack seemed a little less important. *He could wait. Alex deserved some happiness.*

Sure enough, there he sauntered, hands in his pockets, not a care in the world. He saw Tyke and lifted a hand, the greeting dying on his lips when she frowned and waved him away with a furtive gesture from behind her back. Jack wasn't a fool. He'd heard a lot about her family already. *So that's Tyke's mother? Seems nice enough.*

Glad the danger had passed, Tyke relaxed.

'Was he your young man, darling?'

Startled out of her complacency, Tyke stammered. 'Who told you?' Belatedly changing gears. 'What young man?' Catching her mother's eyes she ruefully acknowledged she'd been caught out, admitting as much by explaining, 'Jack's not my young man. We only a met a few weeks ago.'

'It's really not appropriate to see him behind our backs, Tyke.' Young Alex, who she hadn't thought about in years leaned teasingly on her subconscious and waggled an admonishing finger. *'Hypocrite,' she whispered.*

'Hardly behind anyone's back! It seems both you and Maudie know about him. How?'

Alex smiled at her daughter's consternation. 'We didn't know him precisely, more the possibility of something like him.' Alex squeezed Tyke's hand. 'You have been unusually happy, of late, taking a lot of care over your appearance. We women notice these things.'

Tyke didn't know what to say. She'd been congratulating herself no end because she thought Jack had gone quite undetected.

'You don't have to look so worried, darling. You're of an age to be thinking along those lines. Maudie and I were both young once, you know. Neither of us are so senile we can't remember being eighteen.'

'So you've been talking about me?'

'Just a little.' She intended only to be reassuring so Alex recoiled at the look on Tyke's face. 'Tyke?'

'You haven't mentioned anything to Father, have you?'

The fear on her daughter's fear caught Alex's breath.

Tyke misinterpreted her mother's expression and the colour drained from her face. 'Oh, God!' Tyke wrenched her arm from Alex's. 'What will he say? What will he do?'

Such panic paralysed Alex for what seemed like long moments. In reality it was only seconds before she drew Tyke towards her again. 'He doesn't know. It's only been Maudie and I whispering in corners like old gossips.'

Pause. Pulsing and ragged.

Colour slowly returned to Tyke's features. 'Promise?'

'Cross my heart, darling.'

Alex never lied.

Breathing easily again Tyke nodded. 'Thank you, Mama.'

They resumed their walk, arms linked once more. After a few moments Alex leaned towards Tyke. 'So.... Jack? Is he nice?'

Tyke barely drew breath explaining just how nice.

Alex couldn't remember the last time she had enjoyed a walk or her daughter's company so much. *My girl is a woman now. How did that happen so quickly?*

Waiting in Maudie's warm kitchen for their arrival were a dozen children. From some of Wellington's most impoverished families they gathered at the boarding house three times a week to be part of a club. These were just a few of the children whose families had escaped grinding poverty in the countryside to search for work in the city only to be disillusioned once there. Rural and urban children all with destitution and boredom in common. *What could be done with such children? Something worthwhile. Something enjoyable, too.* Kicking the vague idea around with Tyke, Alex had thought of a club, somewhere warm the children could meet. It made sense to hold it at the boarding house, maybe Maudie could stretch things to make a bit of oatmeal or soup. The children could read and write but not like lessons, Tyke insisted, more as if they were playing games; puzzles to be cracked for example. Alex wondered about small competitions, poetry and essays. Maudie's tuppence worth was the idea of working towards a concert to raise a bit of money for the soup kitchen. *'P'raps the little sods could help out there, too.'*

Enthused Alex and Tyke went to work. Separately they spoke to a child here and there, maybe a family. A cut-off point for numbers had to be reached and they expected children would come and go as their families moved on or took them out of the club for various reasons, pride being uppermost. No more than fifteen seemed a manageable number.

What started out as once a week as they tested the water became twice, became three times and settled there. Everyone enjoyed the experience and the children revelled in it.

They arrived wearing ill-fitting clothing and little of that. Some went shoeless, their feet filthy. Maudie sent them all one-by-one into the scullery to wash, passing an old towel around them to dry hands, faces and feet. That done, she herded them into the kitchen for hot soup or sometimes, for a treat, rock cakes, warm from the oven. Today was treat day. The sight of those hungry faces confronted with Maudie's rock cakes was something to be treasured. While Alex and

Tyke removed their outdoor things, Maudie presided over the table, insisting on a show of manners.

'Watch yerselves yer little bleeders or you'll wear the back of my hand off your head.' A sentence always guaranteed to inspire good behaviour.

Because it was winter, the day drew in quickly and by the time the allotted three hours had passed it was dark outside. It was always hard to see the children head back to their bleak lives but as Maudie said, they couldn't do everything and what they did made a difference even for three hours three times a week.

It had been a long day. With the last of the children gone the house was quiet once more. The women settled themselves in the warm kitchen nursing hot cups of tea.

'Another boarder left today. Flitted, the bastard.' Maudie slurped on her cup.

Tyke looked up in surprise. 'Another one? After Mr Pene this morning you mean?'

'Yep.'

'So he left unpaid rent?' Alex couldn't keep the concern from her voice.

'Two months.' Maudie's cup banged down on the saucer. 'I shoulda kicked the bugger out last month. I knew he was a bad 'un.'

Tyke refilled Maudie's cup. 'So what stopped you?'

'It's bloody winter,' Maudie grumbled. 'How could I turf the sod?'

They contemplated the future of their house-keeping with just three boarders left. Alex was wondering whether they could coax another pot of tea out of the tea-leaves in it when someone knocked on the back door.

'I'll go,' Tyke wandered through the scullery and opened the door. The spill of light from the house fell on a white, upturned face, wet with tears. 'Phyllis!'

'Can I come in?'

'Of course.'

They hadn't seen each other for a few months. Tyke working with Alex and the children's club or trying to find paying work hadn't left anytime over for anything else. At the sight of the bedraggled Phyllis she wished she'd made more of an effort to keep in touch. Her friend looked done in, soaked to the skin, shivering with cold, her hair hanging in rat tails around her gaunt face.

'Come through to the kitchen. Maudie and Alex.....'

Phyllis swung off her arm, shaking her head. 'No, please. They won't want me.'

'Don't be silly, Phyl. They like you.'

'They won't anymore.' Phyllis broke down completely, sinking to the floor and crying as if her heart was broken.

A perplexed Tyke reassured her friend who sobbed all the harder. Torn between leaving Phyllis or getting help, she was relieved at the sight of two faces peering inquisitively around the scullery door.

'What's wrong?' Alex took a step towards them, only for Phyllis to howl wildly for them all to keep away.

Alex hesitated.

Maudie didn't. She marched in and knelt beside the distraught young woman. 'What's wrong, girl?'

Phyllis was beyond speech. Her raving hysteria terrified Tyke who watched helplessly. Maudie hoisted Phyllis upright. Her expression changed. Quickly making eye contact with Alex, she supported Phyllis onto her feet and moved slowly through the kitchen. 'My room,' she said emphatically, pointing her head at the kettle. 'Tyke, stay here for a bit.'

'But....'

'I won't tell yer again, girl. Phyllis'll be all right with me.'

No one crossed that tone of Maudie's.

Unable to settle, Tyke paced to and fro as Alex filled a hot water bottle and found a basin.

'Please get me a clean flannel from the airing cupboard.'

Tyke hastened to obey. 'What does Maudie want this all for?'

'Phyllis needs to be warmed up and obviously Maudie wants to check her over.'

'Why can't I help? She's my friend after all.'

'Leave it with Maudie, Tyke. You know she'd have you there if she thought it would help.'

Yes, she would. Tyke shut up.

The clock on the mantelpiece marked time with aching slowness, its regular tick-tock unnaturally loud and pervasive. Having been raised under Maudie's exacting eye, Tyke couldn't just sit and do nothing. She did the dishes and tidied up, automatically checking there was enough bread in the pantry for the next day, finally resorting to wiping down the pantry shelves in an effort to distract from the sound of the clock.

After an interminable time Alex gestured from the doorway. 'Phyllis is asking to see you.'

'Is she all right? What's wrong?'

'Better let her tell you.'

Heart in her mouth, Tyke ran up the stairs to Maudie's room, edging the door ajar and peering round.

Maudie waved her in, bending over her patient to ask, 'Shall I go?'

Phyllis shook her head tiredly and made room on the bed for her friend.

'Phyl?'

Nothing.

'I'll do the talking, eh?' Maudie waited for the nod. 'Tyke, Phyllis is going to have a baby and damn soon if I'm any judge.'

Tyke fought for the maturity she needed as she held Phyllis's hand. 'Mrs Driver....?' she asked huskily.

'Kicked Phyllis out tonight when the pains came and the lass here couldn't hide what was happenin'. She didn't know where else to turn.' Maudie smiled into Phyllis's frightened face. 'But I told her she did the right thing comin' here t'us. She's gonna stay till her baby's born then we'll work things out. Together.'

Tears spilled silently down Phyllis's cheeks. She clung to Tyke who lay down beside her. Taking her cue Maudie left the two alone.

Back in the kitchen she paced as much as Tyke had done, only it was anger driving Maudie, a wide-eyed Alex watching from against the sink bench.

'Her mother knew what her girl was doin' Alex! Knew and took her money. Now when the lass is in dire need, she kicks her out into the world to fend for herself.'

'Maybe she was as frightened as Phyllis.'

Maudie used a word Alex had only heard once or twice before. 'No one is more frightened than the lass up them stairs with Tyke. It's a mother's job not to be frightened!'

In all the years she had known Maudie, Alex had never seen her like this. Maudie's legendary, sometimes exasperating calm was gone, replaced with boiling anger, barely restrained by steely self-control. Alex watched in awe.

'I'm gonna be havin' it out with that bloody woman if it's the last thing I bloody do!'

'Maudie…'

'An' she better not give me no lip 'cause I'll strip the flesh from her bones!'

'Maudie…'

'How could she do this, Alex? How? Fucking hell, I will….'

'Ma!'

The yell brought Maudie up sharp.

Tyke stood in the doorway, eyes like saucers. 'Phyllis is asleep.'

Alex held a chair out. 'That will be for the best. Poor young thing.' She drew another chair up close to her daughter. 'How are you, darling?'

'I don't know. I was shocked at first but now I'm just

worried to death. But what I can do?' The maturity Alex noticed in her daughter earlier in the day had blossomed under this shock.

'It says a lot for your friendship that she knew she could come to you.'

'I'm not so sure,' Tyke said dubiously. 'Before she fell asleep Phyl told me how scared she was that I would turn her away, too.'

'She came, Tyke. Here to you. The only place in the world she felt she had even a chance of acceptance.'

Maudie muttered, 'I'll go up an' sit with her,' and stumped off.

Tyke gazed after her. 'I've never seen Maudie so angry. Never.'

'Me neither.'

'I wish Moss wasn't at the work camp. I wish he was home.'

'Not much he could do tonight.'

'I know. It would just be nice to have him here. I miss him.' Tyke leaned against her mother's shoulder and Alex stroked her soft hair.

'We all do,' she said softly

Silence.

The quiet wasn't companionable, the situation was too fraught, leaving them lost in their own thoughts. Tyke's eyes drooped sleepily when the scream cut through the house. It brought her trembling to her feet only for Alex to push her back down.

'Tyke, please stay here. I'll go.'

'But I have to be there! Phyl will want me!'

'Darling….'

'No. I'm coming, too!' Tyke didn't wait for her mother's approval. She was up the stairs and at the door into Maudie's room before Alex had reached the stairs.

In Maudie's bed, Phyllis was up on her knees, hands clasped to her belly, screaming. Maudie didn't even look round to see who had come in. She pointed to the head of the bed then carefully lay the sobbing Phyllis down on her back.

'Look after her. Hold her hands. I gotta check how things are going.' Maudie lifted Phyllis's skirts and removed her undergarments. Gently she prised her knees apart, then pressed her feet into the mattress to show without words what she wanted. Phyllis's breath came in gasps. Tyke smoothed her friend's hair back from her face, deftly knotting it to keep it tidy. A light touch on her shoulder from Alex who gave her an approving look before turning her attention to Maudie.

'I brought hot water and clean cloths.'

'Good.' Maudie removed Phyllis's skirt completely so she could lay her hands on the baby bulge, cautiously, feeling the shape underneath. 'This baby's breech,' she told them grimly.

'What does that mean?' Tyke demanded, her friend oblivious to everything, lost to the pain of her contractions.

'It means it's comin' out backwards an' that's not good. Sometimes the baby will turn on its own but this one's on its way. Unless I can turn it, it won't go well for the lass.'

Tyke would never forget that night. Never. Phyllis's shrieks, Maudie's calm voice. At times she screwed her eyes tightly shut for Phyllis clenched her hand so tightly, it bruised, her nails scoring Tyke's skin and drawing blood. Working as a team Maudie and Alex did everything they could to ease the girl's suffering and after a terrible night they laid Phyllis's little boy in her arms. Tyke couldn't stop the tears as she watched her friend cradling her son, the love, the utter love on her exhausted features. She offered up silent thanks, grateful the worst was over.

Phyllis wouldn't let the baby out of her arms long enough for Alex to wash him so a bowl was placed on the table beside Tyke and as they waited for the afterbirth, the baby was gently cleaned lying in his mother's arms. All of a sudden Phyllis groaned, her eyes leaving the baby for the first time. Though she couldn't see from where she sat holding Phyllis against her, Tyke knew something had gone wrong. All of a sudden, Phyllis drooped, then collapsed against her. Tyke clutched the baby as her friend slipped into unconsciousness. Cradling the tiny boy, she back away until she pressed against the cold window. When the baby began to cry a mewing, fretful cry Tyke faced the window, concentrating on quieting the hungry boy, trying to block her ears to their muted panic. By degrees the tension eased until Maudie laid a hand on Tyke's shoulder.

'Give us the baby,' she ordered.

As Tyke watched, Maudie replaced the little boy on Phyllis's chest. His screwed up face turned red as his cry became pitchy indignation. Woozily Phyllis ran her hands over him. Acting on instinct she did the one thing that made sense and guided his open mouth to her breast where he latched on hungrily.

'That'll do 'em both the world o'good.' Maudie's satisfaction flickered through her tiredness.

***

'What are you going to name him?' Tyke had claimed the baby from her friend again, mesmerised by his tiny fingers and minute fingernails.

'I don't know.' Phyllis sat propped up in Maudie's bed. She was still too pale though contentment hung about her. 'I did think about Saul.'

'For your dad?'

'Mmmmm. But then I thought about Dad's life, how hard it was and then his suicide and everything.' Phyllis held out her arms and Tyke reluctantly placed the shawl-wrapped bundle in them. 'And I don't want such a life for this little one.' The sleepy baby took hold of his mother's finger. 'Look what he's doing, Tyke!'

Tyke joined them on the bed, equally enthralled. 'You know

sharing someone's name doesn't mean sharing their life.'

'I know. It's just I want life to be better for him than we had. Do you think it's even possible?'

Maudie came in bearing a tray of dinner for Phyllis. 'Knew you'd be up here,' she grumbled at Tyke. 'Shift up and let me get this down.'

Knowing the drill, Tyke placed the baby in the makeshift cradle Hugo had made. Meanwhile Maudie fussed with Phyllis's pillows, making sure she was sitting up comfortably so the tray could be supported safely on her lap.

'Now, listen Missy. Yer've eaten bugger all since the boy was born and yer won't be able t'feed him if yer lose any more of yer strength.' She thrust a spoon into Phyllis's hand. 'So eat.'

'You're a big bully,' Phyllis complained taking up a small forkful of potato.

Maudie watched until the mouthful was swallowed followed by some carrot. 'Right. Just yer carry on, then.' Back downstairs she met Alex in the foyer, a basket over one arm. 'Did yer get some extra milk?'

'I did. You think the baby will need it?'

Together they wandered into the kitchen where Maudie hovered uncharacteristically uncertain. 'No doubt. The lass is wasting away before my eyes and I'm buggered if I know why.'

Alex placed the milk in the cool store. 'Does she have a fever?'

'No.'

'Should we call a doctor?'

'The lass won't hear of it. She says it will shame her family if anyone else knows.'

'Well, then....' Alex's voice faded away.

Pause.

'That's helpful.' Maudie's sarky comment lacked its useful sting. Forcing herself to action she put the kettle on.

Maudie had taken to sleeping in her big chair by the stove in the kitchen, a blanket hauled up to her chin. She was happy enough to leave Phyllis and the boy in her room with the ever vigilant Tyke as a protective guard. Having dragged her mattress beside Maudie's bed, Tyke shared the wakeful hours when the baby needed feeding.

True to Maudie's expectations they began to bottle feed him for Phyllis's milk dried up as she grew weaker.

In the early hours one morning, Maudie was shaken awake. She prised open bleary eyes to see Tyke's worried face bent over her.

'The baby's hungry. He's crying fit to burst and Phyllis won't wake up.'

Maudie's eyes flew open. 'Is she hot to touch?'

'Burning.'

Phyllis never woke. Maudie tried everything. She eventually sent for a doctor who shook his head over the unconscious young woman, took their money and left. Tyke was there with Maudie and Alex when Phyllis drew her last breath.

A baby in her arms. Her dead friend on Maudie's bed.

Alex took care of everything. She visited Phyllis's mother and came away feeling as angry as Maudie on the night of Phyllis's arrival at their door.

Mrs Driver wouldn't hear a word about the baby. 'It's nothing to do with me.'

'He's your grandson.'

Mrs Driver pursed her lips stubbornly, refusing to meet the accusation in Alex's eyes. 'He should never have been brought into the world. Not from the mother he had.'

Something snapped in Alex then. She leaned over the table. 'Your daughter did what she had to do and by God you never refused the money she brought to the household, did you? Did you?' Unable to trust herself anymore, Alex stalked out. She was out of the tumbledown cottage and halfway down the path when running footsteps caught her up and a youth in his mid-teens grabbed her arm.

'Mrs Brodie, this is for Phyl.' He thrust a small, well-loved ragdoll into her hands. Tears shone in his eyes but didn't fall. 'Tell her…. Tell her Bert loves her.'

Gently Alex disengaged her arm. 'Bert, do you want to come to the funeral?'

Bert backed away shaking his head. His mouth opened and he made a strangled sound but no words came. With a gasp he spun around and disappeared the way he came.

So ended Phyllis's life although as Tyke cradled her son in her arms she realised Phyllis would keep on in this world as long as her son lived. She kissed the top of the bald, soft head. *There was a sort of reassurance in that.* Tyke so wanted to keep the little boy. Common sense told her such a thing was impossible. *But how could she let him go?* Alex arranged for the Berhampore Children's Home to take him. *An orphanage. Father had been an orphanage boy and he hated every moment of it. It wasn't fair!* But Tyke had learned enough by now to know life wasn't fair. As Maudie told her so often nor was it meant to be. *'Yer take what it gave yer. Yer coped and were grateful.'*

Such down-to-earth realism didn't help on the day the woman from the Children's Home arrived to take the baby. They had knitted him warm clothes, Tyke lavishing effort on the blanket he was wrapped in. The forbidding woman in the foyer made no comment when Alex explained it all to her. She held out her arms, expecting Tyke to hand the baby over. When the young woman hesitated she frowned. 'I haven't all day, Miss Brodie,' she informed them briskly.

'Please, you will love him, won't you?'

The woman sighed irritably. Not wanting to make things worse, Tyke laid the baby in her arms.

'What's his name?'

Tyke stroked the sleeping boy's head. 'Phillip,' she said softly. 'We call him Phil.'

The woman turned in the doorway, her voice softening just a fraction at the sight of Tyke's miserable face. 'You can visit him if you like. Until we find him a home.'

'Thank you.'

Alex slipped an arm around Tyke's waist as the woman left, the embrace becoming a tight hug when the door closed.

***

Hugo was returning from the wharf in a thoughtful mood. He had caught up with an old friend who was in port for a few days, happy to be shown around Wellington and just as happy to be sailing away from it tomorrow.

'Gawd knows how you stick it, Hugo,' Old Derry had said. 'Dead as door nails.'

Hugo didn't take offence. He had thought it himself when he arrived back in '17. 'You get used to it. I've family here.'

It wasn't all the bullshit they talked which had him thinking. *Bullshit was par for the course when you catch up with old shipmates.* No, it was the comments Old Derry made about the growing tension and change in German ports.

'Something's up under that Hitler. You wanna hear what some of the blokes who fought for the Kaiser have to say. It's all about the Fatherland and making Germany a great country again. They reckon they was stitched up at the end of the great war. Lost territory, they reckon, stolen off them and they want it back.'

A prickle ran down Hugo's spine. 'No one in Europe will want to go to war again. Not in our lifetime.'

His old friend tamped more tobacco down in the bowl of his pipe. 'There's a lot of passion about it is all I'm saying and this Hitler and his Nazis, well, they ain't been backward about grabbing all the power.'

'You think there's something to worry about?'

A wheezy, breathless laugh through a haze of pipe smoke. 'There's always summat t'worry about if you let it.'

So Hugo mulled this over. *Old Derry had a kind of sixth sense for trouble.* Hugo well remembered the riots he had foreshadowed during troubled times in various ports. *He could smell a storm at sea before any other bugger, too. Old Derry had never been a fool.*

Should he share his nagging worry with the women at home? Hugo weighed the pros and cons. *Maybe with old Maud. Never hurt to kick things round with her.*

Hugo also decided to get some stores in. Things were tough but he had a little stash of jewellery tucked away for the rainiest day. *Might be worth spending a bob or two on the future. Stock the larder, kind of thing.* He was running through the items he might get when a piercing whistle broke his meditation.

A filthy dirty Samuel just off work. 'Thought I recognised that seaman's gait of yours.' Samuel removed his cap and wiped the sweat on his forehead. 'Bloody glad to see the back of today.' He'd been lugging wet cement in a wheelbarrow for the past two weeks. 'Shit work, worse money but at least it's something.'

'How long do you think you'll be at it?'

'Dunno. Maybe another month? This is a good time for building.'

Hugo studied him. Samuel was still a good-looking man but the edges of those looks were blurred. Drink had reddened his eyes and weighed them with dark pouches, the skin on his face dragging downwards. Hugo knew Samuel barely slept, trying to keep his black demons away by spending most of his nights out, never saying where *'But s'not difficult to figure out, eh?'* Maudie grumbled. He handed over most of his wages though Hugo also knew Samuel was a lucky gambler, earning a helluva lot more over a card game than he earned working. That money was spent in the pub and one or two other places best not mentioned. All this passed through his brain as he answered. 'Still, better than nothing.'

Samuel snorted. 'Fucking barely. We had a youngster start with us a couple of days ago. Hard worker, by God yes. No faulting him there. Four in the morning starts. By the afternoon of his first day the blood was running from the blisters on his palms. Dripping down his wrists. I didn't think he'd show the next day but know what? He did. He had rags wrapped round both hands and he didn't stop again. Not yesterday, not today, those rags bloodied right through at the end of each shift.' Samuel frowned. 'It's not right. We fought in unions before the war demanding better wages, safer conditions and here we are more worse off than ever.' He rubbed sore eyes with dirty hands. 'Makes you wonder why we bothered fighting at all.'

Hugo said nothing. *What was there to say?*

'Want a bevvie before we head home?'

'Can you afford it?'

'Wouldn't have asked otherwise.'

'Fair enough. Why not?'

They headed towards Ghuznee Street when someone caught Samuel's eye. 'Isn't that Tyke?'

Hugo looked where Samuel pointed and sure enough, a red-headed lass was turning a corner, arm-in-arm with a young man. There had been an ominous tone to Samuel's question so deciding discretion was the better part of keeping Tyke safe, Hugo fudged. 'Don't think so.'

'Looked like her.'

'Nah. Too short.'

To Hugo's relief, Samuel let it go. They reached The Albemarle, shoving the bar door open and walking into a warm welcome.

Tyke couldn't get her breath back. *Had Father seen them?* Frantically, she pulled Jack's hand, almost running to get away. After half a block, she dared to peek back over her shoulder. *No Father or Uncle Hugo. Better to be safe than sorry though.* She tugged Jack forward.

He balked. 'Whoa, Tyke! Where's the fire?'

'Father and Uncle Hugo nearly saw us.'

'So?'

'Father must never know, Jack!' She was so flustered he paused, trying to see things from her point of view.

'You're eighteen.'

'Doesn't matter.'

'What do you mean, doesn't matter? You're nearly an adult.' Jack couldn't help his irritation. He had badgered Tyke to meet her family or for her to meet his and every time he mentioned it she would put him off with excuses. 'Are you ashamed to be seen with me or something?'

Tyke heard the hurt behind his belligerence and softened. 'Don't be daft. It's just…. Father won't like me seeing you.' Reading his expression she hastened to explain. 'Not just you. Any lad. He's…well, he's not easy to live with.' It annoyed Tyke to feel she owed Samuel any loyalty. Her upbringing was too strong, though. He was her father and that was that.

'My old man's not much better.' Jack held her hand as they continued to walk. 'I want you to meet my folks. Mum's already asking me why you don't want to visit her.'

'I do want to.' Tyke insisted.

'Well, then?' Jack's blue eyes gleamed. 'Go on, Tyke. Say yes.'

She hesitated on the brink of refusing. 'If I do meet your mother it doesn't mean you can meet mine.'

Jack sighed. 'It's true, isn't it? What they say about red-heads.' Tyke began to hotly deny this when he held his hands up. 'I take it back. You're very easy going.'

'Thank you.'

'For an unexploded bomb!'

While Tyke abused him, Jack laughed, finally taking his turn to lead the way. 'Come on. You're coming home for a cuppa.' No use protesting, he was adamant.

Giving way to the inevitable Tyke went along with Jack, her heart singing.

***

A month later and Tyke was preparing to visit baby Phillip again. She was standing in the foyer when Maudie bellowed at her from the kitchen.

'I dunno why you put yerself through it, lass. It'll only make it harder when he's adopted.'

Tyke surveyed her reflection in a hand mirror, trying to do so furtively so Maudie wouldn't give her a lecture on the evils of vanity. 'I know. I just want him to know someone loves him.'

'He's barely three months old. He won't know nothin'.'

'Yes, he does. He smiles when he sees me.'

'He'd smile at anyone smilin' at him.'

Tyke stalked back into the kitchen to confront Maudie who was scrubbing the already clean floor. 'Maudie, I refuse to let you make me feel bad about this. I'm going. End of argument.'

With a groan, Maudie eased back onto her haunches. 'Hoity toity miss. A bit o'realism won't go amiss.'

Tyke sniffed. 'There's realism and then there's being a stubborn old biddy.' She strode out, a dumbfounded Maudie gaping after her. It took Tyke a block of walking for it to sink in what she had said. For a second or two she was aghast and then she giggled, picturing the look on Maudie's face. *Bet no one's ever had the courage to call her a stubborn old biddy before.* She smirked. *And lived!*

Jack was to meet her so they could go to Berhampore together. The woman who had collected Phillip was the same one Tyke had to deal with every visit, Mrs Tyrell. Tyke knew from her first visit that Mrs Tyrell believed Phillip was her baby. *Then when Jack came to keep her company, well, her face would have soured cream!* Still, give the woman her dues, she hadn't forbidden them whatever her suspicions leaving Tyke to happily anticipate each call.

A blustery day chased them through Wellington's streets up into Newtown. It tugged so hard at Tyke's hatpins she knew she would have a headache by the end of the day. She skipped over the rubbish blowing around their feet and almost died laughing when Jack's hat was swept off his head and landed in the back door of a passing tram. The man who caught it mocked as Jack trailed behind shouting. It made Tyke's week. When he finally returned to her he jammed the hat down on his head so hard he looked daft.

'I don't care. No way I'm being made a fool of again.'

'Best not look in a mirror anytime soon, then.'

He grabbed for her and she deftly evaded him as they ran the rest of the way, the wind on their backs.

The first sight of the Children's Home was always a sobering one, never mind it was a handsome white two story building set in large grounds. Whether the children were playing outside or peering hopefully through the windows, the sadness of their lives was heart-breaking. Today the little ones chased leaves in the yard, shoving handfuls down each other's backs and squealing.

Jack nudged Tyke. 'Not so sad today.'

Tyke nodded. She admired the relentless optimism children could find in a windy day.

'Come on, doll,' Jack held her hand to get her attention.

Inside bittersweet news awaited them. Phillip was gone. He'd been adopted by a farming family in the Wairarapa.

'They had one boy and couldn't have any more children.' Mrs Tyrell spoke kindly, noting Tyke's stricken face. 'He will be well cared for. Loved, I believe.'

There was no reason for them to stay yet Tyke found her

attention drawn to the children playing outside. 'If I knitted jerseys and things would they be welcome for the others?'

For the first time Mrs Tyrell's smile seemed completely genuine. 'Always, Miss Brodie. Never doubt it.'

Buoyed up with this Tyke enthused a new idea on their way back into the city. 'The club Alex and I run for the poor children? I think I'll teach the girls to knit, too. It will give them a new skill as well as helping others.'

'Good idea.' Jack pulled Tyke onto packed tram. He helped her to a seat and stood gripping the leather strap near his head. 'Come back to my place? I've something for you.'

'Will I like it?' Tyke slanted a mischievous look his way, eliciting a disapproving tut from the elderly woman beside her.

'I'd bet you money on it,' Jack grinned, 'if either of us had any money.'

'Better think of something else then,' Tyke's smile was soft invitation.

The elderly woman moved as far away from them as the seat would allow.

Jack's mum had no cup of tea for them this time.

'We're skint, love.' Maggie told Alex unashamedly, revealing the empty tea caddy. 'Not a skerrick left.'

'I'm happy as I am, Mrs Tyler.'

'Call me Maggie, sweetheart.'

Tyke caught her grin and returned it. 'Maggie it is,' she said.

Jack's surprise proved to be a real eye-opener. He passed over something weighty wrapped in newspaper and after Tyke had dug into it she uncovered a mutton roast.

'Jack! How did you get this?'

'I work in a butcher's don't I?'

'Yes, but…. '

'I didn't steal it if that's your worry. My boss gotta bit of a deal with another farmer selling up and walking off his land.' Jack pointed with his thumb into the tiny kitchen where

Maggie was. 'Got another for us, too. First time the tight old bugger's done anything nice. Wonder where the catch is?'

'Doesn't always have to be a catch. Could just be a nice gesture.'

'Maybe.' Jack's mouth twisted in a sceptical smirk.

Tyke ran her fingers over the rich, marbled meat. 'I can't remember the last time we had a proper roast. Has to be over a year ago.'

They were sitting in the one big room which doubled as the Tyler family's sitting room plus a bedroom for Jack and his brothers.

Jack slid onto the sagging sofa seat next to Tyke. 'Does this mean I win my bet?'

'I would say so.'

'So, what's my prize?' His breath was hot on her cheek as he breathed his words into her ear.

Tyke took refuge behind her usual teasing manner and a pert reply. 'My company.'

Jack was not put off. He lifted the meat off Tyke's lap and held her hand, his thumb circling her palm. 'I'd settle for a kiss,' he whispered.

'What about Maggie?'

'Nah. I don't wanna kiss her.'

'Jack!' Tyke leaned away, muffling her laughter.

This time when he drew her back, his hand slid caressingly about her neck, playing with the curls lying there. Tyke followed where Jack led and when his lips met hers, she responded with a warmth which captivated and entranced.

Later in the afternoon, Tyke unwrapped the mutton onto the kitchen table in front of Maudie. She gave it a proud, possessive slap. 'What d'you think?'

'I think I'll roast it good n'slow with some spuds.' Maudie tapped her cheek ruminating. 'Might even have a bit'o carrot and parsnip with it.'

In all events it was served up on Sunday. A proper Sunday dinner with onion sauce and gravy. They all sat around the table, enjoying the anticipation of a decent meal, sharing their day. When Maudie arrived carrying the joint hot from the stove, they all applauded.

Samuel picked off some of the crunchy fat as he was carving, rolling his eyes with pleasure as he popped it into his mouth. 'Where the hell this come from? A stray sheep wander into the back yard?'

'It's all thanks to Jack.' It was out of Maudie's mouth before she knew what she'd said. Tyke's in-drawn breath alerted her instantly to her mistake.

Seeing the stricken looks Samuel lay down the carving knife and fork with ominous calm. 'Who's Jack?'

Silence.

Each guilty face set wheels turning in Samuel's brain. Hugo sat on his left, wishing he was anywhere else as the question he dreaded was barked at him. 'It was Tyke I saw that afternoon, wasn't it?'

Only Hugo knew what Samuel meant and he didn't want to answer. He sent frantic signals to the horrified Tyke, frozen in her seat.

Finally Alex spoke, laying a calming hand on her daughter's. 'Jack is Tyke's young man.'

'I bloody thought so!' Blood rushed into Samuel face as he hauled Tyke to her feet. 'Why don't I know anything about this? What's he got to hide? What have you got to hide?' His eyes raked her body insultingly.

Tyke was trembling but she held her ground. 'We have nothing to hide. His name's Jack Tyler and he's a butcher's apprentice.'

Samuel pointed at the roast sitting between them. 'And exactly what did you have to do to earn this?'

The eruption of protest in Tyke's defence only enraged Samuel all the more. It was Tyke he focussed on, her response he heard.

'You have a disgusting mind!'

'The bastard didn't even have the manners to come and speak to me.'

'This isn't last century, Father.'

'Don't you dare answer me back!' Samuel swept his plate and cutlery to the floor. 'You will break it off with him.'

'I will not.'

'You will do as I say!' Samuel's punch was lightning fast, sending Tyke crashing back into the wall where she slid to the floor. Alex instantly shielded her. With an enraged roar Samuel picked up the roast and threw it out into the foyer and it slid across the floor. Maudie was on her feet, fists clenched but not before Hugo had grabbed the carving knife and shoved Samuel up against the nearest wall.

'Calm the fuck down, Samuel. You hear me?'

Eye to eye, Hugo was aware of the pulsing anger in the big man. Samuel's eyes were dilated, all black pools and rage. With a strangled cry he elbowed Hugo to one side and threw himself out of the house.

No one moved for long moments until one by one, Tyke leading the way, they began to methodically clear up the mess.

Jack was working late. Not that he minded. As he swabbed down the floors he kept his mind on the coming weekend. He and Tyke were taking their first day trip and after much enjoyable debate had decided on Eastbourne. Rain or shine, they promised, they would take the ferry across.

Whistling, Jack stood back and ran a critical eye over the floor. *Spotless. Nothing else to do but lock up on the way out.* The key was barely in his pocket when a hand slammed down on Jack's arm and dragged him into the shadows.

'What the hell?' Jack wrestled uselessly in the steely grip of a forbiddingly big shape.

'Settle down, boy.'

Jack was thumped against a brick wall, the breath pushed momentarily out of his lungs.

'You will leave my daughter alone.'

'You're Tyke's dad?'

'Unless there's another father you've been bloody avoiding.'

'I haven't been avoiding…..' The words were cut off as Samuel hauled Jack towards him and thrust his knee into his stomach. Before the young man could catch a breath, Samuel launched his attack. When Jack collapsed onto the filthy road, chest heaving, a boot collided with the side of his head. Barely conscious Jack caught Samuel's parting words. 'I won't be so kind next time so make sure there isn't one.'

Jack watched the big man walk away as he passed out.

***

Tyke waited for Jack a way down the Hutt Valley Road where they had organised to meet. *The day was on their side,* she thought happily, enjoying the heat of the sun. Samuel hadn't spoken to her again and she was glad. He wore a nasty, unsettling smirk in her company though making her grateful they rarely met.

The sun climbed higher. Tyke shaded her eyes to peer back towards town. A man sauntered down the other side of the road. *Jack!* She waved, feeling a fool when he stepped out from the shade of an overhanging tree and was revealed to be a stranger.

She waited, foot tapping then idly kicking small stones into the gutter.

Where was he?

The sun was nearly directly above Tyke when she put two and two together.

Father's rage at the thought of her boyfriend.

Jack's no-show.

Heartsick, Tyke began the trek back towards home.

No Moss.

No Phyllis.
No Jack.

***

Murchison

Matthew stood at the top of the hill letting the breeze cool his hot face. Below him spread home farm. The barn, completed three years ago and only recently painted had its own coterie of out-buildings. Matthew had chosen to re-site it nearer the sheepyards and never regretted the decision. As he smiled down from his vantage point on the snugly placed cottage, all was lush green. The well-grown orchard garden, the huge vegetable patch, both bounded by Cally's flowerbeds, a riot of colour wherever the eye fell. Bed linen pegged on the washing line flapped lazily in the warmth of the summer air, dazzling white where the sun hit it. It all looked perfect. It was perfect until Matthew turned to his right - the huge disfiguring scar where the slip had come down in the earthquake. *Grandfather, his old home and his barn all lost four years ago.* Matthew removed his hat to sit on the grass, his dogs immediately lying around him, tongues lolling. *Was it really only four years ago?* He did the simple arithmetic in his head, astounded to be proven right. *Felt a lot longer than four years.*

It had been four years of constant dawn to dark hard slog. In spite of the substantial loss of pastoral land and sheep to the river and slips, the family had held on. As soon as they could, Matthew, Wally and Ben started clearing more land with borrowed machinery. Eventually they managed to buy a broken down old tractor which they rebuilt with such skill it never faltered. Felled trees became fence posts, palings and firewood, the stumps pulled out of the ground and burned. Native bush developed into productive paddocks to graze sheep. *Four short/very long years. Grandfather would be proud.*

Actually, they were doing a bit better than holding on thanks to the workshop his uncles had built down the bottom of the farm nearest the road. Here Wally, Ben and Matthew worked on vehicles in their spare time. It had been a constant balancing act between needing the money their mechanical work brought in to the hard graft required to rebuild the farm. In testament to their strength and focus, Ben had been working in the workshop more or less full time for the past four months.

Down outside the cottage, Cally was taking in the laundry. Fee came out from the big hen run where she'd been clearing out the nesting boxes and giving the chooks clean hay. Janet and Fee kept four house cows, supplying the family with milk, butter and cheese and selling off the surplus. They sold any extra eggs and vegetables, too. The rebuilding of home farm had been a mammoth family effort. If any one of them had faltered, it would have been impossible. Knowing the tension between his mother, Fee and Aunt Janet, Matthew hadn't been too sanguine they could make it work. It said a lot for his sister's temperament that they managed it.

The slight wind carried Fee's voice up to where Matthew sat on the hill above. She was calling for her cats, Arthur and Gawain. *Stupid bloody names! Something to do with characters from one of Fee's interminable books.*

Matthew drew in a deep, deep breath, letting it out slowly to mingle with the scents of the clean, fresh air. *He was bloody proud, too. Proud of them all.*

Further down the road towards the workshop, a figure trudged. Even from up here Matthew could tell it would be another swagger chancing his luck for work or food. *Just as well Grandma would be the one to see to him.* If it was down to Matthew he'd have the scrounging bastard run off their property with the dogs snapping at his heels. He refused to believe these beggars couldn't find work. *Yes, things were tough but a bloke could always find a job. They just didn't want to make the effort.* The sight of the man soured Matthew's mood. Ramming his hat back on his head he returned to the fence post he was digging.

The swagger appeared in the back yard as Cally was folding away the last pillowcase.

'Excuse me, Ma'am.' He removed his cap, twisting it nervously in his hands. 'Any work going?'

'Nothing we can't handle.'

The man nodded and made to leave when Emily spotted him through the open kitchen window and called him back. 'Doesn't mean we can't feed you.'

The swagger's tired face lit up like a beacon.

Cally would have made the man eat on the veranda, if she believed his hard-luck story at all. That was never going to happen under Emily's watch. In no time at all, the swagger sat at the kitchen table. In spite of his hunger he ate carefully, slowly savouring every mouthful.

Emily refilled the man's tea before making him some sandwiches to go. 'And you've found no work at all?'

'Got a few of weeks graft on a farm south of Nelson.' There was bitterness in the man's voice. 'Supposed to get a pound for it. Got a few shillings and a flea in my ear instead.'

'I'm sorry to hear it.'

'Not everyone's like that, Ma'am. There's good folk like yourself, too.'

Cally tutted sensing flagrant flattery and the man coloured hotly, switching his focus to the last, tasty mouthful. When he rose to leave, Emily laid a hand on his sleeve.

'Would you like a wash and brush up first?'

He was as grateful for such an offer as he had been for the food. While he splashed away, they could hear him singing.

Cally's lips twisted. 'He's a beggar taking advantage, Emily. I don't understand why you fall for each and every story these scroungers hand you.'

'Come now. The Depression is hitting everyone hard. What choice do they have?'

They'd had this discussion, ranging from a few words to full arguments more times than either woman could count.

Too weary to bother anymore, Cally placed some bread and butter on a tray, rattling a tea cup in its saucer with more noise than was strictly necessary. 'I'll take this to Jimmy.'

As she passed the scullery door, the swagger came out. He offered a gesture of politeness which Cally deliberately ignored. Instead he turned to the kindly old woman who had fed him so well. 'Thank you for your generosity, Ma'am.'

Emily escorted him to the veranda at the back door, where Fee was removing her boots. She passed him a paper bag of sandwiches and a bottle of cold tea. 'For the journey ahead.'

He felt the weight of the bag and smiled a sweet smile. 'I can't thank you enough.'

'You go well, now,' Emily lifted a hand in farewell as he walked away.

Fee gave Emily a brief hug. 'Anyone in need, Grandma. I've never seen you turn anyone away, even when we barely had enough for ourselves.'

'Well, we had enough, bare or not and such men have nothing.'

It amused Fee how she and Matthew were polar opposites on this issue. She followed Grandma's example whereas Matthew treated the swaggers with all of Cally's disdain. *Was it just their nature or the models set by the people they loved?*

Cally returned from the hallway, banging the untouched tray onto the bench. 'He doesn't want anything.'

'Are you sure, Mother?'

In exasperation Cally pointed at the laden tray. 'See for yourself, Fee. Does it look like he's eaten anything? Or maybe you think I'm just deliberately starving him?'

Ignoring the sarcasm Fee hoisted the tray back up. 'I'll go try again. Just in case.'

Cally didn't know what frustrated her more. The way Fee always doubted she had given Jimmy enough of a chance or the way he invariably ate when either Fee or Janet helped him. *Both*, she decided grumpily. *Don't know why I even bother trying.*

She didn't realise Emily was studying her until the older

woman spoke.

'There's worse things in the world than raising a daughter who loves her Da.'

There bloody well is when the daughter loves no one but her Da! 'Really Emily, I fail to see why you need to comment. I appreciate, neither Fee nor Jimmy can do any wrong in your eyes – unlike myself, but I don't need to have it rammed down my throat every day.' Not wanting to see the hurt in her mother-in-law's eyes Cally stormed out not stopping until she was well clear of the cottage.

She chose not to head down the road towards the workshop, walking in the opposite direction completely. Ben would undoubtedly have his head under a bonnet there but he wouldn't offer her any solace. None of her siblings sympathised with her since Sally had shifted to Nelson to teach. Wally and Ben refused to embroil themselves in things which didn't concern them and Janet…. Cally brought herself up short. *Janet just made things more difficult. Didn't she know Cally realised how much her sister loved Jimmy?* Since she was fifteen or thereabouts Janet had had a crush on the young man courting her sister. Once upon a time Cally thought it was sweet, never wanting to offend Janet by telling her she guessed. *It hadn't been difficult to guess, mind you.* It had been glaringly obvious in Janet's blushes when Jimmy spoke to her or the way she leapt to his defence if Cally dared say something teasing about him. *She'll grow out of it,* Cally had thought fondly.

But Janet hadn't. Even now when Jimmy was a wreck, barely able to get out of his bed, unable to clean or dress himself Janet loved him. She loved the very bones of him. It was Janet who discovered Cally's affair with Jeff. It was Janet to whom Cally confided her despair when Jimmy returned home from the war ruined forever. Janet knew all Cally's trouble, all her suffering. And loved the man who was the cause of it all.

Every year Jeff begged Cally to leave. They could divorce their spouses. Move away. Anywhere. Get married. *Be happy.* She stayed. *Year in, year out, only a spectator to the fading of youth and bloom. How could other women could see any fulfilment in raising children when they were just a reminder, a moment by moment reminder of what youth could be as yours ebbed away.*

Cally rested beside a creek, meandering its pretty way through the paddocks towards the river. Three totara trees formed a shady glade and she gladly welcomed the cool privacy they proffered, sinking to the springy undergrowth to lean back against their mighty trunks.

At some point she would have to go home. *Whatever home meant.*

But not yet.

***

Labour Day in New Zealand had first been held on 28th October 1840 to celebrate the effort of Samuel Parnell, a carpenter in Wellington, to establish an eight hour working day. Since 1910 the public holiday had been commemorated on the fourth Monday in October. On the Benn's farm in Murchison, however, Labour Day had another significance. It was the traditional weekend Emily made the Christmas pudding and cake.

When Emily was a little girl, her grandmother taught her these recipes both of which had been handed down to her.

'You are not just baking something Emily. You are passing down the traditions of your family, thinking of them as they celebrate the most special time of the year.'

All these decades later and Emily could still conjure up her grandmother's face. It wasn't a sweet face, even a kindly one for the life of a mining family was hard and a struggle from one day to the next. It was her smile, Emily remembered, unexpected sweetness, a rainbow shimmering across a dark sky.

Standing in the cottage kitchen, with the spring sun shining through every window, Emily was thrown back to the tiny, dark kitchen in her grandparents' two-up, two-down miner's house just one in a bleak row across a damp Welsh hillside. A lamp on the table was the only light. Warmth came from the stove, the smoky scent of coal permeating the room, the house, the hillside. Little Emily revelled in the almost magical feeling of weighing out the precious ingredients, scrimped and saved for over the preceding months in preparation for Christmas dinner.

It had become easier to relive her youth, she found. She was seventy three now, a great age and somehow those difficult days growing up in a Welsh mining village bloomed ever more brightly. Emily blinked, returning to the here and now and the first thing she saw was the lovely face of her granddaughter, carefully weighing out the suet, cleaned and kept from the last sheep they killed a few days ago.

'Did you know Fee love, these recipes were the only thing left to me from my mother? She and Da were to have travelled to New Zealand with Grandfather and I, only they died in a cholera outbreak six months before we were due to sail.'

Fee paused in the act of tipping currants onto the scales. 'Oh, Grandma! I'm so sorry.'

'It was a very long time ago, love, but thank you.'

Eighteen year old Fee had been helping Emily on Labour Day since she was three. In fact, standing on a chair at the kitchen table in the old farmhouse and eating the sultanas she was supposed to be weighing was her very first memory. 'Do you miss your parents, Grandma?'

'Miss them? Not anymore. The older I become the closer I feel to them, which is a comfort in its way.'

Fee puzzled over this. She reached for the bowl of eggs,

breaking them one after another into the huge bowl they used for this occasion. 'This will be our fifth Christmas without Grandfather and there will be a Grandfather-sized gap where he should be.'

Emily patted Fee's hand. 'It will ease, love. Sure as eggs is eggs.'

As Fee was about to crack another against the side of the bowl, this struck them both as funny and they laughed and laughed, Emily leaning on the table for support. They had barely recovered when Jimmy limped in.

'Stop all this hilarity at once,' he said with mock seriousness. He took in the crowded table, the bowls and bags. 'Ah. Of course. Christmas pudding and Christmas cake baking day.' Jimmy couldn't stand for long these days. He pulled a chair out and sat down, his cane within reach.

'Grandma's letting me do the puddings from scratch, Da.' Fee's pride glaringly obvious. 'Even when they need boiling tomorrow, it will be all up to me.'

'Oh dear,' Jimmy sighed. 'Maybe we should have trifle instead.'

Emily smacked him lightly with the nearest wooden spoon exactly at the moment Fee threw a handful of sultanas at him.

'Attacked in my own kitchen,' he complained.

Cally was on the veranda, leaning against the wall where they couldn't see her. She heard the laughter and the love lilting and lying just underneath its cadences. She wasn't going to stay around listening.

It was a long walk to Jeff's house but it would never be too far.

***

1937/1938

Wellington

Moss was whistling as he prepared for his night out. Clean shirt tucked into newly ironed trousers, he reached for the oil to slick down his hair as Tyke spoke from his open bedroom door.

'You shouldn't do that. You look much better with your hair unoiled.'

Moss studied his reflection critically. 'Really? I dunno....'

'Of course you don't know. You're only too happy to do what your mates do but I'm telling you, you look better without a coating of oil on your barnet.'

'Barnet?'

'Barnet Fair. Hair.' Tyke smirked triumphantly.

Moss sighed, turned his attention back to his reflection. 'Aren't you fed up with all the cockney rhyming shit yet?'

'No. Uncle Hugo's got plenty more'

'I'da thought you'd have grown out of it at twenty three.' He stated the numbers with mocking emphasis.

'And I'd have thought that by thirty you would have the sense not to lather your barnet with oil.'

Moss rolled his eyes, banging the bottle of oil back on the shelf. 'All right. I won't. Jesus, you don't half nag a bloke!' A final preen and he joined her to wander out to the foyer.

'You just want to be thankful I care enough not to let you leave the house on your date with your new girlfriend looking like something the cat threw up.'

'Yeah, yeah.' Moss took his hat and coat off the wicker whatnot. He placed the former on his head, shouted out farewell to his Ma and left in high spirits.

As Tyke turned to head into the kitchen, Maudie was standing in the doorway.

'Why's the fool gone out lookin' like a dog's breakfast for? What's he done to his hair?'

Tyke shrugged negligibly. 'Dunno. He wouldn't listen to

me. I told him it always looks better oiled down and not all curly.'

'Well, he looks a right fool.' Maudie missed Tyke's sly grin. 'I was gonna make a cuppa? Want one?'

'Suppose so.' Tyke drifted about the kitchen aimlessly.

'You goin' out tonight, too?'

'No. I did ask Moss if he wanted to go to the movies but,' Tyke grimaced, 'he had this date organised with Ida. Do you like Ida, Maudie?'

'She seems alright.'

'She smells of mothballs, have you noticed? I think he's too good for her.'

'Yer say that about all his girls.'

Immediately on the defensive Tyke swung round. 'No, I don't. He just dates the wrong kind of women.' She yanked out a chair to sit and drink the tea Maudie had poured out.

'What's the right kind?'

'Can we change the subject? I'm bored with it. Moss can choose whoever he wants. It's not my concern.' Tyke tried to pout and sip her tea at the same time, careful not to make eye contact with Maudie as she mopped up the subsequent mess.

There was cake on the table and they both took a piece. Tyke marvelled how quickly they had become use to such luxury. 1935 had seen the election of the new Labour Party after the Coalition government had postponed the elections for one year in the hope the economy would improve enough for them to be re-elected. They reckoned without the destitute poor and the working class who had been beaten down under their policies and the effects of the Depression. Bare-foot and hungry they came to the polling booths to vote for Labour.

Michael Joseph Savage became Labour's first Prime Minister and the man who had fought for the working classes all his life had the chance to make some real, lasting improvements in their lives by leading this first progressive government. Tyke bit into her piece of cake and chewed. Here was a small but significant consequence of their early policies. There was cake in the pantry again.

The boarding house was full. Hugo and Moss had kicked their business back into life and had never been busier. Tyke helped them every now and again when she was between jobs, which she often was as she couldn't settle to anything. She'd tried nursing, receptionist, nannying, sewing in a factory, office accounts and work in a florist shop where the flowers made her sneeze. She even spent four months typing for the Dominion during the run-up to the last election only to leave in anger at their deliberate anti-Labour advertisements and editorials. Nothing held her interest.

It drove Alex to distraction. She wanted her daughter to have proper work, a career even while Tyke found only boredom or grew to dislike the cattiness of the women she worked with or couldn't cope with Matron demanding instant, unarguing obedience or any one of a hundred complaints.

At the present time she worked with the head gardener at the Botanical Gardens. Everyone was thankful the weather held fair. No one expected Tyke to last if it rained for more than a couple of days in a row.

'Did yer work today?'

'Supposed to have.'

'Tyke....'

'What, Maudie? I'm bored to death.' Tyke pushed her cup and saucer away so she could lean her elbows on the table. 'I hardly see Moss what with him and Uncle Hugo being so busy and now he's taken up with old mothy Ida...' She sighed heavily. 'I'm just sick of everything.'

Maudie was about to take Tyke to task for being a spoiled young madam when the post slot in the front door rattled. Tyke leaped to her feet to get the mail. She returned frowning at one long, white envelope. 'It's from Aunt Cally for Father but she's only just written to Alex about Emily.' Thinking no more about it, she placed it with the other letters in their usual waiting space behind the clock on the mantelpiece.

Uncle Jimmy who she'd never met was dead.

Her father's face when he read the news chilled Tyke. Without a word to any of them he stalked out of the house. While Alex discussed the funeral with Maudie, Tyke made for the comfort of her room, wishing Moss was home so she could talk it over with him. *Would Father react with more violence to things now?* Just the possibility set Tyke's nerves on edge. *Why wasn't Moss home? Surely Ida wasn't that interesting?* Finally, Tyke grabbed her nightgown and dressing gown and headed to the bathroom hoping a long soak might wash away her fears. By the time she was back in her bedroom, the kitchen was quiet meaning Maudie and Alex had retired for the night, too. Tyke sat at her dressing table, brushing her hair to plait it for the night. She wanted to cut it in the new fashion but no one in the house would let her. *She was twenty-three. Why couldn't she just stand up to them and cut it?* Maybe she would have if Moss didn't like her long curls so much.

A scuffling, giggling on the front pavement. Tyke peered through the small window which overlooked the street. A couple were embracing. When they pushed open the front door into the foyer she knew Moss had returned. *With Ida.* A rush of dislike for a woman she hadn't met. Suddenly Tyke determined Moss needed to know about Uncle Jimmy. *Family's more important than floozies,* she thought haughtily.

Down the stairs and through the foyer she paused to press her ear to his bedroom door. Moss's low voiced whispers. More feminine giggles. Tyke raised her fist and knocked.

Silence.

The door pulled back revealing a shirtless Moss. 'Tyke?' Instant concern spread over his face and he closed the door behind him. 'What's up?'

'Uncle Jimmy hanged himself.' She hadn't meant to blurt it

out so childishly.

'Jesus! How's your father?'

'I don't know but we can guess. He probably went straight back to the pub.' Real fear seized her. 'He's angry enough, Moss. What will he be like now?'

Moss hugged her close. 'We'll keep an eye out for you, Tyke. Don't you fret.'

She loved the warmth of his embrace, the safety she felt. When he drew back to smile at her, Tyke placed her arms around his neck and kissed him. It wasn't the sisterly kiss he was expecting but a deep caress, lover-like. Shock held Moss immobile for seconds. Tyke pressed against him, deepening the kiss and that was when Moss tore his mouth from hers.

He pushed her away. 'What the hell are you playing at, Tyke?'

Disorientated she reached out to steady herself but he put more distance between them, wiping at his mouth. 'I....I thought you'd like it.'

Moss shot a guilty look towards the dark kitchen, another to the stairs, half-expecting to see Maudie, Alex or, God forbid, Samuel charging at him. 'Jesus!' His face creased with anger. 'Like it? For fuck's sake!' No longer meeting her eyes he thrust her towards the stairs. 'Go to bed, Tyke.'

'Moss....'

'Just bloody forget about it.'

'But....'

Moss disappeared into his bedroom leaving Tyke to confront the closed door, horrified at what she'd done. She fled to her own room but there was no solace there. The long night crawled by as she lay on her bed, unable to sleep, feeling wretched and very alone.

Had she known it, Moss suffered too. Back in his bedroom it was almost a surprise to see Ida sitting half-dressed on his bed. Still feeling the turmoil of Tyke's kiss he couldn't hide his consternation, unable to return the woman's suggestive smile.

Ida frowned in concern. 'Are you all right, Moss? Who was it?'

'No one. Tyke.'

'Oh, your young step-sister.'

Moss gave Ida a look she couldn't interpret. 'Kinda. Not really. Look, I'll have to call it a night. Sorry.'

'So something is wrong?'

He didn't answer, could barely meet her eyes. 'Shall I walk you home?'

Ida did the buttons up on her frock, scooping up her coat and belongings. 'Don't bother.' She only just managed not to slam the door on her exit.

Moss threw himself onto the bed, lying on his back. *What the hell just happened?*

Like Tyke he felt wretched and dismayed, all the more distressed because he realised just how much he loved Tyke. He had always loved her; the sister who replaced his beloved Peg. Then she kissed him like a woman, not a child and his innocent, comforting ideal splintered. Moss closed his eyes feeling Tyke's warm mouth on his, the press of her body against his. Into his daydream strode Alex, disappointed, outraged. Samuel angry at Moss's betrayal. *And Ma?* The figure of his unpredictable mother hovered in the shadows.

Moss sat up, punched the bed over and over. *Why did it bloody have to change? It couldn't.* There was no choice. He would pretend it hadn't happened. And after a few weeks, maybe a few months, maybe it would be like it never had.

Maybe.

***

Murchison

A couple of months before the letter landed in Tyke's hand, her cousin Fee put on her hat. Reaching for her hatpins she deftly secured them through the felt and into the roll of her thick hair. Turning her head first one way then the other she studied her profile, a hand tucking a few stray hairs back behind her ears. No matter what Hamish whispered to her, she knew she wasn't beautiful. Fee grimaced violently into the mirror. Her smile at the result softened her features so much she eased back on the self-reproach. *She'd settle for prettyish. On a good day.* Several of her friends were already married with children – *more than one in Isabelle's case! Seriously, did Izzy and Kev do anything else?* Fee remained unrepentantly single, much to Cally's dismay, who complained about her being too choosy. *As if the choice of a man good or otherwise was part of her reasoning not to get married.* Though she hadn't shared Hamish's interest with her mother, Fee had mentioned it off-handedly to Aunt Janet one day as they folded sheets prior to ironing them.

Janet reflected for a moment, placing his face. 'Hamish Raynor's a nice enough boy.'

Fee laughed. 'He's twenty-four Aunt Janet! Hardly a boy.'

'Wait till you reached my advanced years, Missy. Then you can comment on what we oldies regard as boyish.'

As Aunt Janet wasn't forty this just increased Fee's amusement. She teased her Aunt relentlessly for several minutes before Janet brought the subject back to the salient point.

'So you're keen on young Hamish, then?'

Fee stopped laughing. *Was she?* 'Maybe.'

'But he's more keen than you are.'

Her niece appreciated it wasn't phrased as a question. 'It sounds a bit arrogant somehow, but yes, I suppose so.' Fee tilted her head to make sure Cally kept out of earshot. 'He keeps wanting us to spend more time together but what's the rush, I say. It's not as if I'm hankering to settle down and get married.'

Janet threw Fee another sheet and they tugged it straight, pulling it tightly, folding it with elaborate care to remove as many of the creases as possible. 'Why not?'

'I don't know. I'm busy enough. Happy enough.' Fee met her aunt's eye. 'I'm not even sure I want children, so as I've said, what's the rush?'

Her aunt nodded and they continued their work. Fee knew she had her approval. Janet wouldn't say anything though and Fee knew why, because as she had grown into adulthood she recognised Janet's devoted care towards Jimmy for what it always had been. Love. Fee never spoke of it even to Matthew. *Why had it taken her so long to see it? And did Da know? Did Mother? All these years of devoted service and what did Aunt Janet get in return?* It never occurred to Fee how for some souls, devoted service was reward in itself. With her secret knowledge came understanding - a woman could find happiness outside the traditional roles defined by society. And knowing someone agreed with her gave Fee the courage to remain single.

With her mind running along these lines, Mary popped into her mind. A while ago the family expected to hear of Mary and Matthew's engagement. For months he had disappeared wearing his best suit, his hair slicked back muttering about seeing Mary. Fee grew bored with the eulogies to Matthew as her friend refused to hear about any of his failings. *She'd learn soon enough,* Fee thought unfeelingly. Just as an engagement seemed inevitable, it all changed. For the past month Matthew never left the farm and the sparkle had gone from her friend's face. In fact, the last time they met up Mary looked positively peaky, prompting Fee to do what she promised she would never do; she asked her brother how things were between him and Mary.

Matthew had blushed a fiery red.

'Mind your own bloody business!'

Hmmmm.

So with the laundry done and Aunt Janet keeping an eye on Da, Fee donned her hat, saluted her reflection and cycled to Mary's.

It was an overcast day, the hilltops lost to mist. The rivers ran high which spoke of heavy rain falling up the valleys. Fee hoped she would be home and dry before it closed in. The farm track to Mary's house was too pitted to cycle so Fee hopped off and pushed her bike the rest of the way. She leaned it under the eaves of the roof before knocking on the front door. Mary's mother was an 'always use the front door' kind of person. To Fee's surprise the normally amiable Mrs Hoddy wasn't the least happy to see her.

'Mary's taken ill.'

'Oh. Can I see her anyway? I could cheer her up a bit.' Fee tried to peer round Mrs Hoddy's bulk to see into the hallway.

'No. Be best if you went.'

The door was closing when Fee heard Mary's voice calling her inside. For a few seconds the door remained stubbornly shut. There were hasty, subdued words on the inside until Mrs Hoddy pulled the door open and stood to one side. 'You can't stay long.'

Inside the hallway was an unhappy Mary. She took Fee's hand and led her to the sunroom she had claimed as a bedroom to give her some privacy from her four brothers.

Fee managed to hold her tongue until the door into the living room was shut but once she had sat on Mary's bed she couldn't contain her curiosity. 'Your mum said you're sick. What's the matter?'

Tears began to spill silently down Mary's face. She wiped at them, blowing her nose on a damp looking handkerchief. 'I'm two months pregnant.'

Fee's jaw fell open.

'You're what?'

'And Matt says the baby isn't his.' Mary's tears fell faster now. 'He refuses to speak about it. I've written him a dozen letters. He sent them all back.' She held them out to Fee, dropping them one by one onto the floor.

'Oh my God, Mary.' Fee didn't know what to say. 'Your mum and dad….?'

'Mum's been wonderful. I thought she would throw me out but she didn't. But Dad.' Mary drew in a shaky breath. 'He doesn't know and I'm dreading Mum telling him. We thought Matt and I would get engaged and everything would be all right but Matt says I've played around and he won't have anything more to do with me.' With a sob Mary crumpled onto the bed. 'What'll happen to me when this gets out? I'll be ruined, Fee!'

There was nothing Fee could say to her friend, but by God, there was something she could say to her brother. With her anger balled like a lead weight in her chest Fee tracked him down to the workshop. Matthew was on his back underneath a truck when his twin stormed in and slammed the door behind her.

'Get up, Matthew.'

'Piss off, Fee. I'm busy.'

Fee counted to ten. It did less than nothing. She grabbed a hammer lying close to hand and chucked it with all her might at the far wall where it clanged and crashed to the floor taking with it a shelf containing tins of nuts, bolts and washers.

'Shit!' Matthew scurried out from under the truck, staring wildly round. 'What happened?'

Fee strode up to him and slapped him across the face. Matthew staggered back, grabbing her hand as it swiped towards him.

'You bastard,' she spat. 'How dare you abandon Mary!' She gave him no time to respond, shoving against his chest, forcing him backwards. 'She's carrying your baby, Matthew. And you treat her like she's nothing more than your whore?'

Again she pushed him but this time Matthew stood his ground. 'How do I know the baby's mine? If she did it with me who's to say she didn't do it with someone else?'

'She loves you!' Fee wasn't sure how Matthew would react but she didn't expect scornful laughter.

'Trust her all you like, Fee but she gave in real quick. A nice girl wouldn't.'

'You encouraged her. You wanted her to.'

Matthew's lip curled. 'So? She didn't have to if she really didn't want to.'

Fee couldn't believe it was her brother saying this. Bad enough it was unfair and untrue. That his attitude would was the one everyone would believe was worst of all. Fee stood right in front of Matthew, trying to control her voice. 'You have to stand by her.'

'I don't have to do anything.'

'She will be ruined if you don't.'

'Then she should've thought about that before sleeping with me.' Matthew picked up a spanner and moved back towards the truck.

Fee grabbed his arm. 'Please, Matt. You took what you wanted and Mary will pay the price.'

'You think I want to be tied down to a wife and kid? At twenty three?'

'Maybe you should have thought about that before you slept with her.'

Frustration burned in Matthew's eyes. The silence spun out until he admitted, 'I don't love her.'

Fee didn't soften. 'Then what you've done is all the more unforgivable.'

Silence.

Matthew ran a filthy hand down his face. 'It's such a fucking mess, Fee,' he pleaded.

She could only answer with the unanswerable. 'It's your mess, brother, of your making.'

With a roar of anger and defeat Matthew swept an arm along the workbench. Tools and materials flew in all directions joining the mess already on the floor.

Fee stopped him, holding his arm as he stood there shoulders heaving. 'You have to do the right thing.'

A final flash of defiance. 'No I don't.'

But it didn't fool his twin. 'Yes. You do.'

Matthew yanked his hand from her grip, leaning against the empty workbench, shoulders stooped, head bowed.

Fee left him. Nothing more she could say. It was up to Matthew now. Mary would have a husband and keep her reputation. *But at what cost?*

***

The wedding was a small affair, the bride in a simple white frock, the groom in a suit. Fee was the only bridesmaid, Mary having no sisters. Only she detected the utter relief masquerading as happiness behind Mary's smile and only she saw anything less than contentment in Matthew's expression. Standing beside the groom and looking too well-scrubbed to be true was Matthew's best man, Hamish. He had already caught Fee's eye once or twice and she was hard put not to play his game. *Did he know about the baby?* When the minister spoke of marriage being for the procreation of children Hamish glanced at Fee and in that split second she had her answer, for his was an easy face to read. *Yes, he did.*

The wedding breakfast was held in the garden at the farm, everyone keeping their fingers crossed for the fine spring morning to hold through the day. Under a forget-me-not blue sky Cally, Fee and Emily laid the food out on trestle tables Wally and Ben had set up earlier in the morning. White linen table cloths were spread then ironed to perfection and the wedding cake Mary's mother made took pride of place at one end. Jimmy sat in an armchair brought outside for the occasion. He hadn't attended the service though he seemed to be enjoying the wedding breakfast.

As everyone milled around, a plate in one hand, Hamish sidled up to Fee. 'That went well.'

'Mmmmm.'

'I wouldn't have bet money on it taking place,' he said softly.

'Me neither.'

'Touch and go for a bit, eh? Glad he went through with it '

Fee watched her brother and his wife standing with Cally who looked radiant. 'Me, too. Although…..'

Hamish bit into a sandwich and nodded. 'I know.' He gave her a perceptive smile and moved away in response to Matthew's call.

Everyone gathered around the cake in preparation for the happy couple to cut it. Fee glanced around, noting expressions and finding Hamish's eyes on her again. Hastily averting her gaze she happened to catch sight of her grandmother. Emily was watching from the veranda, a hand clutched against her chest. She bent her head briefly but not before Fee saw the pain on her face. In moments she was at Emily's side. 'Grandma? Are you all right?'

Emily laid her hand on Fee's arm, leaning her weight against it. 'Don't let's make a fuss, darling. Help me inside while no one's looking. I'll be all right after a sit down.'

Concerned at Emily's white face, Fee led her to her bedroom. 'You look done in, Grandma. How about a lie down? No one will blame you.' Fee's concern racked up a few more notches when Emily agreed without argument. After tucking the snowy embroidered coverlet up under Emily's chin, Fee hastened outside. She wanted to fetch the doctor without raising an alarm. Aunt Janet was sitting with Da and Mary's parents. *Who else could she ask? Where the hell were Wally and Ben? No doubt they were already back in their workshop having been outspokenly resentful at the hours forced away from their beloved machinery.*

As she stood there worrying, Hamish sauntered up and waggled his empty plate. 'Can I get you anything, Fee?' His honest, warm brown eyes smiled at her.

Right then, right there Fee came as close to loving Hamish as she had ever done. Reining in the swamping emotion, she whispered in his ear, 'Grandma needs the doctor.'

***

Emily held on for another couple of weeks. Forbidden any exertion, she watched the bustle of the household from a chair or listened to it as she lay in her bed. One warm spring morning Fee and Jimmy settled her outside under the shade of a walnut tree. When Jimmy checked on her not thirty minutes later, she had passed away from them, looking for all the world like she was sleeping.

They buried her beside John.

The family expected Jimmy to fall into the same darkness after they lost John. He was only too aware of their covert watchfulness, Fee's the hardest of all to bear. He would miss her. Jimmy regretted the pain he knew he would cause but he couldn't cope without Emily.

On a fine spring morning less than a fortnight after she died, Jimmy woke early before anyone else stirred. He could do no more to dress himself than push his feet into his slippers and haul his dressing gown over his shoulders but it was enough. A slow, limping walk took him past where the old homestead once stood. Jimmy paused at the overgrown foundations, reminiscing. *He'd been so happy there.* He left the road, following the familiar route to the gnarled willow tree.

Up in the branches full of pale green new growth sits young Jimmy, his back against the trunk. His dog Colt lies in the grass, on guard and watchful. Sunlight sparkles on the river and in the distance, John whistles to his big working dog, Wolf, just as Emily's voice calls them both in for breakfast.

Jimmy closed his eyes and listened to the baaing of new lambs, the birds in the trees.

So happy.

Fee woke and discovered her Da wasn't in bed. She knew. Something deep inside her knew. She waited for Janet to arrive as she did every morning, not saying anything to Cally or Matthew. Together they found him swinging from a branch of the willow tree.

***

It was late by the time Samuel, Alex and Tyke arrived at the farm, gone midnight, yet the family were all awake and eager to greet them. Samuel found Matthew's likeness to Jimmy unsettling. They clasped warm, firm handshakes, each liking what they saw. *Not much of Jimmy in his daughter though. Who was she most like? There was little of Cally in her features either.* He hugged the tall, reserved Fee, perceptive enough to note the firmness of her chin, the set of her head. *There were depths there.* Then Tyke moved to talk to her cousin and it hit him. *Tyke.* They were unlike in colouring but the similarity couldn't be denied now he'd spotted it. *What will they make of each other?*

Alex offered her condolences on Emily's death. 'I loved her from the first,' her smile soft with reminiscence. 'John, too. Such good people.'

They were introduced quickly to Janet, Wally and Ben, the latter hard put to keep his eyes open after a long day. Vigilant Fee noted her uncle's own drooping eyelids and suggested they call it a night. 'Well, early morning,' she added.

To give their visitors room, Matthew and Mary were staying with Wally, Ben and Janet at their house in town. Alex and Samuel were given their room and Tyke shared Fee's big bed.

The cottage settled into quiet.

Tyke couldn't sleep. As late as it was she was too keyed up to relax. She was glad to have escaped Wellington. Every time she thought of the kiss with Moss she burned with shame, wishing she'd never done it, wondering what had possessed her to do it in the first place.

You know damn fine well what possessed you.

He'd been unlike himself ever since. The warm camaraderie she'd known from her earliest memories was gone and how Tyke missed it, damning herself over and over for making such a terrible misjudgement. *What a fool she was!*

The gentle night breeze wafted the window curtains. A morepork hooted close by, its distinctive, plaintive call unanswered. Beside her, Fee stirred restlessly.

Tyke risked a soft question. 'Cousin? Are you awake?'

'Yes. Just can't nod off.' Fee turned to face Tyke, lifting up on an elbow.

Tyke mirrored her stance, trying to make out her cousin's features through the filtered darkness shot with moonlight. 'I wish we weren't meeting for the first time like this.'

'I know what you mean.'

Pause.

'Fee, can I ask you something personal?'

'Of course.'

'What was he like, your dad?' A heavy silence fell and Tyke hastened to make amends. 'Sorry. You don't have to answer. I didn't mean to upset you.'

'You didn't. It's all right. I was just wondering what to say.' Fee reached for the box on her bedside table. She lit the candle before fumbling with the lid to bring out a much handled photo which she passed to her cousin. 'Mother and Da on their wedding day.'

Tyke smiled. 'He was so good-looking. Such a cheeky grin!'

Fee's words came slowly as she measured each one. 'Da was two men, Tyke. The one who went to war and the one who came back. I have spent all my life longing for him to be the man I never knew and now he's gone, I feel like I spent all these years betraying the man he became because that man never measured up, not for me not for anyone.' Fee's voice dropped. 'And I grieve he always knew.'

To be offered such unsparing honesty by someone she had just met unnerved Tyke, but touched her, too. She shifted a little closer. 'When I was little, Maudie told me Father was still living the war but he never spoke of it. He wouldn't talk about Uncle Jimmy either.'

'Da never breathed one word about what happened to him. He just suffered every single day.'

They fell silent then, neither finding the words to fill the gap. Tyke wondered if she'd have been better not to speak when Fee's hand grasped hers and sharing the warm pressure, they eventually drifted off to sleep.

***

Another death. His brother's open grave almost beckoned Samuel. *If I lift my eyes, I'll see Cass standing there, too.* Cass who always appeared in times of greatest stress. At least there was a burial place to mourn beside, not miles of blasted land turned into mud-filled shell holes or baking hot desert where the sun turned bodies into festering mounds. The strangest silver-lining. *I should have visited you, brother. Should have been here.* Instead, hardship had given Samuel the excuse not to see his younger brother. *But the truth is Jimmy, I didn't want to see what you had become.* Samuel tilted his face to the sky, blinking away the tears.

At his side Alex fought the impulse to offer comfort, aware of her hypocrisy. Too often she'd been sharply rebuffed by Samuel to make the offer lightly. Alex knew she would only be offering him sympathy to be seen doing so. Any compassion she had for her husband died years ago. She and Cally had re-connected. Warily at first, memories of those difficult days when Alex had brought a broken Jimmy home hovering between them. They discovered though how passing years could wash remembrances clear of bitterness. Only regret remained and they were both hardened campaigners in the face of that emotion.

In front of Alex, Tyke and Fee were arm-in-arm, two young women with their lives ahead. *What would those lives be shaped by? Hope? Resentment? Regret?* No mistaking Fee's deep grief for it cut grooves around her mouth and hollowed her eyes. *Not so Matthew.* Alex's gaze lingered on Jimmy's son. His wife stood patiently beside him though he paid her scant heed and had done all day. Matthew seemed oblivious to the scene, quite detached from it. If he grieved there wasn't even a hint of it in his face or demeanour. Alex was grateful Emily wasn't here to witness it. *But then, perhaps he would have put on a show for her. Janet now, her grief was hard to watch. It was so tightly held in, so fiercely guarded you couldn't help but feel it, too.* There was much to admire about Cally's younger sister and certainly Fee loved her. Alex thought the two sisters would have been inseparable today of all days. They barely made eye contact. Janet stood with Fee and Tyke, Cally near Matthew and Mary.

The tangled threads of family relationships.

As people began to move away, Alex approached Matthew. She came within steps of him and stopped as Mary murmured something, something obviously not meant for other ears.

He shook his head, his face twisted in bitterness. 'Why should I? I'm glad he's dead. I only regret the bloody coward didn't die years ago and save us all a lot of heartache.'

Again Mary whispered with urgency and this time Matthew didn't bother to reply. He stalked away.

It took mere seconds for Alex to decide to follow him. He hadn't gone far, just down the short set of steps to the road. She touched his elbow.

'Bloody hell, Mary! I said leave it.' Instead of his wife, Matthew faced Alex. 'Sorry Aunt.' He ran a hand through his short hair. 'Bit of a domestic with the wife.' His rueful smile was engaging.

'It happens. Matthew, can we talk? Just you and me. About your father.'

A shuttered expression closed down Matthew's smile. His was instantly uncomfortable. 'Now?'

'If we could. I gather we're heading to Janet's house for the wake rather than the farm?'

'So?'

'Well, it means maybe we could wander to the river over there and meet everyone soon. I'll make our excuses and let Janet know we shan't be long.'

A bemused Matthew let Alex take charge and in a few minutes they were walking on the rocky banks of the Matakitaki River. They made small talk until Matthew brought them to a halt. 'Aunt, what's this about?' In the ensuing silence he was being weighed and measured. He gave a short, uneasy laugh. 'Should I be worried?'

'What do you know of your father's war experiences?'

Again Matthew closed down. He shot Alex a look half-resentment, half-anger. 'Enough.'

'But you see, I don't think you do. I don't think you've ever known enough and I'd like to enlighten you.'

Matthew swung away, staring at the river but not seeing it. 'Why? Why should I bloody bother?'

'Because you have hated your father all your life. You have feared and hated him, condemning him for something he never was.' She had his unwilling attention now. 'I overheard what you said at his grave site. You called him a coward. And he wasn't. No, by God he never was!'

Now his eyes searched hers. 'Mother never said.'

'Your mother had her own problems dealing with what happened to Jimmy. I'm not here to make judgements on her. I just think it's time you heard the truth.'

The hills across the other side of the river seemed nearer in the clear light today. Somewhere a man whistled to his dogs. A car drove down the road behind them. Matthew was intensely aware of all these things. *What truth did his aunt know? And would it change anything?* He rubbed impatiently at his eyes. *And did he even want to know?*

When he faced Alex once more she had removed her coat to sit on it, her feet resting on large stones at the river's edge. Slowly he lowered down beside her, keeping his eyes on the water. 'All right. I'll listen. I'm not saying it will change how I feel, but...' His voice trailed away.

'It's all I'm asking.'

In her low tone Alex related Jimmy's experiences in the Great Strike; how it scarred him against violence, how conflicted he was when war was declared. 'Yet, he turned up at our door in Wellington so he and your Uncle Samuel could enlist together.' She spoke of Cairo, the riots where Jimmy witnessed more violence against innocent people by New Zealand and Australian soldiers and knew he couldn't be like them. 'You can't know the terrible pressures on young men during wartime, Matthew. If you chose not to fight you were treated like a traitor and a coward. The military could hang you high with no trial. There was very real danger if you declared as a conscientious objector. Nevertheless it's what your father did.' Matthew was utterly still. 'They tortured him. They beat him, starved him and locked him in an English prison with other objectors. He didn't break. He refused to carry a rifle and fight. In the end he became a stretcher bearer on the Western Front.' Tears shimmered in Alex's eyes as she relived and remembered. 'I can't tell you exactly how he became wounded because Jimmy didn't know himself. He was on duty with a friend, Patrick who was also a stretcher bearer. They were bringing in wounded from the shell holes during a bombardment when they were hit.' Alex found her handkerchief and wiped her eyes. 'Patrick died that day. And it was only after months of searching I found your father broken and unnamed in a hospital in France.' For the first time she glanced at her nephew and found his eyes locked on hers. *Jimmy's eyes.* 'He didn't know about you and Fee. Cally's news never reached him. But I told him everything I knew even though I couldn't be sure he heard until the day he came out of his terrible darkness and recognised me.' Alex smiled painfully. 'All he wanted was to come home. But he had to learn to walk all over again, to function. And it was so hard. Time and again his injuries defeated him. Time and again he fought back. To make it home.' A single tear dripped down Matthew's cheek. Alex dabbed it away. 'Jimmy would have agreed with you, Matthew. He always judged himself to be a coward. His was a special kind of bravery and he doubted it every bit as much as everyone around him.'

Her nephew buried his face in his arms. Alex remained silent, gently stroking his head. She listened to the river running towards the sea. *He looks so much like you, Jimmy.*

Eventually Matthew raised his head, his eyes wretched. 'Mother never told me. Even Grandma never said.' But all at once he remembered those times Grandma had tried to speak to him and how he had shut her down. 'I hated him every single day. And now he's dead and it's too late.'

Too late. The most painful two words in the world.

Silence.

Alex gently squeezed his fingers 'Should I have told you?'

'Yes.' His pain was obvious in that single, drawn out syllable.

'You mustn't blame yourself, Matthew. You were a child when you met a frightening stranger.' He made an odd noise but didn't speak. 'Your father would have been the last person to blame you,' she added softly.

Matthew bowed his head. 'That only makes my behaviour all the worse.'

They sat lost in thoughts too complicated to share.

When Matthew stood he held out a hand and helped Alex to her feet. 'They'll be wondering where we are.'

The walk back to his waiting family was the longest walk of Matthew's life.

Cally saw her son re-enter with Alex. He looked haggard, older too as if he carried the cares of the world on his shoulders. Instinct stirred unpleasantly. *What had Alex told him? What had needed to be shared only in private?* Every time she tried to speak with him Matthew excused himself and walked off. The third time it happened, Cally's twinge of unease deepened. She was longing for this gathering to be over, so she could stop pretending she felt any grief and get back to the cottage where her life could begin again. *Maybe she would heed Jeff and they could finally be together.* Even as the thought formed Cally drew back from it. *What would it be like to be just her?*

Impatient to be away, she moved through the family, seeking Matthew's face. Not a sign of him. When both Mary and Fee admitted they hadn't seen him for a while, Cally had no choice but to suffer her sister's heartache.

'I saw him walking back towards the churchyard. Is it important, Cally? Maybe he needs to be alone?'

'I think I know my own son, thank you Janet.' Those sharp words were to haunt her.

Cally found Matthew silhouetted against the blue sky, his head bowed over the grave Jimmy shared with John and Mary. It was already covered, the simple wooden cross dug in until the headstone could be altered.

'Matthew?'

'Leave me alone, Mother.'

Her hand slid under his elbow, Matthew hard put not to flinch at her touch.

'I've been worried since Alex took you away. Did she say something to upset you, darling? I can speak to her if you like.' It wasn't her Matthew who faced her. His eyes were dilated and dark, tension visible in the muscles of his face, the set of his shoulders.

'I don't want to have this conversation now. Just leave me alone.'

'I can't bear to see you so upset. I know you've lost your father but it wasn't as if he was a part of us anymore. Not for years.'

'And whose fault was that?' Resentment underlined every word. 'You never told me what he suffered. I never knew he was a stretcher bearer on the front line.' The words tumbled from Matthew, scorching and raw. 'He was tortured for his beliefs, treated like an animal because he didn't want to kill. My father was on the front line of the Great War and I never knew. You let me believe he was a coward. And worse!' Cally's mouth moved soundlessly. She reached out, her hand trembling only for her son to step back. 'Because of you I never loved him.' The words shattered on the jagged edges of his emotion. Matthew strode away.

Cally called after him. 'Matthew.' Nothing. 'Matthew!'

They couldn't wait for him to return nor did anyone feel the need to panic about a man grown. Janet drove the rest of the family home, their journey a quiet one. As soon as they pulled up by the cottage gate, Fee and Tyke tumbled out of the car door and disappeared into their bedroom.

'Probably for the best,' Janet said, automatically putting the kettle on to boil.

Her comment irritated Cally whose nerves were stretched thin. 'How nice you understand my children so well.'

'What?' Genuine confusion was on Janet's face but somehow Cally managed to haul her emotions in from the teetering edge of an argument.

The four of them sat around the table, Alex and Janet valiantly creating small-talk as Samuel and Cally remained silent, barely even listening.

As soon as his cup was empty, Samuel shoved his chair

back. 'I'm going for a walk.'

No one stopped him, three pairs of eyes on his back as he disappeared out the back door.

Her sister's white face alerted Janet to something being seriously amiss. In all honesty she hadn't expected any show of grief from Cally, so her behaviour since the service was puzzling. As Alex rose to refill the teapot, Janet laid hand on Cally's. 'Are you all right?'

Cally yanked her hand away. 'How can I be, stuck in a room with the two women who have taken my family from me.' Self-pity filled her eyes with tears and they spilled over at the shocked expressions her outburst caused.

Alex shot a look at Janet whose bewilderment was plain to see. Treading carefully, Alex sat back down. 'What do you mean, Cally? We just want to help and….' She broke off at the sound of Cally's laughter.

'Help?' Cally's hand slammed onto the table. 'What did you tell my son today?'

'The truth.'

'Whose truth? Yours? He hates me now. It's bad enough Fee always sided with her father and now Matthew's gone from me, too. Because of your truth!'

Alex and Janet froze, aghast.

'Cally, there were things we didn't tell Matthew because you didn't want him to know. I begged you when he was old enough to understand, to tell him, but you wouldn't.'

Again Cally laughed a terrible laugh. 'Ah, my sister. My wise younger sister.' As Janet rose to her feet, Cally stood too. 'From even before we were married you mooned about him like a bitch on heat and it didn't end when he came home ruined, did it? No. You poured your heart into his, blocking me out, pushing me aside. You deserved each other. The monster and the deceitful bitch!' Janet's slap across her face brought Cally to a gasping stop.

A shocked Alex raised her hands in appeal. 'This isn't the

right time. Please. We're all emotional. Don't say any more things you will regret.'

Cally was shaking so much it seemed incredible she could stay on her feet. From Alex's concern to Janet's anger her eyes flicked to and fro until she found a ragged composure.

'I regret so much already what difference would a few words make?' Dragging tattered self-possession around herself Cally left the venom of her hatred behind.

***

Fee helped Tyke packed her things into her suitcase. 'I wish you weren't leaving.'

'So do I.' Tyke's fervent words were backed by her dread of seeing Moss again. Once or twice she had considered mentioning her confusion about him with the level-headed Fee. Last night she had even opened her mouth only stifle the urge. *Better no one else knew.* Tyke carefully folded her nightgown. 'You could always visit us in Wellington.'

Her cousin visibly brightened. 'I could, couldn't I? I've never been to a city.' Fee remembered Tyke's hairbrush and comb. She picked them up from the dressing table and passed them over.

'Anytime you like, Fee. I'd love it. I would.'

They were supposed to leave in three days' time. It had been on the tip of Tyke's tongue to beg to stay there full time but no one could deny the atmosphere among the adults. Tyke knew they were leaving because her parents and aunts wanted it.

She did a final check around Fee's room to make sure she'd left nothing behind and closed her suitcase with a snap. She would miss her cousins. *Well, to be honest she would miss Fee.* Matthew she had barely seen and the few times she had, he'd been as uncommunicative as Father.

'I'll miss you,' Fee said.

Tyke smiled. 'I was just thinking the same thing.'

One final hug. A promise to write every week and the Brodies left for their journey back to Wellington.

***

Wellington

Maudie had had just about enough of Moss's bad temper. With the rest of the family down south there was only Hugh to act as a buffer between them. She was only grateful the sod worked so bloody hard because it meant the times she saw his scowling face and put up with the slamming doors and general misery was less than it might have been.

Even so, the bugger was proving hard work.

'What the hell's eatin' yer?'

Moss banged the mug he was holding onto the bench. 'Nothing.'

'Don't sound like nuthin'.'

'And yet nothing's what it is.'

Maudie weighed up all the possibilities. 'You seein' that Ida again?'

'No.'

'She seemed all right.'

An exasperated sigh. 'Just drop it, Ma, eh?'

Pause.

'Are yer missin' Tyke?'

'Jesus, Ma! I said drop it!' Which was what he did to his mug of hot tea. It hit the edge of the bench and spilled down his trousers and onto the floor. Moss gave a roar and kicked the mug across the other side of the room before storming out, the front door slamming so loudly Maudie half-expected its window to smash.

Now what the bloody hell was all that about?

When Hugo arrived home he found Maudie sitting on the backdoor step outside the scullery smoking her pipe. With a groan of pleasure he took the weight off his feet and sat beside her. 'Thought you'd given up your pipe.'

'I did while we had no money.' Maudie puffed contentedly. 'Nice to have it back.'

Hugo fished about in his pockets and joined his sister in a

smoke. 'Me and the lad can barely keep up with orders,' he said complacently. 'It's a good year for the black market.'

'Moss is hardly a lad, Hugo. Damn near thirty one. And speaking of the bugger, has he said anythin' to you about anythin'? I can't get a civil word outta him these days.'

'He's been like a bear with a sore head, I'll agree, but no. Sorry, Maud. He's hasn't opened up to me.'

Pause. They both blew smoke rings.

'You know what the French say though, don't you?'

Maudie gave her brother an exasperated glare. 'No, oddly enough I don't bloody know what the bloody Frenchies say.'

' 'Cherchez la femme.' '

'Yer what?'

Hugo pointed his cigarette for emphasis. ' 'Look for the woman.' If a man's in a dark place, ten to one there's a woman at the bottom of his troubles.'

'He hardly knew Ida.'

'Then maybe it's someone you don't know about.' With a final puff on the butt, Hugo ground it out with the toe of his boot and retreated into the house to wash off the day's grime.

Maudie stayed where she was. *The last time Moss had been this bad was all that business with the Chinese girl Jing.* She knew he'd loved her with all the innocent ardour of first love. It tore Moss apart when they were found out and she was ripped from his life. *He's had the occasional girlfriend but nuthin' to compare with Jing. What other woman does he know so well?*

Maudie's pipe had gone out. She continued to puff on it all unawares as her busy mind turned things over.

***

Tyke had been back in Wellington for nearly a month and the city was feeling less and less like home. *What was keeping her here?* Last week she'd started a new job, filing in a lawyer's office. Today she was sacked. Wrong files in the wrong place when the lawyer was due in court. *A mistake anyone could make,* Tyke fumed. When she stalked back home Maudie was hanging laundry in the back yard. As always, Tyke poured out her woes, striding the worn green grass, using language Alex would have disapproved of but which raised no more than an eyebrow from Maudie.

'And I wasn't even given a second chance. If they'd given me a little more training or something, maybe it wouldn't have happened. It's not my bloody fault.'

Maudie removed the final peg from her basket and pegged the last sock. 'Seems t'me, Tyke things ain't never yer fault. 'Bout time yer gave that a bit'o thought.'

'Maudie....'

'No, girl. Yer at an age when others are raising families. Now I ain't sayin' that's gotta be your life but yer've gotta grow up sometime.'

'But...'

'But me no buts. I dunno what's got into yer, Moss either, but that's neither here nor there.' Maudie scooped up the laundry basket and stomped past Tyke. 'Time to grow up, Tyke. Time t'take some responsibility for what yer do.'

If she had shouted and stormed Tyke couldn't have felt worse.

When the rest of the family found out she'd been sacked, well, what could she do but take their reproaches? No matter Father calling her useless, it was no less than Tyke felt anyway. Uncle Hugo didn't take her side this time. For the first time in her life, trouble had come calling and she had no Moss on her side. He had barely made eye contact with her since That Night and was barely at home since they returned from Murchison. She had no help from his quarter. *Something else which was all her fault.*

Sitting cross-legged on her bed, Tyke chewed the end of her pen, trying to find something to write to cousin Fee about. Ink dripped from the nib. It missed the paper completely and soaked into the eiderdown. Too fed up to care, Tyke covered the blot with her paper and pretended it wasn't there.

She had to leave. Lead her own life on her own to prove she could. Whether it was proof to herself or Maudie or everyone else, Tyke couldn't have said, but now the thought had occurred, it took root. Shoving the paper to one side, she slid off the bed and knelt beside her bedside table. Underneath it was the box Moss had carved for her all those years ago. She opened the lid and fingered the silver button from Alex's evening gown which Maudie had given her. *Her first treasure.* As Tyke tucked it under everything, her fingers clutched a little velvet bag which chinked and rustled enticingly. *Her savings.* On her twenty first birthday, Maudie had given her fifty pounds. The amount still took Tyke's breath.

'Yer'll need it one day, girl. Better t'have it ready for when yer do.'

So many things had spun through Tyke's mind. *A new dress. Three new dresses! Shoes which didn't pinch. A holiday for Alex. She could get it all and there would still be money left over.* Nothing seemed right. Something had held her back.

Tyke tipped the pounds and coins onto her lap, fingering the wealth. A fragile root of possibility spread deeper tendrils through her mind.

'Time to grow up, Tyke. Time t'take some responsibility for what yer do.'

Tyke's fist clenched around a ten pound note.

Time to grow up.

The next morning she announced her intention of returning to Murchison.

'I'm fed up with Wellington. Fee said I'd be welcome at their place anytime.' The accompanying glare around the table told each and every one of her family this was more than Tyke felt at home.

Alex was turning over some soothing phrases when Maudie spoke up. 'I'll tell yer true, girl, 'til yer drop that bloody attitude yer'll not be much missed.'

Alex spoke hastily as the storm gathered in Tyke's eyes. 'Darling, if you need to go somewhere to get yourself together, then Fee would be the ideal companion.'

It had been so easy to set the stage but Tyke was left with so many conflicting emotions. *Did Maudie honestly believe that? Did she even care? Thank God they believed her! Then the guilt they had believed her so easily.*

Tyke fought it all down. She remembered Moss with his head bent over his plate. Not once did he glance her way.
'Time to grow up, Tyke. Time t'take some responsibility for what yer do.'

Yes. It was.

***

The post was innocuous enough. One or two bills, a letter for Hugo with a French postmark, then this one. As Maudie handed it to Alex she commented, 'One from Tyke. I wondered when the little bleeder would write.'

Alex smiled, reaching for the letter opener. 'Well, she and Fee got on like a house on fire. No doubt they've been having too much fun to write home.'

'That seems to be most of Tyke's problem. Too much wanting to have fun, not enough getting her head down and workin'.' Maudie grumbled. 'Nuthin' like when I was her age.'

'Oh, Ma. She's young yet.'

'Not so young.' As Maudie watched, Alex's smile dissolved.

Alex couldn't take in what she was reading. The words blurred on the page, smearing together like the ink had run.

'What is it, girl?'

Unable to speak, Alex passed the pages over.

'Dear family

By the time you read this I will be on my way to London. I didn't go to Murchison at all, just passed through on my way to Lyttleton harbour. The kind harbour-master promised to post this a week after we sail.

Everything became too hard. You were right, Mama, you too Maudie. It was time I grew up and lived my own life, wherever it takes me.

Please don't worry about me. I will write when I'm settled. In London! You'll be able to picture where I am, Mama. I hope it hasn't changed so much. I want to see what you saw.

Give love to Moss and tell him I'm sorry. He'll know why.

All my love,

Tyke.'

***

Berlin

Dawn had barely broken when Wilhelm woke, startled into consciousness by an unsettling dream. He was left with no specifics, just a lingering sense of dread. Easing up on one elbow, he wiped his face, trying to focus on externals rather than the nightmare.

His bedroom was also a living space. No heating. He could see his warm breath forming its smoky haze in the chilly air. Outside the door, Kristel was moving around. A metallic bang meant she'd put the kettle on the rusting stove. They had taken these rooms in the months following Jost's arrest. Kristel needed the friendship her cousin gave her and Wilhelm remembered his promise to Jost. He wanted to help where he could, starting with living costs. As the months passed with not a word from Jost, they both feared the worst. So many who disappeared through Dachau's gates died. Although Kristel never gave voice to her worries, Wilhelm could tell she knew. No one worked harder to feed the families of those whose parents were victims of Dachau's insatiable greed.

For five years Hitler and his Nazis had used propaganda and indoctrination to normalise prejudice and fear. The Germany Wilhelm rediscovered at eighteen was gone, that questioning, passionate free-thinking Germany lost. If you didn't follow where Hitler led you were the enemy. If you didn't hate what he hated, feared what he feared, you were the enemy. He drew crowds of thousands, tens of thousands all desperate to believe in the lie – *Germany can be great again. It will be great again. And those who stand in the way of such greatness will force us to war and when they do we will not be found wanting.* Austria had been annexed and there were whispers of marching into Czechoslovakia. Men like Sigmund who had experienced the bloody battlegrounds of the last war shivered as war drums sounded once more in the offices of power.

Wilhelm shook his head to clear it. Picking up his watch, he groaned, throwing his legs out from under the covers. Another day.

Autumn had arrived early, ice in the air signalling a hard winter ahead. Tucking his chin into his scarf, Wilhelm picked up his pace. His work had grown increasingly difficult. Sigmund was hanging on to his position but only just, Joachim champing at his heels. How Emil and Joachim hadn't ousted Sigmund long since was something Wilhelm put down to his uncle's clever vigilance. *They completely underestimated you, Uncle.*

With the Nazis in charge, people were fooled by the look of German prosperity but it came at great cost to so many. Everyone had work now because thousands of K.D.P and S.D.P had been rounded up and removed from the workplace. Jews too had been hounded out of jobs to make way for German workers. Factories worked long hours and with no trade unions to interfere on their behalf, workers were pushed to the limits of their endurance as the regime armed. Accidents increased accordingly, workplace fatalities, too.

Sigmund's factory, like so many, had been taken over to produce weaponry. He looked sick, haunted, the work of his life replaced by Hitler's war machinations.

Wilhelm reached the factory door. Glancing up in surprise he saw light on the second floor. Anger propelled him forward. *Who the hell's in my office?* He marched through his office door, brought up sharply, startled at the sight of Emil Seidel sitting at Wilehlm's desk, openly reading the paperwork he found there.

'Didn't Joachim pass on the list of Jews and socialists employed by you?'

'Yes. Why?'

'I'm just surprised to see them all still working here.' Emil hadn't lifted his eyes from the pages. He appeared completely engrossed, deliberately turning another page.

You arrogant bastard! 'They are good workers. I have no reason to dismiss them.'

'Joachim's list gave you all the reasons you need.' For the first time Emil met Wilhelm's eyes. 'Workers' complaints have increased while output has decreased. Good workers you say? I wonder whether your personal beliefs are affecting your ability to manage this factory satisfactorily.'

Wilhelm slid his hands behind his back where he could ball them into fists, nails biting into palms as he strove for calm. 'My ability and judgement have never been called into question before.'

All Emil's composure fled as he slapped his hands down on the desk. 'You have never made such a serious misjudgement before!' A finger stabbed down onto the paperwork. 'These men are gone. Tomorrow. We will not have traitors or Jews working for us.'

It took massive effort for Wilhelm not to let his anger show on his face. *You marry my cousin, treat us like shit on your boots. Who are the 'us'? The fucking Nazis?* Not by a blink of an eye did his thoughts betray him as he nodded. 'I will speak with Uncle Sigmund.' A reply which promised nothing.

'You do that,' came Emil's smooth reply, 'while you still can.'

His comment sat as sour bile in Wilhelm's stomach as he met privately with Sigmund.

'We've reached crisis point, Uncle. We can no longer protect these men without compromising ourselves to a dangerous degree.'

'And Calev?'

'Will not go. I've begged. I've tried reason. He remains adamant.'

The light from the hearth spilled out around their chairs as they sat by the fire in Sigmund's library, the curtains drawn against the night. No other lights were on. Two worried men surrounded by shadows, the allegory not lost on a sombre Wilhelm.

Sigmund leaned forward to place another log into the depth of the embers, sparks spitting over the marble hearth. One landed on the carpet at the toe of his shoe and he ground it out. 'Things are about to get even worse. I heard today Jews' passports are to be invalidated. No one will say when, only that it will happen. If Calev doesn't get his family out of Germany, the time will come when he will not be able to. We've heard Emil speak of the new camps being built, ready to house thousands. Who are they for, Wilhelm? They have already locked away the opposition.' Sigmund seemed entranced by the flames. 'My contact whispered something to me. *The Jewish solution,*' he said, and would say no more.' Sigmund didn't blink, the orange flames dancing on his features.

'There might be one way to convince Calev.' At Sigmund's hopeful expression, Wilhelm temporised. 'It's not pleasant.'

His uncle dismissed that with a wave of an impatient hand. 'Just speak your mind.'

'Calev stays out of loyalty and friendship. What if we tell him he's a liability? We can no longer sustain his friendship?'

Silence.

'He wouldn't believe it.'

'He would if it came from you.' Silence. 'Calev won't go unless you break him, Uncle.'

Silence.

Sigmund closed his eyes. *A bombed out trench. He's bleeding out from a wound he can't staunch. The arrival of a stranger also wearing a German uniform. A stranger who saves his life at great risk to his own and becomes a lifelong friend. Calev. Closer than family.* Drawing in a ragged breath Sigmund's voice grew husky. 'He's a brother to me.'

Wilhelm replied softly. 'All the more reason to save him.'

Sigmund turned away but not before the firelight caught the sheen of tears.

I admire your strength, Uncle.

After a time, Sigmund cleared his throat. 'How's Kristel?' He could barely speak her name without the hurt showing.

'She's as well as she can be.'

'Freya and I miss her.'

'And she misses you both. Never doubt it.'

Emil and Inge never set up a home of their own. Life was too easy living with Sigmund and Freya. *Another cost to grind his uncle down.* Reluctant to give it all to Emil, Sigmund held on. *For how much longer, Uncle?*

'Thank you for looking after her.'

'We look after each other.'

Sigmund laid a hand over his nephew's. 'Thank you anyway. You have been a blessing in dark times.'

'I have always been grateful for your love and acceptance.'

It was too much. Sigmund left the room, left Wilhelm to the shadows.

Unable to let him face it alone, Wilhelm was at Sigmund's side in the Altmeyer's comfortable home. The family's welcome was heart-breaking, knowing what was to come. Sigmund refused food and drink. He kept his coat on, his face stern and unyielding.

Calev's confusion at this reception was mirrored by his family. 'Old friend. It is cold enough outside without this.' Calev's hand gesture covered Sigmund from head to foot as he smiled.

'I am not here to make pleasantries, Calev.'

'Sigmund....'

'I'm here to dismiss you. You have to go.'

'Must we have this discussion again? Germany is my home. I have fought for this country and I will not be chased away like a thief in the night.'

'Our government has killed or imprisoned their political opponents and those who would resist them. The newspapers and radio only carry stories supportive of the Nazi regime, any journalist who reveals anything questioning the party line disappears. There is no one left to speak out against them, Calev. And with no one to challenge them they have a mandate to violate every democratic law. Whoever they hate, they destroy. They hate and destroyed all their political opposition. And they hate Jews, my friend. You have seen this. They're coming for your people.'

'I will stay.' Calev looked around at his family. 'We will stay.'

'Then you give me no choice.' Sigmund hardened his heart. 'I will no longer employ a Jew.' Calev's wife Nurat gasped as her husband's smile melted away. 'You are a danger to the business and to my family. There is no place for you.' Sigmund clicked his fingers and Wilhelm passed over an envelope. 'I won't have you say I didn't pay what was owed.' Unable to bear the look on Calev's ravaged face, Sigmund turned to the door, pausing with his hand on the latch. 'My son-in-law will ensure you leave Berlin. For the sake of your family, leave Germany.'

From the Altmeyer's they made straight for Joachim's where Sigmund resigned from the company he established all those decades ago.

Wilhelm never saw his uncle smile again.

***

Without Sigmund to back him up, Wilhelm lost the ability to employ those he wanted to protect. Changes were made overnight and every worker with any connection to the K.D.P or S.D.P were laid off. Thanks to Wilhelm, some managed to keep their heads down and earn a living. For the rest, the only way to resist the Nazis was through a struggling resistance movement. Anyone involved risked their lives and knew it. It didn't stop Wilhelm and it didn't stop Kristel. It wasn't a strongly organised resistance, too many deaths and arrests had taken their toll on the remaining militants. With no overt political movement to strengthen or sustain them, those who chose to fight did so underground. Printing presses were set up for small newspapers or if that wasn't possible, pamphlets were handwritten. These were then distributed to let others know they weren't alone. *We too refuse to believe in Nazi propaganda. We too denounce Hitler and his cronies.*

The underground did whatever it could but it wasn't as much as they wanted to do for the danger was very real. They all knew of the young woman found carrying pamphlets. Her husband received her ashes in a small box.

***

Thankfully the streets were busy. Kristel checked her shopping bag, making sure the pamphlets lay flat on the bottom under some second-hand clothes and other odds and ends she had picked up. Walking seemingly without purpose, Kristel strolled in and out of a printer's shop, bumping into a man in the doorway. Half a block from there she wandered into a bookshop. Further on another bookshop, this one selling mostly second-hand and antiquarian books. An innocuous greeting, a request for a book to be ordered and she only had a few pamphlets left. *One more stop then home.* She was halfway to her final destination when she passed a familiar face. He studied her, the look so furtive, Kristel risked a glance back as if checking something in the shop window she was passing. He was staring after her - the same man she bumped into earlier. With a throb of alarm Kristel picked up her pace a little while not appearing to hurry. A florist shop gave her an excuse to buy some flowers, one eye on the pavement as the man passed. He checked his step as he pulled something out of a pocket and studied it. Nothing more than a man checking his bearings who peered in through the florist's window before moving away. Alarmed now, Kristel left the shop, the flowers tucked into her basket. She tried to walk nonchalantly, every nerve screaming at her to run. The man was on the other side of the road but when she turned down an unexpected side-street, he re-crossed. When she looked back over her shoulder he made no pretence, his face grimly determined as he followed her. *One more block then safely home.* Kristel began to run. Veering right she headed for the last corner and ran into someone standing in her path.

Emil.

'I do beg your pardon, Emil. I'm late.'

'So I gathered. Can I help?' He held his hand out for her basket.

Kristel shifted it further down her arm. 'No. It's not heavy.'

'But I insist.'

Kristel took a wary step backwards only to discover her pursuer blocking her exit. 'Emil, I will be late.'

'What for?'

'I'm taking clothes to a family nearby. They will be worried if I'm not on time.'

'If they're the kind of people I believe they are, they have more to worry about than your tardiness.' So much threat deliberately understated.

Kristel could barely swallow. This time when Emil clicked his fingers she passed him the basket. He didn't hesitate, deftly uncovering the last of the pamphlets. Emil held them up to the light before surveying her with triumphant eyes.

'Where did you acquire these?'

Show him no fear. Give him nothing. Kristel met Emil's eyes coolly. 'I found them.'

'Where?'

A considering frown, the pretence of thought. 'I don't remember.'

Silence.

Emil closed the space between them. A hair's breadth from Kristel he confronted her nonchalance with something altogether more unnerving. 'I know you're protecting them. I know you think you're doing the right thing. I know Wilhelm is deeper in the resistance than we ever thought. But,' he reached out to stroke her face, Kristel jerking her head away. Emil's fingers clenched. 'But, your family connections cannot save you.'

'Cannot?'

A chilling smile. 'Will not.'

These men in their stylish grey uniforms were capable of utter ruthlessness. Never had Kristel felt such a swooping rush of fear. Never had she been as brave for Emil never knew it. She drew herself upright, defiance in every syllable. 'Then let the dice fall as they may. I have nothing to say to you.'

'So be it.' With a click of his fingers her brother-in-law watched as Kristel was taken away.

After two days with no sign of Kristel, Wilhelm confronted Joachim.

'You must know where she is.'

Joachim viewed his cousin almost lazily. 'Why must I?'

Pause.

'Because she was taken from the street. None of the people she cares for has seen her. She has not been home. The only conclusion is, she's been taken by the S.A or S.S.'

'If my sister was involving herself in causes which run contrary to the Fuhrer's interests, to Germany's interests, then why are you worried?'

Wilhelm lost his calm, both hands slamming on the desk top as he loomed over it.

'Kristel is family. My family. Your family! Surely you must be concerned if anyone is?'

Silence.

Wilhelm studied the face before him, trying to find the cousin he admired all those years ago. But that man was gone. *Who are you, Joachim?*

'Five years ago Kristel made her choice. She ran from her family and married a man who was a traitor to his country. Why should I concern myself over such a sister?' Pause. Joachim picked up a pen, running it between his fingers. 'You need to take care, cousin. Your sympathies may compromise you. You no longer have my father to appeal to, remember?'

Silence.

Wilhelm eased away from the desk, bitterly disappointed and more than a little lost. He lowered his tone. 'Please, Joachim. If you know where she is, at least tell me she's safe .'

For long moments Joachim said nothing. Something in Wilhelm's expression must have resonated because he laid down the pen, linking his hands on the desktop as he spoke. 'She was given a choice and chose to work in Labour Service in East Prussia. Now, I'm a busy man, so if you'll excuse me?' Joachim indicated the door and Wilhelm left. Joachim never mentioned exactly what choice Kristel had been given other than banishment to East Prussia.

A brother exiling his sister. That's what it means now to be German.

***

Wilhelm knew he should leave Berlin. *What was there to keep him here now?* But Joachim's traitorous refusal to help his sister hardened something in him. There was still an underground opposition, however fragile. He would continue to do what he could. *For Jost. For Kristel. For Aunt Freya and Uncle Sigmund.*

His first thought was for the printing press. If Kristel had been caught delivering pamphlets, maybe she had been forced to say where they came from. *And what about Kristoff?* They had hidden not only the printing press, but given sanctuary to a prominent S.D.P leader who the Nazis had hunted down and left for dead. Kristoff was only now regaining enough strength to be spirited away. He had his new passport and papers and was waiting for the word to get out through the underground.

As worried as he was, Wilhelm waited impatiently to use the dark of the following morning's early hours to make his cautious way to the deserted wine cellar. To his relief, Kristoff was setting the type for the next pamphlet run.

Ah, cousin. Your bravery is an inspiration.

'They've taken Kristel.'

Kristoff paused in his work. 'I'm sorry my friend but surely her family...?' He broke off as Wilhelm shook his head. 'Then I'm even more sorry.'

Finding the sympathy difficult to cope with, Wilhelm gave a curt nod and focussed on the trestle where other pamphlets waited to be distributed. Kristoff left the press and leaned his backside against the table. 'There's word of a-pogrom against the Jews.'

'How'd you hear about it?'

A miniscule shrug. 'I had to get out for a breath of fresh air.'

Anger coloured Wilhelm's face. 'Jesus, Kristoff. You risk being seen!'

'I know. I do, but it's hard, Wilhelm not to be part of the world.'

Wilhelm reined in his temper with a tight smile. 'Well, I suppose you're not a prisoner, are you?'

A smile lit Kristoff's sombre face. 'Not yet. Thanks to my friends.'

'So what about these whispers?'

The smile vanished. 'The S.S are organising something. I overheard a group of Hitler Youth, smirking and bragging, looking forward to 'giving the Jews a message'. We need to get out some kind of warning.'

'About what? A vague rumour? We'd cause panic and if nothing happens what will it say about us?'

'Are you afraid, Wilhelm?'

'Of course I'm bloody afraid! I've spent the last five years feeling afraid. I think, 'It can't get any worse,' and bang! It gets worse. Every year the Nazis target another enemy and I wonder, why won't people fight back? And I know why. Of course I know. They're scared. They know they could well be next. And every day men and women disappear or are murdered and the world still turns.'

Silence.

Kristoff spoke in a low voice. 'I am a socialist and a Jew. Damned twice over and I refuse to let them make me afraid.'

'Then you are a better man than me.' Wilhelm turned away heartsick, busying his hands as he strove not to dwell on Kristel and Jost. And failed.

Silently they worked at their individual tasks. Alwin appeared looking for pamphlets to deliver, shifting uneasily as he waited for Wilhelm to sort through some.

'Why are you so fidgety?'

'Thought someone was following me. They weren't,' Alwin added hastily at the looks he got. 'Just jumpy, I guess.'

'Not necessarily.' Wilhelm made his way out of the cellar to peer around the empty buildings, all looming shadows and menace in the moonlit dark. Cautiously he darted through the broken yard, eyes skimming the doorways he could make out. Soft footfalls sounded and he shoved back between two derelict storage buildings, scarcely breathing. Someone coughed, hastily choking back the sound and there, back towards the entrance he saw two bodies flitting between shadows, the first rays of dawn light picking out the long, rifle barrels. Heart in his mouth Wilhelm dashed back towards the cellar, taking the internal route though it was a little longer. He needed not to be seen. Reaching the stone steps down to the cellar, he hauled the metal gate at the top closed, padlocking it behind him.

Alwin waited on the bottom steps. 'What's up?' he hissed.

'They've found us.'

'Oh, Jesus....'

Kristoff cuffed Alwin in anger. 'You fool! They followed you!'

Poor Alwin stammered. 'I didn't see..... I never....'

Wilhelm grabbed Alwin's shoulder. 'You are not to blame. They could just as easily have followed me. Now, you know what we have to do.' He steered Alwin into the cellar and locked that door behind them, too before facing Kristoff. 'They're minutes away.'

'Armed?'

Wilhelm nodded.

Alwin slid to the floor, hands over his face. 'Oh God. Oh, God. Oh, God...' the words slurred by fear.

Hauling the lad to his feet, Wilhelm pulled his satchel off his shoulder and threw it into a corner. 'We leave through the back way. We split up once we reach the alley. Don't look back.' Alwin's eyes were black pools but he headed for the trapdoor hidden under the clutter in an unused back room. Wilhelm beckoned to Kristoff. 'Come on.'

For the length of several heartbeats Wilhelm thought he wouldn't move until with a final glance round, Kristoff grabbed a sack containing his belongings. When they reached the exit, Alwin was nowhere to be seen. Wilhelm mouthed a silent prayer, helping Kristoff who couldn't haul his body out of the small tunnel. Once on his feet, Kristoff gasped, gripping his side and Wilhelm noticed the stain of seeping blood.

The injured man waved the concern away. 'The stitches tore. Forget it. Let's just get out of here.'

Wilhelm replaced the cover and together they turned into the alleyway, Kristoff's breath covering gasps of pain. Somewhere near them came the ominous metallic click of a loaded rifle. The two men froze as light spilled from the end of the alley where a car was parked. To their right someone stepped from a doorway, a terrified Alwin held securely, pistol at his head. The owner of the rifle moved in. They thought there was just the one but he was joined by two others.

'Traitors.' The word was almost whispered by the man holding Alwin. In a horrifying movement, he rammed the terrified boy against the nearest wall and shot him.

'Bastard!' Kristoff roared and lunged only to be gunned down by rifle fire.

The soft-voiced man stepped into the light revealing Emil, his mouth curving upwards. For the first time Wilhelm knew what it was to feel no fear. He met the other man's eyes and breathed in. Emil lifted his pistol. He squeezed the trigger, his eyes on Wilhelm's body as it tumbled down onto the alley floor.

***

'First they came for the Communists and I did not speak out because I was not a Communist.
Then they came for the Socialists and I did not speak out because I was not a Socialist.
Then they came for the Trade Unionists and I did not speak out because I was not a Trade Unionist.
Then they came for the Jews but I did not speak out because I was not a Jew.
Then they came for me
And there was no one left to speak out for me.'

Pastor Martin Niemoller

Part II

1939-1945

London

Tyke adored London. From the moment she arrived with her suitcase in one hand and a guide to the city in the other it was love at first sight. For the first couple of weeks she had rented a room that was too expensive to keep but would do while she found her bearings. The whole experience was overwhelming, excitingly so. Alex's stories were brought to life - the lions guarding Trafalgar Square, her first sight of the Tower of London. Noisy, dirty, lively. It was everything Wellington, New Zealand wasn't. Tyke viewed it all with awe and unjudgemental eyes right up until the afternoon she was pick-pocketed. The operation had been so slick, the young girl so innocent seeming as she begged, Tyke couldn't even be angry. From that day on though, she tucked her purse into her bodice, lesson learned. As she gawped, Wellington teased her conscience. *I should write. Let them know I'm here at least. They would be fretting, wouldn't they?* But this was her chance to be just Tyke with no preconceptions, just who she was at this moment. Which was all very brave and self-reliant but she missed Moss so much it hurt, every thought of him giving her a queasy ache of pain and pleasure.

Stop it! Right now! You escaped it all. Moss as well. Time to grow up, remember? Eventually to ease her nagging conscience Tyke did write a letter home. She told them she was safe and happy and would write again sometime – no return address on the envelope. She would make contact with the past on her terms only.

Sight-seeing with no income became expensive so Tyke found cheaper digs above a clothing factory in the hustle and bustle of Petticoat Market. She browsed through the different stalls, mesmerised by the speedy patter of every salesman and amused by the fact that although these people were speaking English, she could barely understand a word they were saying. Thanks to Hugo, she had a smattering of the cockney argot but a smattering was all it was.

Then came the day she met Sidney Harris.

It was late one afternoon. Fog swirled around the edges of the city although nothing like the pea-soupers which muffled sound and were so thick people walked around with fingers pressed against a wall or fence unable to see a hand held up to their face. It was substantial enough however to make the air damp and clammy, making Tyke aware of her light-weight coat. *Have to find a warmer one.* Shivering slightly she prepared to call it a day when raucous laughter piqued her curiosity and she wandered a little further to find its source. A young man stood on an upturned box, surrounded by about a dozen women. He was giving them his best sales pitch on some old china. Whatever he said caused hilarity, yet his audience proved as canny as they were keen for a spectacle. He didn't sell one thing. It didn't daunt him though. As one group moved on another formed and off he went, as enthusiastic and funny as ever. Turning from him, Tyke paused in front of a stall selling bits and bobs. Her eyes fell on a tin soldier in a blue coat, a tiny musket in his right hand. With a gasp she picked it up, rotating it around in her fingers. *Just like Father's! She had to have it.*

Catching the eye of the short, stocky stallholder with a deeply pitted face she raised the toy up. 'How much for this?'

He smiled, showing missing teeth. 'Can tell you're a steamer. You neva arsk for a price, gel. You tell me what yer think it's worth.'

Tyke studied the tin soldier with pursed lips. 'Give you a shilling for it.'

On cue the stall-holder erupted into indignation. 'A bleeding shilling! Whaddya think I'm doin' here? Wastin' my bleedin' time? That there's worth two good bob of anyone's money.'

'All right, then. Fair enough.' Tyke fished about in a pocket and pulled out two shillings. 'Here you go.' The man gaped at her. He didn't take the money and Tyke pressed further.

'Don't you want it? It's the right coins, you know.' She became uncomfortable under his incredulous stare. 'What?'

'Bleedin' steamer,' he repeated. Giving Tyke a look of pity he tipped his cap off his crown to scratch the top of his head. 'Where you from, then?'

'New Zealand.'

'It's down the ways, innit? Past Australia, like.'

Pleased to meet someone who recognised her country, Tyke beamed. 'That's right.' Something occurred to her. 'What's a steamer?'

The man's expression softened. 'Look, love,' he took the toy out of her hand. 'This here piece of junk's worth no more than tuppence.'

'Why tell me it's worth two shillings then?'

''Cause you'dve bleedin' paid two shillings for it! I've gorra livin' t'make, haven't I? And a steamer's gullible, gel. Wot's more, you're the biggest steamer I ever met!'

It was outrageous. Tyke burst into laughter as she handed over two pennies and tucked the soldier away in her pocket.

'Here, wot's your name?'

'Tyke.'

Sidney was captivated by the young woman's strange accent, instinctively knowing it would be a draw-card to his stall. 'Want a job?'

'What yer got, cully? Will I be on me plates of meat all day?'

Her mimic entertained him hugely. 'Well, forget being a Cockney, love. I reckon that strange accent of yours'll go down a right treat on my stall. Fancy it? If yer don't like it we'll go our separate ways, no love lost.'

Tyke was thrilled at the prospect of work. 'Go on then.'

Sidney spent the rest of the afternoon giving her lessons in bartering then the very next day stuck Tyke on the stall, always half a step behind to keep an ear out. He needn't have bothered. She proved not only quick-witted but the draw-card he imagined. Hugo's lessons in cockney rhyming slang plus the bits she had already picked up, all coupled with her New Zealand twang made great patter. For the first few weeks while Tyke was a talking point, things flew off the stall, chinaware, books, second-hand clothes and now and again the pieces of silverware Sidney handed her with a wink.

'Sell 'em quick as you can, girl. And don't let no charpering omi get a gander.' He anticipated her question. 'That's a policeman copping a peek to you.'

Tyke's stall became a popular one, everyone wanting to speak to the girl from the bottom of the world.

'Thought you were all blacks down that way?'

'Ain't you all cannibals?'

'You live with kangaroos and whatnot, don't yer. How d'yer catch them? What do they taste like?'

So many questions. Easy to keep the banter flowing. *You catch kangaroos by trapping them with honey. The meat tastes a bit like chicken. We're only cannibals if we can't catch a kangaroo. Yes, you can swim to New Zealand from Australia, but only if the tide's right. Some people swim the distance on a kangaroo's back.*

Tyke's stall emptied of all goods but the shabbiest. Sidney too was hugely entertained by her nonsense and pleased with her honesty and hard work. Now and then he slipped her an extra half-crown or bit of fruit or meat off another stall and after a few weeks his wife Mavis offered a place to stay.

'My Sid always says you gorra keep a good worker happy.'

Tyke happily moved her belongings into their tiny box room, grateful to be part of a family again. It was all tumultuous, hectic fun.

***

It had been a long week, the stall shut up late that Saturday night. Yawning hugely as she sat with Mavis and Sidney over their supper, Tyke thought pleasureably of her Sunday off, making plans to explore the city more.

Sid squeezed Mavis's hand as she cleared the table. 'Duke's Head?'

'Why not? Tyke hasn't been, has she?'

On hearing her name Tyke snapped out of her reverie. 'I haven't been where?'

Sid grinned. 'The East End's best pub, that's all.'

The Duke's Head was heaving with drinkers and rowdy voices and over it all cigarette haze vied with smoke from the blackened fireplace. Mavis used her elbows to get them a place at the bar, immediately turning to greet an old friend. Sidney made sure they all had a drink by asking for, 'Three shanks of wallop, Boo,' before disappearing to play darts. Tyke happily propped up the sticky bar, sipping at her glass and lapping up the sights. She was trying to get the attention of the barmaid for another drink when the piano in the far corner sprang into action and a woman's voice, young and tuneful brought the pub to silence.

''Embrace me, my sweet embraceable you.

Embrace me, my irreplaceable you.''

Tyke edged to one side and saw the singer leaning against the piano, glass of beer in one hand as she sang so sweetly.

''Just one look at you my heart went tipsy in me.

You and you alone bring out the gypsy in me.''

First softly, then with growing power everyone in the pub joined along. The final line, *'My sweet embraceable you!'* was followed by cheering and stamping of feet, cries for more.

The young singer lifted her empty beer glass. 'Keep yer hair on yer noisy bleeders! A girl needs a drink, first.' And she forced a way through the press to stand beside an awe-struck Tyke.

'That was beautiful.' Tyke was painfully aware of sounding breathless.

The sweet, cheeky face melted instantly into a proud grin. 'Thanks, ducks. Gorra do it, don't yer.' A fresh beer appeared in front of her and she winked at the barman roguishly. 'Ta, Boo. On the slate?'

'It's on me, Chezz. You keep them singing and they'll wanna keep drinking.'

'Reckon we should be partners.'

Boo grinned, showing missing teeth. 'Dunno what my old lady'll say to that!'

' 'Good luck wiv him Cherry,' I reckon.'

Boo the barman shook a fist in mock annoyance as he moved away. Tyke couldn't take her eyes off Cherry's blonde hair and brown eyes.

'Got yer box brownie with yer? A photo'll last longer.'

Tyke hastily concentrated on her glass. 'Sorry.'

'Only teasin'. It's when people ain't starin' that yer gorra worry.' She held out a hand. 'I'm Cherry Red.' She leaned towards Tyke confidingly. 'But it's not my real name.'

'Isn't it? What is it, then?'

'Hetty Griffiths.' Cherry screwed up her face.

Tyke laughed. 'I have to say you don't look like a Hetty.'

'And I don't know no singer called Hetty, never mind Griffiths. So I decided to be Cherry. Cherry Red.' She reached into her handbag and pulled out a lipstick. 'I've even gorra bit of slap to match.' A quick swirl to prove the point and refresh the colour. 'Who are you?'

'Jeannie Brodie but you can call me Tyke.'

'Where you from, then? Up North somewhere? Can't place yer accent none.'

The piano bashed out a honky-tonk rhythm, so Tyke lifted her voice. 'New Zealand.'

'Never heard of it.'

'It's in the Pacific Ocean.' Tyke could tell by Cherry's expression her explanation didn't help. 'We're part of the British Empire.'

'Are you? Oh, well, that's all right, then. Means we're friends, don't it? Do you like singing?'

Tyke grimaced. 'When others do it. I sound like a cat screeching.'

Cherry snorted into her beer. 'So happens I love cats. You can listen to me, then.'

It was the start of a wonderful friendship. Tyke woke up back in her bed so could only assume Cherry put her there. Certainly, Mavis had a thing or two to say about the tart from down the Duke's Head being in her house which made Tyke feel very uncomfortable. In spite of Mavis's disapproval, Cherry and Tyke became firm friends. In no time, they found digs together, an attic room in Spitalfields. Tyke kept working with Sidney and Cherry had a job as a nippy waitress in a Lyon's Corner Café. Their evenings they spent in a pub, any pub which took their fancy. It was party time whenever they went out, all thanks to the outgoing Cherry and her voice.

One special night after she raised the roof a bloke sauntered up to her.

'Hey Doll. I'm getting a band together. I reckon you'll be great in it.'

After sizing him from head to toe Cherry went straight to the heart of it. 'Do I get paid?'

'Course you do! We're professionals, Doll and there's always room for a great singer. Whaddya think?'

Cherry could never resist admiring stares and Tommy had a repertoire of those. 'What's your name?'

'Tommy.'

'No second name?'

'Smith.'

'Smith, eh? Suppose I could give it a go. If I don't like it, I'm walking.'

Tommy leaned so close she felt his breath on her cheek. 'So long as I can watch as you sashay away Doll, you got a deal.'

With Cherry fronting Tommy and his Fat Cats, the band went down a treat. There was somewhere to sing most nights and on the occasions there weren't, Cherry sang anyway.

Tyke had never met anyone like her. While the band played, Tyke led the cheering.

One night the girl from New Zealand caught her reflection in the mirror behind the bar. With a contented air she patted her hair, tucked under in the roll-style Cherry taught her and dabbed a finger on her painted lips. She wasn't a gawky, awkward naïve girl from the bottom of the world anymore.

They thought it would last like this forever.

***

3rd September 1939 England declares war on Germany.

'Come back here yer little bleeders!' Cherry's screech rang out over the street.

In answer, her three brothers yanked down their short trousers and showed their bare arses. Before she could move they giggled and dashed off, her curses bouncing off the alley walls. All Tyke could do was laugh, holding her side as a stitch cut her breath, unable to stop.

'Those buggers'll have a wallop if our Dad catches them! Mind, he'll have to stand in line 'cause I'm gonna knock seven bells outta them.' Cherry rounded on Tyke in disgust. 'Fat lotta good you are! Laughing yerself sick at my predicament.'

'I can't help it,' Tyke wiped her streaming eyes. 'That's the funniest thing I've seen in forever.'

Cherry's mum had passed her the responsibility of getting the boys onto the evacuation train. None of them wanted to leave London. In vain Cherry explained the threat of Hitler and his bombs. She told them about raids, gas attacks and general mayhem only to realise much, much too late these were all things her brothers were bound to find exciting.

'Yer could all be killed. Think on it.' Petey, the youngest waggled his head, one finger exploring his left nostril until she clouted him about the ear. 'And stop that. It's disgusting.'

Bran eyed his sister warily. He might be as big as her but Cherry had a punch capable of felling a lad twice her size. Taking a cautious step backwards he marshalled his arguments. 'Mum needs the money we bring in, Chezz. You know that. And wiv Dad joining up, she'll need it even more.'

'It's Mum wants you lot gone.' Morgan jostled his youngest brother who shouldered him back only to get a thick ear. As Petey bellowed Cherry muttered, 'And I can't blame her. Look, they want all kids gone to safety, don't they? Stands to reason.'

'Why don't you have to go?' Bran's expression darkened. 'You're only a coupla years older than me.'

'Them coupla years count, though. So you three gorra get

305

packed and I'll take yer to the station.' Cherry's slim supply of patience was running out.

'Don't wanna go.' Bran's mouth clamped shut on his defiance.

With their oldest brother leading the way, the other two mirrored his stance.

Morgan added, 'Yeah. We ain't going. And you can't make us, Chezz.'

Silence.

An ominous gathering of clouds on their immediate horizon caused Bran to whack Morgan over the head. 'You bloody idiot!'

'Oh can't I?' To the scared boys Cherry seemed to swell to twice her size as she grabbed them all by the neck of their jerseys and shook them. 'You little buggers will get home and get packed or by Christ it'll be a black and blue day for yez!'

Wriggling like fury they managed to jerk free. Then they raced down the alley and that was when Morgan stopped to bare his arse, the others following suit in gales of boisterous laughter.

With her friend glaring down the alleyway, the boys gone from view, Tyke managed to calm down enough to ask, 'So what are you going to do about them?'

'Nuthin. They'll head home and Mum'll have their stuff ready. No way they'll defy me that much.'

In spite of Tyke's scepticism it proved true. By the time she and Cherry arrived at the tenement room, the three boys had been scrubbed by Alice, red faces showing the vigour of the rubbing. At their feet, each boy had a brown paper bag with their meagre belongings inside. Alice knelt in front of them, slipping a string-threaded piece of cardboard about each neck. The tags were headed: *Government Evacuation Scheme* then each boy's name, address, date of birth and the school they attended. That last made them all smirk. They hardly ever went to school.

'Now, Bran. You gorra tell them. You boys ain't to be separated. You look out for each other. Promise.'

Bran blinked furiously, determined not to cry. He bit down on the inside of his cheek so hard it hurt. The ploy worked and his tears retreated, not enough for him to speak safely though so he nodded calmly even as his heart hammered. They'd never left their home even for one night. *And what about them strange buggers in the country? All the animal shit and trees and stuff?* Not only had they never left home, they had never left the city, either. The normally irrepressible Morgan was pale and his throat was working hard, too. Only Petey openly showed his fear, mouth trembling as silent tears spilled down his red cheeks. Cherry watched all this closely. At the sign of Petey's tears the fragile Alice began to crumble.

With their mother on the verge of a collapse, Cherry moved briskly among them. 'Come on Petey. Yer'll have a ball in the country.' She hugged him, feeling pity as he clung to her in desperation, the pity increasing when with massive effort the little boy pulled back from the brink and stood tall, wiping his sleeve across his eyes, then his nose.

Bran, too stepped up, hugging Alice. 'It'll be a great laugh, mum. We'll have tons of food and get as fat as pigs, you'll see.'

'Yer'll remember yer promise?'

'Course. Not that I wanna spend the war minding out for these babies,' Bran scowled, faking scorn.

Morgan raged indignantly as Petey protested loudly that he weren't no baby no more and anyway, he didn't need no looking after. Bran could look after hisself. Bran exchanged a look with Cherry who nodded her gratitude at a job well done.

The railway station was heaving. Women with clipboards dashed here and there, herding children into their appropriate groups, trying to be heard above the clamour. With Tyke's help Cherry managed to grab the attention of a harassed looking woman.

'These here are my brothers. The Griffiths.'

The woman scanned her clipboard. Right. Bran, Morgan and Peter?'

'Petey.'

Making a quick scribble to that effect on her list, the woman gave them a tight smile. 'Their train leaves very soon. Make your way to the carriage over there.' She waved a hand behind them. 'Someone will count you on board. You have everything?'

Two mute nods from Morgan and Petey and a forceful, 'Yes, ma'am,' from Bran.

'Good. Then hurry up and say your goodbyes.' She rushed off leaving the little group standing motionless amidst the waves of bustle.

'Come on, then. Get in and nab good seats.' Cherry led the way, Tyke bringing up the rear.

As they reached the train door, Petey brightened. 'We ain't never been on no train before. I just realised.'

'There yer go. Yer first big adventure.' There was a betraying huskiness to Cherry's voice. She coughed to cover it, grabbing each brother in turn and hugging him tightly. 'Be good and don't let our Mum down none. Or me, neither.'

Bran grinned. 'You do that to yerself, Chezz,' and laughed as she punched his arm.

A final look, a final nod and Bran was gone, herding the younger two boys in front of him.

Cherry and Tyke waited on the platform until the three pale faces appeared at a window, smiling bravely. The whistle blew and the train began to pull slowly away. Cherry waved and waved even after the boys couldn't see her anymore. Finally the tracks were empty and Cherry remained there watching after her brothers.

Gently Tyke tugged her hand. 'Come on, Chezz. How about a cuppa and a scone? My treat.'

'Could do wiv summat a bit stronger than tea.'

'Let's do it, then.'

Cherry hauled a handkerchief from her handbag to blow her nose noisily. 'Don't look so concerned, Tyke. I'll be glad to see the back of the little buggers,' she said, fooling no one least of all Tyke.

***

With so many children having disappeared out of the city, street life seemed strange. A definite sense of mounting threat began to colour life. Blackout regulations were enforced which made moving through the streets at night or in the fog downright dangerous at times for people were killed when vehicles ran up on pavements.

Even as the phoney war continued Cherry carried blithely on through the days, singing with Tommy and the band until a poster caught her eye. 'You know summat? We should do our duty.' She made this solemn pronouncement as she and Tyke sat squashed together on a bus, the poster inches from their noses.

'Like what?' Tyke read the recruitment message dubiously. She didn't fancy slaving in a field somewhere growing potatoes. She was sure it wouldn't be as much fun as the laughing face on the poster led them to believe, especially once winter hit.

'I dunno. Summat anyway. As long as we don't have to answer to no toffee-nosed bitch with a Churchill complex.'

They tried a few types of war work, finally settling on sewing uniforms in a huge warehouse. The sewing machines clattered away hour after hour, their working days made bearable by the camaraderie of their work mates. Tyke learned everything she wanted to know, and a whole lot she didn't, about the male anatomy just by listening to the rowdy conversations. Stewart the foreman walked up and down the long aisles trying to keep 'his women' focussed on the job in hand and he was only partly successful. No one took Old Stew seriously because Big Annie had settled his hash early on with a threat that they weren't no slaves and Stew better get his mind wrapped around the fact or he'd be seeing fucking stars. Stew quickly and without fuss, wrapped his mind around the fact.

The whistles blew signalling the end of the day. Tyke yawned and began to clear up around her machine. As she reached down to the over-flowing material scraps bin, a brown pair of arms beat her to it.

'I'll grab it, love. Get on your way, eh? You'll be back here soon enough tomorrow.'

Tyke's complaint about not needing any help died on her lips when she met the blue/green eyes. Aware of the drawn out pause she hastily gathered her wits. 'Thanks.'

He held out a hand. 'I'm Rob, by the way. Don't think we've been introduced.'

Tyke accepted the hand. 'Tyke.'

'By name and by nature?'

'So some would say.' Without her noticing, they had wandered to the big metal cases out behind the warehouse.

Rob tipped Tyke's bin into one labelled for rags. They stood awkwardly for a moment or two.

'Well, Tyke, see you round, I suppose.'

Taken by surprise at the abruptness of his departure Tyke didn't reply. Disconcerted, she returned to her station to pick up her bag and coat before dashing out to find Cherry who was waiting impatiently at the factory gates. Tyke's enthusiasm lasted all the way back home.

For once Cherry was unable to get a word in. Once in the flat and fed up with hearing about Rob already, she went straight to the mirror, hoping her friend would take the point. *No such bleedin' luck!*

Tyke followed. 'So do you know him?'

'Rob Pearce?' Cherry lifted her shoulders dismissively. 'Yeah. A bit.'

Pause.

Seeing no more information was to be forthcoming, Tyke tapped her foot impatiently and prodded further.

'And?'

'He's all right, I guess. If you like that sort of thing.'

'What sort of thing?' Silence. 'What sort of thing, Chezz?'

'Well, you know, he's not the best looking bloke in the world, is he?'

'I thought he was lovely. He's got the most beautiful blue/green eyes.' Tyke sighed. 'Like the ocean, I thought.'

Cherry burst out laughing. 'You fancy him and you only met him five minutes ago!'

Immediately on the defensive, Tyke glowered. 'No, I don't. I just thought he looked nice.'

'If you say so.' Returning to her own reflection, Cherry pondered sweeping her hair right off her face and tucking it behind her ears. 'We're singing at Boo's tonight. You'll come, won't you?'

'Course I will. Have I ever missed a gig?'

Cherry couldn't decide what to do with her hair. With a tut she crammed it under a net before settling down on the bed. 'Tyke?'

'Mmmm?'

'I think it's gonna happen tonight. You know. With me and Tommy.'

Tyke's eyes widened and her mouth formed an o. 'You sure?'

'Think so. He kinda already asked me.'

'No, I mean are you sure you want to. What about the risk? What about, you know,' in spite of her new-found maturity

Tyke faltered on the word, instinctively pitching her voice lower, 'pregnancy.'

Cherry bumped her shoulder against her playfully. 'There's ways and means or haven't you heard of them?'

'No.'

Cherry laughed, sure she was being teased when the expression on her friend's face pulled her up short. 'You truly don't?'

'No. I don't know what you're talking about.'

'Oh. Right. Well, you take precautions, don't you, to stop a baby starting.' Tyke was a total picture of puzzlement and shock. *She needed enlightening*, Cherry thought. So she enlightened her. 'So, if you get with Rob Pearce you'll know what to do.'

Hot colour flooded Tyke's face and she leapt off the bed. 'There's nothing like that going on.'

'Just in case then.'

Tyke refused to meet Cherry's meaningful ogle. Instead she grabbed her good frock off its hanger behind the door and flounced to the other side of the attic room to change. As she did Cherry's words echoed in her mind and she turned them over.

If she was honest she did want someone else in her life. Someone to trust, to hold and be held by. It was all part of growing up, she knew. *It just didn't make it less daunting or confusing; your own desires butting up against the behaviour expected of you.* Also Maudie's face swam into Tyke's mind. Phyllis's, too.

'Piss off the pair of you,' she muttered.

The gig started off slowly. Not many people out and about tonight. Too many days left before pay day and pockets were empty. Still, Tommy's drums stirred the place up and Cherry's singing drew in passers-by. By midnight there was hardly room to move. They were about to launch into 'Alexander's Ragtime Band' when Tyke caught Cherry's eye. With a bit of explanatory mime she let her know she needed some cool air on her face then elbowed through the throng and made for the comparative quiet of the street. Leaning against a lamppost Tyke drew in a lungful of cool air.

'Didn't know you were a party goer.' Rob Pearce had sauntered up to the door of Boo's before recognising the young woman standing nearby. 'I've heard there's a good band playing here tonight.

Tyke straightened up proudly. 'My friend Cherry's in it. I go to all their gigs.'

'And listen to them from the outside?'

'Of course not. It's just a bit hot in there. They've got a good crowd tonight.'

Rob peered in through the door to check the veracity of this, closing it quickly. 'You're not kidding.' He hovered on the pavement.

'Changed your mind about going in?'

Rob joined her on the other side of the lamppost. 'Maybe I think there's better company to be found out here?'

The odd, swirly feeling in the pit of Tyke's stomach reminded her of meeting Jack. There was something, too about Jack in Rob's eyes. He was very close, so close she could feel the warmth of him. 'What if company could do with a drink?'

Rob pulled a face. 'Suppose I could brave the perils of a packed pub. If company continued to keep me company.'

With a smile, Tyke tucked her hand under his arm. 'It might,' she teased and pushed against the door.

Later, back home and tucked up in the bed she shared with Cherry, Tyke lay on her back, eyes on the moonlight hiding shyly in the attic beams. Too restless to sleep she couldn't keep Rob's face from her mind. He'd been playful, friendly, nothing but a gentleman. It occurred to her there was someone else he reminded her of. *Moss.*

When Cherry finally came in, Tyke had managed to fall into a restive asleep. The creaking door woke her and she roused up onto an elbow and sleepily wiped her hair back from her face. A buoyant Cherry was removing her frock and humming.

'How was it?'

'Lovely.' In her corset and petticoat, Cherry jumped on the bed. 'The best.'

'So you did it?'

Cherry's eyes sparkled with mischief and joy. 'More than once.'

'And you'll do it again?'

Cherry grabbed Tyke, whispered into her face. 'More than once.'

They giggled and laughed so loudly, their neighbour banged on the wall and told them to shut up.

'Shut up yerself yer bastard!'

Nothing and no one quelled the incorrigible Cherry.

***

January 1940 was bitter and the blackout regulations made winter hours an endless, cheerless struggle to navigate the streets. Even the well-known byways to and from work became eerie. People rushed as much as they could in the dark to get home or rarely went out at all. To top it all off, rationing was brought in, rationing books given to every man, woman and child. Almost overnight, black-marketeers responded with a gleeful rubbing of the hands and a stealthy wink.

'Don't you worry about not getting stuff,' Cherry told Tyke confidently and winked. 'I know a coupla people.'

'Who?'

'Can't tell, won't tell.' Cherry grinned.

Evacuated children, blackouts, rationing - The war drums of approaching conflict grew louder.

More men appeared in uniforms and Cherry's eyes were

increasingly drawn to them. 'What do you think, Tyke? Fancy a bloke in uniform?'

A tall man, all crowns and pips marched by. He paused enough to return Cherry's lingering smile.

Tyke watched this byplay. 'Haven't really thought about it. Don't think I care one way or the other. I mean, it's the bloke inside who counts, not what he's wearing.'

Cherry dismissed such belief as New Zealand foolishness. She swung round to Tommy, scuffing his feet as he walked. 'Why don't you join up?' she demanded.

'I can't. Not with my dicky heart,' he grumbled, though to Cherry's ears he didn't sound worried about it.

'I reckon a bloke looks good in uniform. Smart as paint some of them.' She smiled at three new recruits, lotion shining on their recent haircuts. 'You could join the Home Guard if yer can't be a real soldier.'

Tommy scowled at her choice of words. 'What? And be bossed about by some old nonce from the last war? No thanks!'

One of the recruits gave Cherry a jaunty salute. The look on her face soured Tommy's mood completely. Without a goodbye he stomped off, barging past the young soldier and shouldering him off the pavement.

To Cherry's chagrin a few weeks later, Rob appeared in a uniform. True, it was only a Home Guard one but even so, he fancied himself something rotten in it, parading before the two young women.

'Anyone'd think you'd won a Victoria Cross,' Cherry growled jealously.

''Course war work comes first,' Rob began only to be interrupted.

'And what do you do?' Tyke asked, not for the first time.

'I've told you. I can't say.'

'What's so secret about it?' Cherry demanded. 'You a spy or summat?'

Rob's hands cut the air in a definitive gesture. 'No. Of course not. Look, I can't tell you.' He stood tall, admiring his reflection in their mirror. 'The Home Guard is Churchill's defence for the whole of Britain. If the Germans do cross the Channel they'll find us waiting.'

'With guns?'

Some of Rob's bumptiousness seeped away. 'Well, no. But we'll get some eventually.'

'Better hope the enemy don't make it across just yet, then,' Tyke teased, her mockery going astray when she saw she had wounded him. She hastily repaired the damage by kissing him. He didn't return the caress for a moment, then his arms held her tightly. Cherry sighed loudly and left them to it.

Rob's caresses grew increasingly intimate as his hot breath tickled Tyke's ear. 'It's getting dangerous, love. War's coming.'

'It's been coming for months. Maybe it won't get here at all.'

Rob squared his shoulders as his lips moved kiss by kiss down her neck. 'All us blokes, ready to lay down our lives for our country.'

Tyke fought against the pleasurable shiver tingling through her body. 'You won't be. You're staying in England.'

'Once Hitler's bombs start falling on your head you'll know different.'

'Then us women will be risking our lives, too, won't we?'

Rob had backed them slowly up until her legs hit the bed. He pushed with a little more force and they tumbled onto it. Tyke wriggled out from under him, giggling, her laughter silenced when Rob hauled her under him again, kissed her deeply. Happy to play along, Tyke revelled in the passion of the moment. Then his hand slid over her knee, exploring fingers finding their way to her stocking tops. Her hand seized his and brought it to a stop.

Rob pulled his lips from hers. 'Come on, Tyke,' an enticing whisper.

'No.' She smiled when she said it but there was no denying her decision.

He nodded, confined himself to kisses. For a few moments. As his passion grew, Tyke found herself responding, matching him, all the while trying to be sensible. Trying to remember all Cherry's advice. Her body betrayed her and this time when Rob's hand slid possessively under her skirt she didn't stop him, couldn't stop him. Couldn't stop herself.

***

This bloody city!

Moss hated London from the moment he arrived.

He side-stepped a group of soldiers who shoved him onto the road, not acknowledging him in any way. Dodging them, his boot tips caught an uneven pavement edge and almost sent him sprawling. Moss righted himself, glancing about to see if anyone had witnessed this clumsiness but like the scurrying populace, the wardens and soldiers, no one appeared to notice him at all. This was a blessing and a curse. Moss wasn't comfortable in large groups of strangers at the best of times and London at war, even a phoney war, was hardly that. By avoiding all faces he could just about manage an 'I-can't-see-you-so-you-can't-see-me' approach. However his shyness also meant he struggled to speak to strangers and there was no way he was going to stumble on Tyke's whereabouts without asking a few questions. He'd found it easier at the docks because he was acclimatised to seafarers and mariners thanks to Uncle Hugo plus the months spent working his passage to London. *Just gotta toughen up and bite the bullet.* He paused at the metaphor. *There's a bloody war on, isn't there? A bloke better be careful what he wishes for.*

As much as he wanted to find Tyke he was nervous as all hell of seeing her again. *He'd had months to plan things so why was he finding it so difficult to imagine?* Alex's panic at her daughter's disappearance had given Moss the validation he needed to don his battered armour and mount a passing white horse. Hugo furnished a notebook full of helpful hints, contacts and, with a wink and an over-the-shoulder glance, one or two jobs. Moss tucked his savings away under his belongings in an old canvas bag and found working passage on board a merchant ship under the auspices of Old Derry. He was a month into the voyage before it occurred to him - *Tyke might not want to see him.*

'*Tell Moss I'm sorry. He'll know what for.*'

All these months later, there was every chance Tyke had moved on, not just from New Zealand but from them all. *From him. Too late to back out now.* He'd travelled from the other side of the world to find her so find her he would. *What would he say to her?* Even now, after all his time at sea followed by the weeks searching London, Moss had no bloody idea.

Having begun his hunt in the better parts of the city, he gradually headed into the poorer, denser areas until reaching the East End. Here his luck changed. The young woman from New Zealand had made her mark.

'Yer'll be wanting Tyke, then.'

Moss had been asking around for Miss Jeannie Brodie. He hadn't thought of mentioning a young woman from New Zealand until this public bar.

'Yes.' Moss couldn't hide his relief.

He was subjected to a sharp scrutiny. 'What's it worth to yer, cully?'

'Five bob.' Moss ignored the use of cully. He'd heard a lot of words he didn't understand since arriving here. *Best to stick to what he needed.*

In response, the man held out an expectant hand. Moss clinked in the coins which disappeared in a heartbeat.

'Try Petticoat Market, cully. Yer can find anything there.'

But Moss's courage failed him right at the point of discovery. He found his way to Petticoat Market, countless stallholders carrying on as if war hadn't been declared. As Moss glanced at them Tyke's face lit the dark corners of his mind and before setting one foot into the market he bolted. He didn't run far. Suddenly in need of a beer he pushed into a corner pub.

'A pint, please.' A pile of coins were slapped onto the counter top. 'And keep them coming.' Grabbing his dripping glass Moss found a dark corner away from the open fire and scowled moodily at the foamy head of his beer.

Where else could he go? It's not like he knew anyone. Moss drank slowly but steadily as the day darkened into night and the pub filled around him. He barely lifted his head. A saucy woman offered him company, some bloke needed a partner in a game of darts, a lonely old man wanted a chat. Moss ignored them all. His was the only table with a spare chair yet no one dared ask if it was needed, for at the sight of the stranger's angry, preoccupied face they wisely preferred to stand.

Pulling out his battered pocket-watch, Moss scowled to see it was after midnight. He didn't know his way through the streets well during the day, let alone at night when darkness claimed the byways. Instinctively his hand sought out the dagger tucked in its habitual place in his jacket. *Perhaps there'd be a room upstairs for the night.* As he reached this decision, the doors banged open and two couples stumbled drunkenly through them.

'Here, Boo. Give us four shanks of wallop.' Cherry turned in Tommy's arms and kissed him deeply. 'All you gorra do sunshine is pay.'

'Only if you make if worth my while, Doll'

Cherry did.   The other couple followed her amorous example but either they'd had more to drink or were pushed. Either way they stumbled heavily and fell into the crowd before hitting the floor amid cheers and curses. Moss had had enough. Dark or not, he would try and find his way back out of the East End. Shoving towards the door he spared a disdainful glare at the couple on the floor, the woman's dress rucked up high on her thighs as men all around ogled shamelessly.

Recognition hit Moss like a punch. 'Tyke?'

She sat up tugging ineffectually at her hem, one hand shoving at her boyfriend's chest. 'Rob. Give it a rest.'

But her laughing companion tried to lift her skirt higher, their audience egging him on.

'Tyke!'

This time she heard. So stunned was she at the sight of Moss her hands fell limply away. Seeing his chance Rob straddled her. Moss roared, yanked him to his feet only to punch him back down once more. Tyke shrieked and this time Moss hauled her upright, smelling stale alcohol on her breath. He shook her in an effort to sober her up as she fought back.

'For Christ's sake, Tyke, get a hold of yourself!'

'I don't think you should shake her like that.' Cherry stood beside him, eyes on her friend's white face.

'What's it to you?'

Before Cherry could reply, Tyke threw up in spectacular fashion. With a gasp Moss shoved her to arm's length.

'Told yer,' Cherry said with what Moss considered annoying and unnecessary complacency.

Tyke didn't want Moss to go home with them. In fact, she tried to catch Cherry's eye to signal this but her friend seemed more than a little taken with Moss's strong body and good-looking face to even pay Tyke the smallest attention. After settling Tommy and Rob's grumbles at being left behind, the three of them ended up in the poky little flat with its one small window. Moss paced restlessly. Tyke sat on the bed she and Cherry shared, hunched over a bowl.

Her friend hunted for a cloth, using some water from the big china jug to wet it. 'Wipe yer face with this.' Cherry passed it to the groaning Tyke who dabbed listlessly at her mouth.

'How often are you like this? And who was the bloke you were with?' Moss demanded.

'None of your business,' Tyke snapped. 'Why are you even here?'

'If Alex and Maudie could see you now!'

'I can't believe you chased after me. I didn't ask you to come looking for me.'

'What else could I have done? Alex was frantic.'

'I told her where I was. I wrote a letter. It's not like I just disappeared off the face of the earth.'

'Actually, Tyke, you did.'

Silence.

Moss studied Tyke, unhappy at the changes he saw. *The makeup added years to her. So did the fancy hairstyle. As for the clinging frock, the high heels, well. She looked beautiful.* In that moment he hated Tyke for not staying simple and uncomplicated as he had always thought her to be. *Right up until the night she kissed him and changed everything.*

Moss subjected Cherry to the same unblinking scrutiny, rightly surmising she was the catalyst for all this change in Tyke.

If Cherry felt uncomfortable at the glower she gave no sign. Patting Tyke's face she rose from the bed. 'I'll fetch some more water and make us all a cuppa shall I?' Not waiting for a reply, she took the jug from the bench under the window. The door closed on her suggestive wink, her leer embarrassing both Tyke and Moss even as they tried to hide it.

A complicated silence lay heavily in the room, stifling and strange.

Tyke placed the bowl on the floor and eased herself to a sitting position. 'Why did you come here?'

The small room grew smaller around Moss. Far too confining. 'I told you why.'

'Yes. You came for Alex. It's just I don't believe it.'

Moss strained for composure. 'I can't help what you choose

to believe.'

'You've never lied to me before so why now?'

'For Christ's sake, Tyke…..'

Suddenly she was standing in front of him. 'Maybe you're lying to yourself.' He couldn't pull away from her gaze. Tyke moved closer. 'Maybe you lied on that night.'

'Tyke...' Before he could say anymore they were kissing. Moss gloried in the feel of her warm body pressed so passionately against his. There was hunger in their embrace, a need beyond desire. Moss sat on the bed, Tyke straddling his lap and they were lost to everything but right here, right now.

Cherry strode in. 'Hardly any water coming out of the bloody tap! You'd think….' The words died as she took in the frozen tableau, the shock and confusion. Cherry grinned. 'Don't mind me.' The water jug banged onto the wooden bench. 'I'll just….' She gestured to the door but by then Moss was on his feet.

He grabbed his coat and hat. 'Gotta go. See you tomorrow, Tyke?'

She nodded on his exit.

As her friend fell back on the bed with a despairing groan, Cherry leaned over the metal bedstead.

'I know things are different in New Zealand but I thought you told me he was your step-brother?'

'Sort of. Not really.' Tyke wished she had been more forthcoming with Cherry from the get-go. All this time underplaying Moss's part in her life, the confusion of her feelings for him – no wonder Cherry was staring at her like she was mad. 'We were raised in the same house. Moss has looked after me. Always. The brother I always wanted.'

'Strange behaviour for a brother!' Cherry cackled.

Tyke rolled over to catch Cherry's eye, hugging her pillow tightly.

'I've always loved him, Chezz. But one day I understood it wasn't the type of love I'd believed it to be. Or maybe, it changed somehow, somewhere along the way and I only recognised it then.'

Confronted with such sincerity and unable to mock, Cherry lay on the bed beside her friend, eyes fixed on the close, slatted ceiling. 'So who made the first move?'

'Me. And Moss was so shocked, so horrified, I ran. I ran from the other side of the world all the way here to London.'

Cherry held Tyke's hand and squeezed her fingers playfully. 'Well, it didn't seem to me like any bugger was running just now.' As realisation dawned, Tyke smiled, the grin sliding off her face when Cherry added, 'Dunno what Rob'll make of it all, of course. You remember him, right? Your boyfriend, Rob?'

Tyke growled, threw the pillow at Cherry before flouncing out of the room.

'No answer can be an answer in itself, gel.' Cherry told the closed door.

As rough as she felt next morning, Tyke had to rally for work. All she could think about was Moss. *He came all this way to find her. The heat of his kisses, the urgency of their embrace. Was it wrong to want more? To want him?*

'I don't want to go to work.'

'You want to see Moss.'

'What of it?'

'Look, it's pay day tomorrow. It's not like yer don't need the coin, is it?'

'I suppose not.'

At the sight of her friend's confused face Cherry relented. 'Tell yer what, get through today and we'll have a right old knees-up with a plate of jellied eels. My treat.'

Tyke groaned nauseously.

'Shut up, Chezz! You know they made me bloody crook.' Just the memory churned her stomach. 'Don't mention them again.'

With the ecstasy of the true connoisseur, Cherry was oblivious, lost in happy expectation of a favourite meal. 'They'll slide down a treat they will.'

Tyke gagged, clasped a hand to her mouth and dashed to the washing up bowl.

'You've got no taste, that's your problem.' Cherry grumbled unfeelingly, blocking her ears to the sound of retching.

Still feeling queasy at the thought of eels, Tyke made it to the factory moaning every step of the way. The end of the day couldn't come quickly enough so in the way of these things, it seemed to last twice as long. When the whistle sounded Tyke threw her coat over her coveralls, jammed her hat on her head and scurried out before Cherry could catch up. She wanted some time alone to think about Moss. However even as the thought formed, she saw his familiar figure leaning against the gates into the factory. He lifted a hand at the sight of her.

'How'd you find out where I worked?'

'Not many Kiwis around here. You've made quite a name for yourself, Tyke.'

There was something about the way he said it. Tyke looked away, only to relax when he held her hand and whispered, 'It wasn't all bad, you know.' His droll look made her laugh and tucked securely in that laughter was the bond they'd always shared. Attraction had changed the nature but not the depth of it. From such understanding came peace.

Cherry beat them home. She had hot water on the gas ring, ready to make a cup of tea when they wandered in. All it took was an exchange of silent, significant looks between Tyke and Cherry. The latter cleared her throat. 'Tyke, dunno if I said or not but I'll be away tonight. Heading back to Mum's. She's having trouble with Petey.'

'He was evacuated. Thought he'd be laughing it up in the country.'

'So did Mum. He's turned up back home, ain't he. All crying and stuff. Won't tell her what's wrong or nuthin' so I promised I'd have a talk to the wee bleeder.'

A backward wave over her shoulder and Cherry left Tyke and Moss alone in the flat.

With a soft smile Tyke turned the key in the lock. They met in the middle of the room, their embrace as natural as the warm sun. By the time they were on the rumpled bed, Tyke had lost all doubt. It was Moss who drew back from the edge with an effort only he could know. Holding her away from him, her unbound hair falling over his hands he stopped. 'Wait, Tyke. Wait.'

A little disorientated she leaned towards him again but he increased the pressure on her hands. 'Are you sure? About this. Because there'll no going back.'

'I don't want to go back.'

'Really? Back to when we were so easy with each other? No complications?'

She frowned a little, trying to understand what he was getting at. 'Don't you want me, Moss. Is this your way of telling me?'

'No, God almighty.' He drew her against him again briefly. 'But Tyke, this will change everything and if it doesn't work out, how can we go back? It will never be the same.'

Tyke settled more comfortably in his arms. After a pause she ran her hand down his serious face.

'Whatever happens, Moss, whether we carry on or not it's already changed forever. We've changed.'

In answer to his troubled look she kissed him deeply then drew him down onto the bed where they forgot the world.

***

'Have yer told Rob?'
'Not yet.'

'Well when, then?'

'I dunno, Chezz. Sometime. Soon. Never.' Tyke threw her hairbrush onto the floor. 'Look, just leave it. Tell me about Petey. Is he all right?'

'She asked not-so-subtly changing the topic! Rob's not happy, yer know. Tommy says he's already askin' questions.' Cherry picked up the hairbrush and replaced it on the upturned box beside the bed.

'Let him. I thought he was heading up north soon anyway.'

'Tyke....'

'Cherry, please. Can we talk about something else?'

At the pleading look her friend gave her, Cherry sighed and sat beside her on the bed. 'You're asking for trouble.'

'Look at your own life, Chezz. Pots and kettles, I reckon.' Cherry gave Tyke a shamefaced grin. 'Tell me about Petey. I thought you'd just made it up to have an excuse to leave. Something is wrong, though?'

'He got beaten somethin' awful.'

'What?'

'There the boys were standing at some God-forsaken station in the middle of nowhere and this old bat arrives. She looks at her notes then tells them she can't find anyone to take all three of them. It was like it was all their fault, Petey says.'

'No!'

'It gets worse. She separated Petey from Bran and Morgan, even though Bran told the woman they weren't to be. She just told him beggars couldn't be choosers and to be grateful to whoever took them in. Bran tried to be the one on his own but when he argued, he got a whack to make his head spin and before he or Morgan could say or do anything, they took Petey away in a truck. Him and three other boys.'

'Well why couldn't Bran and Morgan go with him instead?'

'The old bitch wouldn't say.'

'That's just cruel!'

'It gets worse,' Cherry repeated, adding emphasis. 'Them

boys had to work in the fields. Petey said he didn't mind actually though he said the animals scared him and made awful noises.'

Compassion tugged at Tyke. *Little Petey being mooed or baaed at – the skinny, undersized cockney lad who'd never seen a real cow or sheep before. What must he have gone through?*

Cherry's normally sunny features twisted. 'Then, once they got the hang of things they were made to work longer hours. Out in the fields before dawn and not allowed back before dark. They were given scraps to eat and if anyone complained they were locked in the cellar.'

'Oh my God.' Tyke rolled over onto her elbow. 'Poor Petey.'

'Yeah. Too many beatings, not enough food. He decided to run for it, though the other lads were too scared to. They were worried they'd get caught and taken somewhere even worse. Petey didn't know where he was and didn't know where the others were so he headed back home. Can't believe the little bugger managed it. He's sworn he's never leaving home again. Not even if the Germans drop a hundred bombs on London.'

'Are you worried about Bran and Morgan?'

'Nah. They're bigger than Petey and give as good as they get. No one'll dare touch Bran or Morgan.' After a pause, Cherry summoned up the courage to ask the question she'd been nerving herself to ask for over a week. 'Tyke?'

'Mmmm?'

'You still chucking your guts up?'

'Sometimes. Those bloody eels of yours, Cherry! I told you.'

'That was a fair while ago now.'

'So? Must have been a bad one among them.' Tyke glowered, rubbing her stomach at the thought. 'And stop going on about them, will you?'

'Yeah but Tyke, when was your last monthly?'

Tyke screwed up her face as she thought.

'Can't exactly remember. I must be over time though, now you mention it.' Cherry said nothing more, just watched Tyke's face as the realisation hit, her eyes widening in horror. 'No.'

'You gorra get checked. I reckon Rob's gone and knocked you up. Didn't you take precautions?'

'Yes, only sometimes I kind of lost track of things.' Tyke's eyes filled with dismay and the approach of panic. 'Cherry, what'll I do?'

Hugging her friend close, Cherry stroked her hair. 'Whatever yer decide, yer won't go through it alone.'

There was no decision to make. Tyke couldn't bring a baby into the world, unmarried, alone.

'What about telling Rob? You could get wed.'

'I don't love him.'

'What's love gorra do with anything?'

'No, Cherry. There's only one thing to do.'

'Akcherly there's two things you've gorra do.'

'What?'

'Find out the damage first – after all it might be nothing. Then, decide what you tell Moss.'

Moss. He could never know. He must never find out. And that meant…..

Tyke paced the flat, laying a hand on the door then turning, reaching the other end of the room and touching the wall there, too. Over and over the same track, mind swirling as she tried not to look at the bed and remember the night she and Moss had spent there.

I thought- this is our moment; we need never look back.

A visit to a midwife made it clear. The damage had been done. Tyke forced herself to be calm. *It hurt to breathe. It really did.* A lump sat in her throat, weighing her down, choking her voice. *Phyllis, hysterical at the scullery door. Dying young. Her baby boy adopted to strangers.* Tyke swallowed down the nausea.

I almost believed in happy endings.

And suddenly Moss was there, smiling in the doorway, a bunch of white violets in one hand. 'Didn't know if you even have a favourite flower but thought, I'll try violets and if you throw them at me I'll take it as a hint.' His face fell at Tyke's unresponsive expression. 'Do you hate them so much? Sorry, Tyke I'll find something else.' Nothing. 'I can go now if you like.' He pointed over his shoulder and she exploded.

'Bloody hell! Stop bloody talking!' *Don't look like that, Moss. Don't look at me.*

He took one step towards her only to falter and stop as she held out her arms, warning him off. 'Tyke?'

'It was a mistake. A big mistake.' *I almost believed in happy endings.*

'I don't understand.'

'It's not difficult.' She hardened her tone further. 'You shouldn't have chased after me. We should never have slept together.' Unable to bear the look on his face Tyke closed her eyes and drew in strength. 'It was a mistake,' she repeated.

Silence.

'But you said....'

'It doesn't matter what I said, Moss.' Certain she had control once more, Tyke confronted him. 'It was a mistake. You have to leave me alone.'

'Tyke....'

Silence.

It was over. *It had to be over.* Tyke turned her back on him, using the table under the window for support, trying to hide her sorrow and when the quiet threatened to break her she spun around.

Moss was gone, the little bunch of white violets dying on the bed.

***

True to her word Cherry stood by Tyke. She found a woman who lived deep in the muddled alleys of the East End and she was there when something went wrong and Tyke began to bleed heavily after the abortion. Thanks to Cherry's quick wits, Tyke made it to hospital and survived, though it was touch and go for a few days.

She lay listlessly on the little bed, listening to the noises around her in the ward. A nurse approached her and Tyke asked the question she had dreaded asking.

'Will I…. will I be able to have another baby?'

The nurse didn't even try to hide her disgust or spare the feelings of the distraught young woman.

'No.'

Tyke gasped but the nurse battered her regrets into sharp relief.

'And nor do whores like you deserve another baby when you kill the ones God gives you.'

For months Cherry couldn't shake Tyke from her depression.

I almost believed in happy endings.

***

Matthew
Singapore

The seas to the south of Java seethed with shipping and the port of Tjilatjap was chaos. Many ships were heading out, escaping the Japanese who had landed on the north coast and both ends of the island. Singapore had fallen. Tjilatjap, an American naval base, was the only port open to Allied shipping. The Japanese had taken all other havens around the island.

Matthew, Dag and Whitey were on board *Stronghold* as she slid into harbour. They anxiously scanned sea and sky. For months Japanese aircraft, surface ships and submarines had been taking a deadly toll on the Allied fleet.

Stronghold's crew were exhausted, worn to shreds. Lack of sleep, the rigours of ongoing tension. They had dodged submarines, provided escort, rescued men from the sea whose ships had been blown to bits and sunk, or left as smoking ruins. They had rescued broken men, dying men. It all took its toll.

Dag was uncharacteristically silent. He had lost a brother on *Jupiter* and wore the loss badly. All Matthew and Whitey could offer was silent sympathy and rum. Neither was helping.

'Well, got duties. See you.' The laconic Dag left Whitey and Matthew attending the approach into harbour.

Matthew had met Whitey during their training at Motuihe Island renamed by the Navy to the H.M.S Tamaki as all naval shore bases were given the names of ships. Physical training, drills, lectures, damn near rioting over small rations, swimming, boxing and swotting up the dreaded Seamanship Manual – it had been challenging and fun, no other word for it. From the years of unrelieved struggle on the farm, Matthew couldn't help but feel free. *No one else needed him. No one here depended on him.* He'd had to remind himself at times during their training it was all to prepare for war. It hadn't seemed real somehow.

Training completed, they arrived at Seletar, the Naval Shore Base, HMS Sultan and it was here they befriended the almost perennially drunk Dag. Any down time, any leave, Dag would be drunk. Becoming his friends meant permanent watch duty keeping Dag from fights and being hauled up on disciplinary charges. With the luxurious base life on the naval base plus leave in Singapore where the New Zealanders discovered how well they were paid compared to their allies from Britain, it had all felt like a great adventure. They were young, ready for excitement and had plenty of money in their pockets. They were seeing the world, and such a different world it was from the farms and backblocks so many of them hailed from.

One night, one chance encounter changed everything for Matthew. The bar was crowded with young men in spotless uniforms. Many of them were accompanied by lovely oriental women who clung possessively to their arms, eyes lowered.

For Dag it wasn't about the women. He figured, 'Dames are a dime a dozen, but a good drink, a special beverage with the kick of a mule,' he sighed, 'that, my friends, is what a man should strive for. The Holy Grail.' Over the course of hours Dag proceeded to strive for his Grail.

Matthew had found a dim corner. Whitey was long gone, heading back to base but Matthew had drunk enough to make him pleasantly genial and also, it was his turn to watch out for Dag. At the moment he was failing in his duty for Dag was the last thing on his mind. The young Chinese woman on Matthew's lap was as light as a feather and as soft, her voice a whisper in his ear which teased and aroused. Her lips nuzzled his neck as her hand caressed his upper thigh and slowly found its practised way higher. Matthew wasn't moving for anyone so he ignored the sudden roar of rage which sounded all too Dag-like. Until the fighting started.

'Take that back, you Australian bastard!'

'Nah.' The gum chewing Aussie threw fuel on the fire by standing tall and yelling, 'Baaa!'in Dag's face. He didn't expect any retaliation. From what he had noticed, the Kiwi could hardly keep to his feet.

Yes, Dag was drunk. However what the Australian patently didn't know was drink never dulled Dag's fighting abilities. In fact, it honed them. The Kiwi's fist slammed into the Australian's jaw, knocking him back against the bar. Quickly upright, the Aussie retaliated. Dag not only ducked under the swinging arm but managed to end up behind him. Two thumps around the bastard's kidneys.

Spinning on his toes, the Australian picked up a chair shouting, 'Fucking sheep shagger!'

Dag gripped onto the legs of the chair and the two of them wrestled, teeth bared.

They didn't realise they were the object of gleeful amusement. A British ranker, busy laying bets on the outcome of the fight, added his two cents worth. 'Aren't all you colonials sheep shaggers?'

Dag froze. So did the Australian. As one they lowered the chair and faced the Brit.

'What did you say, chum?'

The cocky, skinny Brit sneered. 'You're all the same. Second rate British from the arse of the world.'

The Australian and Kiwi turned to each other. They might give each other shit but there was one thing they could both agree on. They loathed the sneering British. By the time a resigned Matthew made his way towards the hubbub, the Brit was crying for his mother and the Australian and Dag were sharing drinks at the bar, slapping each other on the back and laughing.

'Having a good night?' Matthew asked.

He stepped over the sobbing Brit, now curled into a ball on the floor.

Dag grabbed the bottle of rum and poured three generous measures. 'One of the best. Matt, this is Fuzz. He's from Queensland. Top bloke.'

Matthew was happy to prop up the bar and listen to Dag and Fuzz swap stories from home. He was two rums in when he noticed a grizzled sailor slumped over the bar counter, staring at nothing. The stranger had his own bottle to hand, its level down to the last few shots. An odd aura surrounded him, a darkness, something which drew Matthew nearer, curiosity piqued.

'Can I buy you one?'

Instead of replying the man knocked back the remains in his glass. Feeling snubbed, Matthew made to leave only to have the bottle pushed towards him.

'Help yourself. I better not drink the whole fucking thing.' The words weren't slurred exactly, just slushy around the consonants. When he faced Matthew the sombreness revealed eyes which had seen too much.

Matthew poured a small amount, his companion refusing any more. For a while they sat silently.

'You finished training, son?'

'Yep.'

'Looking forward to facing the enemy are you?'

Matthew studied the unshaven face. 'Sure. It's what we've been working towards. Doing our bit.'

'Doing our bit.'

The echoed words were flattened of all feeling. Those world-weary, empty eyes met Matthew's as if trying to read him. Coming to a decision the sailor nodded and reached into his pocket, pulling out a much used wallet. Fumbling a little, he removed half a dozen photos and passed them to a wondering Matthew. 'Before you get too enthusiastic son, you'd better prepare yourself for your enemy. Black and white images of unimaginable horror. Piles of children heaped beside the stone walls they'd been smashed to death against. A woman bayoneted in the street, gutted to reveal a near-term baby.

'Jesus.' Matthew's breath escaped in shock.

'Nanking after the Japs occupation, 1937.'

'How did you get these?'

In answer to Matthew's question the sailor just shook his head. 'Got given them. Spoke to someone who saw it with his own eyes. Women raped to death. Blood everywhere. Piles and piles of dead and dying.' The sailor took one of the photos and lost himself again in the horrors there. 'This is your enemy, son. This is what they can do and believe me, your officers might tell you they can be beaten but, after what I've seen....' He placed the photo down on the bar counter in front of Matthew and emptied the bottle into his glass. 'I'm not sure they can. Not anymore.'

No sleep for Matthew. Not for that night or countless others.

What was he doing in 1937? Re-building the farm in Murchison where life went on with the same unending seasonal repetition. Where his women-folk were safe. Where atrocities like Nanking never touched them. This wasn't just an adventure anymore. This wasn't about receiving the most pay or wearing smart uniforms with shiny shoes. This was war.

Since that night, he, Whitey and Dag had seen their fair share of action and with every Japanese plane shot down or ship sunk, those images of Nanking played out before Matthew. He hadn't shared what he'd been shown with his friends. He wasn't sure why. Maybe it had something to do with the increasing knowledge that the Japanese were beating them. The Allies lost ship after ship and the reality of Nanking drew closer to them all.

And now Singapore was lost.

The bells rang for all hands. Matthew and Whitey turned out. By the time they anchored in port orders had already been established. They were to provide escort for the Dutch ship *Zaandam* and assist loading her with wounded, the sick, women, children and survivors from the *Jupiter* sinking, along with gear and equipment. *Stronghold*, too would take her share. At one point Matthew held a boy in his arms, no more than three, one leg amputated high up his left thigh, his baby-smooth face blistered and burned. Matthew shivered. *Jamsie on his lap, snuggling into his arms, bright, innocent eyes laughing at his father's nonsense.* There was no expression at all in the damaged face of the boy he carried. *A darker image; Jimmy's scalded skin, his screams as he crouches under the kitchen table.*

By nightfall *Zaandam* was overcrowded and heaving with distressed people frantically seeking the safety of an Australian port. Back on board their own ship, *Stronghold's* crew received unwelcome news. There was no fuel available for *Stronghold's* bunkers, and after their latest trials at sea these had already dwindled to a worrying level. No denying their orders, though. No thought of not following them through.

Matthew bitched. 'Here to Perth's a helluva long way for our small ship. Low oil reserves isn't going to bloody help, is it? What if we have to divert? What if.....'

' 'What if. What if.' Come on, Matt.' Whitey said stoically, 'What can't be cured must be endured.'

'And that attitude doesn't bloody help.'

Whitey frowned, puzzled. 'What attitude?'

'Your stiff upper lip bullshit.'

'Would you rather I complained?'

'Yes. Yes, I would.'

'To what end?'

'To me not punching you in the mouth.' But Matthew was grinning.

Their banter had seen them through some frightening moments. No way they would change. Before Whitey could find a suitable comeback, Dag whistled for their attention as he jogged up to them.

'Shit's hit the fan,' he told them by way of a greeting.

'Why?'

'We decoded some of the Nip signals. They've four aircraft carriers, four battleships, eight heavy cruisers and fifteen destroyers heading from Timor along the Java south coast.' Dag shook his head. 'Those bastards want to obliterate every fucking vessel between Timor and Ceylon.'

Whitey never swore but he muttered something under his breath neither friend could quite catch. Three pairs of eyes turned to the *Zaandam*. From where they stood they could hear children and babies crying.

'Looks like we've got our work cut out then, getting them to safety.' Matthew's tone was light and a complete contradiction to what his friends read in his eyes.

Matthew was on duty when further orders came: *Zaandam* to proceed at maximum speed to Perth. *Stronghold* to adjust her course to southeast with the intention of crossing the Japanese battle fleet's path. She was to create the diversion needed for *Zaandam* to escape. Due to *Stronghold's* low oil reserves her speed was set at 12 knots.

Would they make the Australian coast?

The following morning things took a grim turn. A plane was sighted high astern. It kept its position, didn't attack - it could only be a spotter plane from a Japanese cruiser. Orders from their captain not to alter speed or course. And so the day passed. Matthew was off duty mid-afternoon. Taking the opportunity he spent the time he should have been sleeping packing his few possessions. *Just in case.* Reaching into his trunk he pulled out a handful of letters from home, their accompanying photos tucked securely among the pages. Mary's letters read like diary entries, day-to-day matter-of-fact recitals of what was happening on the farm. It was as if she expected him home any day and when he walked into the house stamping the mud off his boots, he would know the shearing needed to be done or the winter's supply of firewood had already been cut and stacked. Running his eyes over the pages Matthew shook his head. He'd never told another soul but he'd felt nothing but relief when he enlisted. Mary bored him. The farm was relentless slog and he had grown tired of his life. *Twenty three. Married. Two kids and sick of it.* Blinking the thoughts away he held a photo. Two year old James, called Jamsie and baby Ruby. Matthew had shied away from Jamsie's babyhood, uninterested in such a helpless scrap of humanity. Then, one afternoon he'd been sitting on the veranda taking his boots off when Jamsie had toddled out to him, called him *Dadda* and collapsed on to Matthew's lap in the sudden way of toddlers. He babbled an incomprehensible story and his father was lost.

From that afternoon if Mary gave permission, Matthew took Jamsie everywhere, letting him toddle and play beside him as he worked. Having a son had given Matthew's marriage and life some sense of purpose. Ruby had only been a couple of months old when he left. Even then, as young as she was, Matthew knew he could never feel for his daughter what he did for Jamsie. *His son.* And that was something else he would never admit to anyone. Even Fee. *Especially Fee, who loved them equally.*

Wrapping the letters and photos in a waterproof bag, Matthew tucked them securely into his jacket pocket before settling down. It seemed impossible but he slept deeply and dreamlessly.

At 6pm he was woken by alarm bells. Even as he gathered his thoughts, Matthew felt the ship throbbing under full power and raced to his action station just behind A gun. His job was to heave the sixty pound shells up through the hatch. Nothing was happening so Matthew cautiously stuck his head out of the gangway to the main deck. On the horizon, all too near was the large Japanese cruiser, *Maia*. As he looked, she fired a full broadside of her ten eight inch guns, a ripple of flame running the length of the ship. The cruiser wasn't alone. Two others were in the background with two large destroyers closing in. *Oh God.*

Stronghold began to lay a thick smoke screen, heavy enough so she could weave through it, using oil from her dwindling reserves. At every break in the smoke, she opened fire. As well as the black smoke, *Stronghold* added dense white smoke from a canister on the stern. This camouflage worked. Without a visible target the Japanese gunfire couldn't be accurate. Matthew was only too aware this action merely bought them a little time. Too soon *Stronghold* had used up all her shells including their practice and smoke shells. Waiting for orders there was nothing to do, giving too much time for thought. Matthew tried not to remember Nanking and the unforgiving ocean covering horizon to horizon.

All *Stronghold* could do she did. Knowing the Japanese had no radar, her crew used the time until nightfall remaining hidden behind their smoke screen, a heavy swell working in their favour. It couldn't last. After half an hour twisting and turning, *Stronghold's* oil was almost finished. Over the tannoy came their final order,

'Stand by to ram.'

Stronghold swung out of the smoke, her four torpedo tubes loaded and trained on one of the cruisers which prepared her own eight and five inch guns. The two destroyers followed her lead. In no time they found *Stronghold's* range and the shells began to land with deadly accuracy. They hit the bridge first, killing all hands. The engine room was next stopping *Stronghold* dead in the water. The next shell exploded near the ammunition crew. Matthew was slammed into the steel side of the ship and knew no more.

When he came to, groaning, he was being carefully shaken, the *Stronghold's* alarms screaming, the explosions deafening.

Whitey was beside him. 'Come on, Matt. We've gotta get something to eat.'

It was surreal.

'Eat?'

'We're heading overboard. Who knows when we'll eat. Come on.'

Dazedly Matthew followed Whitey to the galley. They stepped over dead crewmates, a young Chinese boy with both legs blown off, another disemboweled, his stomach on his lap. Swallowing hard at the sight of blood mixed with a mess of half-cooked fried eggs and baked beans they realized there was no food. *Couldn't eat any now anyway.* A quick check for survivors. Just the one with the bones of his leg poking through his thigh. *Thank God the poor sod was unconcscious.* They carried him to the deck where they seemed to be the only ones left.

It was dark now, the only light coming from the fires. The main steam safety valve on the funnel had blown and the roar was painful. Whitey pointed at the two carly rafts left behind. An oval shaped raft of cork with a canvas covering, a carly had a two foot outer diameter ring and a slat floor suspended from rope mesh inside with internal dimensions measuring no more than six feet by four. Six paddles, a stoneware jug holding three gallons of fresh water and a sealed tin of ship's biscuits were lashed to the slats. It normally took six men to handle but adrenalin surged through Matthew and Whitey. They cut the tie-down ropes and managed to get the two rafts across the deck and over the guard rail as the sea lapped the deck. Grabbing their injured crew mate they threw him into the darkness, hoping like hell he landed on the raft. As Whitey disappeared into the sea Matthew cast a final glance around the dying *Stronghold*. Tough and dependable she had become their home. To lose her was losing family.

Pulling himself together, Matthew went over the side and swam strongly, bumping into the empty raft roughly twenty five metres away. *Whitey must have reached another raft.* This one had landed in the water upside down and the paddles were lashed to the underside of the slat floor with the water jug and biscuits dangling below the raft, about three metres down on a piece of rope. *Nothing he could do about it.* Aching everywhere, Matthew blew up his life jacket and eased himself into the raft. A wave of nausea swamped him, a headache thumping viciously. Fighting the urge to vomit, he cast about for something to take his mind off it and watched other crew members swimming towards him. No Whitey. No Dag. The last to arrive was a fat bloke Matthew didn't know, a passenger taken aboard at Tjilatjap. There was simply was no room for him.

'Let me on board,' he moaned. 'I'm wounded.'

At the sight of his pale face, Matthew slid off the raft beside him.

'Change places with me every couple of hours, all right?'

The relief on the man's face was tremendous. Promptly agreeing, he let Matthew help him on to the raft. It was so overloaded the outer rim was about a foot under water and holding on to the looped rope running around the perimeter was difficult. Matthew ended up to his chin in the ocean, hanging on for dear life. He risked a look behind them. *Stronghold* rode low in the water, eerily illuminated by the light of the still-burning fires. A final explosion and her bow disappeared as she slid under the water.

The survivors were alone on an ill-omened sea.

They bobbed silently in the dark, only the odd moan or groan from the wounded breaking the silence of the splashing waves. After Matthew had judged he'd been in the water a couple of hours he prodded the fat bloke sitting above him.

'My turn, mate.'

All he got in return was an adamant shake of the head.

'No way.'

'What? You fucking promised!'

'Changed my mind.'

'You bastard. Come on, fair's fair.' But the man wouldn't

even look at Matthew. 'Are you even wounded?' No reply. The man turned himself completely around, his back to his rescuer. Matthew shot a look around the others in the raft. Shoulder-to-shoulder they sat. No one spoke. No one made eye contact. No one offered to change places and give him a break.

Bastards the lot of you!

Matthew shivered in the cold water. He had survived, wearing a pair of khaki shorts and bugger all else. He gingerly checked his wounds, feeling heavy shrapnel embedded in his right thigh with other smaller pieces in both legs, his chest and face covered in dozens of tiny wounds. No matter his predicament, he had survived an exploding shell. *And if he managed to do that, he would survive this, too.*

The night dragged on slowly. Too cold for anyone to sleep. Matthew's strength ebbed. It became more and more tiring to keep his face above water. No white caps on the swell of waves, though. *Thank God for small mercies.*

Dawn broke revealing an endless sea. Just the rafts scattered at wide distances. Summoning up some meagre energy, Matthew stretched his legs out and kicked them before drawing them back in as tightly as the pain of his wounds would let him. He did it again and again to try and warm up, to concentrate on something else.

A voice from the raft. 'Hey mate. Seeing as how you're out there, how about you dive down and grab the rations?'

As angry with all the bastards as he was, Matthew had to admit to being just as hungry and thirsty. 'All right,' he said. 'But one of you buggers needs to help me.'

Silence.

'You're kidding, right?' Matthew gave a bitter, incredulous laugh. 'You won't even help to save yourselves?'

Silence.

'Fuck you all. How about giving me a break?'

Nothing.

Then and there Matthew decided he would grab the rations but only when his desperation forced him to. *Bastards.*

The sun rose to its mid-point, blistering skin raw.

How long before we all become shark food? His legs dangled temptingly. Blood from any wounds would signal their presence to any of those perfectly designed killers.

Don't think about it. Don't think about it.

Matthew's tongue was gummed to the roof of his mouth and his lips burned *Could do with a drink.* Again he weighed up the effort required to bring up the water hanging below the raft.

'How about we bring the water up? Biscuits too. I'm happy to go down but I'll need someone hauling from up here.'

Silence.

By late afternoon Matthew's hands were so numb, clinging to the rope would soon be impossible. He was trying not to think of anything at all when someone on the raft yelled.

'Ship! Fucking ship!'

Everyone held their breath and waited for the next swell to lift them. Two masts on the horizon, their tops painted light blue, the colour of all Dutch freighters. Ragged cheering broke out. The freighter closed into the area and stopped a little more than half a mile away. Riding the crests they could see she had stopped alongside a raft and men were beginning to climb up the ladder hanging over the side.

Matthew did some rapid thinking. *She might not see us riding so low in the water. We've no oars to reach her. What if she leaves without seeing us?*

With absolutely no regrets at leaving his raft-mates behind, he swam for it. Encouraged by the view from each succeeding crest of the ship becoming larger, Matthew strained every muscle, thoughts of sharks egging him on. *What if she leaves without seeing us?*

Finally, exhausted, he came alongside the other now empty raft and began to haul himself up the ladder dangling over the side. With his last spurt of energy he threw himself onto the deck where he collapsed, laughing, giddy with the relief of rescue. Shadows fell across as Matthew as he lay on his back. Grinning, he looked up into an Oriental face whose owner jabbed him viciously with a bayonet. This Dutch freighter had been claimed as a war prize by the Japanese.

Oh, Jesus.

Piles of dead, massacred bodies. Blood everywhere. The dead lying in their hundreds, thousands.

Matthew struggled to his feet. His knees refused to lock and they buckled helplessly. He slumped back down onto the deck. The Japanese soldier screamed at him, pouring out a stream of language Matthew had no hope of understanding. He shook his head, unable to move. He was kicked viciously. More screaming, the rifle lifted, butt end towards Matthew who froze, expecting the beating when someone jumped between him and the screaming guard.

Whitey standing tall. 'Don't move, Matt. Don't say a word.'

Matthew couldn't have done either if he tried. From behind the stunned survivors two more Japanese appeared and they were all hustled away, expecting to be shot at any moment. Instead, they were taken to the mess deck and put in the charge of an officer, stern looking, but not given to screaming. They were fed, washed, had their wounds tended to and given a mat to sleep on. Whitey made sure Matthew ate and helped him lie on the mat, throwing over his own, damp jacket over his friend.

Matthew mumbled, 'Never been more pleased to see your ugly mug.'

'Wish I could say the same.'

Matthew gave a hoarse chuckle. 'Dag?'

Silence.

With massive effort Matthew forced his eyelids open. Whitey shook his head, blinking away tears. The stab of pain came and went. Unable to cling to anything, grief or thought, Matthew surrendered to sleep.

Where the hell were they?

No way of knowing where they'd been brought to. From the wharf of what had once been a fair sized town, now mostly bombed into ruins, they were taken through beautiful scenery of lush vegetation and past high gates enclosing a camp surrounded by equally high, barbed wire fences. Once the trucks stopped, the screaming from their captors began anew as every prisoner was dragged off and forced into lines. Punches flew, rifle butts used as they were counted and searched. Watches, money, anything of any value was stripped from the survivors. Matthew had nothing for them to steal. His letters and photos were already lost at sea. 'The bastards will have the fillings from our teeth,' he muttered out of the corner of his mouth.

Whitey didn't dare display a hint of acknowledgment.

The buildings in the camp had the look of army billets and this was reinforced when they saw men in Dutch army uniforms watching from the windows and leaning against doorways. They were divided into the barracks where overcrowding was all too evident. Each two-man cubicle was expected to house six men. Sleeping had to be done in turns.

'Jesus,' Matthew whispered, the final sibilant dragged out far beyond its natural scan. He felt dazed. *What had he truly expected the life of a prisoner of war to be?* He couldn't answer. Dread had frozen his expectations when he landed on the Dutch ship, the Oriental face staring down at him. *Nanking. Piles of bodies bayoneted to an unimaginable death.* Matthew swallowed hard, couldn't keep his gaze from the guards' rifles. *Bayoneted to death.*

The guards marched away and the men slowly unwound. Trying not to stare at those who were already prisoners Matthew and Whitey began to move cautiously around the various buildings.

'Got to get a sense of our new home,' was Whitey's comment.

Matthew matched his nonchalance with flippancy. 'Wonder where the billiard room is?'

'Where do you think it will be? Right next to the smoking room. Philistine.'

The cook house held two huge iron rice pans, the catering done by two English cooks overseen by a Japanese soldier, the first and only one who didn't look as if he loathed them on sight. The latrine block. The wash block. Toilets consisted of footprints set into concrete astride a long, central drain channel and an eight sitter with no seats. Water was supplied to the wash block - water, no soap.

Apart from the well-uniformed Dutch, the other prisoners wore a rag-tag range of bits and pieces of uniform. It dawned on Matthew - *whatever they had on now was all they were expected to live in.* He cast a rueful look at his naval shorts, the only clothes he wore. Already filthy, torn as well. *How long would they last and what would he do when they fell apart?*

Whitey exhaled a long, slow breath as he and Matthew took in their surroundings incredulously.

'Home sweet home,' Matthew muttered

'After what we've seen and been through, my friend, I'm just bloody glad we're alive.'

Whitey never swore. Matthew gaped at him even as he accepted the truth of it.

Macassar Camp on the island of Celebes. That was where they were. Jan gave this information. He'd been a Dutch soldier here until the Japanese occupation. Unlike the prisoners following after them, the Dutch had all their clothing plus spares and all their money.

'You'll be living the life of Riley then, mate.' Matthew said.

Jan, however knew no English slang, merely offering a blank expression and a shrug.

'How many prisoners are there?' Whitey asked.

'Two thousand.' Jan replied solemnly. 'Two thousand prisoners in a camp designed for three hundred soldiers.' His accent was thick but not so indistinct that the enormity of this escaped them.

Having resigned themselves to the arrangements, the arrival of more prisoners meant a rearrangement of living quarters for the *Stronghold* survivors.

'Fingers crossed for the penthouse suite.' Whitey said, twisting two fingers together and holding them up.

A guard swiped him across the head with the end of his rifle and abused him for talking. At least, they assumed it was abuse. They had no Japanese so who knew? Perhaps he was giving them his condolences.

Matthew covered his mouth as if coughing to answer, 'As if they'd let you stay in a penthouse suite. Look at the state of you.' He too wore the rifle butt off the back of his head. Obviously prisoners making any sound at all were to be treated harshly.

No condolences, then.

They were taken to a central block with wings coming off it and each wing was already crammed. When sleeping they would be shoulder-to-shoulder, lined up feet to centre. Every man would have a space roughly the size of himself and no more. They had no furniture. No mats. No coverings of any kind. They had nothing except what they wore.

Food was a small bun in the morning and in the evenings, plain boiled rice eaten out of their hands for there were no bowls or eating utensils. Matthew thanked God for one thing – there was plenty of water from a tap in the yard.

'What doesn't fatten fill,' Whitey stated, wiping his chin.

Matthew glared at him. 'Are you going to be this hearty every damn day?'

'Will you find it very annoying?'

'Yes.'

'Then most probably I will.' Whitey smiled angelically.

Life quickly became monotonous. Tenko, the head count every morning and evening and nothing else to do but wander the camp trying to ignore the increasing pangs of hunger. When a group of prisoners tried to arrange a sing-a-long, they were beaten. A football game with an old traded ball ended the same way. The hungrier they became, the more listless. Groups of men sat slumped against walls, the soaring temperatures sapping what strength they had. Heat became as great an enemy as lack of food or the guards.

Boredom affected the guards too, and they looked to their captives to relieve their boredom. Punishment became a pastime. They took inordinate pleasure in dishing out imaginative punishments merely to have something to do. One of their favourites was the most simple - keep a man standing in the boiling sun until he dropped. If it had been a slow day they made him stand on his head, thoroughly enjoying his distress.

After a few weeks a whisper went round the camp about an expected consignment of Red Cross parcels.

'Every prisoner receives these, don't they? As part of the Geneva Convention?' Whitey was asking around, trying to find some credence in the rumour.

'The Nips don't recognize the Geneva Convention, cobber.' A wiry Australian explained. 'No parcels for us. Better if we'd been taken by the fucking Germans.'

'Maybe the Americans will rescue us.' Whitey raised an eyebrow as their skeptical companion gave a spurt of mocking laughter. 'I overheard a Brit officer saying they were arriving any day.'

'Yeah and maybe the moon's made of cheese,' jeered the Aussie. 'Get used to what you've got, mates. 'Cause this is all there is.'

Matthew fought his despair. *What did they have? Nothing. Not one fucking thing worth a damn.*

Not long after this conversation they were put onto working parties, a hundred men each rotation. Relief at escaping mind-numbing boredom and the overcrowded camp was tempered by the gruelling slog of slaving for the Japanese. Whether they were unravelling miles of barbed wire between the coast and the sea, their skin flayed and torn, loading ships, humping back-breaking loads, or demolishing the bombed out harbour town, prisoners became part of the Japanese war machine.

After a brutal ten hour slog, Matthew was one of the miserable, hungry team being taken back to camp. Their hands were nothing but bloodied mess, every palm throbbing with barbed wire lacerations. Shirt edges were torn as they sought material for bandages. No shirt, no bandages. To increase Matthew's misery, his shorts had been ripped further and he was dwelling on ways to preserve his dignity as they trudged back. Ahead of them walked a group of Chinese locals. Not prisoners, they had been pressured to work for the Japanese. One carried a sack on his back. It was hard for those of European descent to judge expressions on Asiatic faces but there seemed to be sympathy in this man's dark, slanting eyes. This was proved as with a quick, sudden gesture, he reached into his sack and pulled out a small brown bag of rice, shoving it in Matthew's hands. Before Matthew could thank him, a shout erupted behind them, a stream of Japanese. The Chinese man took fright. He ran off, dropping the sack in his panic. He wasn't nearly quick enough. In seconds, three guards had him on the ground, rubbing his face into the dirt.

Matthew was dragged out of line. The small bag of rice ripped out of his hands and upended onto the ground.

'You steal!' Spit landed on Matthew's face but he didn't flinch.

'No.'

The Chinese man was hauled beside Matthew then butted into him, causing the New Zealander to stumble back. Matthew tried to make eye contact with him but the terrified man kept his head bowed. The Japanese guards pushed him to and fro, screaming at him, their helpless prey keeping his eyes on the ground. Having wound themselves up to a frenzy the guards began to attack him, punching him to the ground, kicking him as he twisted into the foetal position in a hopeless effort to evade the blows.

Matthew looked at Jan and unspoken communication passed between them. *Say nothing. Do nothing. Keep quiet you fool!*

But Matthew couldn't stand there and watch this man being half-killed. This man who had only offered a kindly gesture in recognition of suffering. He stepped forward and bellowed. 'Stop!' The shock of one of their prisoners stepping out of line brought every Japanese guard to a stunned halt. 'He did nothing wrong! Nothing!'

For his outspokenness, Matthew wore a rifle butt across his face. He managed to turn his head so the blow didn't connect with his jaw. If it had it would have shattered. Taken on the back of his skull his head reeled and his senses spun drunkenly.

'You silent! You stay!'

Matthew never knew why they didn't kill him there and then.

Jan told him later how much the Japanese loathed the Chinese. 'You were nothing compared to the revenge they wanted to extract from the Chinaman.'

Matthew didn't feel lucky, not then, not until he lived through the fate of the kindly man. They were all forced to watch his terrible beating, then bloodied but not broken they took him to the beach. All along the sand were poles sunk into the mudflats of the receded ocean and these were used by the local fisherman. It was low tide when they tied the Chinese man to one of the poles with barbed wire. Laughing and joking, the Japanese soldiers left him there to suffer the inevitability of the gradually returning waves until they drowned him.

Matthew was given the job of cutting down the dead body and burying it. He began to hate their captors to the depths of his soul.

***

Matthew and Whitey were among the first sent to pull down the splintered walls of the ruined town. They were handed sledgehammers. No wheelbarrows, not even a bucket. Walls were to be smashed and the rubble carried away in bare arms.

'This isn't going to end well,' Matthew said. 'Hardly any clothes, most of us have no shoes. What the hell do the Nips thinks gonna happen to us?'

'Fairly sure they don't care,' was Whitey's comment.

In no time at all, arms and feet bled and blistered. They slaved up to sixteen hours a day and were given no more rations. Prisoners began to sicken and die.

The bastard Nips didn't care. Plenty more prisoners where they came from.

It was late afternoon. Hot as hell and they had been working since dawn. They were pulling down the last section of masonry in what used to be a general store according to Jan. With a grunt of effort, Matthew swung the sledgehammer, standing back as the wall collapsed onto the rubble strewn floor only to disappear. Startled he peered down into the hole it created, coughing at the backdraft of dust.

'A cellar,' he breathed.

Moving as swiftly as he could Matthew found Whitey and Jan sweating in the half-demolished building next door.

'Come quick as you can but don't let anyone see.'

'What've you found?'

'Don't piss about, Whitey. Just come on.'

In no time the three of them had clambered down into the cellar, peering through the murk at the shelves of tinned food and goods.

'It's like Aladdin's cave,' Whitey grinned.

Such a find couldn't be kept to themselves. Word passed around the work group and one by one each man found his way into the cellar to gawp.

'We've gotta get it back to camp.'

'Bugger that! The guards'll flay us alive if they catch us with stolen goods.'

'Nothing stopping us enjoying it here while we work. Bloody Nips don't come near us in these ruins. The only necks they're willing to risk are ours.'

In the end, each shift was told of the magical offerings to be had in the cellar and those prepared to take the risk took supplies back through the inspection at the gates. Amazing ingenuity came to the fore. Hidden pockets were sewn into the inside legs of trousers or in the back of jackets. Bags were made to tie around a waist and dangle between the legs. One Australian who topped six foot three won the award for most resourceful hiding place. He simply placed what he could under his hat. No Japanese guard was over five foot four and when Bluey stood tall, they never bothered to look under his hat.

Not everyone was so lucky. Poor Jan stumbled on returning after one shift. The bag of flour he had secured in his jacket burst open when he fell. With a scream of rage from the guard, he was dragged to the tenko yard. There he had to stand with his arms stretched wide, bags of rice in each hand and left. If he flagged, they beat him. If his arms sagged, they beat him. Hours later when Jan collapsed to the ground he was flogged and kicked to unconsciousness. He never fully recovered from this attack. The head injuries slowed his reactions and Jan never again broke any rule.

When they weren't slaving, tedium remained the biggest threat to their sanity. Endless games of cards or dice were played, trading with the Chinese and the natives, over the back fences in the middle of the night for books, food, supplies. It all became part of the survival game. Whitey surprised Matthew who thought he was beyond surprises. His friend had managed to get his hands on needle and thread. Out of sight of any guard he bent laboriously over the only piece of material he could get, his naval issue handkerchief. On this he embroidered New Zealand. It was done freehand and from memory, with the New Zealand flag on the left and curved around the whole work of art were the words *Home Sweet Home*. Once finished it was something other New Zealand prisoners wanted to see. They handled it gently, staring at the familiar shape of their country and when they handed it back something inside them had been a little replenished. Keeping this precious thing hidden became important. If Whitey was discovered with it he would be killed where he stood. Even though Matthew appreciated what it had come to mean to his friend he asked if it was worth the price he could pay.

Whitey's fingers traced the outline of the North Island. 'It's worth it,' he said softly.

***

Days merged into weeks, into months. Time meant nothing more than the constant struggle to survive. Starving and abused, with no medical supplies, what became important was your buddy. Each man looked out for his buddy. Fed him when he was sick, sharing his own meagre rations. Keeping an eye out, taking his place when he couldn't work. You kept your buddy alive, secure in the knowledge he would do the same for you.

Moss
France.

How did he get into this?

Moss slipped a hand into his jacket and fingered the hilt of his dagger. No need to worry if it was sharp. He'd always kept it honed to its deadliest potential.

Always the possibility it might be needed. Especially now.

At the start of this madness, all he had set out to do was arrange some goods for Hugo, then piss off on the first boat out of port, putting miles between Tyke and the turmoil of his feelings for her. It shouldn't have been difficult. *Except the part about Tyke. That's still difficult.*

When he landed in Normandy there were rumours of Germany's occupation of France but no movement towards it. The Phoney War was in place, some people even believing there was time to halt Hitler's war machine.

Into port. Find contact. Travel to contact. Arrange goods. See goods back onto ship. Bugger off. Simple.

Except here he was in a country under German occupation, hiding during the days, moving during the night helping friends who had connections to the resistance.

Why couldn't he have ignored Lucien's pleas for help and left while there were ships to leave on?

'You're a soft-hearted fool, Moss,' he muttered under his breath.

Actually, he did know why and it wasn't really to do with kindness. It was Tyke. She had allowed him to release those feelings he had locked away and just when he had believed it would all be as he hoped, she took it all away again.

'It was a mistake. You have to leave me alone.'

If he had caught just a look, just a gesture, just one bloody sign she didn't really mean it he would have stayed and argued. But all there had been was coldness and regret. So he left, as angry as he had ever been in his life. Twice now he'd been in this turmoil. When she first kissed him and ran, and now, when he was the one doing the running.

I never understood why you felt you had to leave us so far behind, Tyke. I bloody do now.

Arriving in Le Havre. Losing himself deep in the Normandy countryside among its hills and valleys. And Lucien asking for help as German tanks rolled through towns and villages, taking Paris, cutting the country in half. Lucien and Marceline's anger at their country.

'The French government collaborated. They have sold us to the fascists without mercy.' Lucien pacing, pacing, pacing.

'Not only our government,' Marceline, softer, if no less bitter. 'Too many of our countrymen see no wrong in Hitler. They support him and whoever he says is an enemy, they are the enemy, no questions asked. If we resist him....'

Lucien exploded. 'If?'

'...then we must take care for we could be turned in.'

Moss stepped into the conversation.

'Turned in by who?'

Pause.

'By those who would hate us if they discover what Lucien is.'

'What he is?' Moss studied Lucien. 'What are you?'

Pause. Pulsing, ragged.

'I am a Jew.' Lucien spat out. 'A Jew. Do you want to forget you met me now? Leave? Turn me in?'

As Marceline instantly took Lucien to task for behaving so badly to their guest, Matthew shook his head. 'I don't care about your faith, Lucien.'

Still fired up Lucien refused to give an inch. 'And what do you care about? Anything?' He shrugged off Marceline's restraining hand, kept his eyes on Moss's face as if the answer meant everything.

'Yes.' Moss offered no more, just a steady look for he knew his teasing answer/non-answer would annoy the Frenchman.

After a long pause, Lucien offered the most grudging of smiles but no more accusation as he turned his vehemence back onto fascist collaborators.

Moss listened as if from a distance. Politics had never interested him. He would stand up for the underdog but it never mattered to him what political stripes they wore. *Rich versus poor was his take on life. As for war? He never had any intention of enlisting. There were enough battles for the working class.*

Yet something of Lucien and Marceline's unstinting, unthinking bravery got to him. What began as taking the odd message here and there, or setting up a radio in an out of the way place ended up with him as part of their personal defiance. At first Moss welcomed the challenge as a distraction from his unhappiness. It took a few months until he realised it was the challenge itself he needed, craved even. There was no way out of the country anymore now the merchant ships he could slip on and off were no longer accessible. The only escape route was the same one any person fleeing persecution could use; over the Alps or into Spain via the underground network which had been put into place with impressive speed.

So, here he was; moving through the French countryside on a dark night, wondering at all the odd byways and pathways of his life which led him to this moment.

And Tyke, of course. Always Tyke.

Taking Lucien's roughly drawn map from his pocket, Moss lit a match to read by. He'd had a torch up till a few weeks ago. It was now on its way to safety along with the Jewish family he gave it to. He hoped they all made it. Frowning at the sketch he took his bearings. Moving silently to the top of the hill he peered over the brow to the other side. He could just make out the broad expanse of unshadowed black which was his destination. Stuffing the map away, Moss jogged towards it. Nothing moved. The old barn seemed completely deserted. Reaching the door he whistled softly. There was the lightest pause until the end of the song returned out of the dark.

'Salut? Monsieur? Je suis Moss, s'il vous plait.' This was almost the full extent of his French apart from some swear words.

A head emerged from behind the broken-down farm machinery huddled against the far wall. 'Ici,' the man whispered. *Here.* A small lantern held in his hand provided all the light but it sufficed.

Moss eased the heavy canvas bag from his back with a grateful sigh. He lowered it to the ground as a woman and two small girls joined the man.

'Ma femme,' the man said softly, never pitching his voice above a whisper. 'Et mes filles.' *My wife and my daughters.*

Moss guessed the relationships. He gave the three frightened faces a smile and bow, which made the youngest girl giggle nervously. Opening the bag, Moss brought out bread, cheese and some dried meat, then two thick blankets and tinned food. From his pocket he brought out some sweets which he passed to the eldest girl with a gesture to indicate she had to share with her sister, some cigarettes for the man and another small brown paper bag, its top twisted firmly. This he passed to the woman who opened it and lifted it to her nose.

'Café,' she exclaimed in delight, passing the bag to her husband to share the aroma. 'Merci, Monsieur. Merci.'

'Lucien sent this.' Moss passed the man a letter and waited. When he lifted his head from the page, Moss asked, 'Oui or non?'

'Oui,' nodding vigorously.

'Deux nuits, Monsieur.' Moss held up two fingers to confirm. *Two nights.*

The little family hugged. Candlelight caught the glimmer of tears in the woman's eyes, the silvery trail as they fell down her cheeks yet she was smiling, too. His job done, Moss gathered up the empty canvas bag and lifted a hand in farewell. He hadn't taken more than three steps when the light from the lantern was snuffed carefully out and the family returned to their dark hideaway.

The next morning Moss was able to reassure Lucien of the job done, the family now prepared to begin their journey towards freedom. It wouldn't be safe. They might not make it. Still they had everything to lose by staying so they would try. This was the first time Lucien would use the underground all the way to the border. Both he and Marceline had undertaken part journeys, seeing refugees to a sanctuary, secure in the knowledge the next team would take them on. However, this family refused to trust anyone but Lucien. He would have to see them from safe house to safe house all the way to the Pyrenees.

'I need you to stay with Marceline while I am gone.' Lucien contemplated Moss. There was something completely dependable about him, from their first meeting that sense had been foremost. If Moss gave his word, he would stick to it. It also helped that he carried a lethal dagger and the look of someone who knew exactly how to use it.

Lucien had only met Hugo once, years ago, when his father brought him home to meet the family. From the stories his father told them, it was no surprise Hugo's nephew would offer himself up to this dangerous work. It was also the reason Lucien relied on the New Zealander's nerve and courage to look after Marceline and Luca. *Blood always told.*

Marceline hadn't long given birth to Luca and she wasn't happy Lucien was taking the Jewish family to the border on his own. Her arguments followed the same lines; *others risked their lives so should she.* No matter how passionate her urgings, Lucien wasn't prepared to risk both their lives. *What of their son?* With his wife in mind he told Moss, 'Marceline, she will not be happy. She will argue and when I am gone she will be angrier but I leave her in your care until I am home.' Lucien's smile lightened his normally serious expression. 'Of course, she will still be angry with me but at least I will be here for her to shout at.'

'You can count on me.'

'Merci, mon ami.'

They sat in companionable silence, letting the early morning sun warm their skin and light the corners of this dark thatched cottage by the river. They were close enough to hear the water tumbling over the stones as it wound its way to the sea.

Lucien relaxed, letting his breath out long and slow. His waved a hand to the view. 'I love this. It holds my heart. To think of it in the grip of hands other than French....' He stopped, determined to be peaceful. 'Do you miss your country, Moss?'

'It's people I miss, not places.'

'You have no love for your country?'

'I've never been one for flag waving.'

Lucien pondered this, his eyes on the water and the birds darting down to catch the insects hovering there. 'But our country is our identity. It's where we come from. It defines us.'

Matthew shook his head. 'Nationalism doesn't define me.'

'Then what does?'

A finger jabbed into his own chest. 'Me. I define myself.'

For the first time Lucien detected something else in this amiable New Zealander, something he had kept hidden until forced to reveal it to the light. Moss had been prodded to show passion. Intrigued, Lucien pressed on. 'So you miss nothing in the country of your birth? No one special?'

Yes. Moss lifted his shoulders in a deliberately negligent gesture. 'Family. I miss family.'

The Frenchman didn't pry further. He was happy to change the subject now he knew there would be more to unravel about this interesting Kiwi. 'We need to gather information on the whereabouts of the Germans. The Gestapo are pushing further into the countryside and we do not want to be caught up in Nacht and Nebel.'

Moss searched his mind, found the connection. 'Night and Fog, yes? I heard you speaking to Anat about it; all the disappearances.'

Lucien spat onto the ground, wiping the evidence away with his boot. 'The fucking Gestapo. Thousands are being taken away and never heard of again. On the word of a collaborator they will arrest anyone and no one ever returns, innocent or not. All our men, our workers are being lost and those bastard Germans want more.' Lucien's anger took hold. 'They take eighty per cent of our food to feed their army and themselves and demand more. How can we produce what we need with so few workers? And all the while French people starve and sicken.' Lucien stood up so quickly his chair unbalanced. Tipping backwards it crashed to the floor. Seconds later came the high-pitched cry of newborn Luca. Both men braced themselves.

Sure enough, down the stairs stomped Marceline, hair in disarray, baby Luca in her arms. 'How can he sleep when you make so much noise?' she demanded, narrowed eyes taking in one guilty face then the other.

'It was my fault, love.' Lucien stood at Marceline's side, one rough finger stroking his son's soft face.

Not to be placated Marceline glared. 'Of course it was your fault. It is always your fault. And stop swearing. Luca can hear you.' Making the sound of an angry cat Marceline turned on her heel and disappeared up the steep stairs to the bedroom under the eaves.

Lucien watched until they were out of sight. 'Tomorrow night when I leave, she will take her temper out on you, Moss.'

'If being Maudie's son gave me any insight, it's into the female temper. I'll be just fine.' Moss grew serious. 'Just make bloody sure you come home.'

Lucien was right about Marceline's mood. Moss patiently bore it day after day, taking care of Luca whenever he could to give her a break, giving her time to walk the forest and hills to find peace.

Then came the afternoon Marceline sighed and caught Moss's eye. In the shared glimpse she acknowledged his help, his friendship and moved to lightly kiss his cheek in apology for her temper. They settled down well from then on.

***

Lucien had been gone just over a fortnight when Marceline arrived back from the village, tense and worried.

'That bitch!' she spat, lowering her tone so to not waken Luca as she laid him in his cot.

'Which particular bitch?' Matthew asked calmly. So many of the local women were bitches to Marceline it was difficult to keep track.

'Maria Artois, the Bitch Queen. She asked after Lucien. 'We have not seen him about the village for days, Marceline. Wherever can he be?'' Marceline's mimicry was cruelly accurate, capturing Maria's nasal, whiny tone perfectly. 'I told her he was sick and of course, she spewed out her fake concern. She threatened to visit. I told her no but you know what she is like.'

'I know what you've told me.' Matthew replied with emphasis.

Marceline's hatred of her neighbour was the spur for her concern for Moss. Between them they had decided it would be better if he remained hidden from the locals. The little French language Matthew knew would fool no one into thinking he was born here and strangers were suspect, always. Having become used to his secret life, Matthew revelled in it. If at times he felt like a ghost in the world, all the better for what he had to do. In the meantime, the likes of Maria Artois were to be avoided at all costs.

'When she decides to visit you will have to lie upstairs and be a sick Lucien.'

'Will it fool her?'

Marceline nodded. 'You are a similar build and have the same dark hair. If you keep your back to the door and pretend to sleep, who could tell otherwise?'

Just as well Marceline laid the plan, for a few evenings later they heard someone walking the path towards their cottage. A quick look from the kitchen window revealed the short, rotund all too familiar figure. Moss disappeared up the stairs and lay on the bed, huddled under the covers the top of his head barely showing while Marceline picked Luca up and loosened her blouse to feed him. No sooner had the baby latched on than Maria appeared at the door.

'Oh, the little one is feeding.' Maria had a basket over one arm. She placed it on the table as she leaned over Luca. 'Such thick, dark hair. Did you drink raspberry leaf tea when you were carrying him?'

Marceline swallowed her dislike and found a convincing smile. 'No. I cannot abide the stuff.' She fondled the little head. 'He grew it all by himself. What can I do for you, Maria?

'I am here to visit the poor Lucien.'

'I told you it was not serious.'

'But you were so strange earlier. I worried he was very sick and you did not like to say.' Maria reached into her basket and pulled out a sealed jar. 'I made some of my good broth. There is enough for two or three bowls to tempt his appetite.'

Her chuckle grated on Marceline's ears. 'If you would like to see him, he is in bed, asleep. Please do not wake him. It is better for him to rest.'

'Do you know what is wrong with him? Have you sent for Monsieur le docteur?' Maria's eyes were hungry for detail.

'We do not need a doctor. Lucien has a fever, lack of appetite. He is a little better now he can sleep.'

'I will just pop up.' Without waiting for a reply Maria struggled up the steep stairs, her bulky effort making Marceline smirk behind the woman's back.

Hearing all this, Moss lay motionless.

With a panting gasp, Maria made it to the doorway and poked her head through into the room. 'Are you sleeping, Lucien?'

Silence.

'Lucien?'

Nothing.

Moss gave a realistic mutter, settled more deeply under the covers. After a long pause, he heard Maria's heavy tread back on the stairs. When she spoke to Marceline, he sat up, listening intently.

'Still sound asleep, Marceline.'

'Good. Well, thank you for your visit and the broth. I am sure it will do Lucien the world of good.' *Just leave us alone, you damn nosy bitch.*

Maria picked up her basket. In the doorway she paused. 'Have you seen the stranger hanging around?'

It took a second for Marceline to gather her thoughts, hoping the alert Maria noticed nothing. 'Stranger?'

'Apparently one has been seen around the village in the small hours. A man, I heard.'

Using the pretext to resettle Luca in his cot, Marceline was able to turn away from Maria's intent stare as she pretended to think. 'A strange man? No. I have not seen or heard a thing.' Maria's sharp, black eyes were fixed on Marceline as she faced her once more. 'Do let me know if he is sighted again.'

'I will. Be sure and keep the door locked.'

'Oui.'

'Oh, and the Germans have taken the Marchand family.'

'Les Marchands? Why?'

Maria's beady eyes glittered and her mouth thinned. 'They are Jews. All this time among us and we did not know.'

Marceline's expression didn't change. *We did.* She hated her next thought. *Will they betray Lucien?*

'You and Lucien were good friends of theirs, I think?'

'Like everyone else in the village we knew them, yes.'

'But particularly, I heard.' The sly insinuation in Maria's tone was more than aggravating, it was frightening.

'They are good people.' *The effort not to reach out and slap the fat face eyeing her so inquisitively!*

'You must take care, Marceline. Showing sympathy towards Jews will taint your own reputation.' A tinkling, insincere laugh. 'Not from me, I can assure you. Non. But others.' Maria lay a finger on her lips. 'I could name names but I shall not. But they listen. They judge. You must take care or you will lose everything.'

Suddenly the round, overfed face wasn't comic anymore. It was terrifying. *You know these people. They know you and your family. And they will turn on you like wolves to protect themselves or to claim what is yours.* Marceline suppressed the shiver tingling the length of her spine. Somehow she found the strength to reply, even as her stomach swam sickly. 'I am glad les Marchands have been taken. We do not want their kind here.'

An odd expression flitted across Maria's face but to Marceline's great relief the woman smiled her farewell and left.

Standing on the path, Marceline watched the fat figure recede into the evening shadows. Only when she was certain they were alone again did she close the door. Feeling nauseous she locked it, leaning her weight back against it as Moss came down the stairs.

'Did you hear it all?'

He nodded. 'Did you know the Marchands?'

'Yes.' Marceline slumped into a chair. 'Well enough to know they were kind and would never harm a soul.' She covered her face with icy hands. 'And here they are, judged and condemned by people they shared their lives with, broke bread with, laughed with.' When she raised her eyes to Moss the anguish showed. 'And I damned them, too.'

'You did not. They had already been condemned. You protected Lucien.'

'I feel like a traitor. Even by agreeing with the Artois bitch! How different am I to what she is?'

'You are nothing like Maria Artois. Marceline, you could never be like her. You and Lucien,' Moss paused, 'you are good people in a bad world. It is always easier to follow the crowd. And, you may be forced to bend a little, but they will never break you. Or change you.'

Tears edged her long lashes, Marceline's face was difficult to read. Even when she nodded, Moss didn't think she believed him, or believed in herself. 'I know the family you mean. Lucien wanted to get them away. Did he speak with them?'

'No. He was going to after this trip.' She wiped impatiently at her wet eyes. 'Too late for them now.'

Moss wasn't sure if Marceline meant her tears or the Marchands.

Marceline welcomed a flood of anger. 'Artois bitch! Coming here with her pretend concern. She hates us, you know. Always has. She must never find out Lucien is a Jew. She is on the lookout for anything to condemn us.'

'Why?'

'She wants this land. It used to belong to her father but he got into financial difficulties in the years before the last war and had to sell. Ever since my family moved here she has resented us. When father died Maria came round crying crocodile tears and offering to buy the land to save me the trouble of running it.' She clenched her hands into fists as they lay on the table. 'I was the only one left of our family, both my brothers dead in Flanders. Maria thought I would hand it over. But she was wrong. My father bent his back over the fields. Of course I would do the same! A few months later I met Lucien and we fell in love, married. She will never get her hands on our land.' Marceline scowled, shaking off the old memories to focus on the here and now. 'And you better keep close until the stranger is forgotten.'

'I thought I had been careful.' Moss's tone was rueful.

'This is village life, Moss. Everyone sees everything and knows everything. A secret is hard to keep.' Marceline said grimly.

And the problem was at times like these, secrets were essential to survival.

***

Lucien's return was hailed with relief. He had seen the family safely over the border and took the opportunity on his travels back to gather evidence on the movement of the Germans, which villages and towns remained unoccupied and which they had taken. All information they would need to pass on.

Marceline shared Maria Artois's interest in their little family and this gave Lucien pause. Nothing they could do except be on their guard even more.

But the thing which caused the most debate was Lucien's new beard.

'It makes you look like a pirate.' Marceline laughed as she tugged on it.

'I am thinking of keeping it.'

'Non.' Marceline turned to Moss. 'Moss, support me on this. No beard, oui?'

Making great show of studying his friend, Moss frowned. 'I don't know.' He moved around Lucien, studying his profile from left to right. 'It hides his ugly face.'

After a pause, Lucien let out a guffaw, immediately echoed by baby Luca's cry. Marceline scolded both men, unable to hide her own amusement.

There wasn't much cause for laughter in their lives. All the more reason to enjoy it when they found it.

***

Murchison

Fee carried the last bucket of fresh milk into the kitchen and placed it on the table beside two others. It all had to be separated and the separator itself sat sterilised and ready. Yet....

Outside the day was fresh and cool, the early dawn sky an enticing pink-flushed clear blue. Decision made, Fee covered the milk buckets with cloth and wandered out of the kitchen. Walking down the veranda steps and over the lawn something propelled her forward until she reached the paddocks with their river border. She found a perfect piece of slope and there Fee sat cross-legged on the dew-wet grass. It promised to be a perfect summer day.

In this place, at this moment, it was impossible to imagine a world war raging in Europe. Are you safe in London, Tyke?

Fee could still conjure the shock she had felt reading Alex's letter.

... 'Tyke has escaped her problems by running to London. We've not heard a word from her. Dear Fee, if she writes to you, would you please consider writing to let me know? If you felt you could, I would be very grateful....'

Fee had replied to her aunt the same day. She promised to do what was asked and wondered from then on what could have gone so wrong in her cousin's life that the other side of the world seemed the best option. In spite of the bond they had formed so quickly at their first and only meeting, Tyke had never written. A part of Fee always hoped she would. *Da's funeral. The unbearable tension among the adults. Tyke holding her hand when sleep wouldn't come.* How often had Tyke popped into her mind, especially once the bombing in Britain began? *Hope you're safe, cousin. I hope, I hope.*

Of course it was Matthew who was most often in her thoughts. Almost with every breath Fee worried about him. All around her the lingering earthy scents of summer. Cows lowed, sheep bleated. Birds chased insects in the warming air. *Impossible to imagine Matt on a ship in the Pacific Ocean.*

His letters home had given no indication of his feelings, not that Fee expected them to, knowing her twin as she did. *But couldn't he open up to her? Just a little?* His letters read almost like a travelogue – '*You should see the luxury of our base here in Singapore. I tell you, Fee, we earn more than the Brits and boy! Do they bitch about it!*' It was only in his last letter that Fee read a hint of anything other than buoyant expectation. '*I've learned a bit about the enemy, Fee. The Japs are ferocious little bastards. Just as well we are capable of being ferocious big bastards, eh?*'

She had been amazed when Matthew declared he was joining up. His love for home farm, his family, the workshop, she never thought they wouldn't prove to be enough.

Hamish had been gobsmacked. 'What the hell was Matt thinking of?' The question he still asked Fee on a regular basis.

Not that she could ever give him an answer which made any real sense. It wasn't until Matthew's letters arrived during his training, then Fee began to understand. *He needed to escape.* The years had been long and difficult. Once Matthew enlisted his life simplified and, surrounded by other young men seeking an adventure, it became one for him, too. An adventure without responsibilities. Where other people made the decisions, big and small. Where he could have nights off and drink with no one to judge him.

Where he didn't have to play the husband and father.

Fee shifted her gaze back to their home. *Could she blame him? Was she disappointed in him? It wouldn't matter one way or the other to Matt. His sense of purpose driven by a patriotism adopted or not, gave righteousness to his decision.*

Fee knew too how unhappy her twin had been. Marriage forced on him by circumstances to a woman who bored him, even Jamsies's birth hadn't satisfied Matthew's growing restiveness. *He had never admitted as much to her but he couldn't hide from his twin.* His enlistment merely proved Fee's suspicions correct.

How did Mary feel about it? That was easily answered.
Uncomplicated, simple, hard-working, Mary loved Matthew.
Unless he did something unforgivable she would always love
Matthew. Mary asked nothing more than a home and family.
She had them. If her husband wasn't what she expected or
hoped, hers wasn't the personality to delve when it might
unearth problems. *If Mary was an animal, she'd be an ostrich.*

They had all changed and not changed in the year since
Matthew left. Wally and Ben had rebuilt the workshop next to
their house in town. They still helped out on the farm when
needed but focussed on their workshop. *And what about her?*
With Da gone she stayed. Easy to imagine she was providing
essential care although Mary was no slouch at farm duties and
housework while raising two children without a husband's
support.

You have spent all your life assuming you would look after your
Da. But he's gone, Fee. And you haven't moved on.

Janet had. *Mostly. When viewed from outside.* Apart from
occasional baby-sitting duties which she adored, Janet lived in
town with Wally and Ben. While they did most of the
mechanical work, she tinkered alongside them, did the books,
ran the house and appeared happy. Fee wondered if only she
caught a wistfulness in her aunt's eyes. *Did anyone else notice?*
Janet's grieving was still raw. Too raw to speak of Jimmy even
with Fee. *We miss him and can't talk of him. What a sad state of*
affairs.

And speaking of affairs....

Cally floated in and out, neither with the family or with Jeff –
a position Fee had adjusted to but barely. The jagged wound
of her mother's infidelity hadn't healed since Jimmy's death.
Why the hell didn't Mother just leave?

Janet who knew Cally better than anyone had no
explanation. *'One of life's mysteries,'* she would grimace and
change the subject.

There was always Hamish. His homely, composed face
appeared in her mind. Honest, steady brown eyes, he had a

cheeky spark which could be startling if you weren't expecting it.

'Marry me, Fee.'

Sigh. 'No, thank you.'

'Why not?'

Thoughtful pause.

'I honestly don't know.'

Exasperated pause.

'Well, that's just bloody annoying.'

They had regular conversations varying on this theme. Fee wasn't being cruel. She couldn't give Hamish the answer he wanted, to either his first or second question. She truly didn't know. *It was just....well, it felt like settling.* And she didn't want to settle. *She didn't crave foreign vistas. She didn't need constant excitement. So what was it?*

'Is it me, then?'

'No. It's me.'

'Is there someone else?'

'No! How many times do I have to tell you?'

'Every time, Fee. Until you can give me a better explanation.'

Impatient at herself, Fee shoved up onto her feet to glare at the view she found so captivating minutes ago. Still reluctant to return to the separating, she wandered the river's edge. *Aunt Janet had lived a half-life, devoted to someone who didn't return her feelings. She couldn't live a life which didn't have Jimmy in it so she had been prepared to sacrifice any other options to have the little of him she could.*

There was more on offer for her, Fee knew. *A life with Hamish.* Marriage. Children. Helping him run his own farm which at this time was little more than native bush with a few acres of clearance around his cottage. *Hard work to make it what he wanted. Hamish was a good man. Strong, even-tempered and playful. Joyous, at times. What the hell is wrong with you, Fee? Do you only want to live for Matt's family and never have your own? If you don't want distant horizons then surely Murchison ones should be sufficient?*

She was being contrary. And, if she didn't watch out, faithful Hamish would find someone else to share life with. *That would hurt. Seeing him with another woman.*

Her other self yelled, *'Then take him you stupid cow!'*

Fee grimaced. 'Shouting doesn't help, you know.'

Unsettled and in two minds, Fee kicked stones all the way home. After all, work, as always, waited.

'You're very quiet today.'

'Am I?' Fee churned the butter, unaware of her absent expression.

'Is it anything I can help with?' Mary laid a hand on Fee's arm.

'No. I'm just miles away.'

'He visits today, doesn't he?'

'Sorry?'

'Hamish.' Mary's smile was knowing and it grated. 'Sunday nights. Regular as clockwork.'

Fee kept her eyes on the butter churn, waiting for the wet thudding when thick cream became solid butter. 'I hadn't really noticed.' *A patent lie.* She refused to make eye contact with her sister-in-law, turning the metal handle over and over.

Over and over.

***

'You're very quiet tonight.'

'No I'm bloody not!'

Hamish raised an eyebrow.

'It was merely an observation.'

'A bloody ridiculous one.'

Pause.

They were in the sitting room with the windows wide open to let the summer air waft through the curtains. Mary fussed about in the kitchen having put the children to bed hours ago.

It galled Fee when Mary ostensibly left her and Hamish alone. *As if they would do something which needed privacy.*

Hamish tried to read her expression. It wasn't like Fee to be moody. Moodiness had always been Matt's preserve. *Wonder what was wrong?* 'Would it be quicker if I just took the blame?'

'What for?'

'For whatever's got you all wound up.' Fee's eyes were unusually stormy. Hamish took one big step backwards and raised his hands as if in surrender.

He'd done it again. Made her laugh at herself. 'I'm sorry, Hamish.'

'Good. I'm totally mystified as to why but I'm happy to take my luck where I find it.'

This time her smile was genuine, born of true feelings of companionship. 'How was Home Guarding?'

Hamish rolled his eyes.

'All right, I suppose. It's bloody hard to take it seriously. I mean, our officers bang on about the Japs landing but I can't believe it would be possible. So we march and the officers strut. We practise survival skills, they teach us to observe and how to repel the enemy but mostly we fool around. Paddy and Mick are no end of funny.'

'Good to know we're all in safe hands.'

'I'm learning Morse Code. That's fun.'

'The world's at war and you men are having fun. You're as bad as Matt.'

Hamish stretched his long legs out, relishing the comfort of the surroundings, the nearness of Fee – the sense of home. The day had been a long one though and he had to swallow a yawn, unwilling for it to be misinterpreted as boredom. 'Have you heard from him recently?'

'Just the one letter since he finished training. Want to read it?'

'Sure.'

In the time it took for Fee to find it, Hamish's eyes drooped. When she returned, Fee stood for a moment in the doorway. Arms folded across his chest, feet crossed at the ankles, Hamish's head rested on the sofa back, eyes closed. Utterly peaceful. The corners of Fee's mouth lifted and the thought slid into her mind – *What would it be like to wake up beside you every morning? To share every evening this way?* Returning to the sofa, she eased down on it, careful not to disturb him. Fee leaned closer, taking in the curves of his face, the tanned skin, the shape of his lips.

'It's rude to stare, you know.' His eyes flicked open.

'It's rude to nod off. Didn't realise I was so boring.' Flippancy to cover the rush of embarrassment.

Hamish sat back up, eyes on hers. 'Boring is one thing you could never be.'

Pause.

The letter crunched in Fee's hand, reminding her of its presence. 'Help yourself,' she said as she passed it over.

Hamish skimmed the pages. 'Sounds like he's enjoying himelf.'

'That was my thought, too.'

'So things are hotting up for him because we're losing more control in the Pacific.' His eyes fell again on the sentence about the Japanese. 'Maybe our training isn't so ridiculous after all.'

Fee didn't want to think about that. *Didn't want to think of Matt ending up like Da because of what war might do to him.* She reached for the letter and tucked it into a pocket, determined to push the dark thoughts aside. Hamish looked pensive. Fee shifted closer to him, sure she had his attention once more. 'You haven't asked me to marry you this week.'

A flame burst into life in his eyes though his body language remained casual, deliberately so. 'No. Didn't think you'd noticed.'

Fee slid into his arms, her mouth taking its time in seeking his. 'I always notice.'

Hamish gave himself over to the kiss, the warmth of her tongue teasing his lips. 'Marry me?'

Pause.

A whisper, soft, seductive. 'You know something? I just might.'

***

Neither of them wanted a fuss. A simple exchange of vows in the church where John, Emily and Jimmy were buried followed by a high tea with family. Fee expected to feel panic when Hamish slid the ring over her finger. She waited for regret to strike. Yet after he kissed her, the first face she saw was Janet's. Her aunt was smiling, crying but smiling, too. And Fee realised there was nothing for her to panic about or regret.

Their shift into married life was easy. The excitement of turning their small holding into something like home farm was a shared goal they spent happy hours discussing. All days were busy ones and on the times Hamish had Home Guard duties, Fee came under the Manpower Regulations which saw women replacing men in traditional masculine jobs like truck driving. Thanks to Janet, Fee already had that particular skill so she was able to put it to good use as a land girl. Building up their farm plus war work left little time for relaxation. Hamish and Fee thrived on it all.

One evening after several weeks of not being able to sit down to a dinner together, Fee planned a special night. Hamish was visiting Wally and Ben, checking up on the second-hand tractor they were repairing for him. He had promised to be home by six and it was quarter to. A fragrant casserole simmered in the oven, a loaf of bread made freshly that morning sat on the breadboard. The table was laid with a clean, ironed cloth and the simple cutlery set gleamed having been cleaned with pride. Fee put on a frock, something she rarely wore these days when working women habitually wore trousers. Catching sight of her reflection in the free-standing mirror in their bedroom Fee had to smile, thinking back to the pair of trousers Janet had given her all those years ago and her shyness at the thought of being seen in them. *Still, it made a nice change to wear a pretty frock and stockings.* Happy with the view of herself, Fee heard a knock on the front door. *Who the hell? No one used the front door.*

He was young, no more than thirteen and looked nervous.

'Hunter, isn't it? Barry's son?' Fee's welcoming smile died away as she saw the telegram in his hand.

Hamish was whistling as he arrived home. The tractor would be ready by the weekend and he'd be able to pull those stumps out of south paddock. They'd cleared twenty acres since the wedding, already planning the extra stock they could get on it. Feeling proud Hamish kicked his boots off as he threw open the back door, breathing in the mouth-watering scent of dinner.

As a bachelor he'd managed to feed himself all right. *Got a bit samey after a time though. He only knew how to cook sausages and mashed spud with onions.* If he didn't work so hard, life with Fee would have added not only happiness but a couple of inches to his waistline. A quick scrub in the scullery then a wander into the kitchen to find his wife.

'Fee?'

No reply.

Thinking she wouldn't be far, not with the dinner cooking, Hamish whistled his way into their bedroom and stopped at the sight of glamorously dressed Fee sitting on the end of the bed. 'You look beautiful.' Her stillness alerted him. 'Fee?'

She passed over the telegram. 'It's from the Defence Department. Matt's missing in action.'

Her words didn't sink in, not right away. 'Why did the telegram come to you and not Mary?'

'Matt said when he enlisted he'd named me as his next of kin.'

Hamish didn't bother to read the telegram. Shock knocked the wind out of him and he slumped on the bed beside her. 'Missing isn't dead.'

A surge of anger took Fee by surprise. 'There's no silver lining here, Hamish!' He opened his mouth to be conciliatory when she leapt to her feet. 'And now the bloody dinner's burning!'

Hamish took his time. When he arrived in the kitchen, the perfect casserole lay upended in the sink. Fee was hunched over, arms around her body as if seeking protection. There was no need for words. He took her in his arms and let her cry.

***

The war crash-landed on their lives. From feeling the general annoyance over rationing, then solemnity when reading the lists of the dead, now they had to face the very real possibility that someone they loved might not come home. *Missing in action.* The thought coloured their every day, dragged a shadow behind them wherever they were and tainted their happiness.

Not long after the telegram, Hamish was up on the neighbour's hill. A tree right on their border had fallen, taking a good chunk of fencing with it. With so few hours left in his working days, Hamish dolefully contemplated the extra time needed to repair the damage. *Can't return stock up here until it's fixed. Ken had promised to share the workload. That was something. But the budget would need jigging for the posts and wire – can we get enough wire? If we can't, have we stockpiled enough wooden posts? What they had were ear-marked for the new fences for the south paddock but needs must.*

Jet began barking, an urgent pitch to the tone. *No animals up here, so what had Jet had seen?* The grumbling purr of an aeroplane startled Hamish. *An aeroplane?*

Spinning sharply, Hamish hauled Jet under the nearest bit of scrub cover, eyes fixed on the sky. In moments a plane flew over his head moving low and slow. Its markings were frighteningly unmistakable. The broken fence forgotten, Hamish wasted no time. Racing back home he rang the Murchison Police as per his Home Guard instructions.

'Yeah, we've been told the Japs are reconnoitring. We've heard from Wellington, too. Best keep a watch out. Let us know if you spot anymore.'

It took Hamish a few days to share this with Fee. If he hadn't known how news spread through the valleys he might have been tempted not to say anything. As it was his conscience twinged when Fee thanked him for not sheltering her.

'Most men wouldn't have said anything.'

It was a frightening thing to happen. The war was on their doorstep now.

'You know, in a strange kind of way, Matt seems closer.'

Hamish studied Fee's face as he considered what she meant. 'You don't believe he's dead, do you?'

An emphatic shake of the head. 'Not anymore. I try not to think what might be happening to him but there's a part of me certain he will come home.'

'God, I hope you're right.'

Fee did her damndest not to think of how her father returned from the last war. The one to end all war.

***

Wellington

Maudie stumped out of Courtney Place. She crossed tramlines, dodged vehicles and people, not stopping to chat to familiar faces – something unheard of. Heading towards the metal gates securing the wharf, she was recognised as Hugo's sister and winked through. Once on the waterfront she picked up her pace. By the time Maudie found her brother she was red-faced and puffing.

Hugo was inspecting crates. He looked up at the flurry of movement, concerned at Maudie's sudden, flustered appearance. 'You all right?' It took her a moment to catch a breath. 'Maud, what's up?'

'What's this I hear 'bout the bloody Japs landing in New Zealand?'

'Where'd you hear that?' Hugo rested against a second crate as he frowned.

'Some bugger.'

'Some bugger you know well? It's not like you to believe rumours. Especially from an unfamiliar source.'

Confronted with unflappable calm, Maudie's panic eased. She even felt a little foolish so covered it with gruff nonchalance. 'A bloke from the Defence Department visited one of the boarders. I overheard them talkin'. Thought it was probably nothin'.'

Love prevented Hugo reacting to that. He offered Maudie his seat on the crate so he could carry on checking his wares. 'Well, between you and me it's not an impossibility.'

'But they've not landed?'

'No. There have been Japanese submarines sighted off various coasts on both the North and South Island. Their planes have been reconnoitering, too. All our coastal spotters are on high alert.'

'How worried should we be?'

Hugo looked up from his paperwork, a bottle in one hand. 'Remember Nanking, Maud. And now they've taken

Singapore and half the Pacific? I'd say we should be fairly worried.'

His understatement was somehow more chilling than her earlier feeling of panic. Maudie fidgeted on the crate, her ample proportions making comfort difficult. 'S'always a bugger.'

'What is?'

'Being left with nuthin' t'do but wait.'

Hugo had noticed the increase in Maudie's grumbling about their absent family. Moss's lack of communication was uppermost, *'Even though the bugger promised.'* As for Tyke? *'Run away and leave us with no word. Now she's where the bombs are and we know nothing.'* The more she bitched about them, the greater the proof they were on her mind. In the past, Maudie had focussed on family to get through the tough times. Without Moss and Tyke for her to grumble at, feed, disapprove of and generally annoy, she was a rudderless ship without a sail in a predatory ocean. Most telling of all, Maudie never panicked. The fact she had and rushed to find him spoke volumes to Hugo.

'Maud…..'

'Don't give me no bullshit about them being all right. They're in a war. On the other side of the world away from their family.'

Hugo shoved a wooden cask next to the crate so he could sit beside her. 'They'll come home.'

She cut him off with an impatient gesture. 'Yer can't know that.'

'If anyone can survive, Moss can. Tyke, too.'

'Fuck off, Hugo. That's trite bullshit. Bullets and bombs make no allowances.'

'All we can do is hope.'

'Hope.'

A strange bitterness corrupted the word. As Maudie studiously kept her eyes on the view outside the doors she felt her brother's enquiring regard. *Now was the time to confront the bugger.* 'Yer sent Moss into France, didn't yer?'

Silence.

The secret guilt Hugo had concealed leapt into life. He knew his sister's uncanny ability to expose the undesirable. Her insight was part gift, part problem. He had tried to plan for this day, expecting it, dreading it, turning excuses and reasons over and over, honing them, perfecting them. Now he needed just one, he couldn't think of a single word.

Maudie grew impatient as the silence widened, threatened to swallow them whole. 'Didn't yer?'

Pause.

'How did you guess?'

A snort.

'I'm not a bloody idiot! Where's all this lot come from?' Maudie gestured to the crates and boxes piled behind them against the back wall. 'Bloody French wines. Brandy. Bloody stinking cheeses and God knows what else.' She snatched the bottle out of his hand and thrust it at him. 'Tell me, Hugo. Is my son's life worth black-market shit?' Maudie's arm swung back. Reacting on instinct, Hugo ducked. The bottle flew over his head and exploded against a wall, showering them in splinters of glass and droplets of red wine.

Maudie had never been angry with him. Never truly angry. Ever since he could remember his sister had fought his corner, never him. She had saved his life when they were children, putting nothing above her brother, even her own self-interest. Maudie's words cut into Hugo's wretchedness.

'I didn't want to believe it of yer. Didn't want to think yer'd value stuff over family.'

Silence.

'He was going over there anyway.'

'Not to fucking France, he wasn't!'

'I didn't send him into a war, Maud. It hadn't been declared.'

Maudie was unyielding. 'Yer knew it was a possibility. Yer knew it and sent him anyway.'

Hugo couldn't deny that. He nodded, meeting her eyes, allowing her to see his deep shame. 'It was an opportunity.' Even to him the excuse sounded pitiful. He wished he hadn't spoken at all. 'Moss didn't mind.'

'Of course he wouldn't bloody mind. He'd do anything for family. Anything. It's why he chased after Tyke. But he woulda come home by now. Instead he's in an occupied country and we've not heard a word. Not one bloody thing.'

Silence.

Maudie took the list from Hugo's hand. She ran her eyes down the neat columns, all tallied up, every transaction accounted for. 'I hope it was worth it.' She gazed at the crates and boxes stacked floor to ceiling all around them. 'It's all just shit to me.'

The list fluttered down onto the floor.

Hugo waited until Maudie reached the door before blurting out in sudden unease, 'Do you want me to go?' He truly didn't want to be kicked out of her life. Hugo's heart was in his mouth through the drawn out silence until she shook her head. He hadn't expected that and forced the next words out as if giving her the chance to reconsider. 'Why not?'

Here they were, both in their mid-sixties and all Maudie saw as she glared at her brother was him as a boy, defying their sadistic father for her sake. She hated what Hugo had done but couldn't hate him. He was part of her, maybe most of her. ''cause you and Alex are all the family I got left.'

Hugo caught the sheen of her tears. *My sister never cries.* 'I'm so sorry, Maud.' He whispered the words, remorse beneath and beyond the syllables.

Pause.

A nod and she left him, closing the warehouse door behind her.

***

Tyke
London

Tyke and Cherry tumbled down the steps of the underground station in their panic to escape the screaming sirens and falling bombs. Beside herself with terror, Cherry tripped, falling heavily among the rubble and debris littering the ground. Tyke tugged her to her feet. An explosion shook the ground and the walls they huddled against, lost in the choking clouds of suffocating, smothering dust. Yanking herself free from her friend's restraining grasp, Cherry clamped her hands to her ears. She screamed as she ran, finally reaching the security of the underground railway, already crowded with frightened people.

'Fuck this for a game of soldiers! Gordon Bennett! Look at my bleeding clothes! And my nylons!' Another explosion rent the air. Cherry screamed again, diving to huddle against the nearest wall as Tyke reached her. 'Fucking Germans!' Cherry shrieked.

Another bomb. Another scream.

A middle aged woman clutched her string bag as if it was a barricade between her and the next bombardment. A much patched winter coat covered her legs, her worn dusty shoes were placed just so, ankle-to-ankle. She reacted to every swear word from Cherry as she did each explosion; a wince and a cringe, eyes screwed tightly shut. 'Will you please stop swearing?' Her pompous tone and manner were easily undermined by an all too obvious, shabby gentility.

Tyke hated her on sight.

Cherry was oblivious to everything but her own terror. 'I hate loud noises, Missus. Hate them! I even hate Tommy's bass drum! Boom! Boom de boom!'

The walls shuddered again, the lights above them flickering and swaying. Tyke yanked Cherry onto the concrete floor, holding her friend close as she sobbed.

With an unsympathetic sneer the woman with the shopping tutted. 'You're not the only one who hates the noise.'

Cherry rocked her body to and fro. 'No one hates it more than me. I promise you that for nothing. I'm scared shitless!'

'And the rest of us think it's a picnic, of course.'

Another explosion. Sirens. Screams from the street.

'Oh my God! We're gonna die!' Tears ran through Cherry's smeared mascara, smudged the dirt on her face.

'For goodness sake, girl! If you cannot control yourself, I'll give you something to scream about!'

Tyke met the woman's glower head-on. 'Madam, that hardly helps.'

'Yeah. There's nothing written 'bout no swearing in a time of war.' Cherry's gurgling laugh spouted incongruously through her fear. 'So fuck you, your Majesty'

'Cherry!' Tyke couldn't hide her amusement.

The woman turned her head, shifting further away from them, lips pursed tightly in massive disapproval as the young women giggled at her expense.

The next explosions brought a flurry of people into the shelter, the last one a sight to behold; a woman in her seventies at least, who wore extravagantly dyed red hair in an unruly mop about a lined, grubby face. She wore cut-off gloves and a man's overcoat covering a motley selection of clothes with much-darned stockings bagging about thin legs. Over one arm this apparition lugged a carpet bag almost half her size. As soon as she reached the interior of the shelter, she scrabbled in deep pockets and brought out a flask, raising it to all eyes. 'Anyone else want a snifter? 'Cause I've gorra belt here if yer do.' She grinned a gap-toothed grin around at the hastily averted eyes until meeting one pair she recognised. 'Cherry! How's yer belly off fer spots?'

From a half-crouch Cherry leapt to her feet, dragging Tyke after her. 'Bleeding Vi. Where've you been hiding? Blimey, I needed you a week or so ago, couldn't find your old carcass anywhere. This here's Tyke. She's from New Zealand.' Cherry spoke the words carefully, proud to be friends with someone from a country she'd once never heard of. With a sudden jeer she pointed at her nemesis with the string bag who tried to duck away from the accusing finger. 'Better watch yourself in here, Vi. It's all toffs down with us tonight, isn't that right, your Highness?'

Vi snorted.

'Then here's hoping the Huns drop a bomb on the lot of them. 'Cause it's thanks to the fucking toffs we're in this mess.' She tipped the flask to her lips, wiping her mouth on the back of her hand as she passed the flask to Cherry who drank just as greedily. 'Want some, ducks?' This to Tyke who shook her head. Vi stoppered the flask and peered through the gloom of the shelter. 'Look at all the long faces. Anyone'd think there was a war on or summat.' The disapproving woman sniffed loudly, drawing Vi's attention. 'Here. I knows you. Penelope summat.'

'Briggs-Smythe, if you must know.'

'You ain't no Smythe. You're a Smith, deary. Plain old Smith.'

Penelope used her shoulder as a barrier against the cackling Vi who found a corner beside a pillar. Chuckling under her breath, the old woman made a nest of her belongings before settling among them. Cherry and Tyke followed her example. Shoulder to shoulder they sat with their backs against the wall next to Vi's pillar.

'Do you think Tommy will have to join up?' Cherry asked Tyke. 'What with his dicky heart and all.'

'Better for him an' you if it was the other way round,' Vi leered.

They ignored her as Tyke shrugged. 'I don't know. I guess if he's crook enough....'

'Crook? You've said that word before and I didn't get it. A crook like them shepherds have? '

'No! I mean crook as in sick.' Tyke loved these moments when seemingly obvious words from New Zealand needed explaining. 'They only want the best to join up, don't they?'

Again Vi broke in. 'Only till things get real bad. Then they'll want whoever they can bloody get. Flat feet, bad hearts, need glasses, what's it gonna matter to his nibs when he needs cannon fodder against bleedin' Hitler?'

'His nibs?' Tyke's puzzled frown met Vi's grin.

'Churchill to you, deary.'

Tyke wasn't sure she liked Vi too much. Cherry however, loved her. While Tyke stood back up to stretch, Vi happily gossiped, all Cherry's fear seemingly melted away as she listened. Leaving them to it, Tyke stepped round and over people huddled underground for safety. A man held a sheet in front of a woman using a chamber pot. A child peered round his legs, booted none too gently away. Families squabbled, played cards or dice games, parents shooting anxious glances at the swaying lights above their heads each time they flickered. If they blacked completely, Tyke knew lanterns or candles would be hauled out and life would carry on. Three exhausted nurses slept sitting upright, two heads resting in on the shoulders of the third in the middle. A woman was praying, hands together, lips moving soundlessly.

You'd think God would've found a way to stop this madness.

Tyke stopped at the end of the platform where the tunnel began. She rested against the arch. From here she could see Cherry, her friend animated as she laughed with Vi. *You're a hard case, Chezz.*

Even down here the scream of the sirens could be heard. A child cried heart-brokenly, his mother rocking him in her arms, singing under her breath until he hushed. An elderly couple shared a threadbare blanket, gratefully accepting a hot drink which they traded sip for sip out of their one enamel cup. One old man cuddled an equally aged dog, its silvered chin in the crook of his elbow. People slept. *How could they?* Some read. Plenty stared at nothing. Tyke leaned her head against the wall.

A cackle of street slang and cussing from the irrepressible Vi. With her mop of wild, red hair, *could it be a wig? Surely it must be,* her idiosyncratic style of dressing, she was a sight to see all right. As Tyke watched, the old woman waved a half-empty gin bottle at Cherry, urging her to sing. Cherry grinned, happy to oblige.

' *'Keep the home fires burning,*
While your hearts are yearning.
Now the boys are far away they dream of home…"

Tyke drew in a quick, painful breath. Others joined in, someone added a harmony. A song from the last war. The Great War. *How great will this one be?* Cherry's lovely voice filled the platform. Sweet and true, it could be heard above the rougher ones accompanying it.

Deep in Tyke's pocket was the little soldier she had bought off Sid's stall. It went everywhere with her. Now she drew it into the palm of her hand, fingers confining it.

Uncle Jimmy and Father, both unscarred and youthful in their smart uniforms listened, too. Samuel nudged his brother and they shared a laugh. Shared so much.

Tyke blinked and they vanished.

Was it terrible to admit to being excited? Yes, life was dangerous. It was hard and growing even more so but her little life in New Zealand had diminished until it was little more than a distant gleam of green, like faded, familiar wallpaper on an unfamiliar wall. Only the faces remained. *Moss…..*

Where did you go, Moss? How will I ever see you again?

Tyke laid a hand absently against her stomach, memories of her abortion all too raw. She tried not to think about the repercussions of it. *How could she face life as a woman and not be a mother?* It wasn't something she ever thought about until the possibility was brutally taken away. Tyke impatiently rubbed away the burning tears.

No use crying.

'What's done is done and should be past regret.' Maudie's voice, from years ago, from all those years ago when Tyke was young and the world was endless possibility. *But with age came regret, lingering deep wounds difficult, perhaps impossible to heal.* She felt it most when she was exhausted, like tonight or when she couldn't sleep and those painful thoughts lived as splinters in her mind to haunt her rest.

'Tyke! Hey, Tyke!'

Cherry waved at her, demanding her attention. Glad of the interruption from her dark reflections, Tyke shoved away from the wall. Stepping over recumbent bodies she hurried to where her friend and Vi hovered protectively around a girl who looked about nine.

'This here's Margery Birch. She got separated from her brother Martin.'

Cherry was kneeling beside the distraught youngster, using her sleeve to dab away frightened tears.

Tyke joined Cherry. 'Don't cry, Margery. When the raid's over we'll help you find Martin. The wardens will know exactly what to do, I'm sure.'

The girl gulped, shaking. 'What if Martin's out there looking for me? What if he's got hurt? What if….'

Cherry gripped the girl's hands. 'How old is Martin? Older than you?'

'Two years and three months older.'

'Then the bugger's old enough to look after himself till he can find you.'

Margery considered this with a watery smile. 'Martin is very sensible.'

'There you are, then. It'll be all right.' Cherry reached into her handbag. 'Here, would you like to wear a bit of slap?' She twisted her lipstick, revealing the lush red.

Beside them a haughty voice lifted. 'Only whores wear makeup.'

Cherry and Tyke faced the rigidly respectable Penelope Briggs-Smythe.

With a growl, Cherry loomed over her, lipstick wielded as a weapon. 'If you don't shut your fucking mouth I'm gonna shut it for you. Have you got that, your Majesty?' Satisfied her point was made Cherry turned to the wide-eyed Margery and smiled. 'Come on, ducks. Bit of slap will make all the difference.'

Vi however understood children better than Cherry or Tyke. She foraged in the depths of her carpet bag. 'How about some chocolate, dearie?'

As a beaming Margery accepted the chocolate, Cherry made eye contact with Vi and lowered her voice. 'You haven't got a pair of nylons in there have you?'

With a conspirator's wink, Vi dabbed the side of her nose.

.

It was dawn when the all-clear sounded. From shelters around the city people emerged, bleary eyed and yawning into a dim day, heavy with the smell of smoke and dust. Having despatched Margery into the care of the wardens, Cherry and Tyke bade Vi farewell and trudged through the battered streets to their flat. To their pleased surprise, only one or two buildings in their alley had been damaged, and then with blown out windows.

Cherry lifted a hand and made an obscene gesture to the clouds. 'Oi Fritz! Yer fucking missed! Better luck next time!'

***

They called it a bomber's moon. No matter how beautiful the full moon looked, no matter how her beams danced in puddles or glinted like diamonds on the shattered glass of broken windows, on nights like this she was deadly, too.

Tyke shivered. *Bomber's Moon*. She didn't want to go out tonight. Better they stay home close to their shelter but Cherry was dead set on a night out.

'I'll go bleedin' mad if I stay in another night, Tyke. I've gorra get out. I can't breathe. I can't.'

'All right,' Tyke strove to hide her annoyance. 'You don't have to go all Rita Hayworth about it. I get it. You're bored.'

'S'more than bored.'

'No it isn't. You're just being dramatic.'

'Am I heck!' Cherry clutched her throat with one hand, gesturing to the view out of their little window with the other. 'Somewhere, out there there's a pub and people having fun. When was the last time we went out and had a bit of a knees-up?'

'Last weekend,' was Tyke's laconic reply.

'Never.'

'It was. You got those nylons off Vi then had a row with Tommy over him wanting the band playing at the Windmill.'

'Oh, yeah. All them girls wearing nothing but their smiles. If I catch Tommy there I'll have his guts for garters.' She wrinkled her nose in thought. 'Last weekend you say? That's not so long ago, is it?'

'No.'

'Long enough, though.' Pause. 'My shout.'

'It's always your shout. No wonder you've never got any money.' No matter how exasperated she was, Tyke could never be cross with Cherry for long. One long, pleading look from her. 'Oh, go on, then. But not all night. I'm on earlies tomorrow and if I'm late Madam Fancypants will have my hide. Again. She hates me more than Goering.'

But Cherry was oblivious to everything now there was something to look forward to.

'Let's try a new hairstyle. All pinned off the face at the front and masses of curls at the side and on the neck. Like Hedy Lamarr.'

Such excitement was contagious. Against her better judgement, Tyke was caught in it. Together they primped and preened into their best frocks, hair carefully set, makeup perfect and arm-in-arm they walked the strangely quiet streets. People tried to keep close to home under a bomber's moon. Tyke's frisson of fear stirred at Cherry's squeal.

'Look at all them uniforms'

'You and blokes in sodding uniform! What's Tommy say about it?'

'He can't say nothing and knows it. Come on.' She dragged Tyke into the pub's fuggy, welcoming atmosphere.

It was one of those nights when everyone was out to enjoy themselves no matter what. A young man sat behind the piano and belted out honky-tonk rhythms which made it impossible to keep feet from jigging. Vi was there, screeching laughter and crying for 'summat decent to sing to. Not this honky-tonk shit.' There was plenty of laughter, most of it off-colour though it didn't make Tyke blush like it used to. One young corporal sidled up to her and whispered she would be a star at the Windmill. With a withering glare Tyke let loose a stream of invective, some of it learned, most of it made up but all of it effective. The corporal slunk away, never to be seen again. Smiling at his retreating back, Tyke leaned across the bar.

'Pint of wallop, Boo.'

When the sirens sounded most of the crowd didn't move. People only began to leave when the far-off explosions sounded. Even then Vi and Cherry were reluctant to call it a night.

'You nearly peed yourself in the shelter the other night and look at you now!' Tyke scolded, gesturing to Cherry's shiny gin-grin face. 'Let's go, eh?'

Vi flailed an arm. 'Bugger them bombs! I ain't moving 'cause Old Brown wants to scare the shit outta me. Give us another, Boo. And make it a double this time.'

'Get gone, you mad old biddy. I'm heading into my shelter and you three should, too. Go on.' Boo chivvied them out the door.

From out in the city limits the bombs stomped closer.

'Let's carry on the party, Chezz. Come back to mine.'

'I'm game if Tyke is.'

Tyke shook her head. The explosions grew nearer, the drone of planes louder. 'I'm for the shelter.'

'Well me and Vi ain't afraid, eh Vi?' Cherry waved the glass of gin she had taken out past the usually vigilant Boo.

Vi yanked a bottle out of her carpet bag. 'Gorra nutha one here when that runs out.' She smiled lopsidedly at Tyke. 'Sure you ain't coming?'

The ground shuddered under their feet.

'Not me.'

Without a backward glance Tyke sprinted for the nearest shelter, Vi and Cherry singing their hearts out behind her. Too far from her usual public shelter, Tyke made it to Boo's anderson shelter behind the pub. Dug into the ground, its tin roof covered in dirt, a well-built anderson shelter could save people from anything but a direct hit. Cursing her high heels Tyke clambered awkwardly down the few steps to bang urgently on the locked door.

'Boo! It's me. Tyke. Let me in!'

A huge explosion threw Tyke hard against the heavy door before knocking her onto the brick steps, head ringing.

A frightened Boo opened the door. 'Get in you daft bitches! Told you to get a hurry on.'

Tyke stood there, wide-eyed, rubbing her shoulder and wincing as she put weight on a twisted ankle. Blood trickled down her chin from a bitten bottom lip.

Boo yanked a handkerchief from his pocket, passed it over It was none too clean but she used it to dab at her mouth. 'That was too fucking close!' Boo grabbed her arm. 'Come on, gel.'

'Cherry.'

Boo peered past Tyke. 'You're alone out there? Where the fuck is the silly bitch?'

'She went with Vi. Oh, God.' Tyke stuffed the hanky back into his hands as she kicked her feet out of her high heels. 'Gimme your boots, Boo.'

'What? You off your rocker?'

'Come on! I've got to check on Cherry and Vi.'

Bombs were falling in the streets around them, filling the air with clogging dust. Boo cast a look at the skies and decided. He quickly undid his laces and passed them to Tyke. 'Make sure you get them back to me. I ain't wearing your bloody fancies!'

With her feet secure in Boo's work-boots Tyke tore back out through the alley of the pub onto the street and ran after Cherry and Vi. A shell hit a building opposite. Tyke flung herself into the nearest doorway, arms over her head. She crouched there, waiting for the impact to die away. Coughing and gasping, barely able to make out the street through the cloudy air, she pushed on. Screams and shouts battered her senses. The area she knew so well was suddenly alien as fires silhouetted jagged-edged ruins, the full moon lost in thick haze. Standing amidst the chaos, her heart hammering, Tyke screamed out, 'Cherry!' A fruitless shriek of fear.

Pushing on towards Vi's tenement, Tyke tried not to dwell on her worst thoughts. All around people were helping others out of collapsed buildings or sobbing at the foot of a mountain of rubble, their world lost under it. The street became blocked. Ignoring the shouted warning of a warden, Tyke clambered over piles of rubble, her good frock torn, her legs scratched. She stumbled heavily onto a blown out door and punctured her leg on a nail but didn't feel the pain, not then, didn't notice the blood pouring out of the wound. Eventually Tyke stood panting in front of the destroyed tenement where Vi lived.

'Cherry!' The name gasped on a sob. 'Cherry!' Something caused her to spin round. There against a wall on the other side of the street Cherry lay hunched. In moments Tyke was beside her and it took her no time to realise something was very wrong. Cherry was filthy, her lovely hair matted in dirt and blood from a terrible head wound. She was breathing with difficulty and when Tyke met her eyes she saw no hope there. Carefully she gathered her friend up. Cherry cried out, clutching her side. Tyke gasped at the hunk of splintered wood puncturing the material of her frock. And the blood.

'Chezz, you're bleeding!'

'S'what ...mum..says. 'Cherry bleedin' this....Cherry ...bleedin' that.' She tried to smile, couldn't. 'Vi.' Each breath was a gasp. 'Crushed .... I... I couldn't... shift her...in time.'

'Don't talk, Chezz. Shhh....' Tyke tore a strip off her skirt and wiped Cherry's face with it.

Cherry clutched at Tyke's free hand, clinging desperately. 'Don't .... leave me...Tyke.'

'Don't be bloody daft.'

'I..don't wanna.... bleedin' go alone.'

As the sirens screamed around the destruction of their neighbourhood, Cherry died in Tyke's arms.

***

Matthew
Macassar Camp

The sickening thwack of wood on flesh was heard all over the work camp. Matthew kept his head up, not making a sound as the pick handle walloped onto his buttocks again and again. *20, 21, 22…. Stand tall. Make no sound. Do not fall. Do not fall. Do not fall.* If a man fell they kicked him into unconsciousness with their steel-capped boots. *33, 34, 35….*
The agony was almost too great to bear. *Almost.* So he bore it, grinding his jaw together, tensing every muscle. *46 47, 48, 49….* The worst was to come for the newest guard, the one they called Yoshida stepped forward. He removed the pick handle from his subordinate who handed it over with a deferential bow. Yoshida stood in front of his prey. Matthew stared over his head, sweating profusely, blood dripping down his legs.

'You steal! You cheat!'

In truth he'd done nothing. *This bastard didn't need an excuse to knock them about. No use arguing the point.* Swallowing hard, Matthew made no response, all his energies on not passing out in front of this devil. Yoshida's lips drew back from his mouthful of gold teeth in the rictus of a smile as he thudded the pick handle from hand to hand. 'You suffer.' In a swift movement he was behind his victim. Yoshida raised the pick handle and slammed it into the base of Matthew's spine. How Matthew stayed on his feet he never knew. Agony washed over him in waves. He bit the inside of his mouth so hard he tasted blood but Matthew didn't cry out, he didn't groan. He didn't give the bastard the satisfaction of his pain.

Screaming at his own men Yoshida Tomanao strode away and only when he was out of sight did Matthew move, limping heavily, swaying as he made it to the shade. With Whitey helping him he tried to ease into some position for comfort. *Impossible.* Breath coming in gasps, Matthew stood back on his feet. He leaned against a tree trunk and breathed slowly, deeply. *In....out......in.....out.....* He heard material ripping and forced an eye open. Whitey was tearing a strip off his shirt to use to staunch the blood. Matthew hissed, eyes screwed shut but this wasn't the first time either of them had been in this position. Whitey knew what to do and he cleaned his friend up as best he could, knowing they had maybe a few minutes before Yoshida pushed them all back to work, the wounded Matthew included.

'You've bugger all of your shirt left.'

'Well, you used the remnants of your shorts on me last time. Seems only fair.'

Matthew now wore a long piece of cloth which wrapped between the legs and secured around the waist. Many prisoners wore the same thing. The fandushi it was called and it became their uniform. The Japanese wore the same thing as underclothing and many of these long cloths disappeared from their laundry, in spite of the threats and curses hurled over the prisoners' heads.

Having done what he could, Whitey made sure Matthew had something to drink as well as forcing him to eat their lunchtime handful of rice. It had been cooked earlier in the day and having been left in the sun, had a sour taste to it. Matthew tried to chew a small amount but gagged, passing the remains to Whitey. 'You finish it. God as my witness there's no way I can.'

It had been a terrible month for the camp. With the arrival of Yoshida Tomanao things had grown steadily worse. They knew from his yellow arm-band and his effortless air of command over everyone else, even Lieutenant Commander Ota and Warrant Officer Nagatome he must be Kempetai, Japanese secret police. From the moment he stepped up to their first tenko, Yoshida's sadism knew no bounds. He had marched arrogantly before the lined up prisoners, coming to a halt in front of a Scotsman Matthew only knew as Jock. Yoshida screamed and every man froze, including the other guards. Unleashing a spitting torrent of Japanese at a flunky who bowed and ran, he yanked Jock forward and began pulling on his long sideburns. When the flunky returned he was carrying a set of heavy pliers. First Yoshida lashed out, hitting Jock about the face with them. When he tired of that he used them to tear the sideburns off the man's face, leaving a pulpy, bloodied ruin. Only then did Yoshida smile, exuding the impression of a job well done as he threw the pliers at one of the guards.

There was never any guessing what would set him off. Singing and whistling were banned. Groups were banned. Being caught out of quarters at night was punished. Sometimes it took nothing at all. It seemed impossible but Matthew wasn't the only one to pine nostalgically for life before Yoshida.

The day's slavery done, they were marched back into camp. It looked pristine now for Yoshida was a fiend for exemplary tidiness. If the prisoners weren't on work detail they scrubbed and swept, cleaned and polished. The camp damn near sparkled.

The heat dried Matthew's wounds. They scabbed over enough for him to take small steps, limping as carefully as he could make them to prevent them pulling open and bleeding afresh. Thankful to see the end of the day he and Whitey lined up for their evening meal – a cup of watery 'soup' with the merest sliver of cucumber skin floating in it and another handful of rice. At least this rice had been freshly cooked and was edible. They had barely finished their meal when Matthew noticed Whitey began to shake.

'Are you all right?'

'Dunno. Had a fever all day. Must be that.'

'You idiot! You never said. There you were fussing like an old mother hen over me and you were sick.' Matthew didn't need to lay a hand on Whitey's forehead to know how ill he was. Sweat was pouring off him now and he was shaking so badly he couldn't hold onto his cup. It slipped from his fingers spilling the contents into the dirt.

'What a waste,' Whitey muttered just before he vomited.

A worried Matthew saw his friend to their sleeping quarters. Nothing to cover him with but Whitey's own shirt. Reluctant as he was to leave him, Matthew wanted to find out what was wrong. After searching the Dutch quarters he found Jan.

'Malaria,' Jan told him. 'He needs quinine.'

'Where can I get some?'

'Good luck finding anyone to trade some.'

'Do you know who has a supply?'

Jan looked over each shoulder before drawing Matthew away from the Dutch quarters. 'Our officers have plenty but they won't give you any.'

'Why the hell not?'

'They're hoarding it for themselves, maybe even us lowly Dutchmen but never for any of you.'

Matthew's mouth hung open. 'But....'

Jan cut him off with an impatient gesture. 'Your own officers are just as bad. How many of them sleep under mosquito nets while the rest of you lie uncovered? Don't expect help from officers, Matt. Even your own.'

As Whitey grew worse Matthew discovered Jan spoke the truth. The Dutch officer he cornered wouldn't even admit to having quinine tablets. Only the smug tilt to the man's lips revealed the truth.

'And malaria doesn't go away,' Jan warned Matthew. 'It returns again and again.'

'So what will happen to Whitey?' Matthew flinched at the look of pity Jan shot him.

'He will recover from each bout or he will not.'

There was little to be done. Yoshida put all sick men on half rations and demanded if they could walk they could work. Men died in their dozens but Whitey didn't. He put it down to Matthew's care and his overriding wish. 'I want to go home,' he told Matthew as the fever began to leave him. 'I will go home.' His hold on Matthew's hand was weak but the words held a determination his friend echoed.

***

The day was like any other. Waking, tenko, head to work. They had reached early afternoon when it changed. Whispers spread through the work party; two of their number had escaped. The guards were unaware but none of those remaining wanted to be near them when the realization came. All through a long day, the work party deliberately kept their eyes down and their minds on the job. No one spoke more than a couple of words or broke any rules. Gathered up to return, the tension among them grew. Matthew was thankful for one thing; Whitey continued too weak to work and had stayed in camp.

Bluey the Australian sidled up to him. 'Do you know who flew? Good on them, I reckon.'

Refusing to make eye contact, Matthew gave a short shake of the head as two of their guards approached, laughing. A third joined them and whatever amused them provided a short distraction.

'I don't know anything. And neither should you,' Matthew hissed under his breath. 'This isn't going to go well for any of us so before you offer the stupid fools congratulations, you should think on that.'

By the dawning comprehension on Bluey's face, reprisals hadn't occurred to him; did now though and he looked suddenly ill. As the guards kidded amongst themselves, Matthew could only wonder, *Who will they blame?* And hoped to Christ it wasn't any of them. *Some bloody hope.*

The guards were still joking when they were lined up back in camp for tenko with good- humoured shoving. The first guard went along counting out loud. When he reached the

399

end of the last line, blankness wiped away his humour. Beckoning for one of his comrades, they started again. Same result. Now the prisoners saw the guards' own fear at being hoodwinked. Nothing was worse for any Japanese than loss of face. After much whispering a decision was made and one of them ran off, returning with a near hysterical Yoshida. Up and down the lines he strode, screaming into every face, demanding answers, any trace of understandable English lost as his accent thickened and his rage burned higher. He confronted one of the youngest prisoners, a thin sickly American named Ben who should never have been sent out to work as he was obviously in the early stages of a bout of malaria. Ben's trembling was uncontrollable as Yoshida shrieked into his face. It was too much for the youngster. His knees gave way and he hit the ground giving Yoshida a target for punishment. Ben was dragged to the nearest tree. Wire bound his wrists. Rope was attached and this was thrown over a branch and hauled on until Ben's toes barely grazed the dirt. Then, the beatings began.

Show them no fear. Don't cry. Don't scream. Do nothing.

It was true the Japanese would show respect to the ones who never buckled under a beating. The prisoners who stood tall and showed no fear, no pain were bowed away, even treated with some kindness. But Ben was sick even before the beating started. With every cry Yoshida laid it on harder. Not finished with the poor sufferer, when he was cut down Yoshida dragged Ben to the latrine pit and buried him up to his neck. A guard was left to ensure there was no rescue. The rest of the prisoners were dismissed and the camp torn apart by the guards hunting for the missing prisoners. They found no trace of them at all.

'God pity them if they're found,' Whitey murmured as they watched the hunt from a safe distance.

In the early hours of the morning the camp was disturbed again. Hearing the shouts and clamour some of the braver prisoners cautiously edged around doors and buildings to find the cause. Matthew left Whitey sleeping as he stole out. Through the main gates walked half a dozen natives who were taken to Yoshida standing nearby. As they parted, the two escapees were revealed. Yoshida signalled to one of his officers who quickly handed over what looked like a handful of coins before the men were dismissed back out through the gates. Moving closer Matthew could see the prisoners had already taken a fair beating. It was nothing to what Yoshida would extract from them. The unfortunate men were bound tightly and dragged off to the cells and left for the night. That was their only respite.

Day after day each guard took his turn and the camp reverberated with the agonized screams from the captives. Men volunteered for working parties to escape, for those hours at least, the haunting sounds of torture. It was nearly a week later before the two broken men were taken onto the beach and beheaded. A merciful release. Their bodies were dragged back to camp and shown to the rest of the prisoners as Yoshida stood before them.

'Any you escape we take ten men, execute. Next escape, we take twenty. You not escape. You stay. You work.'

Yes, sir.

By the time Ben was allowed to be hauled out of the latrine pit, he was barely conscious. He was taken away and never seen again.

The screams of those tortured men remained trapped inside Matthew's brain. They tainted the background to every thought until the night he dreamed of his father. The screams became Jimmy's. Jerked awake from the nightmare, Matthew lay there, heart pounding. He fought to keep his breathing as even as possible to not disturb the men sleeping against him. Matthew couldn't keep back the hot tears. For the first time he cried, silently, despairingly.

Forgive me, Dad. Forgive me. I never understood what war could do to a man.

***

How long they had been prisoners?

Days and weeks dissolved into months of heat and hunger, disease and pain. Cut off from all meaningful contact with the outside world, they yearned for any word from home and loved ones. No letters were received here. None sent. Too many hours were wasted in worry over family members who would think they were dead, receiving telegrams 'missing in action' and fearing the worst. As the months slid by with no word, they would be considered dead, mourning replacing memory.

What they all craved was information on how the war was going. Some news filtered through to the camp via a radio the local Chinese had hidden away in a tomb among the graves of the cemetery. Sometimes Malayan newspapers were smuggled in, occasionally a Japanese one and the war's progress could be monitored. They had to shift through the propaganda but the truth emerged with difficulty and over time. If no real news could be had, nothing halted the rumour mill. Everyday a whisper would do the rounds; *The Americans are coming to liberate us!* Faces would wear a hopeful cast, even confronted with the naysayers. Even when night folded in on the day and no Americans had broken through the gates, the whispers would start again tomorrow.

Whitey wondered whether the rumours were begun deliberately. 'They offer hope to those who have forgotten what hope's like.'

'Rumour as a remedy?' Matthew couldn't hide his skepticism.

'Why not? Surely a placebo does the job if a sick person thinks it helps.'

It was from the Chinese radio they heard about a massacre of Japanese prisoners in an internment camp in Featherston, New Zealand. While some gloated, even openly cheered, far-sighted wiser heads took a grimmer view. Matthew was standing with Senior Naval Officer Lieutenant Commander Cooper when Bluey sidled up and passed on the news. 'Leaves fewer of the fuckers in the world, eh sir?'

'So it would seem.'

Bluey watched the loitering guards with narrowed eyes. 'Given half a chance I'd like to do the same to this shower of bastards.'

With an unmistakable gesture of dismissal, the lieutenant moved away, beckoning Matthew to follow. In reply to Bluey's raised eyebrow question, Matthew shrugged. He hurried after the officer who came to a stop near the guardhouse. Following his lead, Matthew stood casually, wondering what the hell they were doing. Finally, there was just the one guard left at the hut, the one they nicknamed Lazy. Not given to screaming or violence, Lazy seemed content to do as little as possible and if sent to deal out punishment, managed to delegate the job. Even now, on duty as he was, Lazy slumped against the entrance to the hut, smoking serenely, eyes closed.

Lieutenant Cooper approached him.

'Excuse me but this young fool needs access to his personnel file.'

'Why?' But even as Lieutenant Cooper began a long-winded explanation, Lazy cut him off with a curt gesture, pointed to the door.

Inside, Matthew closed it behind them as Lieutenant Cooper reached towards the filing cabinet.

'Quick as you can. Find me every one of your compatriots' files.'

Matthew found Whitey's first, his search continuing even as he passed it over. 'Why, sir?'

Lieutenant Cooper opened the file. He scanned the relevant page and reached for a pen. 'As of today, I'm afraid you are born British. No Kiwis at Macassar.'

And suddenly Matthew understood why. 'Good thinking, sir!'

As quickly as possible the changes to nationality were made and after a quick glance to make sure everything was as they found it, the two men left the hut. Disregarded by the slumbering Lazy they lost themselves in the overcrowded camp.

It was only a few days later when Matthew mentally saluted Lieutenant Cooper's foresight. Summoned to the guardhouse, Cooper was screamed at by a demented Yoshida who demanded every New Zealander be identified from the records. He was told quite calmly there were none to be found.

Yoshida stormed off, denied on this one occasion of his retribution.

***

Change came in the shape of a working camp being set up at Maros, fifteen miles from Macassar. Not too far to travel unless you were already exhausted from prison life and made to run. Pressure was put on those who were dragging their feet, and to keep his mind on anything else Matthew thought of something he often did: *Why starve and mistreat your workforce? Where's the sense in it? We'd be more productive fed and cared for.* Grimly they plodded on, Matthew assisting Whitey when he faltered and getting a stripe across his back from the nearest guard for his efforts. They continued uphill until it levelled off once more and made the going easier. The raggedy bunch of thin, wasted men gasped in relief, legs and lungs burning as they toiled on. It was true jungle here, foul swamps in many places. The Dutch ready to warn them this was malaria-central. No escaping it for any of them, they reckoned.

Their new home-away-from-home measured roughly one acre, enclosed as expected by the three metre high barbed wire fence and gates. Three huts sat on concrete floors, with bamboo and thatch the natives called attap, made from palm fronds. The guards had their own small hut and there was a wash-house of sorts, a tiny hut with oil drums containing their boiled drinking water and also the water they washed in every night. What gave them all the chills was the toilet - nothing more than a three metre deep trench with pairs of boards laid across the width.

Whitey gazed down on it. 'The amount of time I'm going to spend here.....'

'Lucky for you the Japs went out of their way to make it a comfortable haven of sanitary delight.'

Whitey was still a bit weak but the punch he threw Matthew's way nearly sent him tumbling into the ditch.

'Wouldn't want to do that in a few days.'

Determined to find a silver lining, they admitted there was something to be said for their new prison. With only a hundred prisoners at any one time the awful overcrowding at Macassar wouldn't be their reality. At thirty men per hut, sleeping would be easier, too, the extra space making up for the bare concrete floor serving as a mattress, but not much. Also, they wouldn't have Yoshida's violence to deal with on a daily basis and given the choice, Matthew knew he would rather sleep on concrete than suffer Yoshida.

***

They were set to work almost immediately building a two kilometre long concrete aerodrome which was to have a grass strip the same length running at right angles to it. Along with this they were to complete a five kilometre road diversion around the aerodrome including a four and a half metre wide, three kilometre long track around the village nearby. Plus, all of these works were to be bordered by monsoon ditches two metres wide and one metre deep. Of course there were no wheelbarrows just picks and shovels, cane baskets and one hundred weak, starving workers.

'Things are looking up,' White murmured. 'Baskets, not bare arms.'

'I know.' Matthew played along. 'Another year or two we might even be given a wheelbarrow.'

'Steady on, Matt. Let's not get too carried away with the thoughts of such unimaginable luxuries.'

Most often their banter garnered them nothing but blank looks. Today, the men either side of them managed a bitter sneer. In spite of anyone else's reaction Matthew and Whitey actively sought to make each other smile at the least. A belly laugh earned a figurative gold star. Deliberately they sought out the nonsensical, they teased and mocked and argued and if their hunt for these things became frantic at times, so what? Every day they witnessed men giving up, losing heart and dying because dying was easier than suffering. In a silent pact Whitey and Matthew determined not to let such an end be theirs.

And so began the slog of shifting a mountain of dirt. The favourite punishment for anyone the guards supposed to be slacking was to stand for up to an hour with a full cane basket held over their heads. A generous-minded guard might call a halt at thirty minutes. One afternoon Matthew was screamed at. As he lifted the basket he called to his fellow prisoners nearby, 'Sweepstake. Bet on how long I can hold this up.' He earned a swat around the head for talking but kept eye contact with those nearest who offered sly grins and nods, fingers and hands flashing their guesses. Matthew tightened every sinew, the basket already slippery with sweat. *Five minutes.* The strain told on aching muscles. *Ten minutes.* Unable to wipe the sweat away, the tickle as it dripped became annoying. *Fifteen minutes.* Puffing now, shifting as unobtrusively as possible, trying to ease the pain. *Twenty minutes.* With a grunt, Matthew dropped the basket to the ground. It earned him some punches and he had to haul the bloody thing back over his head again. He met Whitey's eyes who held up both hands, fingers splayed, opening and closing to show Matthew he'd bet thirty minutes. Whitey gave his friend a disappointed shake of the head while Colin the Brit gave Matthew a cheerful thumbs up. So it became a game among them all, trying to outdo each other for the prize of a small scoop of rice or a piece of stolen fruit. Any man making it to the guard's order to cease earned a round of applause much to the puzzlement of the Japanese.

There had to be humour. There just had to be.

The six foot three Aussie named Bluey and his buddy Stan were two hard cases. Laconic and given to epic bouts of frenzied swearing they had met at Macassar, forming the close bond of friendship lucky men made in terrible times. Neither of them had caught any illness, boasting loudly of native Australian toughness so when Bluey got dysentery it became the joke of the day as he knew it would. They shared the same hut as Matthew and Whitey, the same sleeping corner. None of them had been in bed long when Bluey gave the groan everyone recognised as the stabbing twist in the guts signalling the quick dash to the shit-hole. Swearing under his breath Bluey staggered out and peace settled over the hut again.

Whitey hadn't managed to drop into sleep. Tired as he was, he couldn't switch his mind off so he was awake as the time dragged on and Bluey didn't return. Eventually concern got the better of him and he shook Stan awake. 'Bluey's not back.'

'Stupid bastard's prob'ly gone for a walk.' All the same, a sleepy Stan dragged himself up and wandered outside, yawning. No sign of Bluey at the shit-hole. *Where's the bugger got to?* Taking advantage of his location, Stan took a piss. He'd only started when a voice rose from the trench. 'Oi mate. When you've finished pissing on me, will you help me out?' Bluey had lost his footing and once in, he didn't have the strength to haul himself out.

Barely able to keep to his feet as he contained the gurgling laughter, Stan knelt and gave his friend a hand out of the trench where he had been desperately treading sewage to keep his head from disappearing under. Silently they made their way to the wash-house where Stan sluiced down the exhausted Bluey.

'You should have shouted you daft fucker.'

'Too scared I'd be eating shit. Figured someone would be me soon enough.'

No way they would dream of keeping this episode to themselves. It became the sensation of the hut for several days.

There had to be humour. There just had to be. It was the brave, flickering candle lighting their darkness.

***

Back and forth between Macassar and Maros went sick men. Sent to the hospital to be patched up or rather, until whatever ailed them killed or cured, the prisoners were denied any time to heal before being confronted with the never-ending work. The only difference was where they were sent.

As work at Maros continued, a party of two hundred were rounded up and sent to Pomalaa camp. Passed fit by a Japanese doctor, a large number, including Whitey, already had malaria. Fifty or more had ulcers and septic wounds. Fit enough to be slave labour. Matthew wasn't part of this. He'd been returned to Macassar suffering from an attack of dengue fever, exacerbated by pellagra, which at its worst saw the victim's skin peeling off in strips. Matthew was spared that horror but others weren't. The only thing to take his mind off his own misery was a dangerously sick Whitey being carried back from Pomalaa, barely recognisable from the other grey, gaunt skeletons. Two hundred prisoners had been sent there. Sixteen were dead. Thirteen were dangerously ill and only twenty eight were left able to walk. They had lived in a rat infested, malarial swamp working to reclaim a salt marsh or digging a dam in slime and mud. Starvation rations. For eight months. In short time malaria had swept through the party, followed swiftly by dysentery. Papaya leaves were occasionally provided for the malaria although more often than not the requests were ignored. Halfway through their time the deficiency diseases added to their misery - beriberi, pellagra, blindness, gastric enteritis, skin diseases, also ulcers, scabies, prickly heat, septic bed sores, heat stroke, exhaustion – an appalling list. A month before they returned only nineteen men out of the hundred were fit for work. The arrival of a Japanese officer resulted in food and quinine but it was far too little far too late.

Once back at Macassar, the survivors were taken to the hospital there. Operated by Dutch medical staff it held roughly one hundred men at a time. Every prisoner knew the Dutch prisoners always received preference, the rest losing heart when sick, knowing they would be denied the treatment they desperately needed. It took an English officer with a fiery temper to see the men from Pomalaa administered to.

Whitey's body was swollen with beri-beri. He had pellagra, gaping ulcers and another attack of malaria. Whenever he wasn't working, Matthew was at his friend's side as Whitey fought back to some semblance of health. This once vigorous, fit man who topped six foot two now weighed less than six stone. Matthew could only wonder at the inner strength keeping Whitey alive.

How many of them would survive this hell? And as the months of their captivity slid away and the suffering seemed without end, how many would want to?

***

Moss
France

The children had sunken cheeks, their eyes huge in such wasted faces. Their mother wasn't any better, in fact she was worse because she gave her children the lion's share of any food. As Moss and Marceline were preparing to leave, the sick woman beckoned Marceline near and whispered something to her. Marceline closed her eyes briefly. She gave the woman a long hug, speaking too softly for Moss to hear. All he saw was the relief on the gaunt face.

Once outside Marceline told him. 'She has begun to cough up blood. It is a death knell. I know it and she knows it, too. All her despair is for the children she will leave orphaned.'

'What could you possibly find to say to her?'

'I told her we will take her children to their aunt in Rouen.'

It wasn't much but it was hope of a kind. One tragedy among many.

From their own meagre stores, Marceline and Lucien supported the most desperate families in their reach. Moss had a talent for arriving with a sack bulging with bread or potatoes, carrots or, occasionally, bottles of wine. When asked where he had found such luxuries he would always wink, grin and speak of something else, leaving wide eyes and a sense of wonder in his wake. The truth, as it was all too often, was far more prosaic. After all this time with Lucien and Marceline, plus the bonus of a quick ear Moss now blended into the French countryside with ease. He supplemented his resistance efforts with farm work where a strong back and a willing attitude saw him constantly employed. All produce was stored before shifting it to their armies. Then all a man needed was perfect timing and an eye for the main chance. This was where Moss excelled. Maybe a bored young German soldier would be offered some fine brandy to share with this new friend, waking with a hangover and the warehouse or barn a little less full. Occasionally such a sore head had nothing to do with alcohol and everything to do with the bleeding wound on the back of his unwary skull. Moss roved for miles, never taking too much from anywhere too near home and never drank twice at the same well.

As well as such skills as unlocking doors with no key, Lucien had taught Moss German. Concentrating on being fluent in just enough German was easy. That ability and a uniform stolen from deep in Calvados allowed Moss to venture into towns and villages where Gestapo were stationed. He moved among them like a silhouette on a black wall, gathering medicine and information. The first he passed to Marceline or Lucien, the second to a doctor who assisted them in their work.

***

Moss was on a street in Rouen, his attention taken by a fine metal toy car. Roughly twenty centimetres long, painted red and blue, its driver in position. It was a thing of beauty and just what Moss had been hunting for Luca's second birthday. The car was part of a collection of belongings spread out on a blanket in front of a woman and a boy. The remains of their life now up for sale.

Moss pointed to the car. 'Combien?' *How much?*

The boys answered, 'Trois marks, Monsieur.' *Three marks, sir.*

It was worth so much more and not just in currency. There was wistfulness in the brown eyes meeting Moss's so maturely. Moss appeared to think. He stooped to handle the car, the boy's eyes never leaving it. 'Je vais vous donner vingt marks.' *I will give you twenty marks.*

'Vingt marks, Monsieur?'

'Oui.'

The boy exchanged a glowing look with his mother who was beyond showing any expression. It was left to the boy to stammer their thanks as Moss passed the money and slipped the car into his jacket pocket. 'Ce sera aimé,' he promised. *It will be loved.*

A glimmer of tears, a quick nod in response and Moss walked away.

***

'Why you?'

'Why not me? If not me then who?'

'Us. You and me. Always you tell me no, always you tell me you will do this on your own. It is enough, Lucien. It should always be us. I will not be left behind again leaving you to risk it all.'

Lucien's fist thumped the table top. 'And what of Luca? What of our son?'

'He will be with Moss. He will be cared for. It will not be for long.'

An exasperated Lucien waved a hand at Moss who was leaning against the stairwell trying to be invisible through this latest domestic drama. 'What do you say, Moss? Should a mother leave her son and risk her life?'

Marceline's appeal was unnecessary. A son of Maudie's never considered a woman had a place anywhere other than where she wanted it to be. Moss kept his steady gaze on Lucien. 'Should a father leave his son?'

Again, Lucien's fist hit the table. 'That is beside the point!' he raged.

'No. It is exactly the point.' Marceline reached across the table to grip her husband's fingers. 'Together, Lucien. I will not stay at home while you go.'

'And Moss? He is happy to stay?'

Beating Marceline to the point Moss said, 'I will stay where I'm needed, as always.'

'Playing housemaid?' When Lucien sulked he could be cruel. It never lasted long yet the sting could leave a mark, even if it faded eventually.

'Playing at fatherhood more like. You're lucky to have the role for real, Lucien. I am only honoured you both trust me with your son.'

The unsparing offer of personal regret touched the Frenchman more deeply than he would admit. He slapped Moss's shoulder, kissed him on both cheeks and told him they were lucky to have such a loyal friend. The sting faded as it always did where the mercurial Lucien was concerned.

Nothing more was said about the new venture for a few weeks, the farm needing all hands to bring in the later than usual harvest. The autumn days began to close in as the skies darkened with squadrons of Allied air force and their horizons became the unnatural reds and orange of fiery carnage and destruction.

Then came the evening when Lucien began to gather the few necessary bits and pieces, signalling a late night/early morning departure. He had just packed away map and compass when a worried Marceline appeared on the stairs, Luca in her arms.

'He is not well.'

Meeting them half-way, Lucien laid the back of his hand on the baby's forehead. Hot and clammy too, Luca restless in his mother's arms.

'You had better stay.'

'No. It is only a fever. Moss can cope.'

A frowning Lucien didn't say anymore. As Marceline fussed over Luca, he wandered outside to the barn where he knew Moss would be working to fix the radio needed for this job.

'Luca, he is sick.'

Moss lifted his head from the workbench. 'How sick?'

'A fever.'

'Does Marceline want to stay?'

Lucien gave his best snort.

'What do you think? She wants you to stay. She says the boy is not bad.'

'A mother usually knows. You need to trust her, Lucien.'

'It is not a matter of trust. Of course I trust her. But I love her even more. I hoped once the boy was born she would keep safe with him. She refuses!' Lucien's frustration and confusion made him angry.

Moss laid down his tools and the two men leaned against the bench, arms folded. 'Marceline knows now, Lucien, what it is to give birth to life and has seen what is like when the life you gave to the world is in danger. You know her heart. She feels every mother's loss and worry as her own.'

Lucien's frustration ate away at him. 'I do not understand why our boy is not enough for her.'

A movement at the doorway. Marceline. 'Listen to Moss, Lucien. My child is my life but if I can help another woman's child, then I will, just as you love Luca and risk your life to help another man's son.' She faced her husband who stood for a long moment before burying his face in her neck, her arms holding him closely. 'Too many families have lost their loved ones. We are lucky we still have ours and I cannot stand back when I can step up. I have never asked it of you. Do not continue to expect it of me.' Marceline drew back so she could hold Lucien's face in her hands.

Lucien sighed. He nodded, embraced her again. With his face turned from his wife only Moss saw the toll such a promise demanded.

By the time Marceline and Lucien left, Luca had quietened, his parents happy in their relief. Once the stillness of the night shrouded the cottage Moss studied the baby more closely. He remained hot and fever should make him restless. It worried Moss to see Luca so motionless.

Taking up a comfortable position near the fire, he kept Luca in his arms all through the night, not sleeping, cooling the little face with a damp cloth.

All the next day Luca remained asleep. He should have woken for feeding but when Moss tried, the baby refused and whimpered until allowed to sleep again. No matter how many cold cloths Moss wiped over him, Luca remained worryingly hot. He needed a doctor. The nearest one Marceline suspected of being a collaborator. The one she had reason to trust was a friend, Gerard who lived at La Foret-Auray, an hour and a half's walk away. As night rolled round again and Luca refused to wake or feed, Moss made up his mind. Wrapping the baby warmly, he set off. It was a good night for walking, the moon a sliver of light. When he could do so safely Moss kept to the roads, using the byways only to avoid villages or farms. He was nearly at his destination when it struck him. *Gerard may not even be home. Too late to worry now. If he had to find somewhere to wait, he would.* Moss paused and gazed down on the little, red face. 'Wake up, little man. Wake up.'

The stone village was night-time peaceful. Moving silently as was his wont, Moss found the right door and knocked, not wanting to wake any curious neighbours. Nothing. Reluctant to hammer harder, Moss stood back to look up at the two attic windows. Nothing moved. Swearing under his breath Moss dithered and then he heard the car. Its headlights brightened the road as it drove towards the village from the opposite direction. Quickly, Moss ducked into an alley across from the doctor's house, sliding into the shadows as the car stopped. A glance revealed the doctor himself clambering tiredly from the car. He had barely closed the door when someone approached him, startling him.

'Pardon, Gerard. I've brought Luca to you.'

Gerard's breathing slowly returned to normal. 'Kiwi! Surprising a man in the middle of the night,' he scolded quietly. 'You should know better.'

'I'm sorry. I didn't know what else to do. Luca won't wake. He's feverish and hasn't eaten for nearly two days.'

A quick look around them reassured Gerard. He ushered Moss inside, thankfully locking the door. 'Come on through.'

Moss followed Gerard to his little surgery. It was sparsely furnished and contained only the bare necessities. There was a good supply of drugs, however. Moss and Lucien had seen to that over the past two years.

'Lucien and Marceline are on a job?' Gerard didn't expect a full explanation, happy to accept the brief nod. 'Right, let's have the little lad.'

Grateful to have Luca in good hands, Moss relaxed enough to sit in the comfortable chair by the fire. He crossed his ankles on the handy footstool, glad to rest aching feet. Lifting his right boot, Moss studied the hole growing ever bigger in the sole. *No knowing when he could replace the pair. Better to find a stout piece of leather and lay it on the inside.*

It was warm in the little surgery and Moss hadn't slept for two nights. He tried to keep an eye on what Gerard was doing to Luca but against his will his eyelids dragged downwards. He wrestled them open once, twice before giving up the fight and gladly giving in to sleep.

The street is full of smoke so dense the sun can be seen through it as a blood-red ball. In the distance, artillery explodes, the largest shells shaking the ground under his feet. Moss can hear crying; a woman. He hunts through the deserted buildings and though he hears her sobs, she remains frustratingly out of sight.

'Tyke?'

No reply. The cries are choked off.

'Tyke!'

Moss begins to run, his breath echoing off the close stone walls, filling his ears. A child appears from one of the buildings. She wears a white nightgown and as he stumbles to a halt, Moss sees she is badly injured, clutching a shattered arm. He steps closer, desperate to help. Blood gushes over her lips, pours down her front. As the child collapses, a voice rings out, Tyke screaming for help.

'Moss!'

A log shifted in the fire sending up spattering sparks and sudden flame. Moss's eyes flew open in a rush of unexpected threat, adrenelin forcing him to his feet, heart pounding. All was warmth and calm. Gerard was humming somewhere, off-key and confident. Breathing deliberately to calm down, Moss peered into the cot beside his chair, placed a safe distance from the hearth. There Luca slept, his breathing regular, fever gone. Easing upright Moss went in search of Gerard, surprised to see how bright the light was outside the windows. He must have slept for hours. The little doctor stood in front of his stove where a tantalising aroma of ham and eggs wafted up to Moss.

'Mmmm...' He breathed in ecstatically. 'I hope there's enough for two in your pan, Gerard. And what time is it?'

Fussing like a mother hen, Gerard settled Moss at the table, pouring coffee, real coffee with one hand as he laid a thick slice of bread on a spare plate with the other. In seconds Moss was confronted with a heaped plate. He picked up the knife and fork, filling his mouth even as he mumbled a heartfelt, 'Merci.'

'Better to ask what day it is,' Gerard's smile lifted the edges of his neatly clipped moustache.

Astounded Moss stopped chewing. 'What day is it?'

'Thursday.'

The cutlery hit the plate with a clang. 'I've been asleep one whole day and night?'

Gerard flapped his hands at Moss's plate. 'Eat. You arrived just before four am yesterday. When I saw you'd fallen asleep I didn't have the heart to disturb you. Mind you, I couldn't have woken you if the Gestapo had broken down the door.'

Moss snorted and drank the good, black coffee. 'Where'd you get this?'

Gerard's look was droll. 'From a German officer with venereal disease who wished heartily I would forget his appointment. He wished it so much, you are enjoying ham and fresh eggs. As well I have some cigars tucked up in my wardrobe from his commanding officer who also demanded amnesia.'

'God bless the clap,' Moss mocked, raising the cup to his lips and draining it dry. 'I'm amazed you saved any, mon ami. You usually give it all away.'

'You are lucky, Kiwi. I only received this bounty yesterday.'

Satisfied at last, Moss cleared the table, directing Gerard away from the sink as he washed up. 'I haven't asked about Luca. He seemed to be sleeping peacefully with no fever?'

'The fever broke mid-afternoon yesterday. He had a good supper and woke for more during the night. His breakfast was tucked away just as smartly.' Gerard smiled. 'Luca is a strong boy. He will be perfectly well.' The doctor considered himself well repaid by the look of relief and gratitude on Moss's face. 'And you are both welcome to stay, in fact, as Luca's doctor, I insist on it.' He lifted a hand as Moss opened his mouth. 'Just until tomorrow night, Kiwi. I enjoy the company.'

Moss remembered then how kindly Gerard was a widower who had lost both his sons at the Western Front. He gladly stayed.

When Moss waved goodbye to Gerard, it was dusk, a cold autumn wind swirling the remaining leaves from the trees. Thankfully Luca slept although it had taken most of the evening to wear him out. At nearly two, Luca proudly toddled about, preferring movement to rest, jabbering away at the watching men. When he had finally flagged, Moss bundled him up and prepared to leave.

Before opening the front door Gerard had slipped two packets into Moss's pocket.

'The smallest one is a tonic for Luca. The other is for Madame Coutance, you know her?' Receiving a nod and a grimace, Gerard slapped Moss's arm. 'She is an old dotard but has a good heart. The medicine is for the woman she is hiding in her cellar.'

'Someone Lucien needs to know about?'

This time Gerard shook his head. 'No, thank you for the thought. Madam Coutance has promised the woman she can stay as long as she needs to get well. Between you and me, she will probably stay until the end of the war. Whenever that may be.'

The French farewell of kissing both cheeks still felt strange to Moss and he hadn't warmed well enough to the idea to try it out for himself. Compromising, he returned Gerard's hug and spent the walk home thinking of those risking everything to heal, to help, to shelter and protect, even as the German war machine destroyed their lives.

Moss looked down at Luca's face. 'What world will grow up in, little man?'

It was full dark by the time he reached Madame Coutance's cottage in the shelter of a small valley. No candlelight in the window so Moss placed the package in the usual hidey-hole under the loose brick near the well. He saluted her bravery and continued, preferring the hills to the roads on the way home even knowing it lengthened his journey. There was no panic tonight. Choosing to bypass the nearest village to home, Moss approached from the river and he had to smile when he noted the lighted window.

God bless good fortune. They were home, safe and sound.

Two pistol shots rang out, exploding into the silence of the night. Moss stumbled. Barely keeping his feet, he ducked into the river bed, Luca held tightly in his arms. He must have accidentally squeezed the sleeping child too hard for Luca gave a protesting cry which Moss hastily quelled. Soothing the baby to silence again, heart thumping, he risked a look at the sound of a revving car. Thinking at speed, Moss removed his coat and wrapped Luca in its folds, placing him in a hollowed place burrowed into the riverbank.

Bent double and keeping to the shadows Moss raced across the field, falling onto his stomach as headlamps swung his way as the car turned. *No shouts. No one had seen him.* He stood, moving cautiously as the car raced away down the dirt road. *Was anyone still inside?* Checking around the cottage until sure he was alone, Moss entered through the door and saw them. Lucien's dead body collapsed onto Marceline's, their blood mingling thickly on the flagstone floor. Moss gagged. He moved until his back hit the wall in time for his legs to give way as he slid to the ground, unable to drag his eyes away from his dead friends.

Who betrayed them? A thought slammed into his consciousness. *Did they know about Luca? Would they return?*

Scrabbling to his feet Moss dashed up the stairs. He grabbed warm, thick clothes for Luca, the few tins of food Marceline had hidden away and with his arms full, made his way down stairs to pull his canvas bag from the cupboard. Shoving these things in, he took the dried meat from the pantry plus the new loaf of bread sitting in there. *They must have brought it home in preparation for a family reunion.* A final, painful glance at his butchered friends and Moss ran to the barn. *His other shirt. His shaving things. Money saved. Passport. What else?* He stared wildly around, hand patting his jacket, reassured at the feel of the dagger in its sheath. *Nothing. There was nothing else.*

Moss raced to the riverbank and gathered Luca back into his arms. He headed for the hill and was halfway up when he paused, looked back to the cottage. A car was driving towards it at speed. *Someone must have told them about Luca. Or me.*

No more looking back. Moss ran.

***

8th May 1945
Fighting ends in Europe

Matthew
Macassar Camp

Sweat poured off Matthew in rivulets and he gripped the edge of the bed boards, his teeth locked together as his breath came in short, sharp hisses. Beside him Whitey had pulled the last of the bandage from the gaping ulcer on Matthew's thigh. This wrapping he dropped into a wooden bowl of hot, salty water before inspecting the wound. Under all the rotting flesh on Matthew's thigh, bone showed.

'It's a bad one.'

'Yeah, well, I bloody know that! Just get on with it.'

'Why didn't you say something earlier?'

'Because you were laid out unconscious with another attack.'

Whitey began the job of using a sharpened spoon to scrape away all the suppurating skin and flesh, knowing he had to scrape to the bone. 'I'm not sure if you've noticed or not Matt but there are one or two other blokes around in the camp with us. A couple are even doctors. Not sure you remember what doctors are? They're the ones who can help in times like this.'

Eyes closed against the pain, Matthew shot back, 'Maybe. But I trust you not to make a complete dog's breakfast of it.'

'You should have said something earlier,' Whitey repeated, not really thinking of what he was saying as he concentrated on the mess.

'You shouldn't have got sick, then.'

'So this is my fault?'

'Isn't everything? My ulcer. Your sickness. The weather. The Nips. The war. All. Your. Fault.'

With a final scoop the wound was as clean as Whitey could get it. He surveyed it with satisfaction. 'All the rot gone. Apart from your conversation, of course.' Reaching into the wooden bowl, Whitey rinsed the old bandage as well as he could before re-wrapping the wound. He had just started when Matthew took the bandage off him.

'Last time you did it, the bloody thing came undone in minutes,' he grumbled. 'Something else to blame you for.'

'Nag, nag, nag. Anyone would think you were my mother.' Whitey threw the filthy water out

'Poor woman. She must have been cheering when you shipped out.' Wound re-wrapped, Matthew gingerly stood, testing the feel as he set more weight on the leg. *He'd be limping with a stick for a bit but it'd do.*

Ulcers were a curse and no one escaped them. If the rot wasn't scraped away, gangrene would set in and the only end was amputation, with nothing but ice to dull the agony. The worst case they had witnessed was a poor bloke brought into Macassar from one of the work camps. He had three ulcers, each the size of a saucer, one on each hip, one in his chest. A living skeleton beyond help, though by God the doctors tried. Fresh eggs were traded with the natives, what pitiful medical supplies they had were used but ultimately, there was nothing anyone could do except watch helplessly as the ulcers grew and the stench of death enveloped the whole room. For weeks he lingered until he died, his suffering a torture to behold.

The hospital was a nightmare of hellish anguish. Bodies grossly swollen and bloated to an enormous degree with beri-beri, lower limbs attacked first then everything horribly distended and misshapen as it moved up the body. Scabies and boils, dysentery, conjunctivitis degenerating to blindness. Men were too sick to stand but too afraid to lie down for fear of dying. Most of these diseases and complaints were related to vitamin deficiencies. A spoonful of marmite everyday would make a staggering difference to the prisoners' health, even a handful of green vegetables. The natives knew of lallang grass. Whenever possible this would be gathered or traded and boiled in water. Once the water was cool, it could be drunk and effect an incredible cure. The problem was convincing sick men to drink it as it tasted like something out of the latrine. For those who did try, the problem was keeping it down on wasted stomachs. It was always a challenge to source fresh food but anyone on work parties who could, smuggled in mangoes, bananas, eggs, anything.

It seemed incredible how such sick men were expected to work as hard as healthy ones. As the years passed every man struggled with ill health to a greater or lesser degree and still the Japanese demanded arduous, dangerous levels of slavery. Clinging to the hope of rescue they dragged their broken bodies through the days.

***

The distinctive throb of a four-engined plane spun all heads to the south. They were working on the monsoon ditches at Maros aerodrome, minds on nothing but the stifling heat and the slog when they heard it. The guards slouching nearby became animated, shouting excitedly at each other as the plane flew lower and nearer.

'Ours or theirs?' Matthew shaded his eyes, trying to pick out the markings.

'Ours.' Whitey grinned openly, face turned away from the guards who were staring upwards just as intently.

The guards belatedly came to the same realisation as the plane opened fire with every machine gun it carried. Everyone scattered. They dived into the ditches or paddy-fields all except for one young Japanese guard who seemed transfixed and moved too late. He was shot to pieces, his body falling beside Whitey and Matthew. The plane roared overhead, banking steeply as it climbed. Within moments it was lost to view.

The fury of the guards was severe. Matthew and Whitey were beaten then made to carry the body back to Macassar camp, a stagger or stumble earning them a whack across the shoulders or the butt of a rifle into the backs. The rest of the working party were given no rations that evening or the following morning and several prisoners collapsed, left where they lay.

Despite the punishments, despite the fact they had been shot at, the appearance of the plane stirred their spirits, the rush almost drug-like after years of deprivation. Suddenly, the eyes of the outside world were turned their way, even if briefly.

'Imagine being shot dead by one of our own planes though.' Bluey complained. 'Shit, I'd be pissed off.'

The attack heralded others. Now their days and nights were no longer safe from the air, those mixed feelings grew as the attacks picked up pace.

At first the novelty and excitement of the raids kept them up at night, staring up at the sky. They would huddle at doors and windows, risking a look as the attacks provided them with all the drama and excitement of a performance. The Japanese had four anti-aircraft guns in a park in town plus at least one searchlight. As American bombers flew low, dropping a bomb indiscriminately, the guns fired at them, shell fragments falling on the prisoners no longer crowded around doorways and windows but cowering in the huts and crude shelters. Those shelters were made of coconut tree trunks, old boards and piled up earth. Matthew and Whitey weren't the only ones to prefer to lie under their bed boards until a guard threatening violence, made them leave for the rickety shelters.

Eventually the excitement palled.

A few weeks later, hearing the approaching planes and seeing the searchlights at Macassar town searing the sky, Matthew groaned.

'What's up now?' Whitey sighed.

'Think I'd rather have my sleep.'

'Some people are just never happy.'

As they straggled out towards the shelter, they recognized it was the Australian airforce taking a turn. Whitey and Matthew ducked away for a better view. One bomber arrived from the sea. Lit up brightly it flew low, level and slow. At once the searchlights locked onto it, but the Aussies kept coming. The anti-aircraft guns opened fire, pouring everything they had at the approaching bomber and then Whitey grabbed Matthew's arm.

'There!' he whispered urgently. 'Look, right on the edge of the searchlights. Look!'

Peering desperately Matthew strained to notice anything and then, suddenly he saw it. A second plane, keeping out of the searchlight's beam. No lights on this one. The first bomber was hit, the sound of its damaged engines searing the night but the second held its unseen course until right over the target. With unerring accuracy it dumped its entire load on the guns and searchlights. Thanks to the bravery and skill of the Australian air force, Macassar town lost all its anti-aircraft defences in one night. Matthew could feel Whitey jigging in excitement, his hoarse, swallowed cheering made him laugh. The two of them ended up breathless as a kind of hysteria swamped them. Only when they were certain they had regained control did they slip back into the hut. Every prisoner was awake, too excited to sleep, the excitement heightening as Whitey relayed what they had witnessed.

'I'll never have a bad word to say about the Aussies,' Matthew smiled. He caught Bluey's eye. 'Well, most of them.'

Bluey began to swear and stopped only when he fell asleep.

Eventually it was only a buoyed up Matthew who lay there. His nerves were strung too tight for rest. He replayed the scene over and over, unable to stop grinning. Around the camp he heard shouting guards, panic and his grin widened.

Take that, you fuckers.

***

Of course, the Japanese retaliated.

At Maros aerodrome, it became the prisoners' job to refuel the twin-engine planes. They had been doing this for some time before Matthew had an idea. It wasn't an idea which came without a measure of pain for he had fallen in love with these machines. At every opportunity Matthew studied their engines, making comparisons between them and the truck and car motors he and his uncles had dealt with in Murchison. *What would it be like to fly away in one? There must be such freedom in the sky, high above the world with all its destructive capabilities.* Yet it was humanity's drive to kill and maim which led them further along the road to developing the capacity for flight. *The paradox of human existence.*

Matthew ran a hand down the smooth surface of the plane. 'You shouldn't be a killing machine,' he murmured. 'You should be for escape and joy, for skimming the clouds.'

Whitey's head poked around. 'Who are you talking to?'

'This beauty,' Matthew said, still stroking the metal. 'I think I'm in love.'

'Trust you to fall in love with the enemy.'

'She's not the enemy. The men who order her to kill are the enemy. This lovely creature is a prisoner as much as we are.'

Silence.

'You know, my friend, I think you have finally tipped into insanity.' Whitey shared the top step of the ladder with Matthew. 'This is nothing more than a weapon.'

'They turned her into a weapon. You can't blame her.' Matthew's humour died away, his face suddenly serious. 'And I'm sorry.'

'What for?'

'For the idea I've come up with.'

Whitey studied Matthew, struck by his intent expression. 'What the heck are you going to do to me?'

'I'm not going to do anything to you, you damn fool. I'm going to stop these planes doing what they were designed to do.'

It was ridiculously simple. The guards, whenever possible, sought shade from the scorching sun. They were only too willing to give their orders and leave the prisoners to carry them out under the heat of the day. So, with no eyes on them, Matthew showed his companions what to do. As they added fuel, they mixed in anything they could lay their hands on. Water, handfuls of powered clay, sugar stolen from the guard's stores and, thanks to Bluey who led the way, as much urine as they could each contribute.

'You know, I always wondered what Aussies were best at.' Matthew's tease earned him wet feet and raucous laughter from every Australian nearby.

The ingenuity of those additions provided the prisoners with great scope for their creativity. In a world where they had been reduced to subjugated skeletons, this was power. Only Matthew felt anything other than a sense of liberation, all because of the mechanic within. It pained him to watch these machines cough and choke as the pilots and crew swore and raged. Even if the planes did manage to lift off, more often than not they landed almost instantly. Once grounded they were likely to stay that way for the Japanese didn't have the skills or the tools to dismantle the motors and repair them. Already there were two bombers with ruined engines parked off the runway. And that fact did much to mitigate Matthew's guilt.

'Just as well the bastards have no facilities for overhauls,' he said. 'Even the worst mechanic could spot carburettors chock-full of clay.'

***

The war in the Pacific was on the turn. Thanks to their hidden radio, the Chinese quietly relayed the news as the Japanese lost island after island. The prisoners had become used to having this knowledge, used to the glow of having this knowledge, used to the glow of satisfaction and the faint whiff of hope following each Allied success. It came to an abrupt halt the night when the radio plus the Chinese man manning it were blown to pieces courtesy of a direct hit. From then on they had one gauge for how the war was going for the Japanese - the increased levels of torture in the camp. The worst explosions of violence crushed men inured to the daily exposure to it. Some of the worst examples followed the discovery of hidden pamphlets.   As well as bombs, the Allies were dropping thousands of leaflets which relayed information like the advancement of the Americans through the Pacific Islands or any defeats suffered by the Japanese forces. Though the prisoners were put to work gathering the pamphlets up for burning, to be caught with one on your person was to ensure punishment. After one drop solely concerned with the destruction of the Japanese navy in the Battle of Leyte Gulf, Yoshida's rage knew no bounds. Not even waiting to gather the incriminating evidence up, he rounded up one hundred and twenty prisoners and over two hours they were beaten unmercifully. *99, 100, 101*....The officers kept count of the number of blows. *120,121,122....* History would remember. *170, 171, 172.....*

It must remember.

With no supply ships arriving into Macassar all supplies began to run low.
Another raid. The warehouse holding the supply of rice burned to the ground. What little rice they were given became rotten and stinking, scorched and smoked with gravel mixed in from where it was swept up off the warehouse floor.
At tenko Yoshida screamed at them. 'You bomb the warehouse. Little rice left. You eat the remains.'
And they did because they had to. They were fed with whatever was caught up in the sweepings.   Those ill in

hospital couldn't hope to keep it down. The numbers of dying increased.

History must never forget.

***

6 August 1945

Atomic Bomb dropped on Hiroshima

9 August 1945

Atomic Bomb dropped on Nagasaki

Silence in the skies. No bombers appeared, not one plane. Everything around the camp was hushed and a strange calm settled on them all as work parties ceased. After years of overcrowding, of screamed orders, the shrieks of tortured men, of nineteen hours slavery a day, silence. No one dared put a name to the cause. But anticipation was there in every wasted face and shone in hollowed eyes.

On the 16th August 1945 tenko was called. Every prisoner who was able stood in the yard. Out marched the commandant, surrounded by his remaining guards. The sun beat down and no one spoke as the silence dragged on.

Facing them all, his uniform immaculate, the commandant finally spoke. 'For you, the war is over.'

Without another word or gesture the Japanese all marched out of the camp, closing the gates behind them.

***

2nd September 1945

Japan formally surrenders

End of World War Two

Tyke
London

A weary Tyke made her way home. It had been a difficult shift. *But then, name a day they were anything else?* There was no reason for haste. She had no one to rush home to apart from Anzac and Biscuit and they were mostly self-reliant. So much of the East End was gaping holes and rubble, yet her flat and the three story building it was in remained unscathed. Plenty of people had been bombed out twice or more. Tyke had heard their stories, heart-rending some of them.

'We lost everything and shifted. Then lost it all again. And again.'

'My wife died.'

'My husband died.'

'Gran died, Gramps holding her in his arms.'

'Our girl went missing. We left for the shelter and lost her in the crowds. She never made it home. We haven't seen her since. We look for her every day and every night. Maybe you've seen her?'

'I can't sleep anymore. Not for love nor money.'

'She screams every time the sirens sound and she can't stop. She screams for hours.'

All Tyke's flat had lost was its one window. Cherry had used the top of a table they had found nearby to board it up, that one unscathed piece of wood the only remains of a house and home. She had banged it up in place of glass. It made their room dark but candles fixed the problem.

And Cherry had loved candlelight. It was romantic, she said.

Shaking her head to clear it of the cheeky, well-loved face, Tyke turned the final corner. *Yep. There it still stood. An old brick building standing tall in defiance to Goering and his bombs.* Tyke saluted it tiredly.

The stairs seemed longer these days, a weary trudge to the top rather than the habitual scamper when she and Cherry had first moved in. *I used to think war was exciting. I was so bloody young.* Tyke paused on the stairs. *You're not much older now, you daft cow! Come on, Tyke. Pull your socks up.* And her resolution lasted till the top of the stairs where memories collided with her good intentions and the bone-aching tiredness she felt these days claimed her once more. Key in the lock. *It wasn't locked.* Tyke held her breath wondering what to do for the best. *Fetch a warden in case whoever had broken in was still in there? But the door wasn't broken. How'd they get in? There was only one key. Mind you, there was bugger all for anyone to take. A bit of hard loaf on the table, a small piece of cooked meat, her dinner in the hay-box. If a burglar needed any of her meagre belongings then they were welcome to them. And what about Anzac? Wouldn't he have sorted out any potential burglar?* Chiding herself for cowardice, Tyke pushed the door gently and it swung open. Nothing moved so she walked through, eyes wide.

There on the bed, fast asleep was a man and a small child, Anzac lying at their feet. As Tyke appeared the dog turned his big head her way, his tail thumping softly. Tyke gaped.

Who the bloody hell.....?

In bewildered amazement she drew closer, peering cautiously over the sleepers until she reached the man's face.

Moss!

Of all the bloody things. Moss.

In shock, Tyke cleared the top of the old box beside the bed, the one used for a little table and gently lowered herself onto it, unable to take her eyes from them both. *He looked older, more careworn but didn't they all? And he had a son. Where's the boy's mother?* The little one cried in his sleep and Tyke held her breath. Without waking, Moss drew the little body closer to him, tucking the dark head against his face and the boy quieted again.

Moss.

At the sound of the child's whimpering, Anzac cocked his brindle head to one side his soft, brown eyes meeting Tyke's.

'It's all right, boy,' she whispered leaning carefully over the sleepers to pat his head. 'He's a friend.'

It was full dark by the time Moss blearily prised his eyes open. He lay there, Luca warm in his arms. *Where were they?* A shadow moved against the opposite wall bringing him fully awake. He covered Luca before shifting carefully. 'Who's there?' Moss kept his voice low.

'Goldilocks. But a reverse Goldilocks who wondered who was sleeping in her bed.' Tyke stepped out of the shadows into the spill of candlelight at the head of the bed.

At her side Moss recognised the mongrel who had welcomed them in, covering Luca in wet kisses and making him squeal in joy.

'You're lucky I didn't call a warden when I saw my door was unlocked. How did you get in, by the way? Without breaking the door?'

'I learned some tricks in France. Getting through locked doors without a key was one of the more useful ones.'

Pause.

'I've got a bit of stew warm. You hungry?'

Moss slid off the bed and joined Tyke at the table. 'I could eat a scabby dead dog backwards.' He smiled down at Anzac. 'No offence, mate.'

'Charming image,' Tyke chided. She leaned into the sink and pulled out a wooden box with a tight fitting lid. Prising the lid off, she reached under the layers of sheep wool and tightly balled old rags and hay to pull out a small casserole dish. She lifted the lid and the enticing aromas wafted around them. Moss's stomach gurgled, making them smile.

'It's mostly potato and carrot,' Tyke apologised. 'But there's a bit of rabbit in there if you dig about.'

'It's gourmet cooking at its finest, Tyke.'

She hid the swooping sensation in her chest at the sound of her name. 'Well, you'd know all about gourmet cooking. What with you being recently abroad in France.'

The ridiculousness she conjured up in the sentence tickled them both.

Moss gestured at the sleeping child so they wouldn't laugh out loud. 'Mind you, nothing would wake Luca tonight. After what we've been through lately...' his voice faded.

Seeing his expression, Tyke nudged him. 'Save it for later. Let's eat up, eh? I'll put a bit aside for the wee one.'

They cleaned their plates hungrily. Tyke left a quarter of hers for the dog busy hypnotising her with his stare. To her amusement, Moss saved a bit, too. They watched as the hungry dog chased the plate around the floor.

'Anzac's enthusiastic licking saves a bit of scrubbing on the washing up.'

'Anzac.' Moss turned the word over thoughtfully. 'Good name.'

'It's taken a few years but I'm missing home.' A weight burdened those words.

There was more furniture in the flat than Moss remembered. They sat now on an old two seat sofa with rolled arms, complete with two cushions. The dog eased his way between them, head on Tyke's lap as she gently rubbed his silky ears.

'Where'd you find him?'

'There's an army of stray cats and dogs out there.' She waved an arm to encompass the city outside her flat. 'They get rounded up every so often.' Tyke smiled down on Anzac whose tail waved side-to-side. 'This soppy old thing followed me home after work one day. He was starving, poor bugger. There's a cat somewhere, maybe under the bed. She's called Biscuit. A ginger tabby but don't expect a welcome. She's shy of strangers.'

'Anzac. Biscuit.' Moss reflected on this choice. 'It's a bloody menagerie. What does Cherry make of it? At work now, is she?'

Tyke's brightness ebbed away. 'No. No, Cherry died. Killed in a raid.' She tucked her feet under her, eyes on Anzac.

Moss automatically reached out a hand only to retract it. 'I'm sorry, Tyke.'

'Thanks.' A far-away expression shadowed her face. 'You know I was just remembering on the way home tonight how I used to think war was exciting.' Tears filled her eyes and she tipped her head back so they wouldn't fall. 'What a fool I was.'

Moss didn't speak at once. He rested his head on the sofa back and studied her. 'Lots of us felt the same. Until we learned better. There's a saying, isn't there? Something about experience being the best teacher?' He mouth twisted self-consciously. 'Something like it anyway.'

Pause.

'How old's your son?'

Pause.

'Not quite three but Luca's not my son, not my blood.'

The candle wick needed trimming. What little light it gave off flickered yet neither of them moved to fix it. Tyke shifted her position to see Moss better.

'Tell me.'

'Bit of a sad story,' he warned.

'Aren't they all these days?'

Moss was affected by her obvious fatigue. This was a very different Tyke from one he stormed away from those years ago. *If I had to choose a Tyke, for her sake, I'd wish she was that Tyke, even though she pushed me away. She was happier then.* He couldn't help what he felt. And if he was stirred to compassion he still loved her. Mentally giving himself a shake he spoke. 'It was only by chance I met Luca's father, Lucien. He lived in a tiny Normandy village, Mesnil-Villement. I was on a job, actually. For Hugo.' Moss couldn't help his mouth softening into something resembling a smile. 'You know that bloody man had a couple of jobs for me ready and waiting the moment I told them all at home I was off to find you. I swear the canny old sod knew war was about to kick off. Knew it and had his plans ready-made. Anyway, I met a woman in this wee village and part of the deal meant I had to take a run of stuff back to port. I was heading there when news of the German occupation came. Ships were leaving in panic but I managed to get what Hugo wanted on board one old ship. When my contact at the port knew where I was headed, he gave me a message for some friend of his. It was about the movement of German ships through French ports. The message was for Lucien. Long story short, Tyke. Lucien was Jewish and he and his wife Marceline were resistance, small r not capital R.' His voice drifted away for a few moments. 'Once the Germans arrived in force I wasn't the only one begging them to leave but they always refused. They felt they could help more people using the contacts they had in France than trying to organise anything outside her borders. They were the bravest people I knew.'

Pause.

'You said were.'

Moss nodded. 'Luca had a fever. Marceline and Lucien were on a job and had left him in my care. We had friend, a doctor we knew and trusted who lived at La Foret-Auvray.' He closed his eyes, his voice barely above a whisper. 'It was late when I brought Luca back. It was autumn, the days shortening rapidly. Lucien and Marceline's cottage was down near the river and I had chosen to follow the river the last part of the journey home.' Moss's eyes were dark with reminiscence. 'I saw candlelight in the window and thought how wonderful, Lucien and Marceline were home safely. But, before I got any closer, there were gun shots. One. Two.' Pain twisted his face. 'Luca woke and began to cry, keeping me frozen there. By the time he'd quieted a car had started. Thank God it drove off. When I reached the cottage, Marceline and Lucien were dead.'

His fingers dug into the sofa arm, the image of those dearly loved friends livid, still achingly fresh.

'Dear God,' Tyke whispered in horror. 'The Germans killed

them?

'Fucking Gestapo. Well, nothing I could do anymore. I grabbed my gear, what I could for Luca and we left. Almost a year ago. Feels so much longer. A lifetime.' Moss wiped a hand across the bristles on his unshaven face. 'We got out through the Swiss border and in all the world, this flat was the only place I knew we could be safe. Sorry for the fright we gave you. I hadn't intended to sleep but Luca needed settling and next thing I knew I woke up in your bed.' Grey exhaustion etched deep lines around Moss's mouth and eyes, aging him, hardening him, too.

Tyke found his vulnerability unsettling and reached for humour. 'Well, it wouldn't be the first time, would it?'

Silence.

'Thank you, Tyke.'

Pause.

'Don't be stupid.'

They moved towards each other. Anzac shifted onto both laps, giving a contented sigh. The hug held no passion. They were two weary friends finding comfort in each other's arms.

In spite of Moss's arguments, Tyke made her bed on the sofa, telling him reasonably Luca would take fright at waking with a stranger lying next to him. No denying the logic and Moss couldn't argue anymore. He was asleep as his head hit the pillow.

***

Dear Family

We're coming home. Just as soon as Moss can find us a berth on a ship. Not so many of your old merchant mates left, Uncle Hugo. Too many of them and their ships at the bottom of the Atlantic Ocean. But you know how resourceful Moss is. If he can wrangle it he will.

Oh, and by the way? Moss and I are married. We have a son – Luca who you will love. He's racing to four now and never shuts up.

I miss you. We miss you.

All our love,

Tyke, Moss and Luca.

***

Murchison

The house was quiet yet it felt unfamiliar to Jamsie and all because his father was home. He had no memory of this tall, painfully thin, sick-looking man. He looked only a little like the photos Mum showed him of the time before he went to war. In fact, Jamsie wouldn't believe it was the same man. Ruby was scared of him. The first night father went to bed he wanted to kiss them both goodnight. Jamsie bore it stoically, after all he was seven but Ruby sobbed for their mum like the baby she really still was at five.

No more kisses.

A shriek reverberated through the house. Jamsie leapt out of bed, heart pounding. Forgetting his slippers or dressing gown, he rushed to the hallway to stand there, wide-eyed and frightened as the scream came again and again. With a shock he realised it came from his parents' room. *What should he do?* Heart racing he tried not to give into panic as with the next scream a new cry was added. Ruby had woken up, yelling in fear for Mummy.

In moments, Mary rushed down the hall, almost colliding with her son.

'Mum what's happened?'

'It's your father, love. A nightmare.' Mary paused long enough to hug her son before answering Ruby's distress.

Jamsie listened as his mum whispered reassurance to Ruby until her fright passed. All the while Matthew screamed until Jamsie covered his ears, feverishly trying to block out the sound.

***

Wellington

Maudie unpegged the last piece of washing, folding it carefully before placing it in the basket at her feet. Job done it took her a moment or two to stretch out the crick in her back before lifting the heavy wicker basket onto her wide hip and heading back to the scullery. She met Hugo sitting on the doorstep, puffing away on his favourite pipe.

'Thought yer'd be out and about.'

'I was.'

'So yer gonna hang round here and get under my feet for the rest o'the day?' Maudie glared at her brother before pointedly stepping over him to dump the basket on the scullery floor. 'Where's Samuel?'

Hugo shrugged. 'Where's he usually?'

'Down the bloody pub.'

'See, Maud? You answered your own question.' He copped a whack across his head for his cheek.

'Yer should drag him out and make the bugger put in a day's work.'

'If you want him out, you go get him. I'm wearing the bruises from the last time I tried.'

They exchanged grim looks before Maudie moved into the kitchen. She hadn't even had time to reach the stove when Alex appeared from the hallway.

'Wondered where you were, Ma. I was coming in to put the kettle on.'

'Great minds,' Maudie replied not bothering to finish the adage. She watched the woman who was closer than a daughter as Alex deftly prepared afternoon tea. The years hadn't been kind but Maudie knew it wasn't just time which had added those permanent shadows under Alex's grey eyes and lines to her face. Tied by law and convention to a drunken, abusive husband, Alex kept up the pretence to the world she was happily married. It cut Maudie to the heart to see the cost of such effort and she couldn't have said which gave her the most pain, Alex's brave face or the way she dropped her guard when safe with her Ma or Hugo and the mask was allowed to slip and all the damage showed.

And now there was another generation of broken men finding their way back to the families and lives they left behind. Another generation of hidden abuse, of women and children to pay the price.

Reaching into the pantry, Maudie brought out the remains of a fruitcake which she plonked unceremoniously onto the table Alex had carefully covered in its pristine cloth. 'Hugo's hanging about the place, too.'

Alex's excitement glittered in her eyes. 'We are silly. We don't even know the day they're arriving. *'On our way. See you soon.'* That was the whole telegram.' Seeking reassurance, Alex took it from its resting place on the mantle above the stove, devouring the few words with her eyes. 'Oh, Ma.' A crack in her voice, hastily papered over. 'She will have changed.'

Memory tugged at Maudie, dragging her back down the years. *'He will have changed, Maudie.'* Pushing back against the past Maudie laid a hand over Alex's, intent on the here and now. 'Course she will. She left a girl an' she's a woman now. A wife an' mother.'

'Wife to Moss. Who'd have thought it?' Luckily Alex turned away as the kettle boiled so she missed the shrewd expression on Maudie's face.

Hugo wandered in, stuffing his pipe back into his pocket and with the teapot filled and in its place on the table, the three of them sat talking of everyday matters.

Waiting.

***

Tyke and Moss stepped out of the taxi into Tory St; an over-excited Anzac leaping around them. From inside the taxi, the plaintive meowing of the caged Biscuit was lost in the dog's barking. The cabbie bustled around to the boot to pull out their trunk while Tyke shifted Luca more snugly in her arms. She stood on the street, gazing at the newly painted front door. With Moss's help, the cabbie placed the trunk carefully on the pavement. Saluting his generous tip, he left them.

'Still asleep?' Moss peered down into Luca's face, lifting the boy's cap slightly to see.

Tyke smiled. 'Like a lamb.'

Together they shifted their attention to the newly painted bright blue door. A loud, loved, familiar voice berated someone inside before the front door was yanked open. Maudie stood there, looking behind her, growling.

Her head turned to the street.

And she saw them standing there.

***

1990

Matthew
Stoke, Nelson

He's elderly now. Broken by illness he has no name for. Visions or dreams, he considers them memories and they haunt him. *Angry, violent men beating him, beating them all. Torturing. Killing.*

Mary and he split years ago, eight years after he returned from the war. The children, of course, stayed with their mother. He hasn't seen Jamsie in years though Ruby makes an effort to keep in touch. *Odd how things turn out. It was Jamsie he'd loved the most.*

In later years he was given the luck of the angels. In fact, he was given an angel. The woman he shares his life with now remembered him from those early, hard but different years. She loves him. Cares for him. Shelters and protects him, fighting his corner. She won't marry him, though. Told him early on. She didn't want people saying she was just after his war pension. But, dear God how she loves him! And he loves her. This devotion is the one thing he can cling to with complete certainty.

It's because of her persistence that he sits in front of the doctor's desk. For some reason the dam built from decades of heavy, structured silence has broken and he spills out everything he remembers; the violence, the terrible, appalling torture in a Pacific concentration camp under Japanese rule.

And this wealthy, well-fed doctor listens. It's what he's paid to do. Half his job is administering medication, the other half listening to the reasons for it. So, he sits calmly and unemotionally through the tears and stammering of this sick, elderly man. When the recital comes to an end there's a pause.

'It can't be true, can it Matthew.'

Matthew wipes his streaming face with an unsteady hand. 'Sorry?'

'It's in your mind. These terrible things, they are just in your mind. No one, no man on this earth would treat another human in the way you've described.'

Screaming abuse, savage attacks on skeletal men. Forced marches through fierce, killing heat. Friends lying dead, wasted bodies on wasted grounds.

Coming home. You longed for Home. Being told prisoners of war don't get a full pension. 'You didn't fight on the front lines. You were housed. Fed. You weren't a proper soldier.'

Frightening seas. Burning ships. Men blown to pieces by exploding shells. Disembowelled bodies. Friends lost.

You weren't a proper soldier.

It's all in your mind.

Matthew leaves the doctor's office convinced he's going mad. With his physical health long gone his mind was all he had left and now he's been told he's imagining things.

Those events, so real to him. They. Never. Happened.

She's waiting for him in the waiting room and can tell at first glance, something awful has been added to those shoulders already bowed by so much. He can't speak and he stumbles in his distress but she's there as she always is to take an arm and steady him. Together they leave the doctor's surgery and she takes him home.

She believes him.

She knows what he went through.

And she will continue to fight for him until somebody else believes him too.

***

Author's Note:

Have we learned anything from two World Wars and countless others? The people who treat returned servicemen know we haven't. We take ordinary people and turn them into military weapons and targets and we're more skilled at that now, far more efficient because we understand the human mind so much better. It's called progress. If our soldiers are lucky enough to make it home, their luck runs out pretty damn quickly because as far as the world is concerned all their problems are over.

If only it were so simple.

These men are turned remorselessly into productive killing machines and that switch is a hard one to turn off. Left unsupported, far too many live on our streets as homeless, the lucky ones in sheltered housing. They live with appalling health. They suicide in high numbers, higher than we are led to believe. Girlfriends, wives and families shelter and hide behind smiles.

Shell-shock. Post Traumatic Stress Disorder. Post Traumatic Stress Injury. Call it what you will, its effects remain unchanged.

Our men and women suffer, our children and communities, too.

And the suffering lasts generations.

'You smug-faced crowds with kindling eye
Who cheer when soldier boys march by
Creep home and pray you'll never know
The hell where youth and laughter go.'

From: Suicide in the Trenches by Siegfried Sassoon

Lest We Forget